THE COMPLETE WORKS
OF
HENRY FIELDING, ESQ.

THE NOVELS IN SEVEN VOLUMES
THE PLAYS AND POEMS IN FIVE VOLUMES
THE LEGAL WRITINGS IN ONE VOLUME
THE MISCELLANEOUS WRITINGS IN THREE VOLUMES
COMPLETE IN SIXTEEN VOLUMES

With an Essay on the Life, Genius and Achievement
of the Author, by
WILLIAM ERNEST HENLEY, LL.D.

VOLUME SIX
AMELIA I

The Complete Works of
HENRY FIELDING, ESQ.
With an Essay on the Life, Genius and Achievement of the Author,
by
WILLIAM ERNEST HENLEY, LL.D.

AMELIA

IN TWO VOLUMES

VOL. ONE

Illustrated with
Reproductions of the Rare Designs by
Rooker and Corbould (1793)

BARNES & NOBLE, Inc.
NEW YORK
PUBLISHERS & BOOKSELLERS SINCE 1873

Reprinted in 1967
by Barnes & Noble, Inc.

L. C. Catalog Card Number: 67-15197

Manufactured in the United States of America

CONTENTS

PAGE

To Ralph Allen, Esq.. 11

BOOK I.

CHAPTER I.

Containing the Exordium, etc.. 13

CHAPTER II.

The history sets out. Observations on the excellency of the English
  Constitution, and curious examinations before a Justice of Peace... 14

CHAPTER III.

Containing the inside of a prison..................................... 21

CHAPTER IV.

Disclosing further secrets of the prison-house....................... 26

CHAPTER V.

Containing certain adventures which befel Mr. Booth in the prison. ... 32

CHAPTER VI.

Containing the extraordinary behavior of Miss Matthews on her meeting
  with Booth, and some endeavors to prove, by reason and authority,
  that it is possible for a woman to appear to be what she really is not. 37
      AMELIA, VOL. I.

CHAPTER VII.

PAGE

In which Miss Matthews begins her history............................. 41

CHAPTER VIII.

The history of Miss Matthews continued................................. 47

CHAPTER IX.

In which Miss Matthews concludes her relation......................... 52

CHAPTER X.

Table-talk, consisting of a facetious discourse that passed in the prison. 59

BOOK II.

CHAPTER I.

In which Captain Booth begins to relate his history..................... 66

CHAPTER II.

Mr. Booth continues his story. In this chapter there are some passages that may serve as a kind of touchstone by which a young lady may examine the heart of her lover. I would advise, therefore, that every lover be obliged to read it over in the presence of his mistress, and that she carefully watch his emotions while he is reading............ 70

CHAPTER III.

The narrative continued. More of the touchstone..................... 75

CHAPTER IV.

The story of Mr. Booth continued. In this chapter the reader will perceive a glimpse of the character of a very good divine, with some matters of a very tender kind...................................... 80

CHAPTER V.

Containing strange revolutions of fortune.............................. 83

CHAPTER VI.

PAGE

Containing many surprising adventures............................... 87

CHAPTER VII.

The story of Booth continued. More surprising adventures 92

CHAPTER VIII.

In which our readers will probably be divided in their opinion of Mr.
Booth's conduct... 98

CHAPTER IX.

Containing a scene of a different kind from any of the preceding........ 102

BOOK III.

CHAPTER I.

In which Mr Booth resumes his story....................... 109

CHAPTER II.

Containing a scene of the tender kind................................... 111

CHAPTER III.

In which Mr. Booth sets forward on his journey........................ 117

CHAPTER IV.

A sea piece... 120

CHAPTER V.

The arrival of Booth at Gibraltar, with what there befel him............ 126

CHAPTER VI.

Containing matters which will please some readers...................... 130

CHAPTER VII.

The captain, continuing his story, recounts some particulars which, we
doubt not, to many good people will appear unnatural.............. 134

CHAPTER VIII.

PAGE

The story of Booth continued 139

CHAPTER IX.

Containing very extraordinary matters................................. 148

CHAPTER X.

Containing a letter of a very curious kind 153

CHAPTER XI.

In which Mr. Booth relates his return to England....................... 159

CHAPTER XII.

In which Mr. Booth concludes his story 163

BOOK IV.

CHAPTER I.

Containing very mysterious matter..................................... 172

CHAPTER II.

The latter part of which we expect will please our reader better than the former... 175

CHAPTER III.

Containing wise observations of the author, and other matters.......... 184

CHAPTER IV.

In which Amelia appears in no unamiable light......................... 191

CHAPTER V.

Containing an eulogium upon innocence, and other grave matters...... 195

CONTENTS.

CHAPTER VI.

PAGE

In which may appear that violence is sometimes done to the name of love.. 203

CHAPTER VII.

Containing a very extraordinary and pleasant incident.................. 209

CHAPTER VIII.

Containing various matters 214

CHAPTER IX.

In which Amelia, with her friend, goes to the Oratorio.................. 218

BOOK V.

CHAPTER I.

In which the reader will meet with an old acquaintance................. 225

ADDITIONAL CHAPTER.

Containing a brace of doctors and much physical matter................ 228

CHAPTER II.

In which Booth pays a visit to the noble lord........................... 232

CHAPTER III.

Relating principally to the affairs of Sergeant Atkinson................. 237

CHAPTER IV.

Containing matters that require no preface............................. 241

CHAPTER V.

Containing much heroic matter.. 247

CHAPTER VI.

In which the reader will find matter worthy his consideration........... 252

CHAPTER VII.

PAGE

Containing various matters... 258

CHAPTER VIII.

The heroic behavior of Colonel Bath.................................... 264

CHAPTER IX.

Being the last chapter of the fifth book.............................. 269

BOOK VI.

CHAPTER I.

Panegyrics on beauty, with other grave matters........................ 275

CHAPTER II.

Which will not appear, we presume, unnatural to all married readers.... 280

CHAPTER III.

In which the history looks a little backwards.......................... 284

CHAPTER IV.

Containing a very extraordinary incident.............................. 291

CHAPTER V.

Containing some matters not very unnatural............................ 296

CHAPTER VI.

A scene in which some ladies will possibly think Amelia's conduct exceptionable... 301

CHAPTER VII.

A chapter in which there is much learning............................. 306

CHAPTER VIII.

PAGE

Containing some unaccountable behavior in Mrs. Ellison.............. 311

CHAPTER IX.

Containing a very strange incident........................ 315

A LIST OF THE PRINCIPAL CHARACTERS

AMELIA

CAPTAIN WILLIAM BOOTH	A half-pay officer.
AMELIA BOOTH	Wife to Capt. Booth.
BILLY BOOTH ⎱ EMILY BOOTH ⎰	Their children.
BETTY HARRIS	Sister to Amelia.
MRS. HARRIS	Mother to Amelia.
REV. DR. HARRISON	
MAJOR (afterwards Colonel) BATH	
CAPTAIN (afterwards Colonel) BOB JAMES	
MISS BATH (afterwards Mrs. James)	Sister to Major Bath.
REV. TOM BENNET	
MRS. (MOLLY) BENNET	His wife (afterwards Mrs. Joe Atkinson).
JOE ATKINSON	Foster-brother to Amelia.
MRS. ELLISON	A keeper of a lodging-house.
MISS FANNY MATTHEWS	A woman of the town.
MR. ROGERS ⎱ MR. MURPHY ⎰	Attorneys.
COLONEL TROMPINGTON ⎫ CAPTAIN GEORGE TRENT ⎪ LIEUTENANT BOB BOUND ⎬ CORNET HEBBERS ⎭	Officers.
JONATHAN THRASHER, J. P.	A magistrate.
MR. BONDUM	A bailiff.

Mr. Gotobed	A constable
Monsieur Bagillard	
Susan . . . }	
Betty . . . }	Servants.
Blear-eyed Moll }	
Mr. Robinson } . . .	Prisoners.
Cooper . }	

LIST OF ILLUSTRATIONS

AMELIA, VOL. I

I KNOCKED SOFTLY AT THE DOOR, AND BEING BID TO OPEN IT, I FOUND THE MAJOR IN HIS SISTER'S ANTECHAMBER WARMING HER POSSET (p. 145) . . . . . *Frontispiece*
Engraved by Collyer, from a painting by M. Rooker (1783).

PAGE

RALPH ALLEN (1694-1764) 10
From a contemporary painting.

RALPH ALLEN was a self-made man who won a fortune by devising a mail system of cross-posts for England and Wales ; also owned quarries, and was prominent in local politics. Allen had three or four beautiful residences where he entertained handsomely. Fielding has avowedly drawn his portrait in Squire Allworthy of *Tom Jones;* refers to him slyly in *Joseph Andrews;* and dedicates *Amelia* to him. Allen took a lively interest in the author, and after his death took charge of his family, provided for their education, and left one hundred pounds a year among them. He knew Pope and Pitt also.

FACSIMILE OF TITLE PAGE TO FIRST EDITION (1752) . . 11

A YOUNG FELLOW, WHOSE NAME WAS BOOTH, WAS NOW CHARGED WITH BEATING THE WATCHMAN IN THE EXECUTION OF HIS OFFICE, AND BREAKING HIS LANTERN . . . 19
Engraved by Saunders, from a drawing by J. de Wilde (1793).

EIGHT OR NINE YEARS HAD PASSED SINCE ANY INTERVIEW BETWEEN MR. BOOTH AND MISS MATTHEWS; AND THEIR MEETING NOW IN SO EXTRAORDINARY A PLACE AFFECTED BOTH OF THEM WITH AN EQUAL SURPRISE 37
Engraved by Saunders, from a drawing by R. Corbould (1797).

HE FOUND THE COLONEL IN HIS NIGHT-GOWN, AND HIS GREAT CHAIR ENGAGED WITH ANOTHER OFFICER AT A GAME OF CHESS. HE ROSE IMMEDIATELY, AND HAVING HEARTILY EMBRACED BOOTH, PRESENTED HIM TO HIS FRIEND 254
Engraved by W. Audinett, from a drawing by R. Corbould (1799).

Ralph Allen (1694 1764)

From a contempt ry painting

AMELIA.

BY

Henry Fielding, Esq;

Felices ter & amplius
Quos irrupta tenet Copula.

Γυναικὸς οὐδὲν χρῆμ' ἀνὴρ λήζεται
Ἐσθλῆς ἄμεινον, οὐδὲ ῥίγιον κακῆς.

In FOUR VOLUMES.

VOL. I.

LONDON:

Printed for A. MILLAR, in the *Strand.*
M.DCC.LII.

To RALPH ALLEN, Esq.

SIR : The following book is sincerely designed to promote the cause of virtue, and to expose some of the most glaring evils, as well public as private, which at present infest the country, though there is scarce, as I remember, a single stroke of satire aimed at any one person throughout the whole.

The best man is the properest patron of such an attempt. This, I believe, will be readily granted ; nor will the public voice, I think, be more divided to whom they shall give that appellation. Should a letter, indeed, be thus inscribed, DETUR OPTIMO, there are few persons who would think it wanted any other direction.

I will not trouble you with a preface concerning the work, nor endeavor to obviate any criticisms which can be made on it. The good-natured reader, if his heart should be here affected, will be inclined to pardon many faults for the pleasure he will receive from a tender sensation : and for readers of a different stamp, the more faults they can discover, the more, I am convinced, they will be pleased.

Nor will I assume the fulsome style of common dedicators. I have not their usual design in this epistle, nor will I borrow their language. Long, very long may it be, before a most dreadful circumstance shall make it possible for any pen to draw a just and true character of yourself without incurring a suspicion of flattery in the bosoms of the malignant. This task, therefore, I shall defer till that day (if I should be so unfortunate as ever to see it) when every good man shall pay a tear for the satisfaction of his curiosity—a day which, at present, I believe, there is but one good man in the world who can think of it with unconcern.

Accept, then, sir, this small token of that love, that gratitude, and that respect with which I shall always esteem it my GREATEST HONOR to be,

Sir,

Your most obliged and most obedient humble servant,

HENRY FIELDING.

BOW STREET, Dec. 12, 1751

AMELIA.

BOOK I.

CHAPTER I.

THE various accidents which befell a very worthy couple after their uniting in the state of matrimony will be the subject of the following history. The distresses which they waded through were some of them so exquisite, and the incidents which produced these so extraordinary, that they seemed to require not only the utmost malice, but the utmost invention, which superstition hath ever attributed to Fortune : though whether any such being interfered in the case, or indeed whether there be any such being in the universe, is a matter which I by no means presume to determine in the affirmative. To speak a bold truth, I am, after much mature deliberation, inclined to suspect that the public voice hath, in all ages, done much injustice to Fortune, and hath convicted her of many facts in which she had not the least concern. I question much whether we may not, by natural means, account for the success of knaves, the calamities of fools, with all the miseries in which men of sense sometimes involve themselves, by quitting the directions of Prudence, and following the blind guidance of a predominant passion ; in short, for all the ordinary phenomena which are imputed to fortune, whom perhaps, men accuse with no less absurdity in life than a bad player complains of ill luck at the game of chess.

But if men are sometimes guilty of laying improper blame on this imaginary being, they are altogether as apt to make her amends by ascribing to her honors which she as little deserves. To retrieve the ill consequences of a foolish conduct, and by struggling manfully with distress to subdue it, is one of the noblest efforts of wisdom and virtue. Whoever, therefore, calls such a man fortunate, is guilty of no less impropriety in speech than he would be who should call the statuary or the poet fortunate who carved a Venus or who writ an Iliad.

Life may as properly be called an art as any other ; and the great incidents in it are no more to be considered as mere accidents than the several members of a fine statue or a noble poem. The critics in all these are not content with seeing any thing to be great without knowing why and how it came to be so. By examining carefully the several gradations which conduce to bring every model to perfection, we learn truly to know that science in which the model is formed : as histories of this kind, therefore, may properly be called models of HUMAN LIFE, so, by observing minutely the several incidents which tend to the catastrophe or completion of the whole, and the minute causes whence those incidents are produced, we shall best be instructed in this most useful of all arts, which I call the ART OF LIFE.

CHAPTER II.

THE HISTORY SETS OUT. OBSERVATIONS ON THE EXCELLENCY OF THE ENGLISH CONSTITUTION AND CURIOUS EXAMINATIONS BEFORE A JUSTICE OF THE PEACE.

ON the first of April, in the year ——, the watchmen of a certain parish (I know not particularly which) within the liberty of Westminster brought several persons whom they had apprehended the preceding night before Jonathan Thrasher, Esq., one of the justices of the peace for that liberty.

But here, reader, before we proceed to the trials of these offenders, we shall, after our usual manner, premise some things which it may be necessary for thee to know.

It hath been observed, I think, by many, as well as the celebrated writer of three letters, that no human institution is capable of consummate perfection. An observation which perhaps that writer at least gathered from discovering some defects in the polity even of this well-regulated nation. And indeed if there should be any such defect in a constitution which my Lord Coke long ago told us " the wisdom of all the wise men in the world, if they had all met together at one time, could not have equalled," which some of our wisest men who were met together long before said was too good to be altered in any particular, and which, nevertheless, hath been mending ever since by a very great number of the said wise men ; if, I say, this constitution should be imperfect, we may be allowed, I think, to doubt whether any such faultless model can be found among the institutions of men.

It will probably be objected that the small imperfections which I am about to produce do not lie in the laws themselves, but in the ill execution of them ; but, with submission, this appears to me to be no less an absurdity than to say of any machine that it is excellently made, though incapable of performing its functions. Good laws should execute themselves in a well-regulated state ; at least, if the same legislature which provides the laws doth not provide for the execution of them, they act as Graham would do, if he should form all the parts of a clock in the most exquisite manner, yet put them so together that the clock could not go. In this case, surely we might say that there was a small defect in the constitution of the clock.

To say the truth, Graham would soon see the fault, and would easily remedy it.   The fault, indeed, could be no other than the parts were improperly disposed.

Perhaps, reader, I have another illustration, which will set my intention in a still clearer light before you.   Figure to yourself then a family, the master of which should dispose of the several economical offices in the following manner : viz., should put his butler in the coach-box, his steward behind his coach, his coachman in the butlery, and his footman in the stewardship, and in the same ridiculous manner should misemploy the talents of every other servant ; it is easy to see what a figure such a family must make in the world.

As ridiculous as this may seem, I have often considered some of the lower officers in our civil government to be disposed in this very manner.   To begin, I think, as low as I well can, with the watchman in our metropolis, who, being to guard our streets by night from thieves and robbers, an office which at least requires strength of body, are chosen out of those poor old decrepit people who are, from their want of bodily strength, rendered incapable of getting a livelihood by work.   These men, armed only with a pole, which some of them are scarce able to lift, are to secure the persons and houses of his Majesty's subjects from the attacks of gangs of young, bold, stout, desperate, and well-armed villains.

> Quæ non viribus istis
> Munera conveniunt.

If the poor old fellows should run away from such enemies, no one I think can wonder, unless it be that they were able to make their escape.

The higher we proceed among our public officers and magistrates, the less defects of this kind will perhaps be observable.   Mr. Thrasher, however, the justice before whom the prisoners above mentioned were now brought,

had some few imperfections in his magistratical capacity.
I own I have been sometimes inclined to think that this
office of a justice of peace requires some knowledge of the
law, for this simple reason : because, in every case which
comes before him, he is to judge and act according to law.
Again, as these laws are contained in a great variety of
books, the statutes which relate to the office of a justice of
peace making themselves at least two large volumes in
folio ; and that part of his jurisdiction which is founded on
the common law being dispersed in above a hundred volumes, I cannot conceive how this knowledge should be acquired without reading ; and yet certain it is, Mr. Thrasher
never read one syllable of the matter.

This perhaps was a defect ; but this was not all : for
where mere ignorance is to decide a point between two liti-
gants, it will always be an even chance whether it decides
right or wrong ; but sorry am I to say, right was often in a
much worse situation than this, and wrong hath often had
five hundred to one on his side before that magistrate,
who, if he was ignorant of the laws of England, was yet well
versed in the laws of nature. He perfectly well understood
that fundamental principle so strongly laid down in the in-
stitutes of the learned Rochefoucault, by which the duty of
self-love is so strongly enforced, and every man is taught to
consider himself as the centre of gravity, and to attract all
things thither. To speak the truth plainly, the justice was
never indifferent in a cause but when he could get nothing
on either side.

Such was the justice to whose tremendous bar Mr. Go-
tobed the constable, on the day above mentioned, brought
several delinquents, who, as we have said, had been apprehended by the watch for diverse outrages.

The first who came upon his trial was as bloody a spectre
as ever the imagination of a murderer or a tragic poet conceived. This poor wretch was charged with a battery by a

much stouter man than himself ; indeed the accused person
bore about him some evidence that he had been in an affray,
his clothes being very bloody, but certain open sluices on
his own head sufficiently showed whence all the scarlet
stream had issued, whereas the accuser had not the least
mark or appearance of any wound. The justice asked the
defendant what he meant by breaking the king's peace ?
To which he answered, " Upon my shoul I do love the king
very well, and I have not been after breaking any thing of
his that I do know ; but upon my shoul this man hath brake
my head, and my head did brake his stick ; that is all, gra. "
He then offered to produce several witnesses against this
improbable accusation ; but the justice presently interrupted
him, saying, " Sirrah, your tongue betrays your guilt. You
are an Irishman, and that is always sufficient evidence with
me."

The second criminal was a poor woman, who was taken
up by the watch as a street-walker. It was alleged against
her that she was found walking the streets after twelve
o'clock, and the watchman declared he believed her to be a
common strumpet. She pleaded in her defence (as was
really the truth) that she was a servant, and was sent by her
mistress, who was a little shopkeeper and upon the point of
delivery, to fetch a midwife, which she offered to prove by
several of the neighbors, if she was allowed to send for
them. The justice asked her why she had not done it before ? to which she answered she had no money, and could
get no messenger. The justice then called her several scur-
rilous names, and declaring she was guilty within the statute of street-walking, ordered her to Bridewell for a month.
A genteel young man and woman were then set forward,
and a very grave-looking person swore he caught them in a
situation which we cannot as particularly describe here as he
did before the magistrate, who, having received a wink
from his clerk, declared with much warmth that the fact

AMELIA. VOL. I. Ch. 2. P.12.
Booth's examination before Justice
Thrasher, on the Charge of the Watch.

Copyright 1902. Crowup & Sterling Co.   J. De Wilde, Del.

A young fellow, whose name was Booth, was now charged with beating
the watchman in the execution of his office,
and breaking his lantern.

Engraved by Saunders, from a drawing by J. de Wilde (1793).

was incredible and impossible. He presently discharged the accused parties, and was going, without any evidence, to commit the accuser for perjury ; but this the clerk dissuaded him from, saying he doubted whether a justice of peace had any such power. The justice at first differed in opinion, and said, " He had seen a man stand in the pillory about perjury ; nay, he had known a man in jail for it too ; and how came he there if he was not committed thither ?" " Why, that is true, sir," answered the clerk ; " and yet I have been told by a very great lawyer that a man cannot be committed for perjury before he is indicted ; and the reason is, I believe, because it is not against the peace before the indictment makes it so." " Why, that may be," cries the justice, " and indeed perjury is but scandalous words, and I know a man cannot have no warrant for those, unless you put for rioting * them into the warrant."

The witness was now about to be discharged, when the lady whom he had accused declared she would swear the peace against him, for that he had called her a whore several times. " Oho ! you will swear the peace, madam, will you ?" cries the justice ; " give her the peace, presently ; and pray, Mr. Constable, secure the prisoner, now we have him, while a warrant is made to take him up." All which was immediately performed, and the poor witness, for want of sureties, was sent to prison.

A young fellow, whose name was Booth, was now charged

* *Opus est interprete.* By the laws of England abusive words are not punishable by the magistrate ; some commissioners of the peace, therefore, when one scold hath applied to them for a warrant against another, from a too eager desire of doing justice, have construed a little harmless scolding into a riot, which is in law an outrageous breach of the peace committed by several persons, by three at the least, nor can a less number be convicted of it. Under this word rioting, or riotting (for I have seen it spelt both ways), many thousands of old women have been arrested and put to expense, sometimes in prison, for a little intemperate use of their tongues. This practice began to decrease in the year 1749.

with beating the watchman in the execution of his office and breaking his lantern. This was deposed by two witnesses ; and the shattered remains of a broken lantern, which had been long preserved for the sake of its testimony, were produced to corroborate the evidence. The justice, perceiving the criminal to be but shabbily dressed, was going to commit him without asking any further questions. At length, however, at the earnest request of the accused, the worthy magistrate submitted to hear his defence. The young man then alleged, as was in reality the case, "That as he was walking home to his lodging he saw two men in the street cruelly beating a third, upon which he had stopped and endeavored to assist the person who was so unequally attacked ; that the watch came up during the affray, and took them all four into custody ; that they were immediately carried to the round-house, where the two original assailants, who appeared to be men of fortune, found means to make up the matter, and were discharged by the constable, a favor which he himself, having no money in his pocket, was unable to obtain. He utterly denied having assaulted any of the watchmen, and solemnly declared that he was offered his liberty at the price of half a crown."

Though the bare word of an offender can never be taken against the oath of his accuser, yet the matter of this defence was so pertinent, and delivered with such an air of truth and sincerity, that, had the magistrate been endued with much sagacity, or had he been very moderately gifted with another quality very necessary to all who are to administer justice, he would have employed some labor in cross-examining the watchmen ; at least he would have given the defendant the time he desired to send for the other persons who were present at the affray, neither of which he did. In short, the magistrate had too great an honor for Truth to suspect that she ever appeared in sordid apparel ; nor did he ever sully his sublime notions of that virtue by uniting them with the mean ideas of poverty and distress.

There remained now only one prisoner, and that was the poor man himself in whose defence the last-mentioned culprit was engaged. His trial took but a very short time. A cause of battery and broken lantern was instituted against him, and proved in the same manner ; nor would the justice hear one word in defence ; but though his patience was exhausted, his breath was not, for against this last wretch he poured forth a great many volleys of menaces and abuse.

The delinquents were then all dispatched to prison under a guard of watchmen, and the justice and the constable adjourned to a neighboring ale-house to take their morning repast.

CHAPTER III.

CONTAINING THE INSIDE OF A PRISON.

MR. BOOTH (for we shall not trouble you with the rest) was no sooner arrived in the prison than a number of persons gathered around him, all demanding garnish, to which Mr. Booth not making a ready answer, as indeed he did not understand the word, some were going to lay hold of him, when a person of apparent dignity came up and insisted that no one should affront the gentleman. This person then, who was no less than the master or keeper of the prison, turning toward Mr. Booth, acquainted him that it was the custom of the place for every prisoner upon his first arrival there to give something to the former prisoners to make them drink. This, he said, was what they called garnish, and concluded with advising his new customer to draw his purse upon the present occasion. Mr. Booth answered that he would very readily comply with this laudable custom, was it in his power ; but that in reality he had not a shilling in his pocket, and, what was worse, he had not a shilling in the world. "Oho! if that be the case," cries the keeper, "it is another matter, and I have nothing to say." Upon which he immediately departed, and left poor Booth to the mercy of his companions, who, without loss of time, applied themselves to uncasing, as they termed it, and with such dexterity that his coat was not only stripped off, but out of sight in a minute.

Mr. Booth was too weak to resist and too wise to complain of this usage. As soon, therefore, as he was at liberty, and declared free of the place, he summoned his philosophy, of which he had no inconsiderable share, to his assistance, and resolved to make himself as easy as possible under his present circumstances.

Could his own thoughts indeed have suffered him a moment to forget where he was, the dispositions of the other prisoners might have induced him to believe that he had been in a happier place : for much the greater part of his fellow-sufferers, instead of wailing and repining at their conditions, were laughing, singing, and diverting themselves with various kinds of sports and gambols.

The first person who accosted him was called Blear-eyed Moll, a woman of no very comely appearance. Her eye (for she had but one), whence she derived her nickname, was such as that nickname bespoke ; besides which, it had two remarkable qualities ; for first, as if Nature had been careful to provide for her own defect, it constantly looked towards her blind side ; and secondly, the ball consisted almost entirely of white, or rather yellow, with a little gray spot in the corner, so small that it was scarce discernible. Nose she had none, for Venus, envious perhaps at her former charms, had carried off the gristly part, and some earthly damsel, perhaps from the same envy, had levelled the bone with the rest of her face : indeed it was far beneath the bones of her cheeks, which rose proportionally higher than is usual. About half a dozen ebony teeth fortified that large and long canal which nature had cut from ear to ear, at the bottom of which was a chin preposterously short, nature having turned up the bottom, instead of suffering it to grow to its due length.

Her body was well adapted to her face ; she measured full as much around the middle as from head to foot ; for, besides the extreme breadth of her back, her vast breasts had long since forsaken their native home, and had settled themselves a little below the girdle.

I wish certain actresses on the stage, when they are to perform characters of no amiable cast, would study to dress themselves with the propriety with which Blear-eyed Moll was now arrayed. For the sake of our squeamish reader, we shall not descend to particulars ; let it suffice to say, nothing more ragged or more dirty was ever emptied out of the round-house at St. Giles's.

We have taken the more pains to describe this person for two remarkable reasons ; the one is, that this unlovely creature was taken in the fact with a very pretty young fellow ; the other, which is more productive of moral lesson, is, that however wretched her fortune may appear to the reader, she was one of the merriest persons in the whole prison.

Blear-eyed Moll then came up to Mr. Booth with a smile, or rather grin, on her countenance, and asked him for a dram of gin, and when Booth assured her that he had not a penny of money, she replied, " D—n your eyes, I thought by your look you had been a clever fellow, and upon the snaffling lay * at least ; but, d—n your body and eyes, I find you are some sneaking budge † rascal." She then launched forth a volley of dreadful oaths, interlarded with some language not proper to be repeated here, and was going to lay hold on poor Booth, when a tall prisoner, who

* A cant term for robbery on the highway.
† Another cant term for pilfering.

had been very earnestly eyeing Booth for some time, came
up, and taking her by the shoulder, flung her off at some
distance, cursing her for a b—h, and bidding her let the
gentleman alone.

This person was not himself of the most inviting
aspect. He was long visaged and pale, with a red beard
of above a fortnight's growth. He was attired in a
brownish-black coat, which would have showed more holes
than it did had not the linen, which appeared through it,
been entirely of the same color with the cloth.

This gentleman, whose name was Robinson, addressed
himself very civilly to Mr. Booth, and told him he was sorry
to see one of his appearance in that place : " For as to your
being without your coat, sir," says he, " I can easily account for that ; and indeed dress is the least part which
distinguishes a gentleman." At which words he cast a
significant look on his own coat, as if he desired they should
be applied to himself. He then proceeded in the following manner :

" I perceive, sir, you are but just arrived in this dismal
place, which is indeed rendered more detestable by the
wretches who inhabit it than by any other circumstance ; but
even these a wise man will soon bring himself to bear with
indifference ; for what is, is ; and what must be, must be.
The knowledge of this, which, simple as it appears, is in
truth the height of all philosophy, renders a wise man superior to every evil which can befall him. I hope, sir, no very
dreadful accident is the cause of your coming hither ; but
whatever it was, you may be assured it could not be otherwise ; for all things happen by an inevitable fatality ; and a
man can no more resist the impulse of fate than a wheel-
barrow can the force of its driver."

Besides the obligation which Mr. Robinson had conferred
on Mr. Booth in delivering him from the insults of Blear-
eyed Moll, there was something in the manner of Robinson

which, notwithstanding the meanness of his dress, seemed
to distinguish him from the crowd of wretches who swarmed
in those regions ; and, above all, the sentiments which he
had just declared very nearly coincided with those of Mr.
Booth : this gentleman was what they call a freethinker—
that is to say, a deist, or, perhaps, an atheist ; for though
he did not absolutely deny the existence of a God, yet he
entirely denied his providence. A doctrine which, if it is
not downright atheism, hath a direct tendency toward it ;
and, as Dr. Clarke observes, may soon be driven into it.
And as to Mr. Booth, though he was in his heart an extreme
well-wisher to religion (for he was an honest man), yet his
notions of it were very slight and uncertain. To say truth,
he was in the wavering condition so finely described by
Claudian :

> *labefacta cadebat*
> *Religio, causæque viam* non sponte *sequebar*
> *Alterius ; vacuo quæ currere semina motu*
> *Affirmat ; magnumque novas per inane figuras*
> *Fortuna, non arte, regi ; quæ numina sensu*
> *Ambiguo, vel nulla putat, vel nescia nostri.*

This way of thinking, or rather of doubting, he had contracted from the same reasons which Claudian assigns, and
which had induced Brutus in his latter days to doubt the
existence of that virtue which he had all his life cultivated.
In short, poor Booth imagined that a larger share of misfortunes had fallen to his lot than he had merited ; and this
led him, who (though a good classical scholar) was not deeply
learned in religious matters, into a disadvantageous opinion
of Providence. A dangerous way of reasoning, in which
our conclusions are not only too hasty, from an imperfect
view of things, but we are likewise liable to much error
from partiality to ourselves, viewing our virtues and vices
as through a perspective, in which we turn the glass always
to our own advantage, so as to diminish the one, and as
greatly to magnify the other.

From the above reasons, it can be no wonder that Mr. Booth did not decline the acquaintance of this person, in a place which could not promise to afford him any better. He answered him, therefore, with great courtesy, as indeed he was of a very good and gentle disposition, and after expressing a civil surprise at meeting him there, declared himself to be of the same opinion with regard to the necessity of human actions, adding, however, that he did not believe men were under any blind impulse or direction of fate, but that every man acted merely from the force of that passion which was uppermost in his mind, and could do no otherwise.

A discourse now ensued between the two gentlemen on the necessity arising from the impulse of fate, and the necessity arising from the impulse of passion, which, as it will make a pretty pamphlet of itself, we shall reserve for some future opportunity. When this was ended they set forward to survey the jail and the prisoners, with the several cases of whom Mr. Robinson, who had been some time under confinement, undertook to make Mr. Booth acquainted.

CHAPTER IV.

DISCLOSING FURTHER SECRETS OF THE PRISON-HOUSE.

THE first persons whom they passed by were three men in fetters, who were enjoying themselves very merrily over a bottle of wine and a pipe of tobacco. These, Mr. Robinson informed his friend, were three street robbers, and were all certain of being hanged the ensuing sessions. So inconsiderable an object, said he, is misery to light minds, when it is at any distance.

A little farther they beheld a man prostrate on the ground, whose heavy groans and frantic actions plainly indicated the highest disorder of mind. This person was, it seems, committed for a small felony ; and his wife, who then lay-in, upon hearing the news, had thrown herself from a window two pair of stairs high, by which means he had, in all probability, lost both her and his child.

A very pretty girl then advanced toward them, whose beauty Mr. Booth could not help admiring the moment he saw her, declaring, at the same time, he thought she had great innocence in her countenance. Robinson said she was committed thither as an idle and disorderly person, and a common street-walker. As she passed by Mr. Booth she damned his eyes and discharged a volley of words, every one of which was too indecent to be repeated.

They now beheld a little creature sitting by herself in a corner, and crying bitterly. This girl, Mr. Robinson said, was committed because her father-in-law, who was in the grenadier guards, had sworn that he was afraid of his life, or of some bodily harm which she would do him, and she could get no sureties for keeping the peace ; for which reason justice Thrasher had committed her to prison.

A great noise now arose, occasioned by the prisoners all flocking to see a fellow whipped for petty larceny, to which he was condemned by the court of quarter-sessions ; but this soon ended in the disappointment of the spectators ; for the fellow, after being stripped, having advanced another sixpence, was discharged untouched.

This was immediately followed by another bustle ; Blear-eyed Moll, and several of her companions, having got possession of a man who was committed for certain odious unmanlike practices, not fit to be named, were giving him various kinds of discipline, and would probably have put an end to him had he not been rescued out of their hands by authority.

When this bustle was a little allayed, Mr. Booth took notice of a young woman in rags sitting on the ground, and supporting the head of an old man in her lap, who appeared to be giving up the ghost. These, Mr. Robinson informed him, were father and daughter ; that the latter was com. mitted for stealing a loaf, in order to support the former, and the former for receiving it, knowing it to be stolen.

A well-dressed man then walked surlily by them, whom Mr. Robinson reported to have been committed on an indictment found against him for a most horrid perjury ; but, says he, we expect him to be bailed to-day.   " Good heaven !" cries Booth, " can such villains find bail, and is no person charitable enough to bail that poor father and daughter ?" " Oh ! sir," answered Robinson, " the offence of the daughter, being felony, is held not to be bailable in law, whereas perjury is a misdemeanor only ; and therefore persons who are even indicted for it are, nevertheless, capable of being bailed.   Nay, of all perjuries, that of which this man is indicted is the worst ; for it was with an intention of taking away the life of an innocent person by form of law.   As to perjuries in civil matters, they are not so very criminal." " They are not," said Booth ; " and yet even these are a most flagitious offence, and worthy the highest punishment." " Surely they ought to be distinguished," answered Robinson, " from the others : for what is taking away a little property from a man compared to taking away his life and his reputation, and ruining his family into the bargain ?   I hope there can be no comparison in the crimes, and I think there ought to be none in the punishment.   However, at present, the punishment of all perjury is only pillory and transportation for seven years ; and as it is a traversable and bailable offence, methods are found to escape any punishment at all." *

Booth expressed great astonishment at this, when his attention was suddenly diverted by the most miserable object

* By removing the indictment by *certiorari* into the King's Bench, the trial is so long postponed, and the costs are so highly increased, that prosecutors are often tired out, and some incapacitated from pursuing. *Verbum sapienti.*

that he had yet seen. This was a wretch almost naked, and
who bore in his countenance, joined to an appearance of
honesty, the marks of poverty, hunger, and disease. He
had, moreover, a wooden leg, and two or three scars on his
forehead. "The case of this poor man is indeed unhappy
enough," said Robinson. "He hath served his country, lost
his limb, and received several wounds, at the siege of Gibraltar. When he was discharged from the hospital abroad
he came over to get into that of Chelsea, but could not immediately, as none of his officers were then in England. In
the mean time, he was one day apprehended and committed
hither on suspicion of stealing three herrings from a fish-
monger. He was tried several months ago for this offence,
and acquitted; indeed his innocence manifestly appeared
at the trial; but he was brought back again for his fees,
and here he hath lain ever since."

Booth expressed great horror at this account, and declared, if he had only so much money in his pocket, he
would pay his fees for him; but added that he was not
possessed of a single farthing in the world.

Robinson hesitated a moment, and then said, with a
smile, "I am going to make you, sir, a very odd proposal
after your last declaration; but what say you to a game at
cards? it will serve to pass a tedious hour, and may divert
your thoughts from more unpleasant speculations."

I do not imagine Booth would have agreed to this;
for, though some love of gaming had been formerly
amongst his faults, yet he was not so egregiously addicted
to that vice as to be tempted by the shabby plight of Robinson, who had, if I may so express myself, no charms for
a gamester. If he had, however, any such inclinations, he
had no opportunity to follow them, for before he could
make any answer to Robinson's proposal, a strapping wench
came up to Booth, and taking hold of his arm, asked him
to walk aside with her, saying, "What a pox! are you

such a fresh cull that you do not know this fellow ? why, he is a gambler, and committed for cheating at play. There is not such a pickpocket in the whole quad." *

A scene of altercation now ensued betwen Robinson and the lady, which ended in a bout at fisticuffs, in which the lady was greatly superior to the philosopher.

While the two combatants were engaged, a grave-looking man, rather better dressed than the majority of the company, came up to Mr. Booth, and taking him aside, said, "I am sorry, sir, to see a gentleman, as you appear to be, in such intimacy with that rascal, who makes no scruple of disowning all revealed religion. As for crimes, they are human errors, and signify but little ; nay, perhaps the worse a man is by nature the more room there is for grace. The spirit is active, and loves best to inhabit those minds where it may meet with the most work. Whatever your crime be, therefore, I would not have you despair, but rather rejoice at it ; for perhaps it may be the means of your being called." He ran on for a considerable time with this cant, without waiting for an answer, and ended in declaring himself a Methodist.

Just as the Methodist had finished his discourse a beautiful young woman was ushered into the jail. She was genteel and well dressed, and did not in the least resemble those females whom Mr. Booth had hitherto seen. The constable had no sooner delivered her at the gate than she asked, with a commanding voice, for the keeper ; and when he arrived, she said to him, " Well, sir, whither am I to be conducted ? I hope I am not to take up my lodging with these creatures." The keeper answered, with a kind of surly respect, " Madam, we have rooms for those who can afford to pay for them." At these words she pulled a handsome purse from her pocket, in which many guineas chinked, saying, with an air of indignation, " that she was not come

---

* A cant word for a prison.

thither on account of poverty." The keeper no sooner
viewed the purse than his features became all softened in an
instant ; and with all the courtesy of which he was master,
he desired the lady to walk with him, assuring her that she
should have the best apartment in his house.

Mr. Booth was now left alone, for the Methodist had
forsaken him, having, as the phrase of the sect is, searched
him to the bottom. In fact, he had thoroughly examined
every one of Mr. Booth's pockets, from which he had conveyed away a penknife and an iron snuff-box, these being
all the movables which were to be found.

Booth was standing near the gate of the prison when the
young lady above mentioned was introduced into the yard.
He viewed her features very attentively, and was persuaded
that he knew her. She was indeed so remarkably handsome that it was hardly possible for any who had ever seen
her to forget her. He inquired of one of the under-keepers
if the name of the prisoner lately arrived was not Matthews ; to which he was answered that her name was not
Matthews, but Vincent, and that she was committed for
murder.

The latter part of this information made Mr. Booth suspect his memory more than the former ; for it was very
possible that she might have changed her name ; but he
hardly thought she could so far have changed her nature as
to be guilty of a crime so very incongruous with her former
gentle manners, for Miss Matthews had both the birth and
education of a gentlewoman. He concluded, therefore,
that he was certainly mistaken, and rested satisfied without
any further inquiry.

CHAPTER V.

CONTAINING CERTAIN ADVENTURES WHICH BEFELL MR. BOOTH
IN THE PRISON.

THE remainder of the day Mr. Booth spent in melancholy contemplation on his present condition. He was destitute of the common necessaries of life, and consequently unable to subsist where he was; nor was there a single person in town to whom he could, with any reasonable hope, apply for his delivery. Grief for some time banished the thoughts of food from his mind ; but in the morning nature began to grow uneasy for want of her usual nourishment, for he had not ate a morsel during the last forty hours. A penny loaf, which is, it seems, the ordinary allowance to the prisoners in Bridewell, was now delivered him ; and while he was eating this a man brought him a little packet sealed up, informing him that it came by a messenger who said it required no answer.

Mr. Booth now opened his packet, and after unfolding several pieces of blank paper successively, at last discovered a guinea, wrapped with great care in the inmost paper. He was vastly surprised at this sight, as he had few if any friends from whom he could expect such a favor, slight as it was ; and not one of his friends, as he was apprized, knew of his confinement. As there was no direction to the packet, nor a word of writing contained in it, he began to suspect that it was delivered to the wrong person ; and being one of the most untainted honesty, he found out the man who gave it him, and again examined him concerning the person who brought it, and the message delivered with it. The man assured Booth that he had made no mistake, saying, "If your name is Booth, sir, I am positive you are the gentleman to whom the parcel I gave you belongs."

The most scrupulous honesty would perhaps, in such a

situation, have been well enough satisfied in finding no owner for the guinea, especially when proclamation had been made in the prison that Mr. Booth had received a packet without any direction, to which, if any person had any claim, and would discover the contents, he was ready to deliver it to such claimant. No such claimant being found (I mean none who knew the contents; for many swore that they expected just such a packet, and believed it to be their property), Mr. Booth very calmly resolved to apply the money to his own use.

The first thing after redemption of the coat which Mr. Booth, hungry as he was, thought of, was to supply himself with snuff, which he had long, to his great sorrow, been without. On this occasion he presently missed that iron box which the Methodist had so dexterously conveyed out of his pocket, as we mentioned in the last chapter.

He no sooner missed this box than he immediately suspected that the gambler was the person who had stolen it; nay, so well was he assured of this man's guilt that it may perhaps be improper to say he barely suspected it. Though Mr. Booth was, as we have hinted, a man of very sweet disposition, yet was he rather overwarm. Having, therefore, no doubt concerning the person of the thief, he eagerly sought him out, and very bluntly charged him with the fact.

The gambler, whom I think we should now call the philosopher, received this charge without the least visible emotion either of mind or muscle. After a short pause of a few moments, he answered, with great solemnity, as follows: "Young man, I am entirely unconcerned at your groundless suspicion. He that censures a stranger, as I am to you, without any cause, makes a worse compliment to himself than to the stranger. You know yourself, friend; you know not me. It is true, indeed, you heard me accused of being a cheat and a gamester; but who is my accuser ? Look at my apparel, friend ; do thieves and gamesters wear such clothes as these ? play is my folly, not my vice ; it is my impulse, and I have been a martyr to it. Would a gamester have asked another to play when he could have lost eighteen-pence and won nothing ? however, if you are not satisfied, you may search my pockets ; the outside of all but one will serve your turn, and in that one there is the eighteen-pence I told you of." He then turned up his clothes, and his pockets entirely resembled the pitchers of the Belides.

Booth was a little staggered at this defence. He said the real value of the iron box was too inconsiderable to mention ; but that he had a capricious value for it, for the sake of the person who gave it him ; "for, though it is not," said he, "worth sixpence, I would willingly give a crown to any one who would bring it me again."

Robinson answered, "If that be the case, you have nothing more to do but to signify your intention in the prison, and I am well convinced you will not be long without regaining the possession of your snuff-box.

This advice was immediately followed, and with success, the Methodist presently producing the box, which, he said, he had found, and should have returned it before had he known the person to whom it belonged, adding, with uplifted eyes, that the spirit would not suffer him knowingly to detain the goods of another, however inconsiderable the value was. "Why so, friend ?" said Robinson. "Have I not heard you often say, the wickeder any man was the better, provided he was what you call a believer ?" "You mistake me," cries Cooper (for that was the name of the Methodist) : "no man can be wicked after he is possessed by the spirit. There is a wide difference between the days of sin and the days of grace. I have been a sinner myself." "I believe thee," cries Robinson, with a sneer. "I care not," answered the other, "what an atheist believes. I suppose you would insinuate that I stole the snuff-box ; but I value not your malice ; the Lord knows my innocence." He then walked off with the reward, and Booth, returning to Robinson, very earnestly asked pardon for his groundless suspicion, which the other, without any hesitation, accorded him, saying, "You never accused me, sir ; you suspected some gambler, with whose character I have no concern. I should be angry with a friend or acquaintance who should give a hasty credit to any allegation against me ; but I have no reason to be offended with you for believing what the woman, and the rascal who is just gone, and who is committed here for a pickpocket, which you did not perhaps know, told you to my disadvantage. And if you thought me to be a gambler you had just reason to suspect any ill of me ; for I myself am confined here by the perjury of one of those villains, who, having cheated me of my money at play, and hearing that I intended to apply to a magistrate against him, himself began the attack, and obtained a warrant against me of Justice Thrasher, who, without hearing one speech in my defence, committed me to this place."

Booth testified great compassion at this account ; and, he having invited Robinson to dinner, they spent that day together. In the afternoon Booth indulged his friend with a game at cards ; at first for halfpence and afterward for shillings, when fortune so favored Robinson that he did not leave the other a single shilling in his pocket.

A surprising run of luck in a gamester is often mistaken for somewhat else by persons who are not over-zealous believers in the divinity of fortune. I have known a stranger at Bath, who hath happened fortunately (I might almost say unfortunately) to have four by honors in his hand almost every time he dealt for a whole evening, shunned universally by the whole company the next day. And certain it is that Mr. Booth, though of a temper very little inclined to suspicion, began to waver in his opinion whether the character given by Mr. Robinson of himself, or that which the others gave of him, was the truer.

In the morning hunger paid him a second visit, and found him again in the same situation as before. After some deliberation, therefore, he resolved to ask Robinson to lend him a shilling or two of that money which was lately his own. And this experiment, he thought, would confirm him either in a good or evil opinion of that gentleman.

To this demand Robinson answered, with great alacrity, that he should very gladly have complied, had not fortune played one of her jade tricks with him : " for since my winning of you," said he, " I have been stripped not only of your money but my own. He was going to harangue farther ; but Booth, with great indignation, turned from him.

This poor gentleman had very little time to reflect on his own misery, or the rascality, as it appeared to him, of the other, when the same person who had the day before delivered him the guinea from the unknown hand again accosted him, and told him a lady in the house (so he expressed himself) desired the favor of his company.

Mr. Booth immediately obeyed the message, and was conducted into a room in the prison, where he was presently convinced that Mrs. Vincent was no other than his old acquaintance Miss Matthews.

AMELIA.
Booth comforting Miss Matthews
in her Imprisonment.

Eight or nine years had passed since any interview between Mr. Booth
and Miss Matthews ; and their meeting now in so extraordinary
a place affected both of them with an equal surprise.

Engraved by Saunders, from a drawing by R. Corbould (1797.)

CHAPTER VI.

CONTAINING THE EXTRAORDINARY BEHAVIOR OF MISS MAT-
THEWS ON HER MEETING WITH BOOTH, AND SOME ENDEAV-
ORS TO PROVE, BY REASON AND AUTHORITY, THAT IT IS
POSSIBLE FOR A WOMAN TO APPEAR TO BE WHAT SHE
REALLY IS NOT.

EIGHT or nine years had passed since any interview between Mr. Booth and Miss Matthews ; and their meeting
now in so extraordinary a place affected both of them with
an equal surprise.

After some immaterial ceremonies, the lady acquainted
Mr. Booth that, having heard there was a person in the
prison who knew her by the name of Matthews, she had
great curiosity to inquire who he was, whereupon he had
been shown to her from the window of the house ; that she
immediately recollected him, and being informed of his dis-
tressful situation, for which she expressed great concern,
she had sent him that guinea which he had received the day
before ; and then proceeded to excuse herself for not having
desired to see him at that time, when she was under the
greatest disorder and hurry of spirits.

Booth made many handsome acknowledgments of her
favor ; and added that he very little wondered at the disorder of her spirits, concluding that he was heartily concerned at seeing her there ; but I hope, madam," said he—

Here he hesitated, upon which, bursting into an agony
of tears, she cried out, " O captain ! captain ! many extraordinary things have passed since last I saw you. O
gracious heaven ! did I ever expect that this would be the
next place of our meeting ?"

She then flung herself into her chair, where she gave
loose to her passion, whilst he, in the most affectionate and
tender manner, endeavored to soothe and comfort her ; but

passion itself did probably more for its own relief than all his friendly consolations. Having vented this in a large flood of tears, she became pretty well composed ; but Booth unhappily mentioning her father, she again relapsed into an agony, and cried out, " Why ? why will you repeat the name of that dear man ? I have disgraced him, Mr. Booth ; I am unworthy the name of his daughter." Here passion again stopped her words, and discharged itself in tears.

After this second vent of sorrow or shame, or, if the reader pleases, of rage, she once more recovered from her agonies. To say the truth, these are, I believe, as critical discharges of nature as any of those which are so called by the physicians, and do more effectually relieve the mind than any remedies with which the whole materia medica of philosophy can supply it.

When Mrs. Vincent had recovered her faculties, she perceived Booth standing silent, with a mixture of concern and astonishment in his countenance ; then addressing herself to him with an air of most bewitching softness, of which she was a perfect mistress, she said, " I do not wonder at your amazement, Captain Booth, nor indeed at the concern which you so plainly discover for me ; for I well know the goodness of your nature ; but O, Mr. Booth ! believe me, when you know what hath happened since our last meeting, your concern will be raised, however your astonishment may cease. O sir ! you are a stranger to the cause of my sorrows."

" I hope I am, madam," answered, he " for I cannot believe what I have heard in the prison—surely murder—" at which words she started from her chair, repeating murder ! " Oh ! it is music in my ears ! You have heard then the cause of my commitment, my glory, my delight, my reparation ! Yes, my old friend, this is the arm that drove the penknife to his heart. Unkind fortune, that not one drop of his blood reached my hand. Indeed, sir, I would never have washed it from it. But, though I have not the happiness to see it on my hand, I have the glorious satisfaction of remembering I saw it run in rivers on the floor ; I saw it forsake his cheeks, I saw him fall a martyr to my revenge. And is the killing a villain to be called murder? perhaps the law calls it so. Let it call it what it will, or punish me as it pleases. Punish me! no, no—that is not in the power of man—not of that monster man, Mr. Booth. I am undone, am revenged, and have now no more business for life ; let them take it from me when they will."

Our poor gentleman turned pale with horror at this speech, and the ejaculation of Good heavens! what do I hear? burst spontaneously from his lips ; nor can we wonder at this, though he was the bravest of men ; for her voice, her looks, her gestures, were properly adapted to the sentiments she expressed. Such indeed was her image that neither could Shakespeare describe, nor Hogarth paint, nor Clive act, a fury in higher perfection.

" What do you hear?" reiterated she. " You hear the resentment of the most injured of women. You have heard, you say, of the murder ; but do you know the cause, Mr. Booth? Have you since your return to England visited that country where we formerly knew one another? tell me, do you know my wretched story? tell me that, my friend."

Booth hesitated for an answer ; indeed he had heard some imperfect stories, not much to her advantage. She waited not till he had formed a speech, but cried, " Whatever you may have heard, you cannot be acquainted with all the strange accidents which have occasioned your seeing me in a place which at our last parting was so unlikely that I should ever have been found in ; nor can you know the cause of all that I have uttered, and which, I am convinced, you never expected to have heard from my mouth. If these circumstances raise your curiosity, I will satisfy it."

He answered that curiosity was too mean a word to express his ardent desire of knowing her story. Upon which, with very little previous ceremony, she began to relate what is written in the following chapter.

But before we put an end to this it may be necessary to whisper a word or two to the critics, who have perhaps begun to express no less astonishment than Mr. Booth that a lady in whom we had remarked a most extraordinary power of displaying softness should, the very next moment after the words were out of her mouth, express sentiments becoming the lips of a Dalila, Jezebel, Medea, Semiramis, Parysatis, Tanaquil, Livilla, Messalina, Agrippina, Bruni-childe, Elfrida, Lady Macbeth, Joan of Naples, Christina of Sweden, Katharine Hays, Sarah Malcolm, Con Philips,* or any other heroine of the tender sex which history, sacred or profane, ancient or modern, false or true, hath recorded.

We desire such critics to remember that it is the same English climate in which, on the lovely 10th of June, under a serene sky, the amorous Jacobite, kissing the odoriferous zephyr's breath, gathers a nosegay of white roses to deck the white breast of Celia ; and in which, on the 11th of June, the very next day, the boisterous Boreas, roused by the hollow thunder, rushes horrible through the air, and driving the wet tempest before him, levels the hope of the husbandman with the earth, dreadful remembrance of the consequences of the revolution.

Again, let it be remembered that this is the selfsame Celia, all tender, soft, and delicate, who with a voice, the sweetness of which the Syrens might envy, warbles the harmonious song in praise of the young adventurer ; and again, the next day, or perhaps the next hour, with fiery eyes, wrinkled brows, and foaming lips, roars forth treason and nonsense in a political argument with some fair one of a different principle.

Though last not least.

Or if the critic be a Whig, and consequently dislikes such kind of similes, as being too favorable to Jacobitism, let him be contented with the following story :

I happened in my youth to sit behind two ladies in a side-box at a play, where, in the balcony on the opposite side, was placed the inimitable B—y C—s, in company with a young fellow of no very formal, or indeed sober, appearance. One of the ladies, I remember, said to the other, " Did you ever see any thing look so modest and so innocent as that girl over the way ? what pity it is such a creature should be in the way of ruin, as I am afraid she is, by her being alone with that young fellow !" Now this lady was no bad physiognomist, for it was impossible to conceive a greater appearance of modesty, innocence, and simplicity, than what nature had displayed in the countenance of that girl ; and yet, all appearances notwithstanding, I myself (remember, critic, it was in my youth) had a few mornings before seen that very identical picture of all those engaging qualities in bed with a rake at a bagnio, smoking tobacco, drinking punch, talking obscenity, and swearing and cursing with all the impudence and impiety of the lowest and most abandoned trull of a soldier.

CHAPTER VII.

IN WHICH MISS MATTHEWS BEGINS HER HISTORY.

Miss Matthews, having barred the door on the inside as securely as it was before barred on the outside, proceeded as follows :

" You may imagine I am going to begin my history at the time when you left the country ; but I cannot help reminding you of something which happened before. You will soon recollect the incident ; but I believe you little know the consequence either at that time or since. Alas ! I could keep a secret then ! now I have no secrets ; the

world knows all ; and it is not worth my while to conceal
any thing. Well ! You will not wonder, I believe—I
protest I can hardly tell it you, even now. But I am convinced you have too good an opinion of yourself to be surprised at any conquest you may have made. Few men want
that good opinion—and perhaps very few had ever more
reason for it. Indeed, Will, you was a charming fellow in
those days ; nay, you are not much altered for the worse
now, at least in the opinion of some women, for your complexion and features are grown much more masculine than
they were." Here Booth made her a low bow, most probably with a compliment ; and after a little hesitation she
again proceeded. "Do you remember a contest which
happened at an assembly, betwixt myself and Miss Johnson,
about standing uppermost? you was then my partner, and
young Williams danced with the other lady. The particulars are not now worth mentioning, though I suppose you
have long since forgot them. Let it suffice that you supported my claim, and Williams very sneakingly gave up
that of his partner, who was, with much difficulty, afterward prevailed to dance with him. You said—I am sure
I repeat the words exactly—that ' you would not for the
world affront any lady there ; but that you thought you
might, without any such danger, declare that here was no assembly in which that lady, meaning your humble servant,
was not worthy of the uppermost place ; nor will I,' said you,
' suffer the first duke in England, when she is at the uppermost end of the room, and hath called her dance, to lead
his partner above her.'

"What made this the more pleasing to me was, that I
secretly hated Miss Johnson. Will you have the reason ?
why, then, I will tell you honestly : she was my rival.
That word perhaps astonishes you, as you never, I believe,
heard of any one who made his addresses to me ; and indeed
my heart was, till that night, entirely indifferent to all man-

kind : I mean, then, that she was my rival for praise, for beauty, for dress, for fortune, and consequently for admiration. My triumph on this conquest is not to be expressed any more than my delight in the person to whom I chiefly owed it. The former, I fancy, was visible to the whole company ; and I desired it should be so ; but the latter was so well concealed that no one, I am confident, took any notice of it. And yet you appeared to me that night to be an angel. You looked, you danced, you spoke—everything charmed me.''

" Good heavens !'' cries Booth, " is it possible you should do me so much unmerited honor, and I should be dunce enough not to perceive the least symptom ?''

" I assure you,'' answered she, " I did all I could to prevent you ; and yet I almost hated you for not seeing through what I strove to hide. Why, Mr. Booth, was you not more quick-sighted ? I will answer for you—your affections were more happily disposed of to a much better woman than myself, whom you married soon afterward. I should ask you for her, Mr. Booth ; I should have asked you for her before ; but I am unworthy of asking for her, or of calling her my acquaintance.''

Booth stopped her short as she was running into another fit of passion, and begged her to omit all former matters, and acquaint him with that part of her history to which he was an entire stranger.

She then renewed her discourse as follows : " You know, Mr. Booth, I soon afterward left that town, upon the death of my grandmother, and returned home to my father's house, where I had not been long arrived before some troops of dragoons came to quarter in our neighborhood. Among the officers there was a cornet whose detested name was Hebbers, a name I could scarce repeat had I not at the same time the pleasure to reflect that he is now no more. My father, you know, who is a hearty well-

wisher to the present government, used always to invite the
officers to his house ; so did he these.   Nor was it long before this cornet in so particular a manner recommended himself to the poor old gentleman (I cannot think of him without tears), that our house became his principal habitation,
and he was rarely at his quarters, unless when his superior
officers obliged him to be there.   I shall say nothing of his
person, nor could that be any recommendation to a man ;
it was such, however, as no woman could have made an
objection to.   Nature had certainly wrapped up her odious
work in a most beautiful covering.   To say the truth, he
was the handsomest man, except one only, that I ever saw
—I assure you, I have seen a handsomer—but—well.   He
had, besides, all the qualifications of a gentleman ; was
genteel, and extremely polite ; spoke French well, and
danced to a miracle ; but what chiefly recommended him to
my father was his skill in music, of which you know that
dear man was the most violent lover.   I wish he was not
too susceptible of flattery on that head, for I have heard
Hebbers often greatly commend my father's performance,
and have observed that the good man was wonderfully
pleased with such commendations.   To say the truth, it is
the only way I can account for the extraordinary friendship
which my father conceived for this person—such a friendship
that he at last became a part of our family.

" This very circumstance, which, as I am convinced,
strongly recommended him to my father, had the very contrary effect with me : I had never any delight in music,
and it was not without much difficulty I was prevailed on to
learn to play on the harpsichord, in which I had made a
very slender progress.   As this man, therefore, was frequently the occasion of my being importuned to play against
my will, I began to entertain some dislike for him on that
account ; and as to his person, I assure you, I long continued to look on it with great indifference.

" How strange will the art of this man appear to you presently, who had sufficient address to convert that very circumstance which had at first occasioned my dislike into the first seeds of affection for him !

" You have often, I believe, heard my sister Betty play on the harpsichord ; she was indeed reputed the best performer in the whole country.

" I was the farthest in the world from regarding this perfection of hers with envy. In reality, perhaps, I despised all perfection of this kind : at least, as I had neither skill nor ambition to excel this way, I looked upon it as a matter of mere indifference.

" Hebbers first put this emulation in my head. He took great pains to persuade me that I had much greater abilities of the musical kind than my sister, and that I might with the greatest ease, if I pleased, excel her, offering me, at the same time, his assistance if I would resolve to undertake it.

" When he had sufficiently inflamed my ambition, in which, perhaps, he found too little difficulty, the continual praises of my sister, which before I had disregarded, became more and more nauseous in my ears ; and the rather as, music being the favorite passion of my father, I became apprehensive (not without frequent hints from Hebbers of that nature) that she might gain too great a preference in his favor.

" To my harpsichord then I applied myself night and day with such industry and attention that I soon began to perform in a tolerable manner. I do not absolutely say I excelled my sister, for many were of a different opinion ; but indeed there might be some partiality in all that.

" Hebbers, at least, declared himself on my side, and nobody could doubt his judgment. He asserted openly that I played in the better manner of the two ; and one day, when I was playing to him alone, he affected to burst into a rapture of admiration, and squeezing me gently by

the hand, said, ' There, madam, I now declare you excel your
sister as much in music as,' added he in a whispering sigh,
' you do her, and all the world, in every other charm.'

" No woman can bear any superiority in whatever thing
she desires to excel in.   I now began to hate all the admirers of my sister, to be uneasy at every commendation
bestowed on her skill in music, and consequently to love
Hebbers for the preference which he gave to mine.

" It was now that I began to survey the handsome person
of Hebbers with pleasure.   And here, Mr. Booth, I will
betray to you the grand secret of our sex.   Many women,
I believe, do, with great innocence, and even with great
indifference, converse with men of the finest persons ; but
this I am confident may be affirmed with truth, that, when
once a woman comes to ask this question of herself, Is the
man whom I like for some other reason, handsome ? her
fate, and his too, very strongly depend on her answering in
the affirmative.

" Hebbers no sooner perceived that he made an impression on my heart, of which I am satisfied I gave him too
undeniable tokens, than he affected on a sudden to shun me
in the most apparent manner.   He wore the most melancholy air in my presence, and, by his dejected looks and
sighs, firmly persuaded me that there was some secret
sorrow laboring in his bosom ; nor will it be difficult for
you to imagine to what cause I imputed it.

" Whilst I was wishing for his declaration of a passion in
which I thought I could not be mistaken, and at the same
time trembling whenever we met with the apprehension of
this very declaration, the widow Carey came from London
to make us a visit, intending to stay the whole summer at
our house.

" Those who know Mrs. Carey will scarce think I do
her an injury in saying she is far from being handsome ;
and yet she is as finished a coquette as if she had the highest

beauty to support that character. But perhaps you have seen her ; and if you have, I am convinced you will readily subscribe to my opinion."

Booth answered he had not ; and then she proceeded as in the following chapter.

CHAPTER VIII.

THE HISTORY OF MISS MATTHEWS CONTINUED.

" This young lady had not been three days with us before Hebbers grew so particular with her that it was generally observed ; and my poor father, who, I believe, loved the cornet as if he had been his son, began to jest on the occasion, as one who would not be displeased at throwing a good jointure into the arms of his friend.

" You will easily guess, sir, the disposition of my mind on this occasion ; but I was not permitted to suffer long under it ; for one day, when Hebbers was alone with me, he took an opportunity of expressing his abhorrence at the thoughts of marrying for interest, contrary to his inclinations. I was warm on the subject, and, I believe, went so far as to say that none but fools and villains did so. He replied, with a sigh, Yes, madam, but what would you think of a man whose heart is all the while bleeding for another woman, to whom he would willingly sacrifice the world, but, because he must sacrifice her interest as well as his own, never durst even give her a hint of that passion which was preying on his very vitals ? Do you believe, Miss Fanny, there is such a wretch on earth ? I answered, with an assumed coldness, I did not believe there was. He then took me gently by the hand, and, with a look so tender that I cannot describe it, vowed he was himself that wretch. Then starting, as if conscious of an error committed, he cried with a faltering voice, What am I saying ? Pardon me, Miss Fanny ; since I beg only your pity, I never will ask for more. At these words, hearing my father coming up, I betrayed myself entirely, if indeed I had not done it before. I hastily withdrew my hand, crying, Hush ! for heaven's sake ; my father is just coming in, my blushes, my look, and my accent telling him, I suppose, all which he wished to know.

" A few days now brought matters to an eclaircissement between us ; the being undeceived in what had given me so much uneasiness gave me a pleasure too sweet to be resisted. To triumph over the widow, for whom I had in a very short time contracted a most inveterate hatred, was a pride not to be described. Hebbers appeared to me to be the cause of all this happiness. I doubted not but that he had the most disinterested passion for me, and thought him every way worthy of its return. I did return it, and accepted him as my lover.

" He declared the greatest apprehensions of my father's suspicion, though I am convinced these were causeless had his designs been honorable. To blind these, I consented that he should carry on sham addresses to the widow, who was now a constant jest between us ; and he pretended, from time to time, to acquaint me faithfully with every thing that passed at his interviews with her ; nor was this faithless woman wanting in her part of the deceit. She carried herself to me all the while with a show of affection, and pretended to have the utmost friendship for me. But such are the friendships of women !"

At this remark Booth, though enough affected at some parts of the story, had great difficulty to refrain from laughter ; but, by good luck, he escaped being perceived, and the lady went on without interruption.

" I am come now to a part of my narrative in which it is impossible to be particular without being tedious ; for, as to the commerce between lovers, it is, I believe, much the same in all cases, and there is, perhaps, scarce a single phrase that hath not been repeated ten millions of times.

" One thing, however, as I strongly remarked it then, so I will repeat it to you now. In all our conversations, in moments when he fell into the warmest raptures, and expressed the greatest uneasiness at the delay of his joys, he seldom mentioned the word marriage ; and never once solicited a day for that purpose. Indeed, women cannot be cautioned too much against such lovers ; for though I have heard, and perhaps truly, of some of our sex, of a virtue so exalted that it is proof against every temptation ; yet the generality, I am afraid, are too much in the power of a man to whom they have owned an affection. What is called being upon a good footing is perhaps being upon a very dangerous one ; and a woman who hath given her consent to marry can hardly be said to be safe till she is married.

" And now, sir, I hasten to the period of my ruin. We had a wedding in our family ; my musical sister was married to a young fellow as musical as herself. Such a match, you may be sure, amongst other festivities, must have a ball. Oh ! Mr. Booth, shall modesty forbid me to remark to you what passed on that occasion ? But why do I mention modesty, who have no pretensions to it ? Every thing was said and practised on that occasion as if the purpose had been to inflame the mind of every woman present. That effect, I freely own to you, it had with me. Music, dancing, wine, and the most luscious conversation, in which my poor dear father innocently joined, raised ideas in me of which I shall for ever repent ; and I wished (why should I deny it ?) that it had been my wedding instead of my sister's.

" The villain Hebbers danced with me that night, and he lost no opportunity of improving the occasion. In short, the dreadful evening came. My father, though it was a very unusual thing with him, grew intoxicated with liquor ;

most of the men were in the same condition ; nay, I myself
drank more than I was accustomed to, enough to inflame,
though not to disorder.   I lost my former bedfellow, my
sister, and—you may, I think, guess the rest—the villain
found means to steal to my chamber, and I was undone.

"Two months I passed in this detested commerce, buying, even then, my guilty, half-tasted pleasures at too dear
a rate, with continual horror and apprehension ; but what
have I paid since—what do I pay now, Mr. Booth ?   O
may my fate be a warning to every woman to keep her
innocence, to resist every temptation, since she is certain to
repent of the foolish bargain.   May it be a warning to her to
deal with mankind with care and caution ; to shun the least
approaches of dishonor, and never to confide too much in
the honesty of a man, nor in her own strength, where she
has so much at stake ; let her remember she walks on a
precipice, and the bottomless pit is to receive her if she
slips—nay, if she makes but one false step.

"I ask your pardon, Mr. Booth ; I might have spared
these exhortations, since no woman hears me ; but you will
not wonder at seeing me affected on this occasion."

Booth declared he was much more surprised at her being
able so well to preserve her temper in recounting her story.

"O sir," answered she, "I am at length reconciled to
my fate ; and I can now die with pleasure, since I die
revenged.   I am not one of those mean wretches who can
sit down and lament their misfortunes.   If I ever shed
tears, they are the tears of indignation.   But I will proceed.

"It was my fate now to solicit marriage ; and I failed
not to do it in the most earnest manner. He answered
me at first with procrastinations, declaring, from time to
time, he would mention it to my father, and still excusing
himself for not doing it.   At last he thought on an expedi-
ent to obtain a longer reprieve.   This was by pretending
that he should, in a very few weeks, be preferred to the

command of a troop ; and then, he said, he could with some confidence propose the match.

" In this delay I was persuaded to acquiesce, and was indeed pretty easy, for I had not yet the least mistrust of his honor ; but what words can paint my sensations when one morning he came into my room, with all the marks of dejection in his countenance, and throwing an open letter on the table, said, 'There is news, madam, in that letter which I am unable to tell you ; nor can it give you more concern than it hath given me.'

" This letter was from his captain, to acquaint him that the rout, as they called it, was arrived, and that they were to march within two days. And this, I am since convinced, was what he expected, instead of the preferment which had been made the pretence of delaying our marriage.

" The shock which I felt at reading this was inexpressible, occasioned indeed principally by the departure of a villain whom I loved. However, I soon acquired sufficient presence of mind to remember the main point ; and I now insisted peremptorily on his making me immediately his wife, whatever might be the consequence.

" He seemed thunderstruck at this proposal, being, I suppose, destitute of any excuse : but I was too impatient to wait for an answer, and cried out with much eagerness, 'Sure you cannot hesitate a moment upon this matter.' ' Hesitate, madam !' replied he—' what you ask is impossible. Is this a time for me to mention a thing of this kind to your father ? ' My eyes were now opened all at once—I fell into a rage little short of madness. ' Tell not me,' I cried, ' of impossibilities, nor times, nor of my father—my honor, my reputation, my all are at stake. I will have no excuse, no delay—make me your wife this instant, or I will proclaim you over the face of the whole earth for the greatest of villains.' He answered, with a kind of sneer, ' What will you proclaim, madam ? whose honor will you injure ? '

My tongue faltered when I offered to reply, and I fell into a violent agony, which ended in a fit ; nor do I remember any thing more that passed till I found myself in the arms of my poor affrighted father.

" O Mr. Booth, what was then my situation ! I tremble even now from the reflection. I must stop a moment. I can go no farther." Booth attempted all in his power to soothe her ; and she soon recovered her powers, and proceeded in her story.

CHAPTER IX.

IN WHICH MISS MATTHEWS CONCLUDES HER RELATION.

" Before I had recovered my senses I had sufficiently betrayed myself to the best of men, who, instead of upbraiding me, or exerting any anger, endeavored to comfort me all he could with assurances that all should yet be well. This goodness of his affected me with inexpressible sensations ; I prostrated myself before him, embraced and kissed his knees, and almost dissolved in tears, and a degree of tenderness hardly to be conceived. But I am running into too minute descriptions.

" Hebbers, seeing me in a fit, had left me, and sent one of the servants to take care of me. He then ran away like a thief from the house, without taking his leave of my father, or once thanking him for all his civilities. He did not stop at his quarters, but made directly to London, apprehensive, I believe, either of my father or brother's resentment ; for I am convinced he is a coward. Indeed his fear of my brother was utterly groundless, for I believe he would rather have thanked any man who had destroyed me ; and I am sure I am not in the least behindhand with him in good wishes.

" All his inveteracy to me had, however, no effect on my father, at least at that time ; for, though the good man took sufficient occasions to reprimand me for my past offence, he could not be brought to abandon me. A treaty of marriage was now set on foot, in which my father himself offered me to Hebbers, with a fortune superior to that which had been given with my sister ; nor could all my brother's remonstrances against it, as an act of the highest injustice, avail.

" Hebbers entered into the treaty, though not with much warmth. He had even the assurance to make additional demands on my father, which being complied with, every thing was concluded, and the villain once more received into the house. He soon found means to obtain my forgiveness of his former behavior ; indeed he convinced me, so foolishly blind is female love, that he had never been to blame.

" When every thing was ready for our nuptials, and the day of the ceremony was to be appointed, in the midst of my happiness I received a letter from an unknown hand, acquainting me (guess, Mr. Booth, how I was shocked at receiving it) that Mr. Hebbers was already married to a woman in a distant part of the kingdom.

" I will not tire you with all that passed at our next interview. I communicated the letter to Hebbers, who, after some little hesitation, owned the fact, and not only owned it, but had the address to improve it to his own advantage, to make it the means of satisfying me concerning all his former delays ; which, to say the truth, I was not so much displeased at imputing to any degree of villany as I should have been to impute it to the want of a sufficient warmth of affection ; and though the disappointment of all my hopes, at the very instant of their expected fruition, threw me into the most violent disorders ; yet, when I came a little to myself, he had no great difficulty to persuade me that in every instance, with regard to me, Hebbers had acted from no other motive than from the most ardent and ungovernable love. And there is, I believe, no crime which a woman will not forgive when she can derive it from that fountain. In short, I forgave him all, and am willing to persuade myself I am not weaker than the rest of my sex. Indeed, Mr. Booth, he hath a bewitching tongue, and is master of an address that no woman could resist. I do assure you the charms of his person are his least perfection, at least in my eye."

Here Booth smiled, but happily without her perceiving it.

" A fresh difficulty (continued she) now arose. This was to excuse the delay of the ceremony to my father, who every day very earnestly urged it. This made me so very uneasy that I at last listened to a proposal, which, if any one in the days of my innocence, or even a few days before had assured me I could have submitted to have thought of, I should have treated the supposition with the highest contempt and indignation ; nay, I scarce reflect on it now with more horror than astonishment. In short, I agreed to run away with him—to leave my father, my reputation, every thing which was or ought to have been dear to me, and to live with this villain as a mistress, since I could not be his wife.

" Was not this an obligation of the highest and tenderest kind, and had I not reason to expect every return in the man's power on whom I had conferred it ?

" I will make short of the remainder of my story, for what is there of a woman worth relating after what I have told you ?

" Above a year I lived with this man in an obscure court in London, during which time I had a child by him, whom heaven, I thank it, hath been pleased to take to itself.

" During many months he behaved to me with all the apparent tenderness and even fondness imaginable ; but, alas ! how poor was my enjoyment of this compared to what it would have been in another situation ? When he was present, life was barely tolerable ; but when he was absent, nothing could equal the misery I endured. I passed my hours almost entirely alone, for no company but what I despised would consort with me. Abroad I scarce ever went, lest I should meet any of my former acquaintance, for their sight would have plunged a thousand daggers in my soul. My only diversion was going very seldom to a play, where I hid myself in the gallery, with a daughter of the woman of the house. A girl, indeed, of good sense and many good qualities ; but how much beneath me was it to be the companion of a creature so low ! O heavens ! when I have seen my equals glittering in a side-box, how have the thoughts of my lost honor torn my soul !"

"Pardon me, dear madam," cries Booth, "for interrupting you ; but I am under the utmost anxiety to know what became of your poor father, for whom I have so great a respect, and who, I am convinced, must so bitterly feel your loss."

"O Mr. Booth," answered she, "he was scarce ever out of my thoughts. His dear image still obtruded itself in my mind, and I believe would have broken my heart had I not taken a very preposterous way to ease myself. I am indeed almost ashamed to tell you ; but necessity put it in my head. You will think the matter too trifling to have been remembered, and so it surely was ; nor should I have remembered it on any other occasion. You must know, then, sir, that my brother was always my inveterate enemy, and altogether as fond of my sister. He once prevailed with my father to let him take my sister with him in the chariot, and by that means I was disappointed of going to a ball which I had set my heart on. The disappointment, I assure you, was great at the time ; but I had long since forgotten it. I must have been a very bad woman if I had not, for it was the only thing in which I can remember that my father ever disobliged me. However, I now revived this in my mind, which I artificially worked up into so high an injury that, I assure you, it afforded me no little comfort. When any tender idea intruded into my bosom, I immediately raised this phantom of an injury in my imagination, and it considerably lessened the fury of that sorrow which I should have otherwise felt for the loss of so good a father, who died within a few months of my departure from him.

"And now, sir, to draw to a conclusion. One night, as I was in the gallery at Drury Lane playhouse, I saw below me in a side-box (she was once below me in every place), that widow whom I mentioned to you before. I had scarce cast my eyes on this woman before I was so shocked with the sight that it almost deprived me of my senses ; for the villain Hebbers came presently in and seated himself behind her.

"He had been almost a month from me, and I believed him to be at his quarters in Yorkshire. Guess what were my sensations when I beheld him sitting by that base woman, and talking to her with the utmost familiarity. I could not long endure this sight, and having acquainted my companion that I was taken suddenly ill, I forced her to go home with me at the end of the second act.

"After a restless and sleepless night, when I rose the next morning I had the comfort to receive a visit from the woman of the house, who, after a very short introduction, asked me when I had heard from the captain, and when I expected to see him ? I had not strength or spirits to make her any answer, and she proceeded thus : 'Indeed I did not think the captain would have used me so. My husband was an officer of the army as well as himself ; and if a body is a little low in the world, I am sure that is no reason for folks to trample on a body. I defy the world to say as I ever was guilty of an ill thing.' 'For heaven's sake, madam,' says I, 'what do you mean ?' 'Mean ?' cries she ;

' I am sure if I had not thought you had been Captain Hebbers' lady—his lawful lady too—you should never have set
footing in my house. I would have Captain Hebbers
know that, though I am reduced to let lodgings, I never
have entertained any but persons of character.' In this
manner, sir, she ran on, saying many shocking things not
worth repeating, till my anger at last got the better of my
patience as well as my sorrow, and I pushed her out of the
room.

" She had not been long gone before her daughter came
to me, and, after many expressions of tenderness and pity,
acquainted me that her mother had just found out, by
means of the captain's servant, that the captain was married to another lady, which, if you did not know before,
madam, said she, I am sorry to be the messenger of such
ill news.

" Think, Mr. Booth, what I must have endured to see
myself humbled before such a creature as this—the daughter of a woman who lets lodgings ! However, having recollected myself a little, I thought it would be in vain to
deny any thing ; so, knowing this to be one of the best-
natured and most sensible girls in the world, I resolved to
tell her my whole story, and for the future to make her my
confidante. I answered her, therefore, with a good deal
of assurance, that she need not regret telling me this piece
of ill news, for I had known it before I came to her house.

" ' Pardon me, madam,' replied the girl, ' you cannot possibly have known it so long, for he hath not been married
above a week ; last night was the first time of his appearing
in public with his wife at the play. Indeed, I knew very
well the cause of your uneasiness there ; but would not
mention—— '

" ' His wife at the play ! ' answered I eagerly. ' What
wife ? whom do you mean ? '

" ' I mean the widow Carey, madam,' replied she, ' to

whom the captain was married a few days since. His serv.
ant was here last night to pay for your lodging, and he told
it my mother.'

"I know not what answer I made, or whether I made
any. I presently fell dead on the floor, and it was with
great difficulty I was brought back to life by the poor girl,
for neither the mother nor the maid of the house would
lend me any assistance, both seeming to regard me rathei
as a monster than a woman.

"Scarce had I recovered the use of my senses when I
received a letter from the villain, declaring he had not assurance to see my face, and very kindly advising me to endeavor to reconcile myself to my family, concluding with
an offer, in case I did not succeed, to allow me twenty
pounds a year to support me in some remote part of the
kingdom.

"I need not mention my indignation at these proposals.
In the highest agony of rage I went in a chair to the detested house, where I easily got access to the wretch I had
devoted to destruction, whom I no sooner found within my
reach than I plunged a drawn penknife, which I had prepared in my pocket for the purpose, into his accursed heart.
For this fact I was immediately seized and soon after committed hither ; and for this fact I am ready to die, and
shall with pleasure receive the sentence of the law.

"Thus, sir," said she, "I have related to you my unhappy story, and if I have tired your patience by dwelling
too long on those parts which affected me the most, I ask
your pardon."

Booth made a proper speech on this occasion, and having expressed much concern at her present situation, concluded that he hoped her sentence would be milder than
she seemed to expect.

Her reply to this was full of so much bitterness and indignation that we do not think proper to record the speech

at length, in which, having vented her passion, she all at once put on a serene countenance, and with an air of great complacency said, " Well, Mr. Booth, I think I have now a right to satisfy my curiosity at the expense of your breath. I may say it is not altogether a vain curiosity, for perhaps I have had inclination enough to interest myself in whatever concerns you ; but no matter for that : those days (added she with a sigh) are now over."

Booth, who was extremely good-natured and well-bred, told her that she should not command him twice whatever was in his power ; and then, after the usual apology, was going to begin his history, when the keeper arrived, and acquainted the lady that dinner was ready, at the same time saying, " I suppose, madam, as the gentleman is an acquaintance of yours, he must dine with us too."

Miss Matthews told the keeper that she had only one word to mention in private to the gentleman, and that then they would both attend him. She then pulled her purse from her pocket, in which were upwards of twenty guineas, being the remainder of the money for which she had sold a gold repeating watch, her father's present, with some other trinkets, and desired Mr. Booth to take what he should have occasion for, saying, " You know, I believe, dear Will, I never valued money ; and now I am sure I shall have very little use for it." Booth, with much difficulty, accepted of two guineas, and then they both together attended the keeper.

CHAPTER X.

TABLE-TALK, CONSISTING OF A FACETIOUS DISCOURSE THAT PASSED IN THE PRISON.

THERE were assembled at the table the governor of these (not improperly called infernal) regions ; the lieutenant-governor, vulgarly named the first turnkey ; Miss Matthews, Mr. Booth, Mr. Robinson the gambler, several other prisoners of both sexes, and one Murphy, an attorney.

The governor took the first opportunity to bring the affair of Miss Matthews upon the carpet, and then, turning to Murphy, he said, " It is very lucky this gentleman happens to be present ; I do assure you, madam, your cause cannot be in abler hands. He is, I believe, the best man in England at a defence ; I have known him often succeed against the most positive evidence."

" Fye, sir," answered Murphy, " you know I hate all this ; but if the lady will trust me with her cause, I will do the best in my power. Come, madam, do not be discouraged ; a bit of manslaughter and cold iron, I hope, will be the worst : or perhaps we may come off better with a slice of chance-medley, or *se defendendo.*"

" I am very ignorant of the law, sir," cries the lady.

" Yes, madam," answered Murphy, " it can't be expected you should understand it. There are very few of us who profess it that understand the whole, nor is it necessary we should. There is a great deal of rubbish of little use about indictments and abatements and bars and ejectments and trovers and such stuff, with which people cram their heads to little purpose. The chapter of evidence is the main business ; that is the sheet-anchor ; that is the rudder which brings the vessel safe *in portum.* Evidence is indeed the whole, the *summa totidis,* for *de non apparentibus et non insistentibus eandem est ratio.*"

" If you address yourself to me, sir," said the lady, " you are much too learned, I assure you, for my understanding."

" *Tace,* madam," answered Murphy, " is Latin for a candle ; I commend your prudence. I shall know the particulars of your case when we are alone."

" I hope the lady," said Robinson, " hath no suspicion

of any person here. I hope we are all persons of honor at this table."

"D—n my eyes!" answered a well-dressed woman, "I can answer for myself, and the other ladies ; though I never saw the lady in my life, she need not be shy of us, d—n my eyes ! I scorn to rap * against any lady."

"D—n me, madam !" cried another female, "I honor what you have done. I once put a knife into a cull myself —so my service to you, madam, and I wish you may come off with *se diffidendo* with all my heart."

"I beg, good woman," said Miss Matthews, "you would talk on some other subject, and give yourself no concern about my affairs."

"You see, ladies," cried Murphy, "the gentlewoman doth not care to talk on this matter before company ; so pray do not press her."

"Nay, I value the lady's acquaintance no more than she values mine," cries the first woman who spoke. "I have kept as good company as the lady, I believe, every day in the week. Good woman ! I don't use to be so treated. If the lady says such another word to me, d—n me, I will darken her daylights. Marry come up ! Good woman ! the lady's a whore as well as myself ; and though I am sent hither to milldoll, d—n my eyes, I have money enough to buy it off as well as the lady herself."

Action might perhaps soon have ensued this speech had not the keeper interposed his authority and put an end to any further dispute. Soon after which the company broke up, and none but himself, Mr. Murphy, Captain Booth, and Miss Matthews remained together.

Miss Matthews then, at the entreaty of the keeper, began to open her case to Mr. Murphy, whom she admitted to be her solicitor, though she still declared she was indifferent as to the event of the trial.

* A cant word, meaning to swear, or rather to perjure yourself.

Mr. Murphy, having heard all the particulars with which the reader is already acquainted (as far as related to the murder), shook his head and said, "There is but one circumstance, madam, which I wish was out of the case ; and that we must put out of it ; I mean the carrying the pen-knife drawn into the room with you, for that seems to imply malice prepensive, as we call it in the law ; this circumstance, therefore, must not appear against you ; and if the servant who was in the room observed this, he must be bought off at all hazards. All here you say are friends ; therefore I tell you openly you must furnish me with money sufficient for this purpose. Malice is all we have to guard against."

"I would not presume, sir," cries Booth, "to inform you in the law ; but I have heard, in case of stabbing, a man may be indicted upon the statute ; and it is capital, though no malice appears."

"You say true, sir," answered Murphy ; "a man may be indicted *contra formam statutis;* and that method, I will allow you, requires no malice. I presume you are a lawyer, sir ?"

"No indeed, sir," answered Booth, "I know nothing of the law."

"Then, sir, I will tell you. If a man be indicted *contra formam statutis,* as we say, no malice is necessary, because the form of the statute makes malice ; and then what we have to guard against is having struck the first blow. Pox on't, it is unlucky this was done in a room : if it had been in the street we could have had five or six witnesses to have proved the first blow, cheaper than, I am afraid, we shall get this one ; for when a man knows, from the unhappy circumstances of the case, that you can procure no other witness but himself, he is always dear. It is so in all other ways of business. I am very implicit, you see ; but we are all among friends. The safest way is to furnish me with

money enough to offer him a good round sum at once ; and
I think (it is for your good I speak) fifty pounds is the least
that can be offered him. I do assure you I would offer him
no less was it my own case."

" And do you think, sir," said she, " that I would save
my life at the expense of hiring another to perjure himself ?"

" Ay, surely do I," cries Murphy ; " for where is the
fault, admitting there is some fault in perjury, as you call it ?
and, to be sure, it is such a matter as every man would
rather wish to avoid than not ; and yet, as it may be
managed, there is not so much as some people are apt to
imagine in it ; for he need not kiss the book, and then pray
where's the perjury ? but if the crier is sharper than ordinary, what is it he kisses ? is it any thing but a bit of calf's-
skin ? I am sure a man must be a very bad Christian himself who would not do so much as that to save the life of
any Christian whatever, much more of so pretty a lady.
Indeed, madam, if we can make out but a tolerable case, so
much beauty will go a great way with the judge and the
jury too."

The latter part of this speech, notwithstanding the mouth
it came from, caused Miss Matthews to suppress much of
the indignation which began to arise at the former, and
she answered with a smile, " Sir, you are a great casuist in
these matters ; but we need argue no longer concerning
them, for if fifty pounds would save my life, I assure you
I could not command that sum. The little money I have
in my pocket is all I can call my own, and I apprehend, in
the situation I am in, I shall have very little of that to
spare."

" Come, come, madam," cries Murphy, " life is sweet,
let me tell you, and never sweeter than when we are near
losing it. I have known many a man very brave and un-
daunted at his first commitment, who, when business began

to thicken a little upon him, hath changed his note. It is
no time to be saving in your condition." The keeper,
who, after the liberality of Miss Matthews, and on seeing a
purse of guineas in her hand, had conceived a great opinion
of her wealth, no sooner heard that the sum which he had
in intention entirely confiscated for his own use was attempted to be broke in upon, thought it high time to be
upon his guard. "To be sure," cries he, "Mr. Murphy,
life is sweet, as you say : that must be acknowledged : to
be sure, life is sweet ; but, sweet as it is, no persons can
advance more than they are worth to save it. And indeed,
if the lady can command no more money than that little
she mentions, she is to be commended for her unwillingness
to part with any of it ; for, to be sure, as she says, she will
want every farthing of that to live like a gentlewoman till
she comes to her trial. And, to be sure, as sweet as life is,
people ought to take care to be able to live sweetly while they
do live ; besides, I cannot help saying the lady shows herself to be what she is by her abhorrence of perjury,
which is certainly a very dreadful crime. And though
the not kissing the book doth, as you say, make a great
deal of difference ; and if a man had a great while to live
and repent, perhaps he might swallow it well enough ; yet,
when people comes to be near their end (as who can venture to foretell what will be the lady's case ?) they ought to
take care not to overburden their conscience. I hope the
lady's case will not be found murder ; for I am sure I
always wish well to all my prisoners who show themselves
to be gentlemen or gentlewomen ; yet one should always
fear the worst."

"Indeed, sir, you speak like an oracle," answered the
lady ; "and one subornation of perjury would sit heavier
on my conscience than twenty such murders as I am guilty
of."

"Nay, to be sure, madam," answered the keeper, "nobody can pretend to tell what provocation you must have had ; and certainly it can never be imagined that a lady who behaves herself so handsomely as you have done ever since you have been under my keys should be guilty of killing a man without being very highly provoked to do it.''

Mr. Murphy was, I believe, going to answer when he was called out of the room ; after which nothing passed between the remaining persons worth relating till Booth and the lady retired back again into the lady's apartment.

Here they fell immediately to commenting on the foregoing discourse ; but as their comments were, I believe, the same with what most readers have made on the same occasion, we shall omit them. At last Miss Matthews reminding her companion of his promise of relating to her what had befallen him since the interruption of their former acquaintonce, he began as is written in the next book of this history.

BOOK II.

CHAPTER I.

THE tea-table being removed, and Mr. Booth and the lady left alone, he proceeded as follows :

" Since you desire, madam, to know the particulars of my courtship to that best and dearest of women whom I afterward married, I will endeavor to recollect them as well as I can, at least all those incidents which are most worth relating to you.

" If the vulgar opinion of the fatality in marriage had ever any foundation, it surely appeared in my marriage with my Amelia. I knew her in the first dawn of her beauty, and, I believe, madam, she had as much as ever fell to the share of a woman ; but, though I always admired her, it was long without any spark of love. Perhaps the general admiration which at that time pursued her, the respect paid her by persons of the highest rank, and the numberless addresses which were made her by men of great fortune, prevented my aspiring at the possession of those charms which seemed so absolutely out of my reach. However it was, I assure you the accident which deprived her of the admiration of others made the first great impression on my heart in her favor. The injury done to her beauty by the overturning of a chaise, by which, as you may well remember, her lovely nose was beat all to pieces, gave me an assurance that the woman who had been so much adored

for the charms of her person deserved a much higher adoration to be paid to her mind ; for that she was in the latter
respect infinitely more superior to the rest of her sex than
she had ever been in the former.''

" I admire your taste extremely," cried the lady ; " I
remember perfectly well the great heroism with which your
Amelia bore that misfortune."

" Good heavens ! madam," answered he ; "what a
magnanimity of mind did her behavior demonstrate ! if the
world have extolled the firmness of soul in a man who can
support the loss of fortune ; of a general who can be composed after the loss of a victory ; or of a king who can be
contented with the loss of a crown ; with what astonishment
ought we to behold, with what praises to honor, a young
lady who can with patience and resignation submit to the
loss of exquisite beauty—in other words, to the loss of fortune,
power, glory, every thing which human nature is apt to
court and rejoice in ! what must be the mind which can
bear to be deprived of all these in a moment, and by an
unfortunate trifling accident ; which could support all this,
together with the most exquisite torments of body, and with
dignity, with resignation, without complaining, almost
without a tear, undergo the most painful and dreadful
operations of surgery in such a situation !'' Here he stopped, and a torrent of tears gushed from his eyes—such
tears as are apt to flow from a truly noble heart at the hearing of any thing surprisingly great and glorious. As soon
as he was able he again proceeded thus :

" Would you think, Miss Matthews, that the misfortune
of my Amelia was capable of any aggravation ? I assure
you she hath often told me it was aggravated with a circumstance which outweighed all the other ingredients.
This was the cruel insults she received from some of her
most intimate acquaintance, several of whom, after many
distortions and grimaces, have turned their heads aside,

unable to support their secret triumph, and burst into a loud laugh in her hearing."

" Good heavens !" cried Miss Matthews, " what detestable actions will this contemptible passion of envy prevail on our sex to commit !"

" An occasion of this kind, as she hath since told me, made the first impression on her gentle heart in my favor. I was one day in company with several young ladies, or rather young devils, where poor Amelia's accident was the subject of much mirth and pleasantry. One of these said she hoped miss would not hold her head so high for the future. Another answered, I do not know, madam, what she may do with her head, but I am convinced she will never more turn up her nose at her betters. Another cried, What a very proper match might now be made between Amelia and a certain captain, who had unfortunately received an injury in the same part, though from no shameful cause. Many other sarcasms were thrown out, very unworthy to be repeated. I was hurt with perceiving so much malice in human shape, and cried out very bluntly, Indeed, ladies, you need not express such satisfaction at poor Miss Emily's accident, for she will still be the handsomest woman in England. This speech of mine was afterward variously repeated, by some to my honor, and by others represented in a contrary light ; indeed it was often reported to be much ruder than it was. However, it at length reached Amelia's ears. She said she was very much obliged to me, since I could have so much compassion for her as to be rude to a lady on her account.

" About a month after the accident, when Amelia began to see company in a mask, I had the honor to drink tea with her. We were alone together, and I begged her to indulge my curiosity by showing me her face. She answered in a most obliging manner, ' Perhaps, Mr. Booth, you will as little know me when my mask is off as when it is on ; ' and at the same instant unmasked. The surgeon's skill was the least I considered. A thousand tender ideas rushed all at once on my mind. I was unable to contain myself, and eagerly kissing her hand, I cried, ' Upon my soul, madam, you never appeared to me so lovely as at this instant.' Nothing more remarkable passed at this visit ; but I sincerely believe we were neither of us hereafter indifferent to each other.

" Many months, however, passed after this before I ever thought seriously of making her my wife. Not that I wanted sufficient love for Amelia. Indeed it arose from the vast affection I bore her. I considered my own as a desperate fortune, hers as entirely dependent on her mother, who was a woman, you know, of violent passions, and very unlikely to consent to a match so highly contrary to the interest of her daughter. The more I loved Amelia, the more firmly I resolved within myself never to propose love to her seriously. Such a dupe was my understanding to my heart, and so foolishly did I imagine I could be master of a flame to which I was every day adding fuel.

" O Miss Matthews ! we have heard of men entirely masters of their passions, and of hearts which can carry this fire in them, and conceal it at their pleasure. Perhaps there may be such : but if there are, those hearts may be compared, I believe, to damps, in which it is more difficult to keep fire alive than to prevent its blazing : in mine it was placed in the midst of combustible matter.

" After several visits, in which looks and sighs had been interchanged on both sides, but without the least mention of passion in private, one day the discourse between us when alone happened to turn on love ; I say happened, for I protest it was not designed on my side, and I am as firmly convinced not on hers. I was now no longer master of myself ; I declared myself the most wretched of all martyrs to this tender passion ; that I had long concealed it from its object. At length, after mentioning many particulars, suppressing, however, those which must have necessarily brought it home to Amelia, I concluded with begging her to be the confidante of my amour, and to give me her advice on that occasion.

" Amelia (O I shall never forget the dear perturbation !) appeared all confusion at this instant. She trembled, turned pale, and discovered how well she understood me, by a thousand more symptoms than I could take notice of, in a state of mind so very little different from her own. At last, with faltering accents, she said I had made a very ill choice of a counsellor in a matter in which she was so ignorant. Adding, at last, I believe, Mr. Booth, you gentlemen want very little advice in these affairs, which you all understand better than we do.

" I will relate no more of our conversation at present ; indeed I am afraid I tire you with too many particulars."

" Oh, no !" answered she ; " I should be glad to hear every step of an amour which had so tender a beginning. Tell me every thing you said or did, if you can remember it."

He then proceeded, and so will we in the next chapter.

CHAPTER II.

MR. BOOTH CONTINUES HIS STORY. IN THIS CHAPTER THERE ARE SOME PASSAGES THAT MAY SERVE AS A KIND OF TOUCHSTONE BY WHICH A YOUNG LADY MAY EXAMINE THE HEART OF HER LOVER. I WOULD ADVISE, THEREFORE, THAT EVERY LOVER BE OBLIGED TO READ IT OVER IN THE PRESENCE OF HIS MISTRESS, AND THAT SHE CAREFULLY WATCH HIS EMOTIONS WHILE HE IS READING.

" I WAS under the utmost concern," cries Booth, " when I retired from my visit, and had reflected coolly on what I had said. I now saw plainly that I had made downright love to Amelia ; and I feared, such was my vanity, that I

had already gone too far, and been too successful. Feared!
do I say? could I fear what I hoped? how shall I describe
the anxiety of my mind?"

"You need give yourself no great pain," cried Miss
Matthews, " to describe what I can so easily guess. To be
honest with you, Mr. Booth, I do not agree with your lady's
opinion that the men have a superior understanding in the
matters of love. Men are often blind to the passions of
women : but every woman is as quick-sighted as a hawk
on these occasions ; nor is there one article in the whole science which is not understood by all our sex."

"However, madam," said Mr. Booth, "I now undertook
to deceive Amelia. I abstained three days from seeing
her ; to say the truth, I endeavored to work myself up to a
resolution of leaving her for ever : but when I could not so
far subdue my passion——. But why do I talk nonsense of
subduing passion? I should say, when no other passion
could surmount my love, I returned to visit her ; and now
I attempted the strangest project which ever entered into
the silly head of a lover. This was to persuade Amelia
that I was really in love in another place, and had literally
expressed my meaning when I asked her advice and desired
her to be my confidante.

"I therefore forged a meeting to have been between me
and my imaginary mistress since I had last seen Amelia,
and related the particulars, as well as I could invent them,
which had passed at our conversation.

"Poor Amelia presently swallowed this bait ; and, as she
hath told me since, absolutely believed me to be in earnest.
Poor dear love ! how should the sincerest of hearts have
any idea of deceit? for, with all her simplicity, I assure
you she is the most sensible woman in the world."

"It is highly generous and good in you," said Miss
Matthews, with a sly sneer, " to impute to honesty what
others would perhaps call credulity."

"I protest, madam," answered he, "I do her no more than justice. A good heart will at all times betray the best head in the world. Well, madam, my angel was now, if possible, more confused than before. She looked so silly, you can hardly believe it."

"Yes, yes, I can," answered the lady, with a laugh, "I can believe it. Well, well, go on."

"After some hesitation," cried he, "my Amelia said faintly to me, 'Mr. Booth, you use me very ill; you desire me to be your confidante, and conceal from me the name of your mistress.'"

"Is it possible, then, madam," answered I, "that you cannot guess her, when I tell you she is one of your acquaintance, and lives in this town?"

"My acquaintance!" said she: "La! Mr. Booth—in this town! I—I— I thought I could have guessed for once; but I have an ill talent that way—I will never attempt to guess any thing again."

"Indeed, I do her an injury when I pretend to represent her manner. Her manner, look, voice, every thing, was inimitable; such sweetness, softness, innocence, modesty!

pon my soul, if ever man could boast of his resolution, I think I might now, that I abstained from falling prostrate at her feet, and adoring her. However, I triumphed; pride, I believe, triumphed, or perhaps love got the better of love. We once more parted, and I promised, the next time I saw her, to reveal the name of my mistress.

"I now had, I thought, gained a complete victory over myself; and no small compliments did I pay to my own resolution. In short, I triumphed as cowards and niggards do when they flatter themselves with having given some supposed instance of courage or generosity; and my triumph lasted as long—that is to say, till my ascendant passion had a proper opportunity of displaying itself in its true and natural colors.

" Having hitherto succeeded so well in my own opinion, and obtained this mighty self-conquest, I now entertained a design of exerting the most romantic generosity, and of curing that unhappy passion which I perceived I had raised in Amelia.

" Among the ladies who had expressed the greatest satisfaction at my Amelia's misfortune, Miss Osborne had distinguished herself in a very eminent degree ; she was indeed the next in beauty to my angel—nay, she had disputed the preference, and had some among her admirers who were blind enough to give it in her favor."

" Well," cries the lady, " I will allow you to call them blind ; but Miss Osborne was a charming girl."

" She certainly was handsome," answered he, " and a very considerable fortune ; so I thought my Amelia would have little difficulty in believing me when I fixed on her as my mistress. And I concluded that my thus placing my affections on her known enemy would be the surest method of eradicating every tender idea with which I had been ever honored by Amelia.

" Well, then, to Amelia I went ; she received me with more than usual coldness and reserve ; in which, to confess the truth, there appeared to me more of anger than indifference, and more of dejection than of either. After some short introduction, I revived the discourse of my amour, and presently mentioned Miss Osborne as the lady whose name I had concealed, adding that the true reason why I did not mention her before was that I apprehended there was some little distance between them, which I hoped to have the happiness of accommodating.

" Amelia answered with much gravity, ' If you know, sir, that there is any distance between us, I suppose you know the reason of that distance ; and then, I think, I could not have expected to be affronted by her name. I would not have you think, Mr. Booth, that I hate Miss

Osborne. No! Heaven is my witness, I despise her too much. Indeed, when I reflect how much I loved the woman who hath treated me so cruelly, I own it gives me pain—when I lay, as I then imagined, and as all about me believed, on my death-bed, in all the agonies of pain and misery, to become the object of laughter to my dearest friend. Oh, Mr. Booth, it is a cruel reflection! and could I after this have expected from you—but why not from you, to whom I am a person entirely indifferent, if such a friend could treat me so barbarously?'

" During the greatest part of this speech the tears streamed from her bright eyes. I could endure it no longer. I caught up the word indifferent, and repeated it, saying, ' Do you think then, madam, that Miss Emily is indifferent to me?'

"Yes, surely, I do," answered she: "I know I am; indeed, why should I not be indifferent to you?"

"Have my eyes," said I, "then declared nothing?"

"Oh! there is no need of your eyes," answered she; "your tongue hath declared that you have singled out of all womankind my greatest, I will say my basest, enemy. I own I once thought that character would have been no recommendation to you; but why did I think so? I was born to deceive myself."

" I then fell on my knees before her; and, forcing her hand, cried out, ' O my Amelia! I can bear no longer. You are the only mistress of my affections; you are the deity I adore.' In this style I ran on for above two or three minutes what it is impossible to repeat, till a torrent of contending passions, together with the surprise, overpowered her gentle spirits, and she fainted away in my arms.

" To describe my sensation till she returned to herself is not in my power." "You need not," cried Miss Matthews. " Oh, happy Amelia! why had I not been blessed with such a passion?" "I am convinced, madam," con-

tinued he, " you cannot expect all the particulars of the
tender scene which ensued. I was not enough in my senses
to remember it all. Let it suffice to say that that behavior
with which Amelia, while ignorant of its motive, had been
so much displeased, when she became sensible of that motive, proved the strongest recommendation to her favor,
and she was pleased to call it generous.''

" Generous !'' repeated the lady, " and so it was, almost
beyond the reach of humanity. I question whether you
ever had an equal.''

Perhaps the critical reader may have the same doubt with
Miss Matthews ; and lest he should, we will here make a
gap in our history, to give him an opportunity of accurately
considering whether this conduct of Mr. Booth was natural
or no ; and consequently, whether we have, in this place,
maintained or deviated from that strict adherence to truth
which we profess above all other historians.

CHAPTER III.

THE NARRATIVE CONTINUED. MORE OF THE TOUCHSTONE.

Booth made a proper acknowledgment of Miss Matthews's
civility, and then renewed his story.

" We were upon the footing of lovers ; and Amelia threw
off her reserve more and more, till at length I found all that
return of my affection which the tenderest lover can require.

" My situation would now have been a paradise had not
my happiness been interrupted with the same reflections I
have already mentioned ; had I not, in short, concluded
that I must derive all my joys from the almost certain ruin
of that dear creature to whom I should owe them.

" This thought haunted me night and day, till I at last
grew unable to support it : I therefore resolved in the strongest manner to lay it before Amelia.

" One evening, then, after the highest professions of the most disinterested love, in which heaven knows my sincerity, I took an occasion to speak to Amelia in the following manner :

" ' Too true it is, I am afraid, my dearest creature, that the highest human happiness is imperfect. How rich would be my cup, was it not for one poisonous drop which embitters the whole ! Oh, Amelia ! what must be the consequence of my ever having the honor to call you mine ! You know my situation in life, and you know your own : I have nothing more than the poor provision of an ensign's commission to depend on ; your sole dependence is on your mother ; should any act of disobedience defeat your expectations, how wretched must your lot be with me ! Oh, Amelia ! how ghastly an object to my mind is the apprehension of your distress ! Can I bear to reflect a moment on the certainty of your foregoing all the conveniences of life ? on the possibility of your suffering all its most dreadful inconveniences ? what must be my misery, then, to see you in such a situation, and to upbraid myself with being the accursed cause of bringing you to it ? Suppose, too, in such a season I should be summoned from you. Could I submit to see you encounter all the hazards, the fatigues of war, with me ? you could not yourself, however willing, support them a single campaign. What then ? must I leave you to starve alone, deprived of the tenderness of a husband, deprived too of the tenderness of the best of mothers, through my means ? a woman most dear to me for being the parent, the nurse, and the friend of my Amelia. But oh ! my sweet creature, carry your thoughts a little farther. Think of the tenderest consequences, the dearest pledges of our love. Can I bear to think of entailing beggary on the posterity of my Amelia ? on our—Oh, heavens ! on our children ! On the other side, is it possible even to mention the word—I will not, must not, cannot, cannot part with you.

What must we do, Amelia ? It is now I sincerely ask your advice.'

" ' What advice can I give you,' said she, ' in such an alternative ? Would to heaven we had never met !'

" These words were accompanied with a sigh, and a look inexpressibly tender, the tears at the same time overflowing all her lovely cheeks. I was endeavoring to reply when I was interrupted by what soon put an end to the scene.

" Our amour had already been buzzed all over the town ; and it came at last to the ears of Mrs. Harris : I had indeed observed of late a great alteration in that lady's behavior toward me whenever I visited at the house ; nor could I, for a long time before this evening, ever obtain a private interview with Amelia ; and now, it seems, I owed it to her mother's intention of overhearing all that passed between us.

" At the period then above mentioned Mrs. Harris burst from the closet where she had hid herself, and surprised her daughter, reclining on my bosom in all that tender sorrow I have just described. I will not attempt to paint the rage of the mother, or the daughter's confusion, or my own. ' Here are very fine doings indeed,' cries Mrs. Harris ; ' you have made a noble use, Amelia, of my indulgence, and the trust I repose in you. As for you, Mr. Booth, I will not accuse you ; you have used my child as I ought to have expected ; I may thank myself for what hath happened ;' with much more of the same kind before she would suffer me to speak ; but at last I obtained a hearing, and offered to excuse my poor Amelia, who was ready to sink into the earth under the oppression of grief by taking as much blame as I could on myself. Mrs. Harris answered, ' No, sir, I must say you are innocent in comparison of her ; nay, I can say I have heard you use dissuasive arguments ; and I promise you they are of weight. I have, I thank heaven, one dutiful child, and I shall henceforth think her my only one.' She then forced the poor, trembling, fainting Amelia out of the room, which when she had done, she began very coolly to reason with me on the folly, as well as iniquity, which I had been guilty of, and repeated to me almost every word I had before urged to her daughter. In fine, she at last obtained of me a promise that I would soon go to my regiment, and submit to any misery rather than that of being the ruin of Amelia.

"I now, for many days, endured the greatest torments which the human mind is, I believe, capable of feeling; and I can honestly say I tried all the means, and applied every argument which I could raise, to cure me of my love. And to make these the more effectual, I spent every night in walking backward and forward in the sight of Mrs. Harris's house, where I never failed to find some object or other which raised some tender idea of my lovely Amelia, and almost drove me to distraction."

"And don't you think, sir," said Miss Matthews, "you took a most preposterous method to cure yourself?"

"Alas, madam," answered he, "you cannot see it in a more absurd light than I do; but those know little of real love or grief who do not know how much we deceive ourselves when we pretend to aim at the cure of either. It is with these, as it is with some distempers of the body; nothing is in the least agreeable to us but what serves to heighten the disease.

"At the end of a fortnight, when I was driven almost to the highest degree of despair, and could contrive no method of conveying a letter to Amelia, how was I surprised when Mrs. Harris's servant brought me a card, with an invitation from the mother herself to drink tea that evening at her house!

"You will easily believe, madam, that I did not fail so agreeable an appointment; on my arrival I was introduced into a large company of men and women, Mrs. Harris and my Amelia being part of the company.

" Amelia seemed in my eyes to look more beautiful than ever, and behaved with all the gayety imaginable. The old lady treated me with much civility, but the young lady took little notice of me, and addressed most of her discourse to another gentleman present. Indeed, she now and then gave me a look of no discouraging kind, and I observed her color change more than once when her eyes met mine, circumstances which perhaps ought to have afforded me sufficient comfort, but they could not allay the thousand doubts and fears with which I was alarmed, for my anxious thoughts suggested no less to me than that Amelia had made her peace with her mother at the price of abandoning me forever, and of giving her ear to some other lover. All my prudence now vanished at once, and I would that instant have gladly run away with Amelia, and have married her, without the least consideration of any consequences.

" With such thoughts I had tormented myself for near two hours, till most of the company had taken their leave. This I was myself incapable of doing, nor do I know when I should have put an end to my visit, had not Dr. Harrison taken me away almost by force, telling me in a whisper that he had something to say to me of great consequence. You know the doctor, madam——"

" Very well, sir," answered Miss Matthews, " and one of the best men in the world he is, and an honor to the sacred order to which he belongs."

" You will judge," replied Booth, " by the sequel, whether I have reason to think him so." He then proceeded as in the next chapter.

CHAPTER IV.

THE STORY OF MR. BOOTH CONTINUED. IN THIS CHAPTER
THE READER WILL PERCEIVE A GLIMPSE OF THE CHARAC-
TER OF A VERY GOOD DIVINE, WITH SOME MATTERS OF A
VERY TENDER KIND.

" THE doctor conducted me into his study, and then, desiring me to sit down, began, as near as I can remember, in
these words, or at least to this purpose :

" ' You cannot imagine, young gentleman, that your love
for Miss Emily is any secret in this place ; I have known it
some time, and have been, I assure you, very much your
enemy in this affair.'

" I answered that I was very much obliged to him.

" ' Why, so you are,' replied he ; ' and so perhaps you
will think yourself when you know all. I went about a
fortnight ago to Mrs. Harris, to acquaint her with my apprehensions on her daughter's account ; for, though the
matter was much talked of, I thought it might possibly not
have reached her ears. I will be very plain with you. I
advised her to take all possible care of the young lady, and
even to send her to some place where she might be effectually kept out of your reach while you remained in the
town.'

" ' And do you think, sir,' said I, ' that this was acting
a kind part by me ? or do you expect that I should thank
you on this occasion ? '

" ' Young man,' answered he, ' I did not intend you any
kindness, nor do I desire any of your thanks. My intention
was to preserve a worthy lady from a young fellow of whom
I had heard no good character, and whom I imagined to
have a design of stealing a human creature for the sake of
her fortune.'

" ' It was very kind of you indeed,' answered I, ' to entertain such an opinion of me.'

" ' Why, sir,' replied the doctor, ' it is the opinion which, I believe, most of you young gentlemen of the order of the rag deserve. I have known some instances, and have heard of more, where such young fellows have committed robbery under the name of marriage.'

" I was going to interrupt him with some anger when he desired me to have a little patience, and then informed me that he had visited Mrs. Harris with the above-mentioned design the evening after the discovery I have related ; that Mrs. Harrris, without waiting for his information, had recounted to him all which had happened the evening before ; and indeed she must have an excellent memory, for I think she repeated every word I said, and added that she had confined her daughter to her chamber, where she kept her a close prisoner, and had not seen her since.

" I cannot express, nor would modesty suffer me if I could, all that now passed. The doctor took me by the hand and burst forth into the warmest commendations of the sense and generosity which he was pleased to say discovered themselves in my speech. You know, madam, his strong and singular way of expressing himself on all occasions, especially when he is affected with any thing. ' Sir,' said he, ' if I knew half a dozen such instances in the army, the painter should put red liveries upon all the saints in my closet.'

" From this instant, the doctor told me, he had become my friend and zealous advocate with Mrs. Harris, on whom he had at last prevailed, though not without the greatest difficulty, to consent to my marrying Amelia, upon condition that I settled every penny which the mother should lay down, and that she would retain a certain sum in her hands which she would at any time deposit for my advancement in the army.

" You will, I hope, madam, conceive that I made no hesitation at these conditions, nor need I mention the joy which I felt on this occasion, or the acknowledgment I paid the doctor, who is, indeed, as you say, one of the best of men.

" The next morning I had permission to visit Amelia, who received me in such a manner that I now concluded my happiness to be complete.

" Every thing was now agreed on all sides, and lawyers employed to prepare the writings, when an unexpected cloud arose suddenly in our serene sky, and all our joys were obscured in a moment.

" When matters were, as I apprehended, drawing near a conclusion, I received an express that a sister whom I tenderly loved was seized with a violent fever, and earnestly desired me to come to her. I immediately obeyed the summons, and, as it was then about two in the morning, without staying even to take leave of Amelia, for whom I left a short billet, acquainting her with the reason of my absence.

" The gentleman's house where my sister then was stood at fifty miles distance, and though I used the utmost expedition, the unmerciful distemper had, before my arrival, entirely deprived the poor girl of her senses, as it soon after did of her life.

" Not all the love I bore Amelia, nor the tumultuous delight with which the approaching hour of possessing her filled my heart, could, for a while, allay my grief at the loss of my beloved Nancy. Upon my soul, I cannot yet mention her name without tears. Never brother and sister had, I believe, a higher friendship for each other. Poor dear girl ! whilst I sat by her in her light-head fits, she repeated scarce any other name but mine ; and it plainly appeared that, when her dear reason was ravished away from her, it had left my image on her fancy, and that the last use she made of it was to think on me. ' Send for my dear Billy immediately,' she cried ; ' I know he will come to me in a moment. Will nobody fetch him to me ? pray don't kill me before I see him once more. You durst not use me so if he was here.' Every accent still rings in my ears. Oh, heavens ! to hear this, and at the same time to see the poor delirious creature deriving the greatest horrors from my sight, and mistaking me for a highwayman who had a little before robbed her. But I ask your pardon ; the sensations I felt are to be known only from experience, and to you must appear dull and insipid. At last she seemed for a moment to know me, and cried, ' Oh, heavens ! my dearest brother ! ' upon which she fell into immediate convulsions, and died away in my arms."

Here Mr. Booth stopped a moment, and wiped his eyes ; and Miss Matthews, perhaps out of complaisance, wiped hers.

CHAPTER V.

CONTAINING STRANGE REVOLUTIONS OF FORTUNE.

Booth proceeded thus :

" This loss, perhaps, madam, you will think had made me miserable enough ; but Fortune did not think so ; for, on the day when my Nancy was to be buried, a courier arrived from Dr. Harrison with a letter, in which the doctor acquainted me that he was just come from Mrs. Harris when he dispatched the express, and earnestly desired me to return the very instant I received his letter, as I valued my Amelia. ' Though if the daughter,' added he, ' should take after her mother (as most of them do) it will be perhaps wiser in you to stay away.'

" I presently sent for the messenger into my room, and with much difficulty extorted from him that a great squire in his coach and six was come to Mrs. Harris's, and that the whole town said he was shortly to be married to Amelia.

" I now soon perceived how much superior my love for

Amelia was to every other passion ; poor Nancy's idea disappeared in a moment ; I quitted the dear lifeless corpse, over which I had shed a thousand tears, left the care of her funeral to others, and posted, I may almost say flew, back to Amelia, and alighted at the doctor's house, as he had desired me in his letter.

" The good man presently acquainted me with what had happened in my absence. Mr. Winckworth had, it seems, arrived the very day of my departure, with a grand equipage, and, without delay, had made formal proposals to Mrs. Harris, offering to settle any part of his vast estate, in whatever manner she pleased, on Amelia. These proposals the old lady had, without any deliberation, accepted, and had insisted, in the most violent manner, on her daughter's compliance, which Amelia had as peremptorily refused to give ; insisting, on her part, on the consent which her mother had before given to our marriage, in which she was heartily seconded by the doctor, who declared to her, as he now did to me, ' that we ought as much to be esteemed man and wife as if the ceremony had already passed between us.'

" These remonstrances, the doctor told me, had worked no effect on Mrs. Harris, who still persisted in her avowed resolution of marrying her daughter to Winckworth, whom the doctor had likewise attacked, telling him that he was paying his addresses to another man's wife ; but all to no purpose ; the young gentleman was too much in love to hearken to any dissuasives.

" We now entered into consultation what means to employ. The doctor earnestly protested against any violence to be offered to the person of Winckworth, which, I believe, I had rashly threatened, declaring that, if I made any attempt of that kind, he would for ever abandon my cause. I made him a solemn promise of forbearance. At last he determined to pay another visit to Mrs. Harris, and if he found her obdurate, he said he thought himself at liberty to join us together without any further consent of the mother, which every parent, he said, had a right to refuse, but not retract when given, unless the party himself, by some conduct of his, gave a reason.

" The doctor having made his visit with no better success than before, the matter now debated was, how to get possession of Amelia by stratagem, for she was now a closer prisoner than ever ; was her mother's bed-fellow by night, and never out of her sight by day.

" While we were deliberating on this point a wine merchant of the town came to visit the doctor, to inform him that he had just bottled off a hogshead of excellent old port, of which he offered to spare him a hamper, saying that he was that day to send in twelve dozen to Mrs. Harris.

" The doctor now smiled at a conceit which came into his head ; and taking me aside, asked me if I had love enough for the young lady to venture into the house in a hamper. I joyfully leaped at the proposal, to which the merchant, at the doctor's intercession, consented ; for I believe, madam, you know the great authority which that worthy man had over the whole town. The doctor, moreover, promised to procure a license, and to perform the office for us at his house, if I could find any means of conveying Amelia thither.

" In this hamper, then, I was carried to the house, and deposited in the entry, where I had not lain long before I was again removed and packed up in a cart in order to be sent five miles into the country ; for I heard the orders given as I lay in the entry ; and there I likewise heard that Amelia and her mother were to follow me the next morning.

" I was unloaded from my cart, and set down with the rest of the lumber in a great hall. Here I remained above three hours, impatiently waiting for the evening, when I determined to quit a posture which was becoming very

uneasy, and break my prison ; but Fortune contrived to re-
lease me sooner, by the following means : The house where
I now was had been left in the care of one maid-servant.
This faithful creature came into the hall with the footman who had driven the cart. A scene of the highest fondness having passed between them, the fellow proposed, and
the maid consented, to open the hamper and drink a bottle
together, which, they agreed, their mistress would hardly
miss in such a quantity. They presently began to execute
their purpose. They opened the hamper, and, to their
great surprise, discovered the contents.

"I took an immediate advantage of the consternation
which appeared in the countenances of both the servants,
and had sufficient presence of mind to improve the knowledge of those secrets to which I was privy. I told them
that it entirely depended on their behavior to me whether
their mistress should ever be acquainted, either with what
they had done or with what they had intended to do ; for
that if they would keep my secret I would reciprocally keep
theirs. I then acquainted them with my purpose of lying,
concealed in the house, in order to watch an opportunity of
obtaining a private interview with Amelia.

" In the situation in which these two delinquents stood,
you may be assured it was not difficult for me to seal up
their lips. In short, they agreed to whatever I proposed.
I lay that evening in my dear Amelia's bedchamber, and
was in the morning conveyed into an old lumber-garret,
where I was to wait till Amelia (whom the maid promised,
on her arrival, to inform of my place of concealment) could
find some opportunity of seeing me."

" I ask pardon for interrupting you," cries Miss Matthews, " but you bring to my remembrance a foolish story
which I heard at that time, though at a great distance from
you : That an officer had, in confederacy with Miss Harris,
broke open her mother's cellar and stole away a great quan-

tity of her wine. I mention it only to show you what sort of foundations most stories have."

Booth told her he had heard some such thing himself, and then continued his story as in the next chapter.

CHAPTER VI.

CONTAINING MANY SURPRISING ADVENTURES.

" HERE," continued he, " I remained the whole day in hopes of a happiness the expected approach of which gave me such a delight that I would not have exchanged my poor lodgings for the finest palace in the universe.

" A little after it was dark Mrs. Harris arrived, together with Amelia and her sister. I cannot express how much my heart now began to flutter; for, as my hopes every moment increased, strange fears, which I had not felt before, began now to intermingle with them.

" When I had continued full two hours in these circumstances, I heard a woman's step tripping upstairs, which I fondly hoped was my Amelia; but all on a sudden the door flew open, and Mrs. Harris herself appeared at it, with a countenance pale as death, her whole body trembling, I suppose with anger; she fell upon me in the most bitter language. It is not necessary to repeat what she said, nor indeed can I, I was so shocked and confounded upon this occasion. In a word, the scene ended with my departure without seeing Amelia."

" And pray," cries Miss Matthews, " how happened this unfortunate discovery ?"

Booth answered, " That the lady at supper ordered a bottle of wine, which neither myself," said he, " nor the servants had presence of mind to provide. Being told there was none in the house, though she had been before informed that the things came all safe, she had sent for the maid, who, being unable to devise any excuse, had fallen on her knees, and after confessing her design of opening a bottle, which she imputed to the fellow, betrayed poor me to her mistress.

"Well, madam, after a lecture of about a quarter of an hour's duration from Mrs. Harris, I suffered her to conduct me to the outward gate of her court-yard, whence I set forward in a disconsolate condition of mind toward my lodgings. I had five miles to walk in a dark and rainy night : but how can I mention these trifling circumstances as any aggravation of my disappointment !"

"How was it possible," cried Miss Matthews, "that you could be got out of the house without seeing Miss Harris ?"

"I assure you, madam," answered Booth, "I have often wondered at it myself ; but my spirits were so much sunk at the sight of her mother that no man was ever a greater coward than I was at that instant. Indeed, I believe my tender concern for the terrors of Amelia were the principal cause of my submission. However it was, I left the house, and walked about a hundred yards, when, at the corner of the garden-wall, a female voice, in a whisper, cried out, 'Mr. Booth.' The person was extremely near me, but it was so dark I could scarce see her ; nor did I, in the confusion I was in, immediately recognize the voice. I answered in a line of Congreve's, which burst from my lips spontaneously, for I am sure I had no intention to quote plays at that time,

"'Who calls the wretched thing that was Alphonso ?'

Upon which a woman leaped into my arms, crying out, 'Oh ! it is indeed my Alphonso, my only Alphonso !' Oh, Miss Matthews, guess what I felt when I found I had my Amelia in my arms. I embraced her with an ecstasy not to be described, at the same instant pouring a thousand tendernesses into her ears ; at least, if I could express so many to her in a minute, for in that time the alarm began at the house ; Mrs. Harris had missed her daughter, and the court was presently full of lights and noises of all kinds.

" I now lifted Amelia over a gate, and jumping after, we crept along together by the side of a hedge, a different way from what led to the town, as I imagined that would be the road through which they would pursue us. In this opinion I was right ; for we heard them pass along that road, and the voice of Mrs. Harris herself, who ran with the rest, notwithstanding the darkness and the rain. By these means we luckily made our escape, and clambering over hedge and ditch, my Amelia performing the part of a heroine all the way, we at length arrived at a little green lane, where stood a vast spreading oak, under which we sheltered ourselves from a violent storm.

" When this was over, and the moon began to appear, Amelia declared she knew very well where she was ; and a little farther striking into another lane to the right, she said that would lead us to a house where we would be both safe and unsuspected. I followed her directions, and we at length came to a little cottage about three miles distant from Mrs. Harris's house.

" As it now rained very violently, we entered this cottage, in which we espied a light, without ceremony. Here we found an elderly woman sitting by herself at a little fire, who had no sooner viewed us than she instantly sprung from her seat, and starting back, gave the strongest tokens of amazement, upon which Amelia said, ' Be not surprised, nurse, though you see me in a strange pickle, I own.' The old woman, after having several times blessed herself, and expressed the most tender concern for the lady who stood dripping before her, began to bestir herself in making up the fire, at the same time entreating Amelia that she might be permitted to furnish her with some clothes, which, she said, though not fine, were clean and wholesome, and much dryer than her own. I seconded this motion so vehemently that

Amelia, though she declared herself under no apprehension of catching cold (she hath indeed the best constitution in the world), at last consented, and I retired without doors under a shed to give my angel an opportunity of dressing herself in the only room which the cottage afforded below-stairs.

"At my return into the room, Amelia insisted on my exchanging my coat for one which belonged to the old woman's son." "I am very glad," cried Miss Matthews, "to find she did not forget you. I own I thought it somewhat cruel to turn you out into the rain."

"Oh, Miss Matthews!" continued he, taking no notice of her observation, "I had now an opportunity of contemplating the vast power of exquisite beauty, which nothing almost can add to or diminish. Amelia, in the poor rags of her old nurse, looked scarce less beautiful than I have seen her appear at a ball or an assembly."

"Well, well," cries Miss Matthews, "to be sure she did ; but pray go on with your story."

"The old woman," continued he, "after having equipped us as well as she could, and placed our wet clothes before the fire, began to grow inquisitive ; and, after some ejaculations, she cried, 'Oh, my dear young madam ! my mind misgives me hugeously ; and pray who is this fine young gentleman ? Oh ! Miss Emmy, Miss Emmy, I am afraid madam knows nothing of all this matter.' 'Suppose he should be my husband, nurse,' answered Amelia. 'Oh ! good ! and if he be,' replies the nurse, 'I hope he is some great gentleman or other, with a vast estate and a coach and six : for to be sure, if he was the greatest lord in the land, you would deserve it all.' But why do I attempt to mimic the honest creature ? In short, she discovered the greatest affection for my Amelia, with which I was much more delighted than I was offended at the suspicions she showed of me, or the many bitter curses which

she denounced against me, if I ever proved a bad husband
to so sweet a young lady.

"I so well improved the hint given me by Amelia that
the old woman had no doubt of our being really married ;
and comforting herself that, if it was not as well as it
might have been, yet madam had enough for us both, and
that happiness did not always depend on great riches, she
began to rail at the old lady for having turned us out of
doors, which I scarce told an untruth in asserting. And
when Amelia said ' she hoped her nurse would not betray
her,' the good woman answered, with much warmth, ' Betray you, my dear young madam ! no, that I would not,
if the king would give me all that he is worth : no, not if
madam herself would give me the great house, and the whole
farm belonging to it.'

"The good woman then went out and fetched a chicken
from the roost, which she killed, and began to pick, without asking any questions. Then, summoning her son, who
was in bed, to her assistance, she began to prepare this
chicken for our supper. This she afterward set before us
in so neat, I may almost say elegant, a manner that whoever would have disdained it either doth not know the sensation of hunger or doth not deserve to have it gratified.
Our food was attended with some ale, which our kind
hostess said she intended not to have tapped till Christmas ;
' but,' added she, ' I little thought ever to have the honor
of seeing my dear honored lady in this poor place.'

"For my own part, no human being was then an object
of envy to me, and even Amelia seemed to be in pretty
good spirits ; she softly whispered to me that she perceived
there might be happiness in a cottage."

"A cottage !" cries Miss Matthews, sighing, "a cottage,
with the man one loves, is a palace."

"When supper was ended," continued Booth, "the
good woman began to think of our further wants, and very

earnestly recommended her bed to us, saying it was a very
neat though homely one, and that she could furnish us with
a pair of clean sheets. She added some persuasives which
painted my angel all over with vermilion. As for myself,
I behaved so awkwardly and foolishly, and so readily
agreed to Amelia's resolution of sitting up all night, that, if
it did not give the nurse any suspicion of our marriage, it
ought to have inspired her with the utmost contempt for me.

" We both endeavored to prevail with nurse to retire to
her own bed, but found it utterly impossible to succeed ;
she thanked heaven she understood breeding better than
that. And so well bred was the good woman that we
could scarce get her out of the room the whole night.
Luckily for us, we both understood French, by means of
which we consulted together, even in her presence, upon the
measures we were to take in our present exigency. At
length it was resolved that I should send a letter by this
young lad, whom I have just before mentioned, to our
worthy friend the doctor, desiring his company at our hut,
since we thought it utterly unsafe to venture to the town,
which we knew would be in an uproar on our account before the morning."

Here Booth made a full stop, smiled, and then said he
was going to mention so ridiculous a distress that he could
scarce think of it without laughing. What this was the
reader shall know in the next chapter.

CHAPTER VII.

THE STORY OF BOOTH CONTINUED. MORE SURPRISING AD-
VENTURES.

" FROM what trifles, dear Miss Matthews," cried Booth,
" may some of our greatest distresses arise ! Do you not
perceive I am going to tell you we had neither pen, ink,
nor paper in our present exigency ?

" A verbal message was now our only resource ; however, we contrived to deliver it in such terms that neither nurse nor her son could possibly conceive any suspicion from it of the present situation of our affairs. Indeed, Amelia whispered me, I might safely place any degree of confidence in the lad ; for he had been her foster-brother, and she had a great opinion of his integrity. He was in truth a boy of very good natural parts ; and Dr. Harrison, who had received him into his family, at Amelia's recommendation, had bred him up to write and read very well, and had taken some pains to infuse into him the principles of honesty and religion. He was not indeed even now discharged from the doctor's service, but had been at home with his mother for some time, on account of the smallpox, from which he was lately recovered.

" I have said so much," continued Booth, " of the boy's character that you may not be surprised at some stories which I shall tell you of him hereafter.

" I am going now, madam, to relate to you one of those strange accidents which are produced by such a train of circumstances that mere chance hath been thought incapable of bringing them together, and which have therefore given birth, in superstitious minds, to Fortune, and to several other imaginary beings.

" We were now impatiently expecting the arrival of the doctor ; our messenger had been gone much more than a sufficient time, which to us, you may be assured, appeared not at all shorter than it was, when nurse, who had gone out of doors on some errand, came running hastily to us, crying out, ' Oh, my dear young madam, her ladyship's coach is just at the door ! ' Amelia turned pale as death at these words ; indeed I feared she would have fainted, if I could be said to fear, who had scarce any of my senses left, and was in a condition little better than my angel's.

" While we were both in this dreadful situation, Amelia

fallen back in her chair with the countenance in which ghosts are painted, myself at her feet with a complexion of no very different color, and nurse screaming out and throwing water in Amelia's face, Mrs. Harris entered the room. At the sight of this scene she threw herself likewise into a chair, and called immediately for a glass of water, which Miss Betty, her daughter, supplied her with; for, as to nurse, nothing was capable of making any impression on her whilst she apprehended her young mistress to be in danger.

"The doctor had now entered the room, and coming immediately up to Amelia, after some expressions of surprise, he took her by the hand, called her his little sugarplum, and assured her there were none but friends present. He then led her tottering across the room to Mrs. Harris. Amelia then fell upon her knees before her mother; but the doctor caught her up, saying, ' Use that posture, child, only to the Almighty ; ' but I need not mention this singularity of his to you who know him so well, and must have heard him often dispute against addressing ourselves to man in the humblest posture which we use toward the Supreme Being.

"I will tire you with no more particulars. We were soon satisfied that the doctor had reconciled us and our affairs to Mrs. Harris ; and we now proceeded directly to church, the doctor having before provided a license for us."

"But where is the strange accident ?" cries Miss Matthews ; "sure you have raised more curiosity than you have satisfied."

"Indeed, madam," answered he, "your reproof is just ; I had like to have forgotten it ; but you cannot wonder at me when you reflect on that interesting part of my story which I am now relating. But before I mention this accident I must tell you what happened after Amelia's escape from her mother's house. Mrs. Harris at first ran out into the lane among her servants, and pursued us (so she imagined) along the road leading to the town ; but that being very dirty, and a violent storm of rain coming, she took shelter in an ale-house about half a mile from her own house, whither she sent for her coach ; she then drove, together with her daughter, to town, where, soon after her arrival, she sent for the doctor, her usual privy counsellor in all her affairs. They sat up all night together, the doctor endeavoring, by arguments and persuasions, to bring Mrs. Harris to reason ; but all to no purpose, though, as he hath informed me, Miss Betty seconded him with the warmest entreaties."

Here Miss Matthews laughed, of which Booth begged to know the reason. She at last, after many apologies, said, " It was the first good thing she ever heard of Miss Betty ; nay," said she, " and asking your pardon for my opinion of your sister, since you will have it, I always conceived her to be the deepest of hypocrites."

Booth fetched a sigh, and said he was afraid she had not always acted so kindly ; and then, after a little hesitation, proceeded :

" You will be pleased, madam, to remember the lad was sent with a verbal message to the doctor, which message was no more than to acquaint him where we were, and to desire the favor of his company, or that he would send a coach to bring us to whatever place he would please to meet us at. This message was to be delivered to the doctor himself, and the messenger was ordered, if he found him not at home, to go to him wherever he was. He fulfilled his orders and told it to the doctor in the presence of Mrs. Harris."

" Oh, the idiot !" cries Miss Matthews. " Not at all," answered Booth. " He is a very sensible fellow, as you will perhaps say hereafter. He had not the least reason to suspect that any secrecy was necessary, for we took the

utmost care he should not suspect it. Well, madam, this
accident, which appeared so unfortunate, turned in the highest degree to our advantage. Mrs. Harris no sooner heard
the message delivered than she fell into the most violent
passion imaginable, and accused the doctor of being in the
plot, and of having confederated with me in the design of
carrying off her daughter.

"The doctor, who had hitherto used only soothing
methods, now talked in a different strain. He confessed
the accusation and justified his conduct. He said he was no
meddler in the family affairs of others, nor should he have
concerned himself with hers, but at her own request; but
that, since Mrs. Harris herself had made him an agent in
this matter, he would take care to acquit himself with
honor, and, above all things, to preserve a young lady for
whom he had the highest esteem; 'for she is,' cries he,
and, by heavens, he said true, 'the most worthy, generous,
and noble of all human beings. You have yourself,
madam,' said he, 'consented to the match. I have, at
your request, made the match;' and then he added some
particulars relating to his opinion of me which my modesty
forbids me to repeat." "Nay, but," cries Miss Matthews,
"I insist on your conquest of that modesty for once. We
women do not love to hear one another's praises, and I will
be made amends by hearing the praises of a man, and of a
man whom, perhaps," added she with a leer, "I shall not
think much the better of upon that account." "In obedience to your commands, then, madam," continued he,
"the doctor was so kind to say he had inquired into my
character, and had found that I had been a dutiful son and
an affectionate brother. Relations, said he, in which whoever discharges his duty well, gives us a well-grounded
hope that he will behave as properly in all the rest. He
concluded with saying that Amelia's happiness, her heart—
nay, her very reputation—were all concerned in this matter,

to which, as he had been made instrumental, he was resolved to carry her through it; and then, taking the license
from his pocket, declared to Mrs. Harris that he would go
that instant and marry her daughter wherever he found
her. This speech, the doctor's voice, his look, and his behavior, all which are sufficiently calculated to inspire awe,
and even terror, when he pleases, frightened poor Mrs.
Harris, and wrought a more sensible effect than it was in
his power to produce by all his arguments and entreaties;
and I have already related what followed.

"Thus the strange accident of our wanting pen, ink, and
paper, and our not trusting the boy with our secret, occasioned the discovery to Mrs. Harris; that discovery put the
doctor upon his metal, and produced that blessed event
which I have recounted to you, and which, as my mother
hath since confessed, nothing but the spirit which he had
exerted after the discovery could have brought about.

"Well, madam, you now see me married to Amelia, in
which situation you will, perhaps, think my happiness incapable of addition. Perhaps it was so; and yet I can
with truth say that the love which I then bore Amelia was
not comparable to what I bear her now." "Happy
Amelia!" cried Miss Matthews. "If all men were like
you, all women would be blessed; nay, the whole world
would be so in a great measure; for, upon my soul, I believe
that from the damned inconstancy of your sex to ours proceeds half the miseries of mankind."

That we may give the reader leisure to consider well
the foregoing sentiment, we will here put an end to this
chapter.

CHAPTER VIII.

IN WHICH OUR READERS WILL PROBABLY BE DIVIDED IN
THEIR OPINION OF MR. BOOTH'S CONDUCT.

BOOTH proceeded as follows :

" The first months of our marriage produced nothing remarkable enough to mention. I am sure I need not tell
Miss Matthews that I found in my Amelia every perfection
of human nature. Mrs. Harris at first gave us some little
uneasiness. She had rather yielded to the doctor than
given a willing consent to the match ; however, by degrees
she became more and more satisfied, and at last seemed perfectly reconciled. This we ascribed a good deal to the kind
offices of Miss Betty, who had always appeared to be my
friend. She had been greatly assisting to Amelia in making her escape, which I had no opportunity of mentioning
to you before, and in all things behaved so well, outwardly
at least, to myself as well as her sister, that we regarded
her as our sincerest friend.

" About half a year after our marriage two additional
companies were added to our regiment, in one of which I
was preferred to the command of a lieutenant. Upon this
occasion Miss Betty gave the first intimation of a disposition
which we have since too severely experienced."

" Your servant, sir," says Miss Matthews ; " then I find
I was not mistaken in my opinion of the lady. No, no,
show me any goodness in a censorious prude, and——"

As Miss Matthews hesitated for a simile or an execration,
Booth proceeded : " You will please to remember, madam,
there was formerly an agreement between myself and Mrs.
Harris that I should settle all my Amelia's fortune on her,
except a certain sum, which was to be laid out in my advancement in the army ; but as our marriage was carried
on in the manner you have heard, no such agreement was

ever executed. And since I was become Amelia's husband not a word of this matter was ever mentioned by the old lady; and as for myself, I declare I had not yet awakened from that delicious dream of bliss in which the possession of Amelia had lulled me."

Here Miss Matthews sighed, and cast the tenderest of looks on Booth, who thus continued his story :

"Soon after my promotion Mrs. Harris one morning took an occasion to speak to me on this affair. She said that, as I had been promoted gratis to a lieutenancy, she would assist me with money to carry me yet a step higher; and if more was required than was formerly mentioned, it should not be wanting, since she was so perfectly satisfied with my behavior to her daughter. Adding that she hoped I had still the same inclination to settle on my wife the remainder of her fortune.

"I answered with very warm acknowledgments of my mother's goodness, and declared, if I had the world, I was ready to lay it at my Amelia's feet. And so, heaven knows, I would ten thousand worlds.

"Mrs. Harris seemed pleased with the warmth of my sentiments, and said she would immediately send to her lawyer and give him the necessary orders; and thus ended our conversation on this subject.

"From this time there was a very visible alteration in Miss Betty's behavior. She grew reserved to her sister as well as to me. She was fretful and captious on the slightest occasion; nay, she affected much to talk on the ill consequences of an imprudent marriage, especially before her mother; and if ever any little tenderness or endearments escaped me in public toward Amelia, she never failed to make some malicious remark on the short duration of violent passions; and when I have expressed a fond sentiment for my wife, her sister would kindly wish she might hear as much seven years hence.

"All these matters have been since suggested to us by reflection ; for, while they actually passed, both Amelia and myself had our thoughts too happily engaged to take notice of what discovered itself in the mind of any other person.

"Unfortunately for us, Mrs. Harris's lawyer happened at this time to be at London, where business detained him upward of a month ; and as Mrs. Harris would on no occasion employ any other, our affair was under an entire suspension till his return.

"Amelia, who was now big with child, had often expressed the deepest concern at her apprehensions of my being some time commanded abroad ; a circumstance, which she declared if it should ever happen to her, even though she should not then be in the same situation as at present, would infallibly break her heart. These remonstrances were made with such tenderness, and so much affected me, that, to avoid any probability of such an event, I endeavored to get an exchange into the horse-guards, a body of troops which very rarely goes abroad, unless where the king himself commands in person. I soon found an officer for my purpose, the terms were agreed on, and Mrs. Harris had ordered the money which I was to pay to be ready, notwithstanding the opposition made by Miss Betty, who openly dissuaded her mother from it, alleging that the exchange was highly to my disadvantage, that I could never hope to rise in the army after it, not forgetting, at the same time, some insinuations very prejudicial to my reputation as a soldier.

"When every thing was agreed on, and the two commissions were actually made out, but not signed by the king, one day, at my return from hunting, Amelia flew to me, and eagerly embracing me, cried out, ' Oh, Billy, I have news for you which delights my soul. Nothing sure was ever so fortunate as the exchange you have made. The regiment you was formerly in is ordered for Gibraltar.'

" I received this news with far less transport than it was delivered. I answered coldly, since the case was so, I heartily hoped the commissions might be both signed. ' What do you say ? ' replied Amelia eagerly ; ' sure you told me every thing was entirely settled. That look of yours frightens me to death.' But I am running into too minute particulars. In short, I received a letter by that very post from the officer with whom I had exchanged, insisting that, though his majesty had not signed the commissions, that still the bargain was valid, partly urging it as a right, and partly desiring it as a favor, that he might go to Gibraltar in my room.

" This letter convinced me in every point. I was now informed that the commissions were not signed, and consequently that the exchange was not completed ; of consequence the other could have no right to insist on going ; and as for granting him such a favor, I too clearly saw I must do it at the expense of my honor. I was now reduced to a dilemma, the most dreadful which I think any man can experience, in which, I am not ashamed to own, I found love was not so overmatched by honor as he ought to have been. The thoughts of leaving Amelia in her present condition to misery, perhaps to death or madness, were insupportable ; nor could any other consideration but that which now tormented me on the other side have combated them a moment."

" No woman upon earth," cries Miss Matthews, " can despise want of spirit in a man more than myself ; and yet I cannot help thinking you was rather too nice on this occasion."

" You will allow, madam," answered Booth, " that whoever offends against the laws of honor in the least instance is treated as the highest delinquent. Here is no excuse, no pardon ; and he doth nothing who leaves any thing undone. But if the conflict was so terrible with myself

alone, what was my situation in the presence of Amelia ?
how could I support her sighs, her tears, her agonies, her
despair ? could I bear to think myself the cruel cause of her
sufferings ? for so I was : could I endure the thought of
having it in my power to give her instant relief, for so it
was, and refuse it her ?

" Miss Betty was now again become my friend. She
had scarce been civil to me for a fortnight last past, yet
now she commended me to the skies, and as severely blamed
her sister, whom she arraigned of the most contemptible
weakness in preferring my safety to my honor : she said
many ill-natured things on the occasion, which I shall not
now repeat.

" In the midst of this hurricane the good doctor came
to dine with Mrs. Harris, and at my desire delivered his
opinion on the matter."

Here Mr. Booth was interrupted in his narrative by the
arrival of a person whom we shall introduce in the next
chapter.

CHAPTER IX.

CONTAINING A SCENE OF A DIFFERENT KIND FROM ANY OF
THE PRECEDING.

THE gentleman who now arrived was the keeper ; or, if
you please (for so he pleased to call himself), the governor
of the prison.

He used so little ceremony at his approach that the bolt,
which was very slight on the inside, gave way, and the door
immediately flew open. He had no sooner entered the room
than he acquainted Miss Matthews that he had brought her
very good news, for which he demanded a bottle of wine as
his due.

This demand being complied with, he acquainted Miss
Matthews that the wounded gentleman was not dead, nor
was his wound thought to be mortal : that loss of blood,

and perhaps his fright, had occasioned his fainting away :
" but I believe, madam," said he, " if you take the proper
measures you may be bailed to-morrow. I expect the lawyer here this evening, and if you put the business into his
hands I warrant it will be done. Money to be sure must
be parted with, that's to be sure. People to be sure will
expect to touch a little in such cases. For my own part, I
never desire to keep a prisoner longer than the law allows,
not I ; I always inform them they can be bailed as soon as
I know it ; I never make any bargain, not I ; I always love
to leave those things to the gentlemen and ladies themselves. I never suspect gentlemen and ladies of wanting
generosity."

Miss Matthews made a very slight answer to all these
friendly professions. She said she had done nothing she
repented of, and was indifferent as to the event. " All I
can say," cries she, " is, that if the wretch is alive there is
no greater villain in life than himself ;" and instead of
mentioning any thing of the bail, she begged the keeper to
leave her alone again with Mr. Booth. The keeper replied,
" Nay, madam, perhaps it may be better to stay a little
longer here, if you have not bail ready, than to buy them
too dear. Besides, a day or two hence, when the gentleman is past all danger of recovery, to be sure some folks
that would expect an extraordinary fee now cannot expect
to touch any thing. And to be sure you shall want nothing
here. The best of all things are to be had here for money,
both eatable and drinkable : though I say it, I sha'n't turn
my back to any of the taverns for either eatables or wind.
The captain there need not have been so shy of owning
himself when he first came in ; we have had captains and
other great gentlemen here before now ; and no shame to
them, though I say it. Many a great gentleman is sometimes found in places that don't become them half so well,
let me tell them that, Captain Booth, let me tell them that."

"I see, sir," answered Booth, a little discomposed, "that you are acquainted with my title as well as my name."

"Ay, sir," cries the keeper, "and I honor you the more for it. I love the gentlemen of the army. I was in the army myself formerly ; in the Lord of Oxford's horse. It is true I rode private ; but I had money enough to have bought in quartermaster, when I took it into my head to marry, and my wife she did not like that I should continue a soldier : she was all for a private life ; and so I came to this business."

"Upon my word, sir," answered Booth, "you consulted your wife's inclinations very notably ; but pray will you satisfy my curiosity in telling me how you became acquainted that I was in the army ? for my dress I think could not betray me."

"Betray !" replied the keeper ; "there is no betraying here, I hope —I am not a person to betray people. But you are so shy and peery you would almost make one suspect there was more in the matter. And if there be, I promise you you need not be afraid of telling it me. You will excuse me giving you a hint ; but the sooner the better, that's all. Others may be beforehand with you, and first come first served on these occasions, that's all. Informers are odious, there's no doubt of that, and no one would care to be an informer if he could help it, because of the ill-usage they always receive from the mob ; yet it is dangerous to trust too much ; and when safety and a good part of the reward too are on one side, and the gallows on the other—I know which a wise man would choose."

"What the devil do you mean by all this ?" cries Booth.

"No offence, I hope," answered the keeper : "I speak for your good ; and if you have been upon the snaffling lay —you understand me, I am sure."

"Not I," answered Booth, "upon my honor."

"Nay, nay," replied the keeper, with a contemptuous sneer, "if you are so peery as that comes to, you must take the consequence. But for my part, I know I would not trust Robinson with twopence untold."

"What do you mean?" cries Booth; "who is Robinson?"

"And you don't know Robinson!" answered the keeper with great emotion. To which Booth replying in the negative, the keeper, after some tokens of amazement, cried out, "Well, captain, I must say you are the best at it of all the gentlemen I ever saw. However, I will tell you this: the lawyer and Mr. Robinson have been laying their heads together about you above half an hour this afternoon. I overheard them mention Captain Booth several times, and, for my part, I would not answer that Mr. Murphy is not now gone about the business; but if you will impeach any to me of the road, or any thing else, I will step away to his worship Thrasher this instant, and I am sure I have interest enough with him to get you admitted an evidence."

"And so," cries Booth, "you really take me for a highwayman?"

"No offence, captain, I hope," said the keeper; "as times go, there are many worse men in the world than those. Gentlemen may be driven to distress, and when they are, I know no more genteeler way than the road. It hath been many a brave man's case, to my knowledge, and men of as much honor too as any in the world."

"Well, sir," said Booth, "I assure you I am not that gentleman of honor you imagine me."

Miss Matthews, who had long understood the keeper no better than Mr. Booth, no sooner heard his meaning explained than she was fired with greater indignation than the gentleman had expressed. "How dare you, sir," said she to the keeper, "insult a man of fashion, and who hath had the honor to bear his majesty's commission in the army?

as you yourself own you know. If his misfortunes have sent him hither, sure we have no laws that will protect such a fellow as you in insulting him." "Fellow!" muttered the keeper—" I would not advise you, madam, to use such language to me." " Do you dare threaten me ?" replied Miss Matthews in a rage. " Venture in the least instance to exceed your authority with regard to me, and I will prosecute you with the utmost vengeance.

A scene of very high altercation now ensued, till Booth interposed and quieted the keeper, who was perhaps enough inclined to an accommodation ; for, in truth, he waged unequal war. He was besides unwilling to incense Miss Matthews, whom he expected to be bailed out the next day, and who had more money left than he intended she should carry out of the prison with her ; and as for any violent or unjustifiable methods, the lady had discovered much too great a spirit to be in danger of them. The governor, therefore, in a very gentle tone, declared that if he had given any offence to the gentleman, he heartily asked his pardon ; that if he had known him to be really a captain, he should not have entertained any such suspicions ; but the captain was a very common title in that place, and belonged to several gentlemen that had never been in the army, or, at most, had rid private like himself. " To be sure, captain," said he, " as you yourself own, your dress is not very military" (for he had on a plain fustian suit) ; " and besides, as the lawyer says, *noscitur a sosir*, is a very good rule. And I don't believe there is a greater rascal upon earth than that same Robinson that I was talking of. Nay, I assure you, I wish there may be no mischief hatching against you. But if there is I will do all I can with the lawyer to prevent it. To be sure, Mr. Murphy is one of the cleverest men in the world at the law ; that even his enemies must own, and as I recommend him to all the business I can (and it is not a little to be sure that arises in this place), why one good turn deserves another. And I may expect that he will not be concerned in any plot to ruin any friend of mine, at least when I desire him not. I am sure he could not be an honest man if he would.''

Booth was then satisfied that Mr. Robinson, whom he did not yet know by name, was the gamester who had won his money at play. And now Miss Matthews, who had very impatiently borne this long interruption, prevailed on the keeper to withdraw. As soon as he was gone Mr. Booth began to felicitate her upon the news of the wounded gentleman being in a fair likelihood of recovery. To which, after a short silence, she answered, '' There is something, perhaps, which you will not easily guess, that makes your congratulations more agreeable to me than the first account I heard of the villain's having escaped the fate he deserves ; for I do assure you, at first, it did not make me amends for the interruption of my curiosity. Now I hope we shall be disturbed no more till you have finished your whole story. You left off, I think, somewhere in the struggle about leaving Amelia—the happy Amelia.'' '' And can you call her happy at such a period ?'' cries Booth. '' Happy, ay, happy, in any situation,'' answered Miss Matthews, '' with such a husband. I, at least, may well think so, who have experienced the very reverse of her fortune ; but I was not born to be happy. I may say with the poet,

> '' ' The blackest ink of fate was sure my lot,
> And when fate writ my name, it made a blot.' ''

'' Nay, nay, dear Miss Matthews,'' answered Booth, '' you must and shall banish such gloomy thoughts. Fate hath, I hope, many happy days in store for you.'' '' Do you believe it, Mr. Booth ?'' replied she ; '' indeed you know the contrary — you must know — for you can't have forgot. No Amelia in the world can have quite obliterated—forgetfulness is not in our own power. If it was, indeed, I have reason to think—but I know not what I am saying. Pray do proceed in that story.''

Booth so immediately complied with this request that it is possible he was pleased with it. To say the truth, if all which unwittingly dropped from Miss Matthews was put together, some conclusions might, it seems, be drawn from the whole, which could not convey a very agreeable idea to a constant husband. Booth, therefore, proceeded to relate what is written in the third book of this history.

BOOK III.

CHAPTER I.

IN WHICH MR. BOOTH RESUMES HIS STORY.

" If I am not mistaken, madam," continued Booth, " I was just going to acquaint you with the doctor's opinion when we were interrupted by the keeper.

" The doctor, having heard counsel on both sides—that is to say, Mrs. Harris for my staying, and Miss Betty for my going, at last delivered his own sentiments. As for Amelia, she sat silent, drowned in her tears ; nor was I myself in a much better situation.

" ' As the commissions are not signed,' said the doctor, ' I think you may be said to remain in your former regiment ; and therefore I think you ought to go on this expedition ; your duty to your king and country, whose bread you have eaten, requires it ; and this is a duty of too high a nature to admit the least deficiency. Regard to your character, likewise, requires you to go ; for the world, which might justly blame your staying at home if the case was even fairly stated, will not deal so honestly by you : you must expect to have every circumstance against you heightened, and most of what makes for your defence omitted ; and thus you will be stigmatized as a coward without any palliation. As the malicious disposition of mankind is too well known, and the cruel pleasure which they take in destroying the reputations of others, the use we are to make of this knowledge is to afford no handle to reproach ; for, bad as the world is, it seldom falls on any man who hath not given some slight cause for censure, though this perhaps is often aggravated ten thousand-fold, and when we blame the malice of the aggravation we ought not to forget our own imprudence in giving the occasion. Remember, my boy, your honor is at stake ; and you know how nice the honor of a soldier is in these cases. This is a treasure which he must be your enemy indeed who would attempt to rob you of. Therefore, you ought to consider every one as your enemy who, by desiring you to stay, would rob you of your honor.'

" ' Do you hear that, sister ? ' cries Miss Betty. ' Yes, I do hear it,' answered Amelia, with more spirit than I ever saw her exert before, ' and would preserve his honor at the expense of my life. I will preserve it if it should be at that expense ; and since it is Dr. Harrison's opinion that he ought to go, I give my consent. Go, my dear husband,' cried she, falling upon her knees ; ' may every angel of heaven guard and preserve you ! ' I cannot repeat her words without being affected," said he, wiping his eyes ; " the excellence of that woman no words can paint : Miss Matthews, she hath every perfection in human nature.

" I will not tire you with the repetition of any more that passed on that occasion, nor with the quarrel that ensued between Mrs. Harris and the doctor ; for the old lady could not submit to my leaving her daughter in her present condition. She fell severely on the army, and cursed the day in which her daughter was married to a soldier, not sparing the doctor for having had some share in the match. I will omit, likewise, the tender scene which passed between Amelia and myself previous to my departure."

" Indeed, I beg you will not," cries Miss Matthews ; " nothing delights me more than scenes of tenderness. I should be glad to know, if possible, every syllable which was uttered on both sides."

" I will indulge you then," cries Booth, " as far as is in my power. Indeed I believe I am able to recollect much the greatest part, for the impression is never to be effaced from my memory."

He then proceeded as Miss Matthews desired ; but, lest all our readers should not be of her opinion, we will, according to our usual custom, endeavor to accommodate ourselves to every taste, and shall therefore place this scene in a chapter by itself, which we desire all our readers who do not love, or who perhaps do not know the pleasure of tenderness, to pass over, since they may do this without any prejudice to the thread of the narrative.

CHAPTER II.

CONTAINING A SCENE OF THE TENDER KIND.

" THE doctor, madam," continued Booth, " spent his evening at Mrs. Harris's house, where I sat with him whilst he smoked his pillow pipe, as his phrase is. Amelia was retired about half an hour to her chamber before I went to her. At my entrance I found her on her knees, a posture in which I never disturbed her. In a few minutes she arose, came to me, and embracing me, said she had been praying for resolution to support the cruellest moment she had ever undergone or could possibly undergo. I reminded her how much more bitter a farewell would be on a death-bed, when we never could meet, in this world at least, again. I then endeavored to lessen all those objects which alarmed her most, and particularly the danger I was to encounter, upon which head I seemed a little to comfort her ; but the probable length of my absence, and the certain length of my voyage, were circumstances which no oratory of mine could even palliate. ' O heavens ! ' said she, bursting into tears, ' can I bear to think that hundreds, thousands for aught I know, of miles or leagues, that lands and seas are between us ? What is the prospect from that mount in our garden where I have sat so many happy hours with my Billy ? what is the distance between that and the farthest hill which we see from thence compared to the distance which will be between us ? You cannot wonder at this idea ; you must remember, my Billy, at this place, this very thought came formerly into my foreboding mind. I then begged you to leave the army. Why would you not comply ?—did I not tell you then that the smallest cottage we could survey from the mount would be, with you, a paradise to me ? it would be so still—why can't my Billy think so ? am I so much his superior in love ? where is the dishonor, Billy ? or, if there be any, will it reach our ears in our little hut ? are glory and fame, and not his Amelia, the happiness of my husband ? go then, purchase them at my expense. You will pay a few sighs, perhaps a few tears, at parting, and then new scenes will drive away the thoughts of poor Amelia from your bosom ; but what assistance shall I have in my affliction ? not that any change of scene could drive you one moment from my remembrance ; yet here every object I behold will place your loved idea in the liveliest manner before my eyes. This is the bed in which you have reposed ; that is the chair on which you sat. Upon these boards you have stood. These books you have read to me. Can I walk among our beds of flowers without viewing your favorites, nay, those which you have planted with your own hands ? can I see one beauty from our beloved mount which you have not pointed out to me ? ' Thus she went on, the woman, madam, you see, still prevailing.'' '' Since you mention it,'' says Miss Matthews, with a smile, '' I own the same observation occurred to me. It is too natural to us to consider ourselves only, Mr. Booth.'' '' You shall hear,'' he cried. '' At last the thoughts of her present condition suggested themselves. ' But if,' said she, ' my situation, even in health, will be so

intolerable, how shall I, in the danger and agonies of child-
birth, support your absence ? ' Here she stopped, and,
looking on me with all the tenderness imaginable, cried
out, ' And am I then such a wretch to wish for your presence at such a season ? ought I not to rejoice that you are
out of the hearing of my cries or the knowledge of my
pains ? if I die, will you not have escaped the horrors of a
parting ten thousand times more dreadful than this ? Go,
go, my Billy ; the very circumstance which made me most
dread your departure hath perfectly reconciled me to it.   I
perceive clearly now that I was only wishing to support my
own weakness with your strength, and to relieve my own
pains at the price of yours.   Believe me, my love, I am
ashamed of myself.'   I caught her in my arms with raptures not to be expressed in words, called her my heroine ;
sure none ever better deserved that name ; after which we remained for some time speechless, and locked in each other's
embraces."   " I am convinced," said Miss Matthews,
with a sigh, " there are moments in life worth purchasing
with worlds."

" At length the fatal morning came.   I endeavored to
hide every pang of my heart, and to wear the utmost gayety
in my countenance.   Amelia acted the same part.   In
these assumed characters we met the family at breakfast ;
at their breakfast, I mean, for we were both full already.
The doctor had spent above an hour that morning in discourse with Mrs. Harris, and had, in some measure, reconciled her to my departure.   He now made use of every art
to relieve the poor distressed Amelia ; not by inveighing
against the folly of grief, or by seriously advising her not
to grieve ; both of which were sufficiently performed by
Miss Betty.   The doctor, on the contrary, had recourse to
every means which might cast a veil over the idea of grief,
and raise comfortable images in my angel's mind.   He endeavored to lessen the supposed length of my absence by

discoursing on matters which were more distant in time.
He said he intended next year to rebuild a part of his par-
sonage-house. ' And you, captain,' says he, ' shall lay the
corner-stone, I promise you,' with many other circumstances of the like nature, which produced, I believe, some
good effect on us both.

" Amelia spoke but little ; indeed, more tears than words
dropped from her ; however, she seemed resolved to bear
her affliction with resignation. But when the dreadful
news arrived that the horses were ready, and I having
taken my leave of all the rest, at last approached her, she
was unable to support the conflict with nature any longer,
and, clinging round my neck, she cried, ' Farewell, farewell for ever ; for I shall never, never see you more.' At
which words the blood entirely forsook her lovely cheeks,
and she became a lifeless corpse in my arms.

" Amelia continued so long motionless that the doctor,
as well as Mrs. Harris, began to be under the most terrible
apprehensions ; so they informed me afterward, for at that
time I was incapable of making any observation. I had indeed very little more use of my senses than the dear creature whom I supported. At length, however, we were all
delivered from our fears ; and life again visited the loveli-
est mansion that human nature ever afforded it.

" I had been, and yet was, so terrified with what had
happened, and Amelia continued yet so weak and ill that I
determined, whatever might be the consequence, not to
leave her that day, which resolution she was no sooner
acquainted with than she fell on her knees, crying, ' Good
heaven ! I thank thee for this reprieve at least. Oh !
that every hour of my future life could be crammed into
this dear day ! '

" Our good friend the doctor remained with us. He
said he had intended to visit a family in some affliction ;
' but I don't know,' says he, ' why I should ride a dozen

miles after affliction, when we have enough here.' Of all
mankind the doctor is the best of comforters. As his excessive good-nature makes him take vast delight in the
office, so his great penetration into the human mind,
joined to his great experience, renders him the most wonderful proficient in it ; and he so well knows when to
soothe, when to reason, and when to ridicule, that he never
applies any of those arts improperly, which is almost universally the case with the physicians of the mind, and
which it requires very great judgment and dexterity to
avoid.

" The doctor principally applied himself to ridiculing the
dangers of the siege, in which he succeeded so well that he
sometimes forced a smile even into the face of Amelia.
But what most comforted her were the arguments he used
to convince her of the probability of my speedy if not immediate return. He said the general opinion was that the
place would be taken before our arrival there, in which
case we should have nothing more to do than to make the
best of our way home again.

" Amelia was so lulled by these arts that she passed the
day much better than I expected. Though the doctor
could not make pride strong enough to conquer love, yet
he exalted the former to make some stand against the latter ; insomuch that my poor Amelia, I believe, more than
once flattered herself, to speak the language of the world,
that her reason had gained an entire victory over her passion ; till love brought up a reinforcement, if I may use
that term, of tender ideas, and bore down all before him.

" In the evening the doctor and I passed another half-
hour together, when he proposed to me to endeavor to
leave Amelia asleep in the morning, and promised me to be
at hand when she awaked, and to support her with all the
assistance in his power. He added that nothing was more
foolish than for friends to take leave of each other. It is

true indeed, says he, in the common acquaintance and friendship of the world, this is a very harmless ceremony; but between two persons who really love each other the church of Rome never invented a penance half so severe as this which we absurdly impose on ourselves.

"I greatly approved the doctor's proposal; thanked him, and promised, if possible, to put it in execution. He then shook me by the hand, and heartily wished me well, saying, in his blunt way, 'Well, boy, I hope to see thee crowned with laurels at thy return; one comfort I have at least, that stone walls and a sea will prevent thee from running away.'

"When I had left the doctor I repaired to my Amelia, whom I found in her chamber, employed in a very different manner from what she had been the preceding night; she was busy in packing up some trinkets in a casket, which she desired me to carry with me. This casket was her own work, and she had just fastened it as I came to her.

"Her eyes very plainly discovered what had passed while she was engaged in her work; however, her countenance was now serene, and she spoke, at least, with some cheerfulness. But after some time, 'You must take care of this casket, Billy,' said she. 'You must indeed, Billy—for——' here passion almost choked her, till a flood of tears gave her relief, and then she proceeded—'for I shall be the happiest woman that ever was born when I see it again.' I told her, with the blessing of God, that day would soon come. 'Soon!' answered she. 'No, Billy, not soon; a week is an age; but yet the happy day may come. It shall, it must, it will! Yes, Billy, we shall meet never to part again, even in this world, I hope.' Pardon my weakness, Miss Matthews, but, upon my soul, I cannot help it," cried he, wiping his eyes. "Well, I wonder at your patience, and I will try it no longer. Amelia, tired out with so long a struggle between variety of passions, and having not closed her eyes during three successive nights, toward the morning fell into a profound sleep. In which sleep I left her, and having dressed myself with all the expedition imaginable, singing, whistling, hurrying, attempting by every method to banish thought, I mounted my horse, which I had over night ordered to be ready, and galloped away from that house where all my treasure was deposited.

" Thus, madam, I have, in obedience to your commands, run through a scene which, if it hath been tiresome to you, you must yet acquit me of having obtruded upon you. This I am convinced of, that no one is capable of tasting such a scene who hath not a heart full of tenderness, and perhaps not even then, unless he hath been in the same situation."

CHAPTER III.

IN WHICH MR. BOOTH SETS FORWARD ON HIS JOURNEY.

" WELL, madam, we have now taken our leave of Amelia. I rode a full mile before I once suffered myself to look back ; but now being come to the top of a little hill, the last spot I knew which could give me a prospect of Mrs. Harris's house, my resolution failed : I stopped and cast my eyes backward. Shall I tell you what I felt in that instant ? I do assure you I am not able. So many tender ideas crowded at once into my mind that, if I may use the expression, they almost dissolved my heart. And now, madam, the most unfortunate accident came first into my head. This was, that I had in the hurry and confusion left the dear casket behind me. The thought of going back at first suggested itself ; but the consequences of that were too apparent. I therefore resolved to send my man, and in the meantime to ride on softly on my road. He immediately executed my orders, and after some time, feeding my eyes with that delicious and yet heartfelt prospect, I at last turned my horse to descend the hill, and proceeded about a hundred yards, when, considering with myself that I should lose no time by a second indulgence, I again turned back, and once more feasted my sight with the same painful pleasure till my man returned, bringing me the casket, and an account that Amelia still continued in the sweet sleep I left her. I now suddenly turned my horse for the last time, and with the utmost resolution pursued my journey.

"I perceived my man at his return—but before I mention any thing of him it may be proper, madam, to acquaint you who he was. He was the foster-brother of my Amelia. This young fellow had taken it into his head to go into the army; and he was desirous to serve under my command. The doctor consented to discharge him; his mother at last consented to his importunities, and I was very easily prevailed on to list one of the handsomest young fellows in England.

"You will easily believe I had some little partiality to one whose milk Amelia had sucked; but as he had never seen the regiment, I had no opportunity to show him any great mark of favor. Indeed he waited on me as my servant; and I treated him with all the tenderness which can be used to one in that station.

"When I was about to change into the horse-guards the poor fellow began to droop, fearing that he should no longer be in the same corps with me, though certainly that would not have been the case. However, he had never mentioned one word of his dissatisfaction. He is indeed a fellow of a noble spirit; but when he heard that I was to remain where I was, and that we were to go to Gibraltar together, he fell into transports of joy little short of madness. In short, the poor fellow had imbibed a very strong affection for me; though this was what I knew nothing of till long after.

"When he returned to me then, as I was saying, with the casket, I observed his eyes all over blubbered with tears. I rebuked him a little too rashly on this occasion. ' Heyday ! ' says I, ' what is the meaning of this ? I hope I have not a milk-sop with me. If I thought you would show such a face to the enemy I would leave you behind.' ' Your honor need not fear that, answered he ; I shall find nobody there that I shall love well enough to make me cry.' I was highly pleased with this answer, in which I thought I could discover both sense and spirit. I then asked him what had occasioned those tears since he had left me (for he had no sign of any at that time), and whether he had seen his mother at Mrs. Harris's ? He answered in the negative, and begged that I would ask him no more questions, adding that he was not very apt to cry, and he hoped he should never give me such another opportunity of blaming him. I mention this only as an instance of his affection toward me, for I never could account for those tears any otherwise than by placing them to the account of that distress in which he left me at that time. We travelled full forty miles that day without baiting, when, arriving at the inn where I intended to rest that night, I retired immediately to my chamber, with my dear Amelia's casket, the opening of which was the nicest repast, and to which every other hunger gave way.

" It is impossible to mention to you all the little matters with which Amelia had furnished this casket. It contained medicines of all kinds, which her mother, who was the Lady Bountiful of that country, had supplied her with. The most valuable of all to me was a lock of her dear hair, which I have from that time worn in my bosom. What would I have then given for a little picture of my dear angel, which she had lost from her chamber about a month before ! and which we had the highest reason in the world to imagine her sister had taken away ; for the suspicion lay

only between her and Amelia's maid, who was of all creatures the honestest, and whom her mistress had often trusted with things of much greater value ; for the picture,
which was set in gold, and had two or three little diamonds
round it, was worth about twelve guineas only, whereas
Amelia left jewels in her care of much greater value."

"Sure," cries Miss Matthews, "she could not be such a
paltry pilferer."

"Not on account of the gold or the jewels," cries
Booth. "We imputed it to mere spite, with which, I
assure you, she abounds ; and she knew that, next to Amelia herself, there was nothing which I valued so much as
this little picture ; for such a resemblance did it bear of the
original that Hogarth himself did never, I believe, draw a
stronger likeness. Spite, therefore, was the only motive
to this cruel depredation ; and indeed her behavior on the
occasion sufficiently convinced us both of the justice of our
suspicion, though we neither of us durst accuse her ; and
she herself had the assurance to insist very strongly (though
she could not prevail) with Amelia to turn away her innocent maid, saying she would not live in the house with a
thief."

Miss Matthews now discharged some curses on Miss
Betty, not much worth repeating, and then Mr. Booth proceeded in his relation.

CHAPTER IV.

A SEA PIECE.

"The next day we joined the regiment, which was soon
after to embark. Nothing but mirth and jollity were in
the countenance of every officer and soldier ; and as I now
met several friends whom I had not seen for above a year
before, I passed several happy hours, in which poor Amelia's image seldom obtruded itself to interrupt my pleasure.

To confess the truth, dear Miss Matthews, the tenderest of passions is capable of subsiding ; nor is absence from our dearest friends so insupportable as it may at first appear. Distance of time and place do really cure what they seem to aggravate ; and taking leave of our friends resembles taking leave of the world ; concerning which it hath been often said that it is not death, but dying, which is terrible." Here Miss Matthews burst into a fit of laughter, and cried, "I sincerely ask your pardon ; but I cannot help laughing at the gravity of your philosophy." Booth answered that the doctrine of the passions had been always his favorite study ; that he was convinced every man acted entirely from that passion which was uppermost. "Can I then think," said he, "without entertaining the utmost contempt for myself, that any pleasure upon earth could drive the thoughts of Amelia one instant from my mind ?

"At length we embarked aboard a transport, and sailed for Gibraltar ; but the wind, which was at first fair, soon chopped about, so that we were obliged, for several days, to beat to windward, as the sea phrase is. During this time the taste which I had of a seafaring life did not appear extremely agreeable. We rolled up and down in a little narrow cabin, in which were three officers, all of us extremely sea-sick, our sickness being much aggravated by the motion of the ship, by the view of each other, and by the stench of the men. But this was but a little taste indeed of the misery which was to follow ; for we were got about six leagues to the westward of Scilly, when a violent storm arose at north-east, which soon raised the waves to the height of mountains. The horror of this is not to be adequately described to those who have never seen the like. The storm began in the evening, and as the clouds brought on the night apace, it was soon entirely dark ; nor had we, during many hours, any other light than what was caused by the jarring elements, which frequently sent forth

flashes, or rather streams, of fire ; and whilst these presented
the most dreadful objects to our eyes, the roaring of the
winds, the dashing of the waves against the ship and each
other, formed a sound altogether as horrible for our ears ;
while our ship, sometimes lifted up, as it were, to the skies,
and sometimes swept away at once as into the lowest abyss,
seemed to be the sport of the winds and seas.   The captain
himself almost gave up all for lost, and expressed his apprehension of being inevitably cast on the rocks of Scilly,
and beat to pieces.   And now, while some on board were
addressing themselves to the Supreme Being, and others
applying for comfort to strong liquors, my whole thoughts
were entirely engaged by my Amelia.   A thousand tender
ideas crowded into my mind.   I can truly say that I had
not a single consideration about myself in which she was
not concerned.   Dying to me was leaving her ; and the
fear of never seeing her more was a dagger stuck in my
heart.   Again, all the terrors with which this storm, if it
reached her ears, must fill her gentle mind on my account,
and the agonies which she must undergo when she heard
of my fate, gave me such intolerable pangs that I now
repented my resolution, and wished, I own I wished, that I
had taken her advice, and preferred love and a cottage to
all the dazzling charms of honor.

" While I was tormenting myself with those meditations,
and had concluded myself as certainly lost, the master came
into the cabin, and with a cheerful voice assured us that we
had escaped the danger, and that we had certainly passed to
the westward of the rock.   This was comfortable news to
all present ; and my captain, who had been some time on
his knees, leaped suddenly up, and testified his joy with a
great oath.

" A person unused to the sea would have been astonished
at the satisfaction which now discovered itself in the master
or in any on board ; for the storm still raged with great

violence, and the daylight, which now appeared, presented us with sights of horror sufficient to terrify minds which were not absolute slaves to the passion of fear ; but so great is the force of habit that what inspires a landman with the highest apprehension of danger gives not the least concern to a sailor, to whom rocks and quicksands are almost the only objects of terror.

" The master, however, was a little mistaken in the present instance ; for he had not left the cabin above an hour before my man came running to me, and acquainted me that the ship was half full of water ; that the sailors were going to hoist out the boat and save themselves, and begged me to come that moment along with him, as I tendered my preservation. With this account, which was conveyed to me in a whisper, I acquainted both the captain and ensign ; and we all together immediately mounted the deck, where we found the master making use of all his oratory to persuade the sailors that the ship was in no danger, and at the same time employing all his authority to set the pumps a-going, which he assured them would keep the water under, and save his dear Lovely Peggy (for that was the name of the ship), which he swore he loved as dearly as his own soul.

" Indeed this sufficiently appeared ; for the leak was so great, and the water flowed in so plentifully, that his Lovely Peggy was half filled before he could be brought to think of quitting her ; but now the boat was brought alongside the ship, and the master himself, notwithstanding all his love for her, quitted his ship, and leaped into the boat. Every man present attempted to follow his example, when I heard the voice of my servant roaring forth my name in a kind of agony. I made directly to the ship-side, but was too late, for the boat, being already overladen, put directly off. And now, madam, I am going to relate to you an instance of heroic affection in a poor fellow toward his master, to which love itself, even among persons of superior education, can produce but few similar instances. My poor man, being unable to get me with him into the boat, leaped suddenly into the sea, and swam back to the ship ; and when I gently rebuked him for his rashness, he answered he chose rather to die with me than to live to carry the account of my death to my Amelia : at the same time bursting into a flood of tears, he cried, ' Good heavens ! what will that poor lady feel when she hears of this ! ' This tender concern for my dear love endeared the poor fellow more to me than the gallant instance which he had just before given of his affection toward myself.

" And now, madam, my eyes were shocked with a sight the horror of which can scarce be imagined ; for the boat had scarce got four hundred yards from the ship when it was swallowed up by the merciless waves, which now ran so high that out of the number of persons which were in the boat none recovered the ship, though many of them we saw miserably perish before our eyes, some of them very near us, without any possibility of giving them the least assistance.

" But, whatever we felt for them, we felt, I believe, more for ourselves, expecting every minute when we should share the same fate. Among the rest, one of our officers appeared quite stupefied with fear. I never indeed saw a more miserable example of the great power of that passion : I must not, however, omit doing him justice, by saying that I afterward saw the same man behave well in an engagement, in which he was wounded, though there likewise he was said to have betrayed the same passion of fear in his countenance.

" The other of our officers was no less stupefied (if I may so express myself) with foolhardiness, and seemed almost insensible of his danger. To say the truth, I have, from this and some other instances which I have seen, been

almost inclined to think that the courage as well as coward-
ice of fools proceeds from not knowing what is or what is
not the proper object of fear ; indeed, we may account for
the extreme hardiness of some men in the same manner as
for the terrors of children at a bugbear. The child knows
not but that the bugbear is the proper object of fear, the
blockhead knows not that a cannon-ball is so.

" As to the remaining part of the ship's crew and the
soldiery, most of them were dead drunk, and the rest were
endeavoring, as fast as they could, to prepare for death in
the same manner.

" In this dreadful situation we were taught that no human
condition should inspire men with absolute despair ; for, as
the storm had ceased for some time, the swelling of the sea
began considerably to abate, and we now perceived the
man of war which convoyed us at no great distance
astern. Those aboard her easily perceived our distress,
and made toward us. When they came pretty near they
hoisted out two boats to our assistance. These no sooner
approached the ship than they were instantaneously filled,
and I myself got a place in one of them, chiefly by the aid
of my honest servant, of whose fidelity to me on all occasions I cannot speak or think too highly. Indeed, I got
into the boat so much the more easily, as a great number
on board the ship were rendered, by drink, incapable of
taking any care for themselves. There was time, however,
for the boat to pass and repass ; so that, when we came to
call over names, three only, of all that remained in the ship
after the loss of her own boat, were missing.

" The captain, ensign, and myself were received with
many congratulations by our officers on board the man of
war. The sea-officers too, all except the captain, paid us
their compliments, though these were of the rougher kind,
and not without several jokes on our escape. As for the
captain himself, we scarce saw him during many hours ;

and when he appeared, he presented a view of majesty beyond any that I had ever seen. The dignity which he preserved did indeed give me rather the idea of a Mogul, or a Turkish emperor, than of any of the monarchs of Christendom. To say the truth, I could resemble his walk on the deck to nothing but the image of Captain Gulliver strutting among the Lilliputians ; he seemed to think himself a being of an order superior to all around him, and more especially to us of the land service. Nay, such was the behavior of all the sea-officers and sailors to us and our soldiers that, instead of appearing to be subjects of the same prince, engaged in one quarrel, and joined to support one cause, we landsmen rather seemed to be captives on board an enemy's vessel. This is a grievous misfortune, and often proves so fatal to the service that it is great pity some means could not be found of curing it.''

Here Mr. Booth stopped a while to take breath. We will therefore give the same refreshment to the reader.

CHAPTER V.

THE ARRIVAL OF BOOTH AT GIBRALTAR, WITH WHAT THERE BEFELL HIM.

'' The adventures,'' continued Booth, '' which happened to me from this day till my arrival at Gibraltar are not worth recounting to you. After a voyage the remainder of which was tolerably prosperous, we arrived in that garrison, the natural strength of which is so well known to the whole world.

'' About a week after my arrival it was my fortune to be ordered on a sally party, in which my left leg was broke with a musket-ball ; and I should most certainly have either perished miserably, or must have owed my preservation to some of the enemy, had not my faithful servant carried me off on his shoulders, and afterward, with the assistance of one of his comrades, brought me back into the garrison.

"The agony of my wound was so great that it threw me into a fever from whence my surgeon apprehended much danger. I now began again to feel for my Amelia, and for myself on her account ; and the disorder of my mind, occasioned by such melancholy contemplations, very highly aggravated the distemper of my body, insomuch that it would probably have proved fatal had it not been for the friendship of one Captain James, an officer of our regiment, and an old acquaintance, who is undoubtedly one of the pleasantest companions and one of the best-natured men in the world. This worthy man, who had a head and a heart perfectly adequate to every office of friendship, stayed with me almost day and night during my illness ; and by strengthening my hopes, raising my spirits, and cheering my thoughts, preserved me from destruction.

"The behavior of this man alone is a sufficient proof of the truth of my doctrine, that all men act entirely from their passions ; for Bob James can never be supposed to act from any motives of virtue or religion, since he constantly laughs at both ; and yet his conduct toward me alone demonstrates a degree of goodness which perhaps few of the votaries of either virtue or religion can equal."

"You need not take much pains," answered Miss Matthews, with a smile, "to convince me of your doctrine. I have been always an advocate for the same. I look upon the two words you mention to serve only as cloaks, under which hypocrisy may be the better enabled to cheat the world. I have been of that opinion ever since I read that charming fellow Mandevil."

"Pardon me, madam," answered Booth ; "I hope you do not agree with Mandevil neither, who hath represented human nature in a picture of the highest deformity. He hath left out of his system the best passion which the mind can possess, and attempts to derive the effects or energies of that passion from the base impulses of pride or fear. Whereas it is as certain that love exists in the mind of man as that its opposite hatred doth ; and the same reasons will equally prove the existence of the one as the existence of the other."

"I don't know, indeed," replied the lady ; "I never thought much about the matter. This I know, that when I read Mandevil I thought all he said was true ; and I have been often told that he proves religion and virtue to be only mere names. However, if he denies there is any such thing as love, that is most certainly wrong. I am afraid I can give him the lie myself."

"I will join with you, madam, in that," answered Booth, "at any time."

"Will you join with me ?" answered she, looking eagerly at him—"Oh, Mr. Booth ! I know not what I was going to say—What—Where did you leave off ? I would not interrupt you—but I am impatient to know something."

"What, madam ?" cries Booth ; "if I can give you any satisfaction——"

"No, no," said she, "I must hear all ; I would not for the world break the thread of your story. Besides, I am afraid to ask—Pray, pray, sir, go on."

"Well, madam," cries Booth, "I think I was mentioning the extraordinary acts of friendship done me by Captain James ; nor can I help taking notice of the almost unparalleled fidelity of poor Atkinson (for that was my man's name), who was not only constant in the assiduity of his attendance, but during the time of my danger demonstrated a concern for me which I can hardly account for, as my prevailing on his captain to make him a sergeant was the first favor he ever received at my hands, and this did not happen till I was almost perfectly recovered of my broken leg. Poor fellow ! I shall never forget the extravagant

joy his halbert gave him ; I remember it the more because
it was one of the happiest days of my own life ; for it was
upon this day that I received a letter from my dear Amelia,
after a long silence, acquainting me that she was out of all
danger from her lying-in.

" I was now once more able to perform my duty, when
(so unkind was the fortune of war), the second time I
mounted the guard, I received a violent contusion from the
bursting of a bomb. I was felled to the ground, where
I lay breathless by the blow, till honest Atkinson came to
my assistance, and conveyed me to my room, where a surgeon immediately attended me.

" The injury I had now received was much more dangerous in my surgeon's opinion than the former ; it caused me
to spit blood, and was attended with a fever, and other bad
symptoms ; so that very fatal consequences were apprehended.

" In this situation the image of my Amelia haunted me
day and night ; and the apprehensions of never seeing her
more were so intolerable that I had thoughts of resigning
my commission and returning home, weak as I was, that I
might have, at least, the satisfaction of dying in the arms of
my love. Captain James, however, persisted in dissuading
me from any such resolution. He told me my honor was too
much concerned, attempted to raise my hopes of recovery to
the utmost of his power ; but chiefly he prevailed on me by
suggesting that, if the worst which I apprehended should
happen, it was much better for Amelia that she should be
absent than present in so melancholy an hour. ' I know,'
cried he, ' the extreme joy which must arise in you from
meeting again with Amelia, and the comfort of expiring in
her arms ; but consider what she herself must endure upon
the dreadful occasion, and you would not wish to purchase
any happiness at the price of so much pain to her.' This
argument at length prevailed on me ; and it was, after many

long debates, resolved that she should not even know my present condition till my doom either for life or death was absolutely fixed."

" Oh ! heavens ! how great ! how generous !" cried Miss Matthews. " Booth, thou art a noble fellow ; and I scarce think there is a woman upon earth worthy so exalted a passion."

Booth made a modest answer to the compliment which Miss Matthews had paid him. This drew more civilities from the lady, and these again more acknowledgments, all which we shall pass by, and proceed with our history.

CHAPTER VI.

CONTAINING MATTERS WHICH WILL PLEASE SOME READERS.

" Two months and more had I continued in a state of uncertainty, sometimes with more flattering, and sometimes with more alarming symptoms ; when one afternoon poor Atkinson came running into my room, all pale and out of breath, and begged me not to be surprised at his news. I asked him eagerly what was the matter, and if it was any thing concerning Amelia ? I had scarce uttered the dear name when she herself rushed into the room, and ran hastily to me, crying, ' Yes, it is, it is your Amelia herself.'

" There is nothing so difficult to describe, and generally so dull when described, as scenes of excessive tenderness."

" Can you think so ?" says Miss Matthews ; " surely there is nothing so charming ! Oh, Mr. Booth, our sex is d—ned by the want of tenderness in yours. Oh, were they all like you—certainly no man was ever your equal."

" Indeed, madam," cries Booth, " you honor me too much. But—well—when the first transports of our meeting were over, Amelia began gently to chide me for having concealed my illness from her ; for, in three letters which I had writ her since the accident had happened, there was not the least mention of it, or any hint given by which she could possibly conclude I was otherwise than in perfect health. And when I had excused myself, by assigning the true reason, she cried, ' O Mr. Booth ! and do you know so little of your Amelia as to think I could or would survive you ? Would it not be better for one dreadful sight to break my heart all at once than to break it by degrees ? O Billy ! can any thing pay me for the loss of this embrace ? ' But I ask your pardon —how ridiculous doth my fondness appear in your eyes !"

" How often," answered she, " shall I assert the contrary ? What would you have me say, Mr. Booth ? Shall I tell you I envy Mrs. Booth of all the women in the world ? would you believe me if I did ? I hope you—what am I saying ? Pray, make no farther apology, but go on."

" After a scene," continued he, " too tender to be conceived by many, Amelia informed me that she had received a letter from an unknown hand acquainting her with my misfortune, and advising her, if she ever desired to see me more, to come directly to Gibraltar. She said she should not have delayed a moment after receiving this letter had not the same ship brought her one from me written with rather more than usual gayety, and in which there was not the least mention of my indisposition. This, she said, greatly puzzled her and her mother, and the worthy divine endeavored to persuade her to give credit to my letter, and to impute the other to a species of wit with which the world greatly abounds. This consists entirely in doing various kinds of mischief to our fellow-creatures, by belying one, deceiving another, exposing a third, and drawing in a fourth to expose himself—in short, by making some the objects of laughter, others of contempt, and indeed not seldom by subjecting them to very great inconveniences, perhaps to ruin, for the sake of a jest.

" Mrs. Harris and the doctor derived the letter from this

species of wit. Miss Betty, however, was of a different
opinion, and advised poor Amelia to apply to an officer
whom the governor had sent over in the same ship, by
whom the report of my illness was so strongly confirmed,
that Amelia immediately resolved on her voyage.

" I had a great curiosity to know the author of this letter, but not the least trace of it could be discovered. The
only person with whom I lived in any great intimacy was
Captain James, and he, madam, from what I have already
told you, you will think to be the last person I could
suspect ; besides, he declared upon his honor that he knew
nothing of the matter, and no man's honor is, I believe,
more sacred. There was indeed an ensign of another regiment who knew my wife, and who had sometimes visited
me in my illness ; but he was a very unlikely man to interest himself much in any affairs which did not concern him ;
and he too declared he knew nothing of it."

" And did you never discover this secret ?" cried Miss
Matthews.

" Never to this day," answered Booth.

" I fancy," said she, " I could give a shrewd guess.
What so likely as that Mrs. Booth, when you left her,
should have given her foster-brother orders to send her
word of whatever befell you ? Yet stay—that could not be
neither ; for then she would not have doubted whether she
should leave dear England on the receipt of the letter. No,
it must have been by some other means ; yet that I own appeared extremely natural to me ; for if I had been left by
such a husband I think I should have pursued the same
method."

" No, madam," cried Booth, " it must have been conveyed by some other channel ; for my Amelia, I am certain,
was entirely ignorant of the manner ; and as for poor Atkinson, I am convinced he would not have ventured to take
such a step without acquainting me. Besides, the poor fel-

low had, I believe, such a regard for my wife, out of gratitude for the favors she hath done his mother, that I make no doubt he was highly rejoiced at her absence from my melancholy scene. Well, whoever writ it is a matter very immaterial ; yet, as it seemed so odd and unaccountable an incident, I could not help mentioning it.

"From the time of Amelia's arrival nothing remarkable happened till my perfect recovery, unless I should observe her remarkable behavior, so full of care and tenderness that it was perhaps without a parallel."

"O no, Mr. Booth," cries the lady ; "it is fully equalled, I am sure, by your gratitude. There is nothing, I believe, so rare as gratitude in your sex, especially in husbands. So kind a remembrance is indeed more than a return to such an obligation ; for where is the mighty obligation which a woman confers, who, being possessed of an inestimable jewel, is so kind to herself as to be careful and tender of it ? I do not say this to lessen your opinion of Mrs. Booth. I have no doubt but that she loves you as well as she is capable. But I would not have you think so meanly of our sex as to imagine there are not a thousand women susceptible of true tenderness toward a meritorious man. Believe me, Mr. Booth, if I had received such an account of an accident having happened to such a husband, a mother and a parson would not have held me a moment. I should have leaped into the first fishing-boat I could have found, and bid defiance to the winds and waves. Oh ! there is no true tenderness but in a woman of spirit. I would not be understood all this while to reflect on Mrs. Booth. I am only defending the cause of my sex ; for, upon my soul, such compliments to a wife are a satire on all the rest of womankind."

"Sure you jest, Miss Matthews," answered Booth, with a smile ; "however, if you please, I will proceed in my story."

CHAPTER VII.

THE CAPTAIN, CONTINUING HIS STORY, RECOUNTS SOME PAR-
TICULARS WHICH, WE DOUBT NOT, TO MANY GOOD PEOPLE
WILL APPEAR UNNATURAL.

"I was scarce sooner recovered from my indisposition
than Amelia herself fell ill. This, I am afraid, was occasioned by the fatigues which I could not prevent her from
undergoing on my account; for, as my disease went off
with violent sweats, during which the surgeon strictly ordered that I should lie by myself, my Amelia could not be
prevailed upon to spend many hours in her own bed. During my restless fits she would sometimes read to me several
hours together; indeed it was not without difficulty that she
ever quitted my bedside. These fatigues, added to the uneasiness of her mind, overpowered her weak spirits, and
threw her into one of the worst disorders that can possibly
attend a woman—a disorder very common among the
ladies, and our physicians have not agreed upon its name.
Some call it the fever on the spirits, some a nervous fever,
some the vapors, and some the hysterics."

"O say no more," cries Miss Matthews; "I pity you, I
pity you from my soul. A man had better be plagued with
all the curses of Egypt than with a vaporish wife."

"Pity me! madam," answered Booth; "pity rather
that dear creature who, from her love and care of my unworthy self, contracted a distemper the horrors of which
are scarce to be imagined. It is indeed a sort of compli-
cation of all diseases together, with almost madness added
to them. In this situation, the siege being at an end, the
governor gave me leave to attend my wife to Montpelier,
the air of which was judged to be most likely to restore her
to health. Upon this occasion she wrote to her mother to
desire a remittance, and set forth the melancholy condition

of her health, and her necessity for money, in such terms as would have touched any bosom not void of humanity, though a stranger to the unhappy sufferer. Her sister answered it, and I believe I have a copy of the answer in my pocket. I keep it by me as a curiosity, and you would think it more so could I show you my Amelia's letter." He then searched his pocket-book, and finding the letter among many others, he read it in the following words :

" ' DEAR SISTER : My mamma, being much disordered, hath commanded me to tell you she is both shocked and surprised at your extraordinary request, or, as she chooses to call it, order for money. You know, my dear, she says that your marriage with this red-coat man was entirely against her consent and the opinion of all your family (I am sure I may here include myself in that number) ; and yet, after this fatal act of disobedience, she was prevailed on to receive you as her child ; not, however, nor are you so to understand it, as the favorite which you was before. She forgave you ; but this was as a Christian and a parent ; still preserving in her own mind a just sense of your disobedience and a just resentment on that account. And yet, notwithstanding this resentment, she desires you to remember that, when you a second time ventured to oppose her authority, and nothing would serve you but taking a ramble (an indecent one, I can't help saying) after your fellow, she thought fit to show the excess of a mother's tenderness, and furnished you with no less than fifty pounds for your foolish voyage. How can she, then, be otherwise than surprised at your present demand ? which, should she be so weak to comply with, she must expect to be every month repeated, in order to supply the extravagance of a young rakish officer. You say she will compassionate your sufferings ; yes, surely she doth greatly compassionate them, and so do I too, though you was neither so kind nor so civil as to suppose I should. But I forgive all your slights to me.

as well now as formerly. Nay, I not only forgive, but I pray daily for you. But, dear sister, what could you expect less than what hath happened? you should have believed your friends, who were wiser and older than you. I do not here mean myself, though I own I am eleven months and some odd weeks your superior; though, had I been younger, I might perhaps have been able to advise you; for wisdom and what some may call beauty do not always go together. You will not be offended at this, for I know in your heart you have always held your head above some people whom perhaps other people have thought better of; but why do I mention what I scorn so much? No, my dear sister, heaven forbid it should ever be said of me that I value myself upon my face — not but if I could believe men perhaps—but I hate and despise men—you know I do, my dear, and I wish you had despised them as much; but *jacta est jalea*, as the doctor says. You are to make the best of your fortune — what fortune, I mean, my mamma may please to give you, for you know all is in her power. Let me advise you, then, to bring your mind to your circumstances, and remember (for I can't help writing it, as it is for your own good) the vapors are a distemper which very ill become a knapsack. Remember, my dear, what you have done; remember what my mamma hath done; remember we have something of yours to keep, and do not consider yourself as an only child; no, nor as a favorite child; but be pleased to remember,

    " ' Dear sister,

       " ' Your most affectionate sister,

          " ' and most obedient humble servant,

                " ' E. HARRIS.' "

"O brave Miss Betty!" cried Miss Matthews; "I always held her in high esteem; but I protest she exceeds even what I could have expected from her."

" This letter, madam," cries Booth, " you will believe, was an excellent cordial for my poor wife's spirits. So dreadful indeed was the effect it had upon her that, as she had read it in my absence, I found her, at my return home, in the most violent fits ; and so long was it before she recovered her senses that I despaired of that blessed event ever happening ; and my own senses very narrowly escaped from being sacrificed to my despair. However, she came at last to herself, and I began to consider of every means of carrying her immediately to Montpelier, which was now become much more necessary than before.

" Though I was greatly shocked at the barbarity of the letter, yet I apprehended no very ill consequence from it ; for, as it was believed all over the army that I had married a great fortune, I had received offers of money, if I wanted it, from more than one. Indeed, I might have easily carried my wife to Montpelier at any time ; but she was extremely averse to the voyage, being desirous of our returning to England, as I had leave to do ; and she grew daily so much better that, had it not been for the receipt of that cursed—which I have just read to you, I am persuaded she might have been able to return to England in the next ship.

" Among others there was a colonel in the garrison who had not only offered but importuned me to receive money of him ; I now therefore repaired to him ; and, as a reason for altering my resolution, I produced the letter, and at the same time acquainted him with the true state of my affairs. The colonel read the letter, shook his head, and, after some silence, said he was sorry I had refused to accept his offer before, but that he had now so ordered matters, and disposed of his money, that he had not a shilling left to spare from his own occasions.

" Answers of the same kind I had from several others, but not one penny could I borrow of any ; for I have been since firmly persuaded that the honest colonel was not con-

tent with denying me himself, but took effectual means, by
spreading the secret I had so foolishly trusted him with, to
prevent me from succeeding elsewhere ; for such is the
nature of men that whoever denies himself to do you a
favor is unwilling that it should be done to you by any other.

" This was the first time I had ever felt that distress
which arises from the want of money—a distress very dreadful indeed in a married state ; for what can be more miserable than to see any thing necessary to the preservation of a
beloved creature, and not be able to supply it ?

" Perhaps you may wonder, madam, that I have not
mentioned Captain James on this occasion ; but he was at
that time laid up at Algiers (whither he had been sent by
the governor) in a fever.   However, he returned time
enough to supply me, which he did with the utmost readiness on the very first mention of my distress ; and the good
colonel, notwithstanding his having disposed of his money,
discounted the captain's draft.   You see, madam, an instance in the generous behavior of my friend James, how
false are all universal satires against humankind.   He is indeed one of the worthiest men the world ever produced.

" But perhaps you will be more pleased still with the
extravagant generosity of my sergeant.   The day before
the return of Mr. James the poor fellow came to me with
tears in his eyes, and begged I would not be offended at
what he was going to mention.   He then pulled a purse
from his pocket, which contained, he said, the sum of
twelve pounds, and which he begged me to accept, crying
he was sorry it was not in his power to lend me whatever I
wanted.   I was so struck with this instance of generosity
and friendship in such a person that I gave him an opportunity of pressing me a second time before I made him an
answer.   Indeed I was greatly surprised how he came to
be worth that little sum, and no less at his being acquainted
with my own wants.   In both which points he presently

satisfied me. As to the first, it seems he had plundered a
Spanish officer of fifteen pistoles ; and as to the second, he
confessed he had it from my wife's maid, who had overheard some discourse between her mistress and me. Indeed
people, I believe, always deceive themselves who imagine
they can conceal distressed circumstances from their servants ; for these are always extremely quick-sighted on such
occasions."

"Good heavens !" cries Miss Matthews, "how astonish-
ing is such behavior in so low a fellow !"

"I thought so myself," answered Booth ; "and yet I
know not, on a more strict examination into the matter, why
we should be more surprised to see greatness of mind discover itself in one degree or rank of life than in another.
Love, benevolence, or what you will please to call it, may
be the reigning passion in a beggar as well as in a prince ;
and wherever it is, its energies will be the same.

"To confess the truth, I am afraid we often compliment
what we call upper life with too much injustice at the expense of the lower. As it is no rare thing to see instances
which degrade human nature in persons of the highest birth
and education, so I apprehend that examples of whatever is
really great and good have been sometimes found amongst
those who have wanted all such advantages. In reality,
palaces, I make no doubt, do sometimes contain nothing
but dreariness and darkness, and the sun of righteousness
hath shone forth with all its glory in a cottage."

CHAPTER VIII.

THE STORY OF BOOTH CONTINUED.

MR. BOOTH thus went on :

"We now took leave of the garrison, and having landed
at Marseilles, arrived at Montpelier, without any thing happening to us worth remembrance, except the extreme sea-

sickness of poor Amelia ; but I was afterward well repaid for the terrors which it occasioned me by the good consequences which attended it ; for I believe it contributed even more than the air of Montpelier to the perfect re-establishment of her health."

" I ask your pardon for interrupting you," cries Miss Matthews, " but you never satisfied me whether you took the sergeant's money. You have made me half in love with that charming fellow."

" How can you imagine, madam," answered Booth, " I should have taken from a poor fellow what was of so little consequence to me, and at the same time of so much to him ? Perhaps, now, you will derive this from the passion of pride."

" Indeed," says she, " I neither derive it from the passion of pride nor from the passion of folly : but methinks you should have accepted the offer, and I am convinced you hurt him very much when you refused it. But pray proceed in your story." Then Booth went on as follows :

" As Amelia recovered her health and spirits daily, we began to pass our time very pleasantly at Montpelier ; for the greatest enemy to the French will acknowledge that they are the best people in the world to live amongst for a little while. In some countries it is almost as easy to get a good estate as a good acquaintance. In England, particularly, acquaintance is of almost as slow growth as an oak ; so that the age of man scarce suffices to bring it to any perfection, and families seldom contract any great intimacy till the third, or at least the second generation. So shy indeed are we English of letting a stranger into our houses that one would imagine we regarded all such as thieves. Now the French are the very reverse. Being a stranger among them entitles you to the better place, and to the greater degree of civility ; and if you wear but the appearance of a gentleman, they never suspect you are not one.

Their friendship indeed seldom extends as far as their purse ; nor is such friendship usual in other countries. To say the truth, politeness carries friendship far enough in the ordinary occasions of life, and those who want this accomplishment rarely make amends for it by their sincerity ; for pluntness, or rather rudeness, as it commonly deserves to be called, is not always so much a mark of honesty as it is taken to be.

" The day after our arrival we became acquainted with Mons. Bagillard. He was a Frenchman of great wit and vivacity, with a greater share of learning than gentlemen are usually possessed of. As he lodged in the same house with us, we were immediately acquainted, and I liked his conversation so well that I never thought I had too much of his company. Indeed, I spent so much of my time with him that Amelia (I know not whether I ought to mention it) grew uneasy at our familiarity, and complained of my being too little with her, from my violent fondness for my new acquaintance ; for, our conversation turning chiefly upon books, and principally Latin ones (for we read several of the classics together), she could have but little entertainment by being with us. When my wife had once taken it into her head that she was deprived of my company by M. Bagillard, it was impossible to change her opinion ; and though I now spent more of my time with her than I had ever done before, she still grew more and more dissatisfied, till at last she very earnestly desired me to quit my lodgings, and insisted upon it with more vehemence than I had ever know her express before. To say the truth, if that excellent woman could ever be thought unreasonable, I thought she was so on this occasion.

" But in what light soever her desires appeared to me, as they manifestly arose from an affection of which I had daily the most endearing proofs, I resolved to comply with her, and accordingly removed to a distant part of the town ; for

it is my opinion that we can have but little love for the
person whom we will never indulge in an unreasonable demand.   Indeed, I was under a difficulty with regard to
Mons. Bagillard ; for, as I could not possibly communicate
to him the true reason for quitting my lodgings, so I found
it as difficult to deceive him by a counterfeit one ; besides,
I was apprehensive I should have little less of his company
than before.   I could indeed have avoided this dilemma
by leaving Montpelier, for Amelia had perfectly recovered
her health ; but I had faithfully promised Captain James
to wait his return from Italy, whither he was gone some
time before from Gibraltar ; nor was it proper for Amelia
to take any long journey, she being now near six months
gone with child.

" This difficulty, however, proved to be less than I had
imagined it ; for my French friend, whether he suspected
any thing from my wife's behavior, though she never, as I
observed, showed him the least incivility, became suddenly
as cold on his side.   After our leaving the lodgings he never
made above two or three formal visits ; indeed his time was
soon after entirely taken up by an intrigue with a certain
countess, which blazed all over Montpelier.

" We had not been long in our new apartments before an
English officer arrived at Montpelier, and came to lodge in
the same house with us.   This gentleman, whose name was
Bath, was of the rank of a major, and had so much singularity in his character that perhaps you never heard of
any like him.   He was far from having any of those book-
ish qualifications which had before caused my Amelia's dis-
quiet.   It is true his discourse generally turned on matters
of no feminine kind, war and martial exploits being the
ordinary topics of his conversation ; however, as he had a
sister with whom Amelia was greatly pleased, an intimacy
presently grew between us, and we four lived in one family.

" The major was a great dealer in the marvellous, and

was constantly the little hero of his own tale. This made
him very entertaining to Amelia, who, of all persons in the
world, hath the truest taste and enjoyment of the ridiculous; for, whilst no one sooner discovers it in the character
of another, no one so well conceals her knowledge of it
from the ridiculous person. I cannot help mentioning a
sentiment of hers on this head, as I think it doth her great
honor. 'If I had the same neglect,' said she, 'for ridiculous people with the generality of the world, I should rather
think them the object of tears than laughter; but, in reality, I have known several who, in some parts of their characters, have been extremely ridiculous, in others have been
altogether as amiable. For instance,' said she, ' here is the
major, who tells us of many things which he hath never
seen, and of others which he hath never done, and both in
the most extravagant excess; and yet how amiable is his
behavior to his poor sister, whom he hath not only brought
over hither for her health, at his own expense, but is come
to bear her company.' I believe, madam, I repeat her very
words, for I am very apt to remember what she says.

" You will easily believe, from a circumstance I have just
mentioned in the major's favor, especially when I have told
you that his sister was one of the best of girls, that it was
entirely necessary to hide from her all kind of laughter at
any part of her brother's behavior. To say the truth, this
was easy enough to do ; for the poor girl was so blinded
with love and gratitude, and so highly honored and rever-
enced her brother, that she had not the least suspicion that
there was a person in the world capable of laughing at
him.

" Indeed, I am certain she never made the least discovery
of our ridicule, for I am well convinced she would have
resented it : for, besides the love she bore her brother, she
had a little family pride, which would sometimes appear.
To say the truth, if she had any fault it was that of vanity,

but she was a very good girl upon the whole ; and none of us are entirely free from faults."

" You are a good-natured fellow, Will," answered Miss Matthews ; " but vanity is a fault of the first magnitude in a woman, and often the occasion of many others."

To this Booth made no answer, but continued his story.

" In this company we passed two or three months very agreeably, till the major and I both betook ourselves to our several nurseries, my wife being brought to bed of a girl, and Miss Bath confined to her chamber by a surfeit, which had like to have occasioned her death."

Here Miss Matthews burst into a loud laugh, of which, when Booth asked the reason, she said she could not forbear at the thoughts of two such nurses. " And did you really," says she, " make your wife's caudle yourself."

" Indeed, madam," said he, " I did ; and do you think that so extraordinary ?"

" Indeed I do," answered she ; " I thought the best husbands had looked on their wives' lying-in as a time of festival and jollity. What ! did you not even get drunk in the time of your wife's delivery ? tell me honestly how you employed yourself at this time."

" Why, then, honestly," replied he, " and in defiance of your laughter, I lay behind her bolster and supported her in my arms ; and, upon my soul, I believe I felt more pain in my mind than she underwent in her body. And now answer me as honestly : Do you really think it a proper time of mirth, when the creature one loves to distraction is undergoing the most racking torments, as well as in the most imminent danger ? and—but I need not express any more tender circumstances."

" I am to answer honestly," cried she. " Yes, sincerely," cries Booth. " Why, then, honestly and sincerely," says she, " may I never see heaven if I don't think you an angel of a man !"

"Nay, madam," answered Booth—"but indeed you do me too much honor; there are many such husbands. Nay, have we not an example of the like tenderness in the major? though as to him, I believe, I shall make you laugh. While my wife lay-in, Miss Bath being extremely ill, I went one day to the door of her apartment to inquire after her health, as well as for the major, whom I had not seen during a whole week. I knocked softly at the door, and being bid to open it, I found the major in his sister's ante-chamber warming her posset. His dress was certainly whimsical enough, having on a woman's bedgown and a very dirty flannel nightcap, which, being added to a very odd person (for he is a very awkward, thin man, near seven feet high), might have formed, in the opinion of most men, a very proper object of laughter. The major started from his seat at my entering into the room, and with much emotion, and a great oath, cried out, ' Is it you, sir ? ' I then inquired after his and his sister's health. He answered that his sister was better, and he was very well, ' though I did not expect, sir,' cried he, with not a little confusion, ' to be seen by you in this situation.' I told him I thought it impossible he could appear in a situation more becoming his character. ' You do not ? ' answered he. ' By G—, I am very much obliged to you for that opinion ; but I believe, sir, however my weakness may prevail on me to descend from it, no man can be more conscious of his own dignity than myself.' His sister then called to him from an inner room ; upon which he rang the bell for her servant, and then, after a stride or two across the room, he said, with an elated aspect, ' I would not have you think, Mr. Booth, because you have caught me in this deshabille, by coming upon me a little too abruptly—I cannot help saying a little too abruptly—that I am my sister's nurse. I know better what is due to the dignity of a man, and I have shown it in a line of battle. I think I have made a figure there, Mr. Booth, and becoming my character ; by G—, I ought not to be despised too much if my nature is not totally without its weaknesses.' He uttered this, and some more of the same kind, with great majesty, or, as he called it, dignity. Indeed, he used some hard words that I did not understand, for all his words are not to be found in a dictionary. Upon the whole, I could not easily refrain from laughter ; however, I conquered myself, and soon after retired from him, astonished that it was possible for a man to possess true goodness, and be at the same time ashamed of it.

"But if I was surprised at what had passed at this visit, how much more was I surprised the next morning, when he came very early to my chamber, and told me he had not been able to sleep one wink at what had passed between us ! ' There were some words of yours,' says he, ' which must be further explained before we part. You told me, sir, when you found me in that situation, which I cannot bear to recollect, that you thought I could not appear in one more becoming my character ; these were the words—I shall never forget them. Do you imagine that there is any of the dignity of a man wanting in my character ? do you think that I have, during my sister's illness, behaved with a weakness that savors too much of effeminacy ? I know how much it is beneath a man to whine and whimper about a trifling girl as well as you or any man ; and if my sister had died, I should have behaved like a man on the occasion. I would not have you think I confined myself from company merely upon her account. I was very much disordered myself. And when you surprised me in that situation—I repeat again, in that situation—her nurse had not left the room three minutes, and I was blowing the fire for fear it should have gone out.' In this manner he ran on almost a quarter of an hour before he would suffer me to speak. At last, looking steadfastly in his face, I asked him if I must conclude that he was in earnest ? ' In earnest ! ' says he, repeating my words, ' do you then take my character for a jest ? ' ' Lookee, sir,' said I, very gravely, ' I think we know one another very well ; and I have no reason to suspect you should impute it to fear when I tell you I was so far from intending to affront you, that I meant you one of the highest compliments. Tenderness for women is so far from lessening that it proves a true manly character. The manly Brutus showed the utmost tenderness to his Portia ; and the great king of Sweden, the bravest, and even fiercest of men, shut himself up three whole days in the midst of a campaign, and would see no company on the death of a favorite sister.' At these words I saw his features soften, and he cried out, ' D—n me, I admire the king of Sweden of all the men in the world ; and he is a rascal that is ashamed of doing any thing which the king of Sweden did. And yet, if any king of Sweden in France was to tell me that his sister had more merit than mine, by G— I'd knock his brains about his ears. Poor little Betsey ! she is the honestest, worthiest girl that ever was born. Heaven be praised, she is recovered ; for if I had lost her, I never should have enjoyed another happy moment.' In this manner he ran on some time, till the tears began to overflow, which, when he perceived, he stopped ; perhaps he was unable to go on, for he seemed almost choked ; after a short silence, however, having wiped his eyes with his handkerchief, he fetched a deep sigh, and cried, ' I am ashamed you should see this, Mr. Booth ; but d—n me, nature will get the better of dignity.' I now comforted him with the example of Xerxes, as I had before done with that of the king of Sweden ; and soon after we sat down to breakfast together with much cordial friendship ; for I assure you, with all his oddity, there is not a better-natured man in the world than the major."

" Good-natured indeed !" cries Miss Matthews, with

great scorn. "A fool! how can you mention such a fellow with commendation?"

Booth spoke as much as he could in defence of his friend; indeed, he had represented him in as favorable a light as possible, and had particularly left out those hard words with which, as he hath observed a little before, the major interlarded his discourse. Booth then proceeded as in the next chapter.

CHAPTER IX.

CONTAINING VERY EXTRAORDINARY MATTERS.

"Miss Bath," continued Booth, "now recovered so fast that she was abroad as soon as my wife. Our little partie quarrée began to grow agreeable again, and we mixed with the company of the place more than we had done before. Mons. Bagillard now again renewed his intimacy, for the countess, his mistress, was gone to Paris, at which my wife at first showed no dissatisfaction; and I imagined that, as she had a friend and companion of her own sex (for Miss Bath and she had contracted the highest fondness for each other), that she would the less miss my company. However, I was disappointed in this expectation; for she soon began to express her former uneasiness, and her impatience for the arrival of Captain James, that we might entirely quit Montpelier.

"I could not avoid conceiving some little displeasure at this humor of my wife, which I was forced to think a little unreasonable." "A little, do you call it?" says Miss Matthews: "Good heavens! what a husband are you!" "How little worthy," answered he, "as you will say hereafter, of such a wife as my Amelia. One day, as we were sitting together, I heard a violent scream, upon which my wife, starting up, cried out, 'Sure that's Miss Bath's voice;' and immediately ran toward the chamber whence

it proceeded. I followed her ; and when we arrived we
there beheld the most shocking sight imaginable—Miss
Bath lying dead on the floor, and the major all bloody
kneeling by her, and roaring out for assistance. Amelia,
though she was herself in little better condition than her
friend, ran hastily to her, bared her neck, and attempted to
loosen her stays, while I ran up and down, scarce knowing
what I did, calling for water and cordials, and dispatching
several servants one after another for doctors and surgeons.

" Water, cordials, and all necessary implements being
brought, Miss Bath was at length recovered, and placed in
her chair, when the major seated himself by her. And
now, the young lady being restored to life, the major, who,
till then, had engaged as little of his own as of any other
person's attention, became the object of all our considera-
tions, especially his poor sister's, who had no sooner recovered sufficient strength than she began to lament her brother, crying out that he was killed, and bitterly bewailing
her fate, in having revived from her swoon to behold so
dreadful a spectacle. While Amelia applied herself to
soothe the agonies of her friend, I began to inquire into the
condition of the major, in which I was assisted by a surgeon, who now arrived. The major declared, with great
cheerfulness, that he did not apprehend his wound to be in
the least dangerous, and therefore begged his sister to be
comforted, saying he was convinced the surgeon would
soon give her the same assurance ; but that good man was
not so liberal of assurances as the major had expected ;
for as soon as he had probed the wound he afforded no more
than hopes, declaring that it was a very ugly wound, but
added, by way of consolation, that he had cured many much
worse.

" When the major was dressed, his sister seemed to posses?
his whole thoughts, and all his care was to relieve her grief.
He solemnly protested that it was no more than a flesh

wound, and not very deep, nor could, as he apprehended, be in the least dangerous ; and as for the cold expressions of the surgeon, he very well accounted for them from a motive too obvious to be mentioned. From these declarations of her brother, and the interposition of her friends, and, above all, I believe, from that vast vent which she had given to her fright, Miss Bath seemed a little pacified. Amelia therefore at last prevailed ; and as terror abated, curiosity became the superior passion. I therefore now began to inquire what had occasioned that accident whence all the uproar arose.

"The major took me by the hand, and looking very kindly at me, said, 'My dear Mr. Booth, I must begin by asking your pardon, for I have done you an injury for which nothing but the height of friendship in me can be an excuse, and therefore nothing but the height of friendship in you can forgive.' This preamble, madam, you will easily believe, greatly alarmed all the company, but especially me. I answered, 'Dear major, I forgive you, let it be what it will ; but what is it possible you can have done to injure me ?' 'That,' replied he, 'which I am convinced a man of your honor and dignity of nature, by G—, must conclude to be one of the highest injuries. I have taken out of your own hands the doing yourself justice. I am afraid I have killed the man who hath injured your honor. I mean that villain Bagillard—but I cannot proceed ; for you, madam,' said he to my wife, 'are concerned, and I know what is due to the dignity of your sex.' Amelia, I observed, turned pale at these words, but eagerly begged him to proceed. 'Nay, madam,' answered he, 'if I am commanded by a lady, it is a part of my dignity to obey.' He then proceeded to tell us that Bagillard had rallied him upon a supposition that he was pursuing my wife with a view of gallantry, telling him that he could never succeed, giving hints that, if it had been possible, he should have succeeded himself, and ending with calling my poor Amelia an accomplished prude, upon which the major gave Bagillard a box on the ear, and both immediately drew their swords.

" The major had scarce ended his speech when a servant came into the room, and told me there was a friar below who desired to speak with me in great haste. I shook the major by the hand, and told him I not only forgave him, but was extremely obliged to his friendship ; and then, going to the friar, I found that he was Bagillard's confessor, from whom he came to me, with an earnest desire of seeing me, that he might ask my pardon and receive my forgiveness before he died for the injury he had intended me. My wife at first opposed my going, from some sudden fears on my account ; but when she was convinced they were groundless she consented.

" I found Bagillard in his bed ; for the major's sword had passed up to the very hilt through his body. After having very earnestly asked my pardon, he made me many compliments on the possession of a woman who, joined to the most exquisite beauty, was mistress of the most impregnable virtue, as a proof of which he acknowledged the vehemence as well as ill success of his attempts, and, to make Amelia's virtue appear the brighter, his vanity was so predominant he could not forbear running over the names of several women of fashion who had yielded to his passion, which, he said, had never raged so violently for any other as for my poor Amelia ; and that this violence, which he had found wholly unconquerable, he hoped would procure his pardon at my hands. It is unnecessary to mention what I said on the occasion. I assured him of my entire forgiveness ; and so we parted. To say the truth, I afterward thought myself almost obliged to him for a meeting with Amelia the most luxuriously delicate that can be imagined.

" I now ran to my wife, whom I embraced with raptures

of love and tenderness. When the first torrent of these
was a little abated, ' Confess to me, my dear,' said she,
' could your goodness prevent you from thinking me a little
unreasonable in expressing so much uneasiness at the loss of
your company, while I ought to have rejoiced in the
thoughts of your being so well entertained ? I know you
must ; and then consider what I must have felt, while I
knew I was daily lessening myself in your esteem, and
forced into a conduct which I was sensible must appear to
you, who was ignorant of my motive, to be mean, vulgar,
and selfish. And yet, what other course had I to take with
a man whom no denial, no scorn could abash ? But if this
was a cruel task, how much more wretched still was the
constraint I was obliged to wear in his presence before you,
to show outward civility to the man whom my soul detested, for fear of any fatal consequence from your suspicion ; and this too while I was afraid he would construe
it to be an encouragement ? Do you not pity your poor
Amelia when you reflect on her situation ? ' ' Pity ! '
cried I ; ' my love ! is pity an adequate expression for
esteem, for adoration ? But how, my love, could he carry
this on so secretly ?—by letters ?' ' O no, he offered me
many ; but I never would receive but one, and that I returned him. Good G— ! I would not have such a letter in
my possession for the universe ; I thought my eyes contaminated with reading it.' '' '' O brave !'' cried Miss
Matthews ; '' heroic, I protest.

> '' ' Had I a wish that did not bear
>   The stamp and image of my dear,
>   I'd pierce my heart through ev'ry vein,
>   And die to let it out again.' ''

  '' And can you really,'' cried he, '' laugh at so much tenderness ?'' '' I laugh at tenderness ! O Mr. Booth !''
answered she, '' thou knowest but little of Calista.'' '' I
thought formerly,'' cried he, '' I knew a great deal, and

thought you, of all women in the world, to have the greatest—of all women!" "Take care, Mr. Booth," said she. "By heaven! if you thought so, you thought truly. But what is the object of my tenderness—such an object as——" "Well, madam," says he, "I hope you will find one." "I thank you for that hope, however," says she, "cold as it is. But pray go on with your story;" which command he immediately obeyed.

CHAPTER X.

CONTAINING A LETTER OF A VERY CURIOUS KIND.

"THE major's wound," continued Booth, "was really as slight as he believed it; so that in a very few days he was perfectly well; nor was Bagillard, though run through the body, long apprehending to be in any danger of his life. The major then took me aside, and wishing me heartily joy of Bagillard's recovery, told me I should now, by the gift (as it were) of heaven, have an opportunity of doing myself justice. I answered I could not think of any such thing; for that when I imagined he was on his death-bed I had heartily and sincerely forgiven him. 'Very right,' replied the major, 'and consistent with your honor, when he was on his death-bed; but that forgiveness was only conditional, and is revoked by his recovery.' I told him I could not possibly revoke it, for that my anger was really gone. 'What hath anger,' cried he, 'to do with the matter? the dignity of my nature hath been always my reason for drawing my sword; and when that is concerned I can as readily fight with the man I love as with the man I hate.' I will not tire you with the repetition of the whole argument, in which the major did not prevail; and I really believe I sunk a little in his esteem upon that account, till Captain James, who arrived soon after, again perfectly reinstated me in his favor.

" When the Captain was come there remained no cause of our longer stay at Montpelier ; for, as to my wife, she was in a better state of health than I had ever know her ; and Miss Bath had not only recovered her health but her bloom, and from a pale skeleton was become a plump, handsome young woman. James was again my cashier ; for, far from receiving any remittance, it was now a long time since I had received any letter from England, though both myself and my dear Amelia had written several, both to my mother and sister ; and now, at our departure from Montpelier, I bethought myself of writing to my good friend the doctor, acquainting him with our journey to Paris, whither I desired he would direct his answer.

" At Paris we all arrived without encountering any adventure on the road worth relating ; nor did any thing of consequence happen here during the first fortnight ; for, as you know neither Captain James nor Miss Bath, it is scarce worth telling you that an affection, which afterward ended in a marriage, began now to appear between them, in which it may appear odd to you that I made the first discovery of the lady's flame, and my wife of the captain's.

" The seventeenth day after our arrival at Paris I received a letter from the doctor, which I have in my pocket-book ; and, if you please, I will read it you, for I would not willingly do any injury to his words."

The lady, you may easily believe, desired to hear the letter, and Booth read it as follows :

" ' MY DEAR CHILDREN : For I will now call you so, as you have neither of you now any other parent in this world. Of this melancholy news I should have sent you earlier notice if I had thought you ignorant of it, or indeed if I had known whither to have written. If your sister hath received any letters from you she hath kept them a secret, and perhaps out of affection to you hath reposited them in

the same place where she keeps her goodness, and, what I
am afraid is much dearer to her, her money. The reports
concerning you have been various ; so is always the case in
matters where men are ignorant ; for when no man knows
what the truth is, every man thinks himself at liberty to report what he pleases. Those who wish you well, son
Booth, say simply that you are dead : others, that you ran
away from the siege, and was cashiered. As for my
daughter, all agree that she is a saint above ; and there are
not wanting those who hint that her husband sent her
thither. From this beginning you will expect, I suppose,
better news than I am going to tell you ; but pray, my dear
children, why may not I, who have always laughed at my
own afflictions, laugh at yours, without the censure of
much malevolence ? I wish you could learn this temper
from me ; for, take my word for it, nothing truer ever
came from the mouth of a heathen than that sentence :

'——*Leve fit quod bene fertur onus.*' *

And though I must confess I never thought Aristotle
(whom I do not take for so great a blockhead as some who
have never read him) doth not very well resolve the doubt
which he hath raised in his Ethics, viz., How a man in the
midst of King Priam's misfortunes can be called happy?
yet I have long thought that there is no calamity so great
that a Christian philosopher may not reasonably laugh at it.
If the heathen Cicero, doubting of immortality (for so wise
a man must have doubted of that which had such slender
arguments to support it), could assert it as the office of wisdom, *Humanas res despicere atque infra se positas arbi-
trari.*†

" ' Which passage, with much more to the same purpose,
you will find in the third book of his Tusculan Questions.

* The burthen becomes light by being well borne.
† To look down on all human affairs as matters below his consideration.

" ' With how much greater confidence may a good Christian despise, and even deride, all temporary and short transitory evils ! If the poor wretch who is trudging on to his miserable cottage can laugh at the storms and tempests, the rain and whirlwinds, which surround him, while his richest hope is only that of rest, how much more cheerfully must a man pass through such transient evils whose spirits are buoyed up with the certain expectation of finding a noble palace and the most sumptuous entertainment ready to receive him ! I do not much like the simile ; but I cannot think of a better. And yet, inadequate as the simile is, we may, I think, from the actions of mankind, conclude that they will consider it as much too strong ; for, in the case I have put of the entertainment, is there any man so tender or poor-spirited as not to despise, and often to deride, the fiercest of these inclemencies which I have mentioned ? but in our journey to the glorious mansions of everlasting bliss, how severely is every little rub, every trifling accident, lamented ! and if Fortune showers down any of her heavier storms upon us, how wretched do we presently appear to ourselves and to others ! The reason of this can be no other than that we are not in earnest in our faith ; at the best, we think with too little attention on this our great concern. While the most paltry matters of this world, even those pitiful trifles, those childish gewgaws, riches and honors, are transacted with the utmost earnestness and most serious application, the grand and weighty affair of immortality is postponed and disregarded, nor ever brought into the least competition with our affairs here. If one of my cloth should begin a discourse of heaven in the scenes of business or pleasure, in the court of requests, at Garraway's, or at White's, would he gain a hearing, unless perhaps of some sorry jester who would desire to ridicule him ? would he not presently acquire the name of the mad parson, and be thought by all men worthy of Bed-

lam? or would he not be treated as the Romans treated
their Aretalogi,* and considered in the light of a buffoon?
But why should I mention those places of hurry and
worldly pursuit? What attention do we engage even in
the pulpit? Here, if a sermon be prolonged a little beyond the usual hour, doth it not set half the audience
asleep? as I question not I have by this time both my children. Well, then, like a good-natured surgeon, who pre-
pares his patient for a painful operation by endeavoring as
much as he can to deaden his sensation, I will now communicate to you, in your slumbering condition, the news
with which I threatened you. Your good mother, you are
to know, is dead at last, and hath left her whole fortune to
her elder daughter. This is all the ill news I have to tell
you. Confess now, if you are awake, did you not expect it
was much worse; did not you apprehend that your charming child was dead? Far from it; he is in perfect health,
and the admiration of everybody: what is more, he will be
taken care of, with the tenderness of a parent, till your
return. What pleasure must this give you! if indeed any
thing can add to the happiness of a married couple who are
extremely and deservedly fond of each other, and, as you
write me, in perfect health. A superstitious heathen
would have dreaded the malice of Nemesis in your situation; but as I am a Christian, I shall venture to add another circumstance to your felicity, by assuring you that
you have, besides your wife, a faithful and zealous friend.
Do not, therefore, my dear children, fall into that fault
which the excellent Thucydides observes is too common in
human nature, to bear heavily the being deprived of the
smaller good, without conceiving, at the same time, any
gratitude for the much greater blessings which we are
suffered to enjoy. I have only farther to tell you, my son,

---

* A set of beggarly philosophers who diverted great men at their table
with burlesque discourses on virtue.

that, when you call at Mr. Morand's, Rue Dauphine, you will find yourself worth a hundred pounds. Good heaven! how much richer are you than millions of people who are in want of nothing! Farewell, and know me for your sincere and affectionate friend.'

"There, madam," cries Booth, "how do you like the letter?"

"Oh! extremely," answered she; "the doctor is a charming man; I always loved dearly to hear him preach. I remember to have heard of Mrs. Harris's death above a year before I left the country, but never knew the particulars of her will before. I am extremely sorry for it, upon my honor."

"Oh, fie! madam," cries Booth; "have you so soon forgot the chief purport of the doctor's letter?"

"Ay, ay," cried she; "these are very pretty things to read, I acknowledge; but the loss of fortune is a serious matter; and I am sure a man of Mr. Booth's understanding must think so." "One consideration, I must own, madam," answered he, "a good deal baffled all the doctor's arguments. This was the concern for my little growing family, who must one day feel the loss; nor was I so easy upon Amelia's account as upon my own, though she herself put on the utmost cheerfulness, and stretched her invention to the utmost to comfort me. But sure, madam, there is something in the doctor's letter to admire beyond the philosophy of it; what think you of that easy, generous, friendly manner in which he sent me the hundred pounds?"

"Very noble and great indeed," replied she. "But pray go on with your story, for I long to hear the whole."

CHAPTER XI.

IN WHICH MR. BOOTH RELATES HIS RETURN TO ENGLAND.

"NOTHING remarkable, as I remember, happened during our stay at Paris, which we left soon after and came to London. Here we rested only two days, and then, taking leave of our fellow-travellers, we set out for Wiltshire, my wife being so impatient to see the child which she had left behind her that the child she carried with her was almost killed with the fatigue of the journey.

"We arrived at our inn late in the evening. Amelia, though she had no great reason to be pleased with any part of her sister's behavior, resolved to behave to her as if nothing wrong had ever happened. She therefore sent a kind note to her the moment of our arrival, giving her her option whether she would come to us at the inn, or whether we should that evening wait on her. The servant, after waiting an hour, brought us an answer, excusing her from coming to us so late, as she was disordered with a cold, and desiring my wife by no means to think of venturing out after the fatigue of her journey, saying she would, on that account, defer the great pleasure of seeing her till the morning, without taking any more notice of your humble servant than if no such person had been in the world, though I had very civilly sent my compliments to her. I should not mention this trifle if it was not to show you the nature of the woman, and that it will be a kind of key to her future conduct.

"When the servant returned, the good doctor, who had been with us almost all the time of his absence, hurried us away to his house, where we presently found a supper and a bed prepared for us. My wife was eagerly desirous to see her child that night; but the doctor would not suffer it; and as he was at nurse at a distant part of the town, and the doctor assured her he had seen him in perfect health that evening, she suffered herself at last to be dissuaded.

" We spent that evening in the most agreeable manner, for the doctor's wit and humor, joined to the highest cheerfulness and good nature, made him the most agreeable companion in the world, and he was now in the highest spirits, which he was pleased to place to our account. We sat together to a very late hour, for so excellent is my wife's constitution that she declared she was scarce sensible of any fatigue from her late journeys.

" Amelia slept not a wink all night, and in the morning early the doctor accompanied us to the little infant. The transports we felt on this occasion were really enchanting, nor can any but a fond parent conceive, I am certain, the least idea of them. Our imaginations suggested a hundred agreeable circumstances, none of which had perhaps any foundation. We made words and meaning out of every sound, and in every feature found out some resemblance to my Amelia, as she did to me.

" But I ask your pardon for dwelling on such incidents, and will proceed to scenes which, to most persons, will be more entertaining.

" We went hence to pay a visit to Miss Harris, whose reception of us was, I think, truly ridiculous ; and as you know the lady, I will endeavor to describe it particularly. At our first arrival we were ushered into a parlor, where we were suffered to wait almost an hour. At length the lady of the house appeared in deep mourning, with a face, if possible, more dismal than her dress, in which, however, there was every appearance of art. Her features were indeed screwed up to the very height of grief. With this face, and in the most solemn gait, she approached Amelia, and coldly saluted her. After which she made me a very distant formal courtesy, and we all sat down. A short silence now ensued, which Miss Harris at length broke with a deep sigh, and said, ' Sister, here is a great alteration in this place since you saw it last ; heaven hath been pleased to take my poor mother to itself.' (Here she wiped her eyes, and then continued.) ' I hope I know my duty, and have learned a proper resignation to the divine will ; but something is to be allowed to grief for the best of mothers ; for so she was to us both ; and if at last she made any distinction, she must have had her reasons for so doing. I am sure I can truly say I never wished, much less desired it.' The tears now stood in poor Amelia's eyes ; indeed, she had paid too many already for the memory of so unnatural a parent. She answered, with the sweetness of an angel, that she was far from blaming her sister's emotions on so tender an occasion ; that she heartily joined with her in her grief, for that nothing which her mother had done in the latter part of her life could efface the remembrance of that tenderness which she had formerly shown her. Her sister caught hold of the word efface, and rung the changes upon it. ' Efface ! ' cried she, ' O Miss Emily (for you must not expect me to repeat names that will be for ever odious), I wish indeed every thing could be effaced. Effaced ! O that that was possible ! we might then have still enjoyed my poor mother ; for I am convinced she never recovered her grief on a certain occasion.' Thus she ran on, and after many bitter strokes upon her sister, at last directly charged her mother's death on my marriage with Amelia. I could be silent then no longer. I reminded her of the perfect reconciliation between us before my departure, and the great fondness which she expressed for me ; nor could I help saying, in very plain terms, that if she had ever changed her opinion of me, as I was not conscious of having deserved such a change by my own behavior, I was well convinced to whose good offices I owed it. Guilt hath very quick ears to an accusation. Miss Harris immediately answered to the charge. She said, such suspicions were no more than she expected ; that they were of a piece with every other part of my conduct, and gave her one consolation, that they served to account for her sister Emily's unkindness, as well to herself as to her poor deceased mother, and in some measure lessened the guilt of it with regard to her, since it was not easy to know how far a woman is in the power of her husband. My dear Amelia reddened at this reflection on me, and begged her sister to name any single instance of unkindness or disrespect in which she had ever offended. To this the other answered (I am sure I repeat her words, though I cannot mimic either the voice or air with which they were spoken), ' Pray, Miss Emily, which is to be the judge, yourself or that gentleman ? I remember the time when I could have trusted to your judgment in any affair ; but you are now no longer mistress of yourself, and are not answerable for your actions. Indeed, it is my constant prayer that your actions may not be imputed to you. It was the constant prayer of that blessed woman, my dear mother, who is now a saint above—a saint whose name I can never mention without a tear, though I find you can hear it without one. I cannot help observing some concern on so melancholy an occasion ; it seems due to decency ; but perhaps (for I always wish to excuse you) you are forbid to cry.' The idea of being bid or forbid to cry struck so strongly on my fancy that indignation only could have prevented me from laughing. But my narrative, I am afraid, begins to grow tedious. In short, after hearing, for near an hour, every malicious insinuation which a fertile genius could invent, we took our leave, and separated as persons who would never willingly meet again.

" The next morning after this interview Amelia received a long letter from Miss Harris, in which, after many bitter invectives against me, she excused her mother, alleging that she had been driven to do as she did in order to prevent Amelia's ruin, if her fortune had fallen into my hands.

She likewise very remotely hinted that she would be only a trustee for her sister's children, and told her that on one condition only she would consent to live with her as a sister. This was, if she could by any means be separated from that man, as she was pleased to call me, who had caused so much mischief in the family.

" I was so enraged at this usage that, had not Amelia intervened, I believe I should have applied to a magistrate for a search-warrant for that picture, which there was so much reason to suspect she had stolen ; and which I am convinced, upon a search, we should have found in her possession."

" Nay, it is possible enough," cries Miss Matthews ; " for I believe there is no wickedness of which the lady is not capable."

" This agreeable letter was succeeded by another of the like comfortable kind, which informed me that the company in which I was, being an additional one raised in the beginning of the war, was reduced ; so that I was now a lieutenant on half-pay.

" Whilst we were meditating on our present situation the good doctor came to us. When we related to him the manner in which my sister had treated us, he cried out, ' Poor soul ! I pity her heartily ; ' for this is the severest resentment he ever expresses ; indeed, I have often heard him say that a wicked soul is the greatest object of compassion in the world." A sentiment which we shall leave the reader a little time to digest.

CHAPTER XII.

IN WHICH MR. BOOTH CONCLUDES HIS STORY.

" THE next day the doctor set out for his parsonage, which was about thirty miles distant, whither Amelia and myself accompanied him, and where we stayed with him all the time of his residence there, being almost three months.

" The situation of the parish under my good friend's care is very pleasant. It is placed among meadows, washed by a clear trout-stream, and flanked on both sides with downs. His house, indeed, would not much attract the admiration of the virtuoso. He built it himself, and it is remarkable only for its plainness ; with which the furniture so well agrees, that there is no one thing in it that may not be absolutely necessary, except books, and the prints of Mr. Hogarth, whom he calls a moral satirist.

" Nothing, however, can be imagined more agreeable than the life that the doctor leads in this homely house, which he calls his earthly paradise. All his parishioners, whom he treats as his children, regard him as their common father. Once in a week he constantly visits every house in the parish, examines, commends, and rebukes, as he finds occasion. This is practised likewise by his curate in his absence ; and so good an effect is produced by this their care, that no quarrels ever proceed either to blows or law-suits ; no beggar is to be found in the whole parish ; nor did I ever hear a very profane oath all the time I lived in it.

" But to return from so agreeable a digression, to my own affairs, that are much less worth your attention. In the midst of all the pleasures I tasted in this sweet place, and in the most delightful company, the woman and man whom I loved above all things, melancholy reflections concerning my unhappy circumstances would often steal into my thoughts. My fortune was now reduced to less than forty pounds a year ; I had already two children, and my dear Amelia was again with child.

" One day the doctor found me sitting by myself, and employed in melancholy contemplations on this subject. He told me he had observed me growing of late very serious ; that he knew the occasion, and neither wondered at nor blamed me. He then asked me if I had any prospect

of going again into the army ; if not, what scheme of life
I proposed to myself ?

" I told him that, as I had no powerful friends, I could
have but little expectations in a military way ; that I was
as incapable of thinking of any other scheme, as all business
required some knowledge or experience, and likewise money
to set up with ; of all which I was destitute.

" ' You must know then, child,' said the doctor, ' that I
have been thinking on this subject as well as you ; for I can
think, I promise you, with a pleasant countenance.' These
were his words. ' As to the army, perhaps means might be
found of getting you another commission ; but my daughter seems to have a violent objection to it ; and to be plain,
I fancy you yourself will find no glory make you amends
for your absence from her. And for my part,' said he,
' I never think those men wise who, for any worldly interest, forego the greatest happiness of their lives. If I
mistake not,' says he, ' a country life, where you could be
always together, would make you both much happier
people.'

" I answered, that of all things I preferred it most ; and
I believed Amelia was of the same opinion.

" The doctor, after a little hesitation, proposed to me to
turn farmer, and offered to let me his parsonage, which was
then become vacant. He said it was a farm which required
but little stock, and that little should not be wanting.

" I embraced this offer very eagerly, and with great
thankfulness, and immediately repaired to Amelia to communicate it to her, and to know her sentiments.

" Amelia received the news with the highest transports
of joy ; she said that her greatest fear had always been of
my entering again into the army. She was so kind as to
say that all stations of life were equal to her, unless as one
afforded her more of my company than another. ' And
as to our children,' said she, ' let us breed them up to an

humble fortune, and they will be contented with it ; for none,' added my angel, ' deserve happiness, or indeed are capable of it, who make any particular station a necessary ingredient.'

" Thus, madam, you see me degraded from my former rank in life ; no longer Captain Booth, but farmer Booth at your service.

" During my first year's continuance in this new scene of life, nothing, I think, remarkable happened ; the history of one day would indeed be the history of the whole year."

" Well, pray then," said Miss Matthews, " do let us hear the history of that day ; I have a strange curiosity to know how you could kill your time ; and do, if possible, find out the very best day you can."

" If you command me, madam," answered Booth, " you must yourself be accountable for the dulness of the narrative. Nay, I believe you have imposed a very difficult task on me ; for the greatest happiness is incapable of description.

" I rose, then, madam——"

" Oh, the moment you waked, undoubtedly," said Miss Matthews.

" Usually," said he, " between five and six."

" I will have no usually," cried Miss Matthews ; " you are confined to a day, and it is to be the best and happiest in the year."

" Nay, madam," cries Booth, " then I must tell you the day in which Amelia was brought to bed, after a painful and dangerous labor ; for that I think was the happiest day of my life."

" I protest," said she, " you are become farmer Booth indeed. What a happiness have you painted to my imagination ! you put me in mind of a newspaper, where my lady such-a-one is delivered of a son, to the great joy of some illustrious family."

"Why then, I do assure you, Miss Matthews," cries Booth, "I scarce know a circumstance that distinguished one day from another. The whole was one continued series of love, health, and tranquillity. Our lives resembled a calm sea——"

"The dullest of all ideas," cries the lady.

"I know," said he, "it must appear dull in description, for who can describe the pleasures which the morning air gives to one in perfect health; the flow of spirits which springs up from exercise; the delights which parents feel from the prattle and innocent follies of their children; the joy with which the tender smile of a wife inspires a husband; or lastly, the cheerful, solid comfort which a fond couple enjoy in each other's conversation? All these pleasures and every other of which our situation was capable we tasted in the highest degree. Our happiness was, perhaps, too great; for fortune seemed to grow envious of it and interposed one of the most cruel accidents that could have befallen us by robbing us of our dear friend the doctor."

"I am sorry for it," said Miss Mathews. "He was indeed a valuable man, and I never heard of his death before."

"Long may it be before any one hears of it!" cries Booth. "He is, indeed, dead to us; but will, I hope, enjoy many happy years of life. You know, madam, the obligations he had to his patron the earl; indeed, it was impossible to be once in his company without hearing of them. I am sure you will neither wonder that he was chosen to attend the young lord in his travels as his tutor, nor that the good man, however disagreeable it might be (as in fact it was) to his inclination, should comply with the earnest request of his friend and patron.

"By this means I was bereft not only of the best companion in the world, but of the best counsellor; a loss of which I have since felt the bitter consequence; for no

greater advantage, I am convinced, can arrive to a young
man, who hath any degree of understanding, than an intimate converse with one of riper years, who is not only able
to advise, but who knows the manner of advising.   By this
means alone, youth can enjoy the benefit of the experience
of age, and that at a time of life when such experience will
be of more service to a man than when he hath lived long
enough to acquire it of himself.

" From want of my sage counsellor, I now fell into many
errors.   The first of these was in enlarging my business,
by adding a farm of one hundred a year to the parsonage,
in renting which I had also as bad a bargain as the doctor
had before given me a good one.   The consequence of
which was, that whereas, at the end of the first year, I was
worth upward of fourscore pounds ; at the end of the second I was near half that sum worse (as the phrase is) than
nothing.

" A second folly I was guilty of in uniting families with
the curate of the parish, who had just married, as my wife
and I thought, a very good sort of a woman.   We had not,
however, lived one month together before I plainly perceived this good sort of a woman had taken a great prejudice against my Amelia, for which, if I had not known
something of the human passions, and that high place which
envy holds among them, I should not have been able to
account, for, so far was my angel from having given her any
cause of dislike, that she had treated her not only with
civility, but kindness.

" Besides superiority in beauty, which I believe all
the world would have allowed to Amelia, there was another
cause of this envy, which I am almost ashamed to mention,
as it may well be called my greatest folly.   You are to know
then, madam, that from a boy I had been always fond of
driving a coach, in which I valued myself on having some
skill.   This, perhaps, was an innocent, but I allow it to

have been a childish, vanity. As I had an opportunity, therefore, of buying an old coach and harness very cheap (indeed they cost me but twelve pounds), and as I considered that the same horses which drew my wagons would likewise draw my coach, I resolved on indulging myself in the purchase.

" The consequence of setting up this poor old coach is inconceivable. Before this, as my wife and myself had very little distinguished ourselves from the other farmers and their wives, either in our dress or our way of living, they treated us as their equals ; but now they began to consider us as elevating ourselves into a state of superiority, and immediately began to envy, hate, and declare war against us. The neighboring little squires, too, were uneasy to see a poor renter become their equal in a matter in which they placed so much dignity ; and, not doubting but it arose in me from the same ostentation, they began to hate me likewise, and to turn my equipage into ridicule, asserting that my horses, which were as well matched as any in the kingdom, were of different colors and sizes, with much more of that kind of wit, the only basis of which is lying.

" But what will appear most surprising to you, madam, was, that the curate's wife, who, being lame, had more use of the coach than my Amelia (indeed she seldom went to church in any other manner), was one of my bitterest enemies on the occasion. If she had ever any dispute with Amelia, which all the sweetness of my poor girl could not sometimes avoid, she was sure to introduce with a malicious sneer, ' Though my husband doth not keep a coach, madam.' Nay, she took this opportunity to upbraid my wife with the loss of her fortune, alleging that some folks might have had as good pretensions to a coach as other folks, and a better too, as they brought a better fortune to their husbands, but that all people had not the art of making brick without straw.

"You will wonder, perhaps, madam, how I can remember such stuff, which, indeed, was a long time only matter of amusement to both Amelia and myself ; but we at last experienced the mischievous nature of envy, and that it tends rather to produce tragical than comical events. My neighbors now began to conspire against me. They nicknamed me in derision the Squire Farmer. Whatever I bought, I was sure to buy dearer, and when I sold I was obliged to sell cheaper, than any other. In fact, they were all united, and while they every day committed trespasses on my lands with impunity, if any of my cattle escaped into their fields, I was either forced to enter into a lawsuit or to make amends fourfold for the damage sustained.

"The consequences of all this could be no other than that ruin which ensued. Without tiring you with particulars, before the end of four years I became involved in debt near three hundred pounds more than the value of all my effects. My landlord seized my stock for rent, and, to avoid immediate confinement in prison, I was forced to leave the country with all that I hold dear in the world, my wife and my poor little family.

"In this condition I arrived in town five or six days ago. I had just taken a lodging in the verge of the court, and had writ my dear Amelia word where she might find me, when she had settled her affairs in the best manner she could. That very evening, as I was returning home from a coffee-house, a fray happening in the street, I endeavored to assist the injured party, when I was seized by the watch, and, after being confined all night in the round - house, was conveyed in the morning before a justice of peace, who committed me hither ; where I should probably have starved, had I not from your hands found a most unaccountable preservation. And here, give me leave to assure you, my dear Miss Matthews, that, whatever advantage I may have reaped from your misfortune, I sincerely lament it ; nor would I have purchased any relief to myself at the price of seeing you in this dreadful place."

He spake these last words with great tenderness ; for he was a man of consummate good nature, and had formerly had much affection for this young lady ; indeed, more than the generality of people are capable of entertaining for any person whatsoever.

BOOK IV.

CHAPTER I.

CONTAINING VERY MYSTERIOUS MATTER.

Miss Matthews did not in the least fall short of Mr. Booth in expressions of tenderness. Her eyes, the most eloquent orators on such occasions, exerted their utmost force ; and at the conclusion of his speech she cast a look as languishingly sweet as ever Cleopatra gave to Antony. In real fact, this Mr. Booth had been her first love, and had made those impressions on her young heart which the learned in this branch of philosophy affirm, and perhaps truly, are never to be eradicated.

When Booth had finished his story a silence ensued of some minutes ; an interval which the painter would describe much better than the writer. Some readers may, however, be able to make pretty pertinent conjectures by what I have said above, especially when they are told that Miss Matthews broke the silence by a sigh, and cried, "Why is Mr. Booth unwilling to allow me the happiness of thinking my misfortunes have been of some little advantage to him ? sure the happy Amelia would not be so selfish to envy me that pleasure. No ; not if she was as much the fondest as she is the happiest of women." "Good heavens ! madam," said he, "do you call my poor Amelia the happiest of women ?" "Indeed I do," answered she briskly. "O Mr. Booth ! there is a speck of white in her fortune which, when it falls to the lot of a sensible woman,

makes her full amends for all the crosses which can attend
her. Perhaps she may not be sensible of it; but if it had
been my blessed fate—O Mr. Booth! could I have
thought, when we were first acquainted, that the most
agreeable man in the world had been capable of making the
kind, the tender, the affectionate husband—the happy
Amelia, in those days, was unknown; heaven had not
then given her a prospect of the happiness it intended her;
but yet it did intend it her; for sure there is a fatality in
the affairs of love; and the more I reflect on my own life,
the more I am convinced of it. O heavens! how a thousand little circumstances crowd into my mind! When you
first marched into our town, you had then the colors in
your hand; as you passed under the window where I stood,
my glove, by accident, dropped into the street; you
stopped, took up my glove, and, putting it upon the spike
belonging to your colors, lifted it up to the window. Upon
this a young lady who stood by said, " So miss, the young
officer hath accepted your challenge." I blushed then, and
I blush now, when I confess to you I thought you the prettiest young fellow I had ever seen; and, upon my soul, I
believe you was then the prettiest fellow in the world."
Booth here made a low bow, and cried, " O dear madam,
how ignorant was I of my own happiness!" " Would you
really have thought so ?" answered she. " However, there
is some politeness if there be no sincerity in what you
say." Here the governor of the enchanted castle interrupted them, and, entering the room without any ceremony, acquainted the lady and gentleman that it was lock-
ing-up time; and, addressing Booth by the name of captain, asked him if he would not please to have a bed; adding that he might have one in the next room to the lady,
but that it would come dear; for he never let a bed in that
room under a guinea, nor could he afford it cheaper to his
father.

No answer was made to this proposal; but Miss Mat-thews, who had already learned some of the ways of the house, said she believed Mr. Booth would like to drink a glass of something; upon which the governor immediately trumpeted forth the praises of his rack-punch, and, without waiting for any farther commands, presently produced a large bowl of that liquor.

The governor, having recommended the goodness of his punch by a hearty draught, began to revive the other mat-ter, saying that he was just going to bed, and must first lock up. "But suppose," said Miss Matthews, with a smile, "the captain and I should have a mind to sit up all night." "With all my heart," said the governor; "but I expect a consideration for those matters. For my part, I don't inquire into what doth not concern me; but single and double are two things. If I lock up double I expect half a guinea, and I'm sure the captain cannot think that's out of the way; it is but the price of a bagnio."

Miss Matthews's face became the color of scarlet at those words. However, she mustered up her spirits, and, turn-ing to Booth, said, "What say you, captain? for my own part, I had never less inclination to sleep; which hath the greater charms for you, the punch or the pillow?" "I hope, madam," answered Booth, "you have a better opin-ion of me than to doubt my preferring Miss Matthews's conversation to either." "I assure you," replied she, "it is no compliment to you to say I prefer yours to sleep at this time."

The governor, then, having received his fee, departed; and turning the key, left the gentleman and the lady to themselves.

In imitation of him we will lock up likewise a scene which we do not think proper to expose to the eyes of the public. If any over-curious readers should be disappointed on this occasion, we will recommend such readers to the apologies with which certain gay ladies have lately been pleased to oblige the world, where they will possibly find every thing recorded that passed at this interval.

But, though we decline painting the scene, it is not our intention to conceal from the world the frailty of Mr. Booth, or of his fair partner, who certainly passed that evening in a manner inconsistent with the strict rules of virtue and chastity.

To say the truth, we are much more concerned for the behavior of the gentleman than of the lady, not only for his sake, but for the sake of the best woman in the world, whom we should be sorry to consider as yoked to a man of no worth nor honor.

We desire, therefore, the good-natured and candid reader will be pleased to weigh attentively the several unlucky circumstances which concurred so critically that Fortune seemed to have used her utmost endeavors to ensnare poor Booth's constancy. Let the reader set before his eyes a fine young woman, in a manner, a first love, conferring obligations and using every art to soften, to allure, to win, and to inflame ; let him consider the time and place ; let him remember that Mr. Booth was a young fellow in the highest vigor of life ; and, lastly, let him add one single circumstance, that the parties were alone together ; and then, if he will not acquit the defendant, he must be convicted, for I have nothing more to say in his defence.

CHAPTER II.

THE LATTER PART OF WHICH WE EXPECT WILL PLEASE OUR READER BETTER THAN THE FORMER.

A WHOLE week did our lady and gentleman live in this criminal conversation, in which the happiness of the former was much more perfect than that of the latter ; for, though the charms of Miss Matthews, and her excessive endearments, sometimes lulled every thought in the sweet lethargy of pleasure, yet in the intervals of his fits his virtue alarmed and roused him, and brought the image of poor injured Amelia to haunt and torment him. In fact, if we regard this world only, it is the interest of every man to be either perfectly good or completely bad. He had better destroy his conscience than gently wound it. The many bitter reflections which every bad action costs a mind in which there are any remains of goodness are not to be compensated by the highest pleasures which such an action can produce.

So it happened to Mr. Booth. Repentance never failed to follow his transgressions ; and yet so perverse is our judgment, and so slippery is the descent of vice when once we are entered into it, the same crime which he now repented of became a reason for doing that which was to cause his future repentance ; and he continued to sin on because he had begun. His repentance, however, returned still heavier and heavier, till at last it flung him into a melancholy, which Miss Matthews plainly perceived, and at which she could not avoid expressing some resentment in obscure hints and ironical compliments on Amelia's superiority to her whole sex, who could not cloy a gay young fellow by many years' possession. She would then repeat the compliments which others had made to her own beauty, and could not forbear once crying out, " Upon my soul, my dear Billy, I believe the chief disadvantage on my side is my superior fondness ; for love, in the minds of men, hath one quality, at least, of a fever, which is to prefer coldness in the object. Confess, dear Will, is there not something vastly refreshing in the cool air of a prude ?" Booth fetched a deep sigh, and begged her never more to mention Amelia's name. " O Will," cries she, " did that request proceed from the motive I could wish, I should be the happiest of womankind." " You would not, sure, madam," said Booth, " desire a sacrifice which I must be a

villain to make to any ?" "Desire !" answered she ; " are
there any bounds to the desire of love ? have not I been
sacrificed ? hath not my first love been torn from my bleeding heart ? I claim a prior right. As for sacrifices, I can
make them too, and would sacrifice the whole world at the
least call of my love."

Here she delivered a letter to Booth, which she had received within an hour, the contents of which were these :

" DEAREST MADAM : Those only who know what love is
can have any conception of the horrors I felt at hearing of
your confinement at my arrival in town, which was this
morning. I immediately sent my lawyer to inquire into
the particulars, who brought me the agreeable news that the
man, whose heart's blood ought not to be valued at the rate
of a single hair of yours, is entirely out of all danger, and
that you might be admitted to bail. I presently ordered
him to go with two of my tradesmen, who are to be bound
in any sum for your appearance, if he should be mean
enough to prosecute you. Though you may expect my
attorney with you soon, I will not delay sending this, as I
hope the news will be agreeable to you. My chariot will
attend at the same time to carry you wherever you please.
You may easily guess what a violence I have done to myself in not waiting on you in person ; but I, who know
your delicacy, feared it might offend, and that you might
think me ungenerous enough to hope from your distresses
that happiness which I am resolved to owe to your free gift
alone, when your good nature shall induce you to bestow on
me what no man living can merit. I beg you will pardon
all the contents of this hasty letter, and do me the honor of
believing me,

　　　　" Dearest madam,
　　　　　　" Your most passionate admirer,
　　　　　　　　" and most obedient humble servant,
　　　　　　　　　　　　" DAMON."

Booth thought he had somewhere before seen the same hand, but in his present hurry of spirits could not recollect whose it was, nor did the lady give him any time for reflection ; for he had scarce read the letter when she produced a little bit of paper and cried out, "Here, sir, here are the contents which he fears will offend me." She then put a bank-bill of a hundred pounds into Mr. Booth's hands, and asked him with a smile if he did not think she had reason to be offended with so much insolence ?

Before Booth could return any answer the governor arrived, and introduced Mr. Rogers the attorney, who acquainted the lady that he had brought her discharge from her confinement, and that the chariot waited at the door to attend her wherever she pleased.

She received the discharge from Mr. Rogers, and said she was very much obliged to the gentleman who employed him, but that she would not make use of the chariot, as she had no notion of leaving that wretched place in a triumphant manner ; in which resolution when the attorney found her obstinate he withdrew, as did the governor, with many bows and as many ladyships.

They were no sooner gone than Booth asked the lady why she would refuse the chariot of a gentleman who had behaved with such excessive respect ? She looked earnestly upon him, and cried, "How unkind is that question ! do you imagine I would go and leave you in such a situation ? thou knowest but little of Calista. Why, do you think I would accept this hundred pounds from a man I dislike unless it was to be serviceable to the man I love ? I insist on your taking it as your own and using whatever you want of it."

Booth protested in the solemnest manner that he would not touch a shilling of it, saying he had already received too many obligations at her hands, and more than ever he should be able, he feared, to repay. "How unkind," answered she, " is every word you say ! why will you mention obligations ? love never confers any. It doth every thing for its own sake. I am not therefore obliged to the man whose passion makes him generous ; for I feel how inconsiderable the whole world would appear to me if I could throw it after my heart."

Much more of this kind passed, she still pressing the bank-note upon him, and he as absolutely refusing, till Booth left the lady to dress herself, and went to walk in the area of the prison.

Miss Matthews now applied to the governor to know by what means she might procure the captain his liberty. The governor answered, " As he cannot get bail, it will be a difficult matter ; and money to be sure there must be ; for people no doubt expect to touch on these occasions. When prisoners have not wherewithal as the law requires to entitle themselves to justice, why they must be beholden to other people to give them their liberty ; and people will not, to be sure, suffer others to be beholden to them for nothing, whereof there is good reason ; for how should we all live if it was not for these things ?" " Well, well," said she, " and how much will it cost ?" " How much !" answered he, " how much ! why, let me see." Here he hesitated some time, and then answered " That for five guineas he would undertake to procure the captain his discharge." That being the sum which he computed to remain in the lady's pocket ; for, as to the gentleman's, he had long been acquainted with the emptiness of it.

Miss Matthews, to whom money was as dirt (indeed she may be thought not to have known the value of it), delivered him the bank-bill, and bid him get it changed ; for if the whole, says she, will procure him his liberty, he shall have it this evening.

" The whole, madam !" answered the governor, as soon as he had recovered his breath, for it almost forsook him at

the sight of the black word hundred. "No, no ; there
might be people indeed, but I am not one of those. A
hundred ! no, nor nothing like it. As for myself, as I
said, I will be content with five guineas, and I am sure
that's little enough. What other people will expect I cannot exactly say. To be sure his worship's clerk will expect to touch pretty handsomely ; as for his worship him
self, he never touches any thing—that is, not to speak of ;
but then the constable will expect something, and the
watchmen. must have something, and the lawyers on both
sides, they must have their fees for finishing." "Well,"
said she, "I leave all to you. If it costs me twenty
pounds, I will have him discharged this afternoon. But
you must give his discharge into my hands without letting
the captain know any thing of the matter."

The governor promised to obey her commands in every
particular ; nay, he was so very industrious that, though
dinner was just then coming upon the table, at her earnest
request he set out immediately on the purpose, and went, as
he said, in pursuit of the lawyer.

All the other company assembled at table as usual, where
poor Booth was the only person out of spirits. This was imputed by all present to a wrong cause ; nay, Miss Matthews
herself either could not or would not suspect that there was
any thing deeper than the despair of being speedily discharged that lay heavy on his mind.

However, the mirth of the rest, and a pretty liberal
quantity of punch, which he swallowed after dinner (for
Miss Matthews had ordered a very large bowl at her own
expense to entertain the good company at her farewell), so
far exhilarated his spirits that, when the young lady and he
retired to their tea, he had all the marks of gayety in his
countenance, and his eyes sparkled with good humor.

The gentleman and lady had spent about two hours in
tea and conversation, when the governor returned, and pri-

vately delivered to the lady the discharge for her friend, and the sum of eighty-two pounds five shillings, the rest having been, he said, disbursed in the business, of which he was ready at any time to render an exact account.

Miss Matthews, being again alone with Mr. Booth, she put the discharge into his hands, desiring him to ask her no questions ; and adding, " I think, sir, we have neither of us now any thing more to do at this place." She then summoned the governor, and ordered a bill of that day's expense, for long scores were not usual there ; and at the same time ordered a hackney coach, without having yet determined whither she would go, but fully determined she was, wherever she went, to take Mr. Booth with her.

The governor was now approaching with a long roll of paper, when a faint voice was heard to cry out hastily, " Where is he ?" and presently a female spectre, all pale and breathless, rushed into the room, and fell into Mr. Booth's arms, where she immediately fainted away.

Booth made a shift to support his lovely burden ; though he was himself in a condition very little different from hers. Miss Matthews likewise, who presently recollected the face of Amelia, was struck motionless with the surprise ; nay, the governor himself, though not easily moved at sights of horror, stood aghast, and neither offered to speak nor stir.

Happily for Amelia, the governess of the mansions had, out of curiosity, followed her into the room, and was the only useful person present on this occasion : she immediately called for water, and ran to the lady's assistance, fell to loosening her stays, and performed all the offices proper at such a season ; which had so good an effect that Amelia soon recovered the disorder which the violent agitation of her spirits had caused, and found herself alive and awake in her husband's arms.

Some tender caresses and a soft whisper or two passed privately between Booth and his lady ; nor was it without great difficulty that poor Amelia put some restraint on her fondness in a place so improper for a tender interview. She now cast her eyes round the room, and, fixing them on Miss Matthews, who stood like a statue, she soon recollected her, and, addressing her by her name, said, " Sure madam, I cannot be mistaken in those features ; though meeting you here might almost make me suspect my memory."

Miss Matthews's face was now all covered with scarlet. The reader may easily believe she was on no account pleased with Amelia's presence ; indeed, she expected from her some of those insults of which virtuous women are generally so liberal to a frail sister : but she was mistaken ; Amelia was not one

> Who thought the nation ne'er would thrive
> Till all the whores were burnt alive.

Her virtue could support itself with its own intrinsic worth, without borrowing any assistance from the vices of other women ; and she considered their natural infirmities as the objects of pity, not of contempt or abhorrence.

When Amelia therefore perceived the visible confusion in Miss Matthews she presently called to remembrance some stories which she had imperfectly heard ; for, as she was not naturally attentive to scandal, and had kept very little company since her return to England, she was far from being a mistress of the lady's whole history. However, she had heard enough to impute her confusion to the right cause ; she advanced to her, and told her she was extremely sorry to meet her in such a place, but hoped that no very great misfortune was the occasion of it.

Miss Matthews began, by degrees, to recover her spirits. She answered, with a reserved air, " I am much obliged to you, madam, for your concern ; we are all liable to misfortunes in this world. Indeed, I know not why I should be much ashamed of being in any place where I am in such good company."

Here Booth interposed. He had before acquainted Amelia in a whisper that his confinement was at an end. "The unfortunate accident, my dear," said he, "which brought this young lady to this melancholy place is entirely determined ; and she is now as absolutely at her liberty as myself."

Amelia, imputing the extreme coldness and reserve of the lady to the cause already mentioned, advanced still more and more in proportion as she drew back ; till the governor, who had withdrawn some time, returned, and acquainted Miss Matthews that her coach was at the door ; upon which the company soon separated. Amelia and Booth went together in Amelia's coach, and poor Miss Matthews was obliged to retire alone, after having satisfied the demands of the governor, which in one day only had amounted to a pretty considerable sum ; for he, with great dexterity, proportioned the bills to the abilities of his guests.

It may seem, perhaps, wonderful to some readers, that Miss Matthews should have maintained that cold reserve toward Amelia, so as barely to keep within the rules of civility, instead of embracing an opportunity which seemed to offer of gaining some degree of intimacy with a wife whose husband she was so fond of ; but, besides that her spirits were entirely disconcerted by so sudden and unexpected a disappointment ; and besides the extreme horrors which she conceived at the presence of her rival, there is, I believe, something so outrageously suspicious in the nature of all vice, especially when joined with any great degree of pride, that the eyes of those whom we imagine privy to our failings are intolerable to us, and we are apt to aggravate their opinions to our disadvantage far beyond the reality.

CHAPTER III.

CONTAINING WISE OBSERVATIONS OF THE AUTHOR, AND
OTHER MATTERS.

THERE is nothing more difficult than to lay down any fixed and certain rules for happiness ; or indeed to judge with any precision of the happiness of others from the knowledge of external circumstances. There is sometimes a little speck of black in the brightest and gayest colors of fortune, which contaminates and deadens the whole. On the contrary, when all without looks dark and dismal, there is often a secret ray of light within the mind, which turns every thing to real joy and gladness.

I have in the course of my life seen many occasions to make this observation, and Mr. Booth was at present a very pregnant instance of its truth. He was just delivered from a prison, and in the possession of his beloved wife and children ; and (which might be imagined greatly to augment his joy) fortune had done all this for him within an hour, without giving him the least warning or reasonable expectation of the strange reverse in his circumstances ; and yet it is certain that there were very few men in the world more seriously miserable than he was at this instant. A deep melancholy seized his mind, and cold damp sweats overspread his person, so that he was scarce animated ; and poor Amelia, instead of a fond warm husband, bestowed her caresses on a dull, lifeless lump of clay. He endeavored, however, at first, as much as possible, to conceal what he felt, and attempted, what is the hardest of all tasks, to act the part of a happy man ; but he found no supply of spirits to carry on this deceit, and would have probably sunk under his attempt, had not poor Amelia's simplicity helped him to another fallacy, in which he had much better success.

This worthy woman very plainly perceived the disorder in her husband's mind ; and, having no doubt of the cause of it, especially when she saw the tears stand in his eyes at the sight of his children, threw her arms round his neck, and, embracing him with rapturous fondness, cried out, " My dear Billy, let nothing make you uneasy. Heaven will, I doubt not, provide for us and these poor babes. Great fortunes are not necessary to happiness. For my own part, I can level my mind with any state ; and for those poor little things, whatever condition of life we breed them to, that will be sufficient to maintain them in. How many thousands abound in affluence whose fortunes are much lower than ours ! for it is not from nature, but from education and habit, that our wants are chiefly derived. Make yourself easy therefore, my dear love ; for you have a wife who will think herself happy with you, and endeavor to make you so, in any situation. Fear nothing, Billy ; industry will always provide us a wholesome meal, and I will take care that neatness and cheerfulness shall make it a pleasant one.''

Booth presently took the cue which she had given him. He fixed his eyes on her for a minute with great earnestness and inexpressible tenderness ; and then cried, " Oh, my Amelia, how much are you my superior in every perfection ! how wise, how great, how noble are your sentiments ! why can I not imitate what I so much admire ? why can I not look with your constancy on those dear little pledges of our loves ? All my philosophy is baffled with the thought that my Amelia's children are to struggle with a cruel, hard, unfeeling world, and to buffet those waves of fortune which have overwhelmed their father. Here, I own I want your firmness, and am not without an excuse for wanting it ; for am I not the cruel cause of all your wretchedness ? have I not stepped between you and fortune, and been the cursed obstacle to all your greatness and happiness ?"

" Say not so, my love," answered she. " Great I might have been, but never happy with any other man. Indeed, dear Billy, I laugh at the fears you formerly raised in me ; what seemed so terrible at a distance, now it approaches nearer, appears to have been a mere bugbear, and let this comfort you, that I look on myself at this day as the happiest of women ; nor have I done any thing which I do not rejoice in, and would, if I had the gift of prescience, do again."

Booth was so overcome with this behavior that he had no words to answer. To say the truth, it was difficult to find any worthy of the occasion. He threw himself prostrate at her feet, whence poor Amelia was forced to use all her strength as well as entreaties to raise and place him in his chair.

Such is ever the fortitude of perfect innocence, and such the depression of guilt in minds not utterly abandoned. Booth was naturally of a sanguine temper ; nor would any such apprehensions as he mentioned have been sufficient to have restrained his joy at meeting with his Amelia. In fact, a reflection on the injury he had done her was the sole cause of his grief. This it was that enervated his heart, and threw him into agonies, which all that profusion of heroic tenderness that the most excellent of women intended for his comfort served only to heighten and aggravate ; as the more she rose in his admiration, the more she quickened his sense of his own unworthiness.

After a disagreeable evening, the first of that kind that he had ever passed with his Amelia, in which he had the utmost difficulty to force a little cheerfulness, and in which her spirits were at length overpowered by discerning the oppression on his, they retired to rest, or rather to misery, which need not be described.

The next morning at breakfast, Booth began to recover a little from his melancholy, and to taste the company of his children. He now first thought of inquiring of Amelia by what means she had discovered the place of his confinement. Amelia, after gently rebuking him for not having himself acquainted her with it, informed him that it was known all over the country, and that she had traced the original of it to her sister; who had spread the news with a malicious joy, and added a circumstance which would have frightened her to death, had not her knowledge of him made her give little credit to it, which was, that he was committed for murder. But, though she had discredited this part, she said the not hearing from him during several successive posts made her too apprehensive of the rest; that she got a conveyance therefore for herself and children to Salisbury, from whence the stage coach had brought them to town; and, having deposited the children at his lodging, of which he had sent her an account on his first arrival in town, she took a hack and came directly to the prison where she heard he was, and where she found him.

Booth excused himself, and with truth, as to his not having writ; for, in fact, he had writ twice from the prison, though he had mentioned nothing of his confinement; but as he sent away his letters after nine at night, the fellow to whom they were intrusted had burnt them for the sake of putting the twopence in his own pocket, or rather in the pocket of the keeper of the next gin-shop.

As to the account which Amelia gave him, it served rather to raise than to satisfy his curiosity. He began to suspect that some person had seen both him and Miss Matthews together in the prison, and had confounded her case with his; and this the circumstance of murder made the more probable. But who this person should be he could not guess. After giving himself, therefore, some pains in forming conjectures to no purpose, he was forced to rest contented with his ignorance of the real truth.

Two or three days now passed without producing any thing remarkable ; unless it were that Booth more and more recovered his spirits, and had now almost regained his former degree of cheerfulness, when the following letter arrived, again to torment him :

"Dear Billy : To convince you I am the most reasonable of women, I have given you up three whole days to the unmolested possession of my fortunate rival ; I can refrain no longer from letting you know that I lodge in Dean Street, not far from the church, at the sign of the Pelican and Trumpet, where I expect this evening to see you.

"Believe me I am, with more affection than any other woman in the world can be, my dear Billy,

"Your affectionate, fond, doting

"F. Matthews."

Booth tore the letter with rage, and threw it into the fire, resolving never to visit the lady more, unless it was to pay her the money she had lent him, which he was determined to do the very first opportunity, for it was not at present in his power.

This letter threw him back into his fit of dejection, in which he had not continued long when a packet from the country brought him the following from his friend Dr. Harrison :

"Lyons, January 21, N. S.

"Sir : Though I am now on my return home, I have taken up my pen to communicate to you some news I have heard from England, which gives me much uneasiness, and concerning which I can indeed deliver my sentiments with much more ease this way than any other. In my answer to your last, I very freely gave you my opinion, in which it was my misfortune to disapprove of every step you had

taken ; but those were all pardonable errors. Can you be
so partial to yourself, upon cool and sober reflection, to
think what I am going to mention is so ? I promise you, it
appears to me a folly of so monstrous a kind, that, had I
heard it from any but a person of the highest honor, I
should have rejected it as utterly incredible. I hope you
already guess what I am about to name ; since, heaven
forbid, your conduct should afford you any choice of such
gross instances of weakness. In a word, then, you have
set up an equipage. What shall I invent in your excuse,
either to others or to myself ? In truth, I can find no excuse for you, and, what is more, I am certain you can find
none for yourself. I must deal therefore very plainly and
sincerely with you. Vanity is always contemptible ; but
when joined with dishonesty, it becomes odious and detestable. At whose expense are you to support this equipage ?
is it not entirely at the expense of others ? and will it not
finally end in that of your poor wife and children ? you
know you are two years in arrears to me. If I could impute this to any extraordinary or common accident I think
I should never have mentioned it ; but I will not suffer my
money to support the ridiculous, and, I must say, criminal
vanity of any one. I expect, therefore, to find, at my return, that you have either discharged my whole debt, or
your equipage. Let me beg you seriously to consider your
circumstances and condition in life, and to remember that
your situation will not justify any the least unnecessary expense. *Simply to be poor*, says my favorite Greek histo-
rian, *was not held scandalous by the wise Athenians, but
highly so to owe that poverty to our own indiscretion.*

"Present my affections to Mrs. Booth, and be assured
that I shall not, without great reason, and great pain too,
ever cease to be,

"Your most faithful friend,

"R. HARRISON."

Had this letter come at any other time, it would have given Booth the most sensible affliction ; but so totally had the affair of Miss Matthews possessed his mind, that, like a man in the most raging fit of the gout, he was scarce capable of any additional torture ; nay, he even made an use of this latter epistle, as it served to account to Amelia for that concern which he really felt on another account. The poor deceived lady, therefore, applied herself to give him comfort where he least wanted it. She said he might easily perceive that the matter had been misrepresented to the doctor, who would not, she was sure, retain the least anger against him when he knew the real truth.

After a short conversation on this subject, in which Booth appeared to be greatly consoled by the arguments of his wife, they parted. He went to take a walk in the Park, and she remained at home to prepare him his dinner.

He was no sooner departed than his little boy, not quite six years old, said to Amelia, " La ! mamma, what is the matter with poor papa ? what makes him look so as if he was going to cry ? he is not half so merry as he used to be in the country." Amelia answered, " Oh ! my dear, your papa is only a little thoughtful ; he will be merry again soon." Then looking fondly on her children, she burst into an agony of tears, and cried, " Oh, heavens ! what have these poor little infants done ? why will the barbarous world endeavor to starve them by depriving us of our only friend ? Oh, my dear, your father is ruined, and we are undone !" The children presently accompanied their mother's tears, and the daughter cried, " Why, will anybody hurt poor papa ? hath he done any harm to anybody ?" " No, my dear child," said the mother ; " he is the best man in the world, and therefore they hate him." Upon which the boy, who was extremely sensible at his years, answered, " Nay, mamma, how can that be ? have not you often told me that if I was good everybody would love me?" "All good people will," answered she. "Why don't they love papa then?" replied the child, "for I am sure he is very good." "So they do, my dear," said the mother, "but there are more bad people in the world, and they will hate you for your goodness." "Why, then, bad people," cries the child, "are loved by more than the good." "No matter for that, my dear," said she; "the love of one good person is more worth having than that of a thousand wicked ones; nay, if there was no such person in the world, still you must be a good boy; for there is one in heaven who will love you, and His love is better for you than that of all mankind."

This little dialogue, we are apprehensive, will be read with contempt by many; indeed, we should not have thought it worth recording was it not for the excellent example which Amelia here gives to all mothers. This admirable woman never let a day pass without instructing her children in some lesson of religion and morality. By which means she had, in their tender minds, so strongly annexed the ideas of fear and shame to every idea of evil of which they were susceptible, that it must require great pains and length of habit to separate them. Though she was the tenderest of mothers, she never suffered any symptom of malevolence to show itself in their most trifling actions without discouragement, without rebuke, and, if it broke forth with any rancor, without punishment. In which she had such success, that not the least marks of pride, envy, malice, or spite discovered itself in any of their little words or deeds.

CHAPTER IV.

IN WHICH AMELIA APPEARS IN NO UNAMIABLE LIGHT.

AMELIA, with the assistance of a little girl, who was their only servant, had dressed her dinner, and she had likewise dressed herself as neat as any lady who had a regular set of

servants could have done, when Booth returned, and
brought with him his friend James, whom he had met with
in the Park ; and who, as Booth absolutely refused to dine
away from his wife, to whom he had promised to return,
had invited himself to dine with him.   Amelia had none of
that paltry pride which possesses so many of her sex, and
which disconcerts their tempers, and gives them the air and
looks of furies, if their husbands bring in an unexpected
guest, without giving them timely warning to provide a
sacrifice to their own vanity.   Amelia received her husband's friend with the utmost complaisance and good
humor : she made indeed some apology for the homeliness
of her dinner ; but it was politely turned as a compliment
to Mr. James's friendship, which could carry him where he
was sure of being so ill entertained ; and gave not the least
hint how magnificently she would have provided *had she
expected the favor of so much good company.*   A phrase
which is generally meant to contain not only an apology for
the lady of the house, but a tacit satire on her guests for
their intrusion, and is at least a strong insinuation that they
are not welcome.

Amelia failed not to inquire very earnestly after her old
friend Mrs. James, formerly Miss Bath, and was very
sorry to find that she was not in town.   The truth was, as
James had married out of a violent liking of, or appetite
to, her person, possession had surfeited him, and he was
now grown so heartily tired of his wife, that she had very
little of his company ; she was forced therefore to content
herself with being the mistress of a large house and
equipage in the country ten months in the year by herself.
The other two he indulged her with the diversions of the
town ; but then, though they lodged under the same roof,
she had little more of her husband's society than if they
had been one hundred miles apart.   With all this, as she
was a woman of calm passions, she made herself contented ;

for she had never had any violent affection for James : the match was of the prudent kind, and to her advantage ; for his fortune, by the death of an uncle, was become very considerable ; and she had gained every thing by the bargain but a husband, which her constitution suffered her to be very well satisfied without.

When Amelia, after dinner, retired to her children, James began to talk to his friend concerning his affairs. He advised Booth very earnestly to think of getting again into the army, in which he himself had met with such success, that he had obtained the command of a regiment to which his brother-in-law was lieutenant-colonel. These preferments they both owed to the favor of fortune only ; for, though there was no objection to either of their military characters, yet neither of them had any extraordinary desert ; and, if merit in the service was a sufficient recommendation, Booth, who had been twice wounded in the siege, seemed to have the fairest pretensions ; but he remained a poor half-pay lieutenant, and the others were, as we have said, one of them a lieutenant-colonel, and the other had a regiment. Such rises we often see in life, without being able to give any satisfactory account of the means, and therefore ascribe them to the good fortune of the person.

Both Colonel James and his brother-in-law were members of parliament ; for, as the uncle of the former had left him, together with his estate, an almost certain interest in a borough, so he chose to confer this favor on Colonel Bath ; a circumstance which would have been highly immaterial to mention here, but as it serves to set forth the goodness of James, who endeavored to make up in kindness to the family what he wanted in fondness for his wife.

Colonel James then endeavored all in his power to persuade Booth to think again of a military life, and very kindly offered him his interest toward obtaining him a company in the regiment under his command. Booth must have been a madman, in his present circumstances, to have hesitated one moment at accepting such an offer, and he well knew Amelia, notwithstanding her aversion to the army, was much too wise to make the least scruple of giving her consent. Nor was he, as it appeared afterward, mistaken in his opinion of his wife's understanding ; for she made not the least objection when it was communicated to her, but contented herself with an express stipulation, that wherever he was commanded to go (for the regiment was now abroad) she would accompany him.

Booth, therefore, accepted his friend's proposal with a profusion of acknowledgments ; and it was agreed that Booth should draw up a memorial of his pretensions, which Colonel James undertook to present to some man of power, and to back it with all the force he had.

Nor did the friendship of the colonel stop here. " You will excuse me, dear Booth," said he, " if, after what you have told me" (for he had been very explicit in revealing his affairs to him), " I suspect you must want money at this time. If that be the case, as I am certain it must be, I have fifty pieces at your service." This generosity brought the tears into Booth's eyes ; and he at length confessed that he had not five guineas in the house ; upon which James gave him a bank-bill for twenty pounds, and said he would give him thirty more the next time he saw him.

Thus did this generous colonel (for generous he really was to the highest degree) restore peace and comfort to this little family ; and by this act of beneficence make two of the worthiest people two of the happiest that evening.

Here, reader, give me leave to stop a minute, to lament that so few are to be found of this benign disposition ; that, while wantonness, vanity, avarice, and ambition are every day rioting and triumphing in the follies and weakness, the ruin and desolation of mankind, scarce one man in a thousand is capable of tasting the happiness of others. Nay, give me leave to wonder that pride, which is constantly struggling, and often imposing on itself, to gain some little pre-eminence, should so seldom hint to us the only certain as well as laudable way of setting ourselves above another man, and that is, by becoming his benefactor.

CHAPTER V.

CONTAINING AN EULOGIUM UPON INNOCENCE, AND OTHER GRAVE MATTERS.

Booth passed that evening, and all the succeeding day, with his Amelia, without the interruption of almost a single thought concerning Miss Matthews, after having determined to go on the Sunday, the only day he could venture without the verge in the present state of his affairs, and pay her what she had advanced for him in the prison. But she had not so long patience ; for the third day, while he was sitting with Amelia, a letter was brought to him. As he knew the hand, he immediately put it into his pocket unopened, not without such an alteration in his countenance, that had Amelia, who was then playing with one of the children, cast her eyes toward him, she must have remarked it. This accident, however, luckily gave him time to recover himself ; for Amelia was so deeply engaged with the little one, that she did not even remark the delivery of the letter. The maid soon after returned into the room, saying the chairman desired to know if there was any answer to the letter. " What letter ?" cries Booth. " The letter I gave you just now," answered the girl. " Sure," cries Booth, " the child is mad ; you gave me no letter." " Yes, indeed, I did, sir," said the poor girl. " Why then as sure as fate," cries Booth, " I threw it into the fire in my reverie ; why, child, why did you not tell me it was a letter? bid the chairman come up—stay, I will go down my-self; for he will otherwise dirt the stairs with his feet.''

Amelia was gently chiding the girl for her carelessness when Booth returned, saying it was very true that she had delivered him a letter from Colonel James, and that perhaps it might be of consequence. ''However,'' says he, '' I will step to the coffee-house, and send him an account of this strange accident, which I know he will pardon in my present situation.''

Booth was overjoyed at this escape, which poor Amelia's total want of all jealousy and suspicion made it very easy for him to accomplish; but his pleasure was considerably abated when, upon opening the letter, he found it to contain, mixed with several very strong expressions of love, some pretty warm ones of the upbraiding kind; but what most alarmed him was a hint that it was in her (Miss Matthews's) power to make Amelia as miserable as herself. Besides the general knowledge of

——Furens quid fœmina possit,

he had more particular reasons to apprehend the rage of a lady who had given so strong an instance of how far she could carry her revenge. She had already sent a chairman to his lodgings with a positive command not to return without an answer to her letter. This might of itself have possibly occasioned a discovery; and he thought he had great reason to fear that, if she did not carry matters so far as purposely and avowedly to reveal the secret to Amelia, her indiscretion would at least effect the discovery of that which he would at any price have concealed. Under these terrors he might, I believe, be considered as the most wretched of human beings.

O innocence, how glorious and happy a portion art thou to the breast that possesses thee! thou fearest neither the eyes nor the tongues of men. Truth, the most powerful of

all things, is thy strongest friend ; and the brighter the
light is in which thou art displayed, the more it discovers
thy transcendent beauties. Guilt, on the contrary, like a
base thief, suspects every eye that beholds him to be privy
to his transgressions, and every tongue that mentions his
name to be proclaiming them. Fraud and falsehood are
his weak and treacherous allies ; and he lurks trembling in
the dark, dreading every ray of light, lest it should discover him, and give him up to shame and punishment.

While Booth was walking in the Park with all these horrors in his mind he again met his friend Colonel James,
who soon took notice of that deep concern which the other
was incapable of hiding. After some little conversation,
Booth said, "My dear colonel, I am sure I must be the
most insensible of men if I did not look on you as the best
and the truest friend ; I will, therefore, without scruple,
repose a confidence in you of the highest kind. I have
often made you privy to my necessities ; I will now
acquaint you with my shame, provided you have leisure
enough to give me a hearing : for I must open to you a
long history, since I will not reveal my fault without informing you, at the same time, of those circumstances
which, I hope, will in some measure excuse it."

The colonel very readily agreed to give his friend a patient hearing. So they walked directly to a coffee-house at
the corner of Spring-Garden, where, being in a room by
themselves, Booth opened his whole heart, and acquainted
the colonel with his amour with Miss Matthews, from the
very beginning to his receiving that letter which had
caused all his present uneasiness, and which he now delivered into his friend's hand.

The colonel read the letter very attentively twice over
(he was silent indeed long enough to have read it oftener) ;
and then, turning to Booth, said, " Well, sir, and is it so
grievous a calamity to be the object of a young lady's

affection ; especially of one whom you allow to be so extremely handsome ?"   "Nay, but, my dear friend," cries
Booth, " do not jest with me ; you who know my Amelia."
" Well, my dear friend," answered James, " and you know
Amelia and this lady too.   But what would you have me
do for you ?"   " I would have you give me your advice,"
says Booth, " by what method I shall get rid of this dreadful woman without a discovery."   " And do you really,"
cries the other, " desire to get rid of her ?"   " Can you
doubt it," said Booth, " after what I have communicated
to you, and after what you yourself have seen in my family ? for I hope, notwithstanding this fatal slip, I do not
appear to you in the light of a profligate."   " Well," answered James, " and, whatever light I may appear to you
in, if you are really tired of the lady, and if she be really
what you have represented her, I'll endeavor to take her
off your hands ; but I insist upon it that you do not deceive
me in any particular."   Booth protested in the most solemn manner that every word which he had spoken was
strictly true ; and being asked whether he would give his
honor never more to visit the lady, he assured James that
he never would.   He then, at his friend's request, delivered him Miss Matthews's letter, in which was a second
direction to her lodgings, and declared to him that, if he
could bring him safely out of this terrible affair, he should
think himself to have a still higher obligation to his
friendship than any which he had already received from
it.

Booth pressed the colonel to go home with him to dinner ; but he excused himself, being, as he said, already
engaged.   However, he undertook in the afternoon to do
all in his power that Booth should receive no more alarms
from the quarter of Miss Matthews, whom the colonel undertook to pay all the demands she had on his friend.
They then separated.   The colonel went to dinner at the

King's Arms, and Booth returned in high spirits to meet his Amelia.

The next day, early in the morning, the colonel came to the coffee-house and sent for his friend, who lodged but at a little distance. The colonel told him he had a little exaggerated the lady's beauty; however, he said, he excused that, "for you might think, perhaps," cries he, " that your inconstancy to the finest woman in the world might want some excuse. Be that as it will," said he, " you may make yourself easy, as it will be, I am convinced, your own fault, if you have ever any further molestation from Miss Matthews."

Booth poured forth very warmly a great profusion of gratitude on this occasion ; and nothing more anywise material passed at this interview, which was very short, the colonel being in a great hurry, as he had, he said, some business of very great importance to transact that morning.

The colonel had now seen Booth twice without remembering to give him the thirty pounds. This the latter imputed entirely to forgetfulness ; for he had always found the promises of the former to be equal in value with the notes or bonds of other people. He was more surprised at what happened the next day, when, meeting his friend in the Park, he received only a cold salute from him ; and though he passed him five or six times, and the colonel was walking with a single officer of no great rank, and with whom he seemed in no earnest conversation, yet could not Booth, who was alone, obtain any further notice from him.

This gave the poor man some alarm ; though he could scarce persuade himself that there was any design in all this coldness or forgetfulness. Once he imagined that he had lessened himself in the colonel's opinion by having discovered his inconstancy to Amelia ; but the known character of the other presently cured him of his suspicion, for he was a perfect libertine with regard to women ; that being

indeed the principal blemish in his character, which otherwise might have deserved much commendation for good-
nature, generosity, and friendship. But he carried this
one to a most unpardonable height ; and made no scruple
of openly declaring that, if he ever liked a woman well
enough to be uneasy on her account, he would cure himself, if he could, by enjoying her, whatever might be the
consequence.

Booth could not therefore be persuaded that the colonel
would so highly resent in another a fault of which he was
himself most notoriously guilty. After much consideration he could derive this behavior from nothing better than
a capriciousness in his friend's temper, from a kind of inconstancy of mind, which makes men grow weary of their
friends with no more reason than they often are of their
mistresses. To say the truth, there are jilts in friendship
as well as in love ; and, by the behavior of some men in
both, one would almost imagine that they industriously
sought to gain the affections of others with a view only of
making the parties miserable.

This was the consequence of the colonel's behavior to
Booth. Former calamities had afflicted him, but this
almost distracted him ; and the more so as he was not able
well to account for such conduct, nor to conceive the reason of it.

Amelia, at his return, presently perceived the disturbance in his mind, though he endeavored with his utmost
power to hide it ; and he was at length prevailed upon by
her entreaties to discover to her the cause of it, which she
no sooner heard than she applied as judicious a remedy to
his disordered spirits as either of those great mental physicians, Tully or Aristotle, could have thought of. She
used many arguments to persuade him that he was in an
error, and had mistaken forgetfulness and carelessness for a
designed neglect.

But, as this physic was only eventually good, and as its efficacy depended on her being in the right, a point in which she was not apt to be too positive, she thought fit to add some consolation of a more certain and positive kind. "Admit," said she, "my dear, that Mr. James should prove the unaccountable person you have suspected, and should, without being able to allege any cause, withdraw his friendship from you (for surely the accident of burning his letter is too trifling and ridiculous to mention), why should this grieve you? the obligations he hath conferred on you, I allow, ought to make his misfortunes almost your own; but they should not, I think, make you see his faults so very sensibly, especially when, by one of the greatest faults in the world committed against yourself, he hath considerably lessened all obligations; for sure, if the same person who hath contributed to my happiness at one time doth every thing in his power maliciously and wantonly to make me miserable at another, I am very little obliged to such a person. And let it be a comfort to my dear Billy, that, however other friends may prove false and fickle to him, he hath one friend, whom no inconstancy of her own, nor any change of his fortune, nor time, nor age, nor sickness, nor any accident, can ever alter; but who will esteem, will love, and dote on him for ever." So saying, she flung her snowy arms about his neck, and gave him a caress so tender that it seemed almost to balance all the malice of his fate.

And, indeed, the behavior of Amelia would have made him completely happy, in defiance of all adverse circumstances, had it not been for those bitter ingredients which he himself had thrown into his cup, and which prevented him from truly relishing his Amelia's sweetness, by cruelly reminding him how unworthy he was of this excellent creature.

Booth did not long remain in the dark as to the conduct

of James, which, at first, appeared to him to be so great a
mystery ; for this very afternoon he received a letter from
Miss Matthews which unravelled the whole affair. By this
letter, which was full of bitterness and upbraiding, he discovered that James was his rival with that lady, and was,
indeed, the identical person who had sent the hundred-
pound note to Miss Matthews, when in the prison. He had
reason to believe, likewise, as well by the letter as by other
circumstances, that James had hitherto been an unsuccess-
ful lover ; for the lady, though she had forfeited all title to
virtue, had not yet so far forfeited all pretensions to delicacy as to be, like the dirt in the street, indifferently common to all. She distributed her favors only to those she
liked, in which number that gentleman had not the happiness of being included.

When Booth had made this discovery, he was not so little versed in human nature as any longer to hesitate at the
true motive to the colonel's conduct ; for he well knew
how odious a sight a happy rival is to an unfortunate lover.
I believe he was, in reality, glad to assign the cold treat.
ment he had received from his friend to a cause which,
however injustifiable, is at the same time highly natural ;
and to acquit him of a levity, fickleness, and caprice, which
he must have been unwillingly obliged to have seen in a
much worse light.

He now resolved to take the first opportunity of accost-
ing the colonel, and of coming to a perfect explanation
upon the whole matter. He debated likewise with himself
whether he should not throw himself at Amelia's feet, and
confess a crime to her which he found so little hopes of
concealing, and which he foresaw would occasion him so
many difficulties and terrors to endeavor to conceal.
Happy had it been for him had he wisely pursued this
step ; since, in all probability, he would have received immediate forgiveness from the best of women ; but he had

not sufficient resolution, or, to speak perhaps more truly, he had too much pride, to confess his guilt, and preferred the danger of the highest inconveniences to the certainty of being put to the blush.

CHAPTER VI.

IN WHICH MAY APPEAR THAT VIOLENCE IS SOMETIMES DONE TO THE NAME OF LOVE.

WHEN that happy day came, in which unhallowed hands are forbidden to contaminate the shoulders of the unfortunate, Booth went early to the colonel's house, and, being admitted to his presence, began with great freedom, though with great gentleness, to complain of his not having dealt with him with more openness. " Why, my dear colonel," said he, " would you not acquaint me with that secret which this letter hath disclosed ?" James read the letter, at which his countenance changed more than once ; and then, after a short silence, said, " Mr. Booth, I have been to blame, I own it ; and you upbraid me with justice. The true reason was, that I was ashamed of my own folly. D—n me, Booth, if I have not been a most consummate fool, a very dupe to this woman ; and she hath a particular pleasure in making me so. I know what the impertinence of virtue is, and I can submit to it ; but to be treated thus by a whore ! You must forgive me, dear Booth, but your success was a kind of triumph over me, which I could not bear. I own, I have not the least reason to conceive any anger against you ; and yet, curse me if I should not have been less displeased at your lying with my own wife ; nay, I could almost have parted with half my fortune to you more willingly than have suffered you to receive that trifle of my money which you received at her hands. However, I ask your pardon, and I promise you I will never more think of you with the least ill-will on the account of

this woman ; but as for her, d—n me if I do not enjoy
her by some means or other, whatever it costs me ; for I
am already above two hundred pounds out of pocket without having scarce had a smile in return.''

Booth expressed much astonishment at this declaration ;
he said he could not conceive how it was possible to have
such an affection for a woman who did not show the least
inclination to return it.   James gave her a hearty curse,
and said, '' Pox of her inclination ; I want only the possession of her person, and that, you will allow, is a very fine
one.   But, besides my passion for her, she hath now piqued
my pride ; for how can a man of my fortune brook being
refused by a whore ?''   '' Since you are so set on the business,'' cries Booth, '' you will excuse my saying so ; I fancy
you had better change your method of applying to her ;
for, as she is, perhaps, the vainest woman upon earth, your
bounty may probably do you little service, nay, may rather
actually disoblige her.   Vanity is plainly her predominant
passion, and, if you will administer to that, it will infallibly
throw her into your arms.   To this I attribute my own unfortunate success.   While she relieved my wants and distresses she was daily feeding her own vanity ; whereas, as
every gift of yours asserted your superiority, it rather
offended than pleased her.   Indeed, women generally love
to be of the obliging side ; and, if we examine their favorites, we shall find them to be much oftener such as they
have conferred obligations on than such as they have received them from.''

There was something in this speech which pleased the
colonel ; and he said, with a smile, '' I don't know how it
is, Will, but you know women better than I.''   '' Perhaps,
colonel,'' answered Booth, '' I have studied their minds
more.''   '' I don't, however, much envy your knowledge,'' replied the other, '' for I never think their minds
worth considering.   However, I hope I shall profit a little

by your experience with Miss Matthews. Damnation seize
the proud insolent harlot ! the devil take me if I don't love
her more than I ever loved a woman !''

The rest of their conversation turned on Booth's affairs.
The colonel again reassumed the part of a friend, gave him
the remainder of the money, and promised to take the first
opportunity of laying his memorial before a great man.

Booth was greatly overjoyed at this success. Nothing
now lay on his mind but to conceal his frailty from Amelia,
to whom he was afraid Miss Matthews, in the rage of her
resentment, would communicate it. This apprehension
made him stay almost constantly at home ; and he trembled at every knock at the door. His fear, moreover, betrayed him into a meanness which he would have heartily
despised on any other occasion. This was to order the
maid to deliver him any letter directed to Amelia ; at the
same time strictly charging her not to acquaint her mistress
with her having received any such orders.

A servant of any acuteness would have formed strange
conjectures from such an injunction ; but this poor girl
was of perfect simplicity ; so great, indeed, was her simplicity, that, had not Amelia been void of all suspicion of
her husband, the maid would have soon after betrayed her
master.

One afternoon, while they were drinking tea, little Betty,
so was the maid called, came into the room, and, calling
her master forth, delivered him a card which was directed
to Amelia. Booth, having read the card, on his return into
the room chid the girl for calling him, saying, '' If you can
read, child, you must see it was directed to your mistress.''
To this the girl answered pertly enough, '' I am sure, sir,
you ordered me to bring every letter first to you.'' This
hint, with many women, would have been sufficient to
have blown up the whole affair ; but Amelia, who heard
what the girl said, through the medium of love and confi-

dence, saw the matter in a much better light than it deserved, and, looking tenderly on her husband, said, " Indeed, my love, I must blame you, for a conduct which,
perhaps, I ought rather to praise, as it proceeds only from
the extreme tenderness of your affection.   But why will you
endeavor to keep any secrets from me ? believe me, for my
own sake, you ought not ; for, as you cannot hide the consequences, you make me always suspect ten times worse than
the reality.   While I have you and my children well before my eyes, I am capable of facing any news which can
arrive ; for what ill news can come (unless, indeed, it concerns my little babe in the country) which doth not relate
to the badness of our circumstances ? and those, I thank
heaven, we have now a favorable prospect of retrieving.
Besides, dear Billy, though my understanding be much in-
ferior to yours, I have sometimes had the happiness of
luckily hitting on some argument which hath afforded you
comfort.   This, you know, my dear, was the case with regard to Colonel James, whom I persuaded you to think
you had mistaken, and you see the event proved me in the
right." So happily, both for herself and Mr. Booth, did
the excellence of this good woman's disposition deceive
her, and force her to see every thing in the most advantage-
ous light to her husband.

The card, being now inspected, was found to contain the
compliments of Mrs. James to Mrs. Booth, with an account
of her being arrived in town, and having brought with her
a very great cold.   Amelia was overjoyed at the news of
her arrival, and having dressed herself in the utmost hurry,
left her children to the care of her husband, and ran away
to pay her respects to her friend, whom she loved with
the most sincere affection.   But how was she disappointed
when, eager with the utmost impatience, and exulting with
the thoughts of presently seeing her beloved friend, she
was answered at the door that the lady was not at home !

nor could she, upon telling her name, obtain any admission. This, considering the account she had received of the lady's cold, greatly surprised her ; and she returned home very much vexed at her disappointment.

Amelia, who had no suspicion that Mrs. James was really at home, and, as the phrase is, was denied, would have made a second visit the next morning, had she not been prevented by a cold which she herself now got, and which was attended with a slight fever. This confined her several days to her house, during which Booth officiated as her nurse, and never stirred from her.

In all this time she heard not a word from Mrs. James, which gave her some uneasiness, but more astonishment. The tenth day, when she was perfectly recovered, about nine in the evening, when she and her husband were just going to supper, she heard a most violent thundering at the door, and presently after a rustling of silk upon her staircase, at the same time a female voice cried out pretty loud, " Bless me ! what, am I to climb up another pair of stairs ?" upon which Amelia, who well knew the voice, presently ran to the door, and ushered in Mrs. James, most splendidly dressed, who put on as formal a countenance, and made as formal a courtesy to her old friend, as if she had been her very distant acquaintance.

Poor Amelia, who was going to rush into her friend's arms, was struck motionless by this behavior ; but re-collecting her spirits, as she had an excellent presence of mind, she presently understood what the lady meant, and resolved to treat her in her own way. Down therefore the company sat, and silence prevailed for some time, during which Mrs. James surveyed the room with more attention than she would have bestowed on one much finer. At length the conversation began, in which the weather and the diversions of the town were well canvassed. Amelia, who was a woman of great humor, performed her part to

admiration ; so that a bystander would have doubted, in
every other article than dress, which of the two was the
most accomplished fine lady.

After a visit of twenty minutes, during which not a
word of any former occurrences was mentioned, nor indeed
any subject of discourse started, except only those two
above mentioned, Mrs. James rose from her chair and
retired in the same formal manner in which she had approached.   We will pursue her for the sake of the contrast
during the rest of the evening.   She went from Amelia
directly to a rout, where she spent two hours in a crowd of
company, talked again and again over the diversions and
news of the town, played two rubbers at whist, and then
retired to her own apartment, where, having passed another
hour in undressing herself, she went to her own bed.

Booth and his wife, the moment their companion was
gone, sat down to supper on a piece of cold meat, the
remains of their dinner.   After which, over a pint of wine,
they entertained themselves for a while with the ridiculous
behavior of their visitant.   But Amelia, declaring she
rather saw her as the object of pity than anger, turned the
discourse to pleasanter topics.   The little actions of their
children, the former scenes and future prospects of their
life, furnished them with many pleasant ideas ; and the
contemplation of Amelia's recovery threw Booth into raptures.   At length they retired, happy in each other.

It is possible some readers may be no less surprised at
the behavior of Mrs. James than was Amelia herself, since
they may have perhaps received so favorable an impression
of that lady from the account given of her by Mr. Booth,
that her present demeanor may seem unnatural and inconsistent with her former character.   But they will be
pleased to consider the great alteration in her circumstances, from a state of dependency on a brother, who was
himself no better than a soldier of fortune, to that of being

wife to a man of a very large estate and considerable rank in life. And what was her present behavior more than that of a fine lady who considered form and show as essential ingredients of human happiness, and imagined all friendship to consist in ceremony, courtesies, messages, and visits ? in which opinion, she hath the honor to think with much the larger part of one sex, and no small number of the other.

CHAPTER VII.

CONTAINING A VERY EXTRAORDINARY AND PLEASANT INCIDENT.

THE next evening Booth and Amelia went to walk in the Park with their children. They were now on the verge of the parade, and Booth was describing to his wife the several buildings around it, when, on a sudden, Amelia, missing her little boy, cried out, " Where's little Billy ?" Upon which Booth, casting his eyes over the grass, saw a foot soldier shaking the boy at a little distance. At this sight, without making any answer to his wife, he leaped over the rails, and, running directly up to the fellow, who had a firelock with a bayonet fixed in his hand, he seized him by the collar and tripped up his heels, and, at the same time, wrested his arms from him. A sergeant upon duty, seeing the affray at some distance, ran presently up, and, being told what had happened, gave the sentinel a hearty curse, and told him he deserved to be hanged. A bystander gave this information ; for Booth was returned with his little boy to meet Amelia, who staggered toward him as fast as she could, all pale and breathless, and scarce able to support her tottering limbs. The sergeant now came up to Booth, to make an apology for the behavior of the soldier, when, of a sudden, he turned almost as pale as Amelia herself. He stood silent whilst Booth was employed in comforting and recovering his wife ; and then, addressing himself to him, said, "Bless me! lieutenant, could I imagine it had been your honor; and was it my little master that the rascal used so? I am glad I did not know it, for I should certainly have run my halbert into him."

Booth presently recognized his old faithful servant Atkinson, and gave him a hearty greeting, saying he was very glad to see him in his present situation. "Whatever I am," answered the sergeant, "I shall always think I owe it to your honor." Then taking the little boy by the hand he cried, "What a vast fine young gentleman master is grown!" and, cursing the soldier's inhumanity, swore heartily he would make him pay for it.

As Amelia was much disordered with her fright, she did not recollect her foster-brother till he was introduced to her by Booth; but she no sooner knew him than she bestowed a most obliging smile on him; and, calling him by the name of honest Joe, said she was heartily glad to see him in England. "See, my dear," cries Booth, "what preferment your old friend is come to. You would scarce know him, I believe, in his present state of finery." "I am very well pleased to see it," answered Amelia, "and I wish him joy of being made an officer with all my heart." In fact, from what Mr. Booth said, joined to the sergeant's laced coat, she believed that he had obtained a commission. So weak and absurd is human vanity, that this mistake of Amelia's possibly put poor Atkinson out of countenance, for he looked at this instant more silly than he had ever done in his life; and, making her a most respectful bow, muttered something about obligations, in a scarce articulate or intelligible manner.

The sergeant had, indeed, among many other qualities, that modesty which a Latin author honors by the name of ingenuous: nature had given him this, notwithstanding the meanness of his birth; and six years' conversation in the army had not taken it away. To say the truth, he was a

noble fellow ; and Amelia, by supposing he had a commission in the guards, had been guilty of no affront to that
honorable body.

Booth had a real affection for Atkinson, though, in fact,
he knew not half his merit. He acquainted him with his
lodgings, where he earnestly desired to see him.

Amelia, who was far from being recovered from the terrors into which the seeing her husband engaged with the
soldier had thrown her, desired to go home : nor was she
well able to walk without some assistance. While she supported herself, therefore, on her husband's arm, she told
Atkinson she should be obliged to him if he would take
care of the children. He readily accepted the office ; but,
upon offering his hand to miss, she refused, and burst into
tears. Upon which the tender mother resigned Booth to
her children, and put herself under the sergeant's protection, who conducted her safe home, though she often declared she feared she should drop down by the way ; the
fear of which so affected the sergeant (for besides the honor
which he himself had for the lady, he knew how tenderly
his friend loved her) that he was unable to speak ; and, had
not his nerves been so strongly braced that nothing could
shake them, he had enough in his mind to have set him a
trembling equally with the lady.

When they arrived at the lodgings the mistress of the
house opened the door, who, seeing Amelia's condition,
threw open the parlor and begged her to walk in, upon
which she immediately flung herself into a chair, and all
present thought she would have fainted away. However,
she escaped that misery, and, having drank a glass of water
with a little white wine mixed in it, she began in a little
time to regain her complexion, and at length assured Booth
that she was perfectly recovered, but declared she had
never undergone so much, and earnestly begged him never
to be so rash for the future. She then called her little boy

and gently chid him, saying, " You must never do so more, Billy ; you see what mischief you might have brought upon your father, and what you have made me suffer." " La ! mamma," said the child, " what harm did I do ? I did not know that people might not walk in the green fields in London. I am sure if I did a fault, the man punished me enough for it, for he pinched me almost through my slender arm." He then bared his little arm, which was greatly discolored by the injury he had received. Booth uttered a most dreadful execration at this sight, and the sergeant, who was now present, did the like.

Atkinson now returned to his guard and went directly to the officer to acquaint him with the soldier's inhumanity, but he, who was about fifteen years of age, gave the sergeant a great curse and said the soldier had done very well, for that idle boys ought to be corrected. This, however, did not satisfy poor Atkinson, who, the next day, as soon as the guard was relieved, beat the fellow most unmercifully, and told him he would remember him as long as he stayed in the regiment.

Thus ended this trifling adventure, which some readers will, perhaps, be pleased at seeing related at full length. None, I think, can fail drawing one observation from it, namely, how capable the most insignificant accident is of disturbing human happiness, and of producing the most unexpected and dreadful events. A reflection which may serve to many moral and religious uses.

This accident produced the first acquaintance between the mistress of the house and her lodgers ; for hitherto they had scarce exchanged a word together. But the great concern which the good woman had shown on Amelia's account at this time, was not likely to pass unobserved or unthanked either by the husband or wife. Amelia, therefore, as soon as she was able to go upstairs, invited Mrs. Ellison (for that was her name) to her apartment, and desired the favor of her stay to supper. She readily complied, and they passed a very agreeable evening together, in which the two women seemed to have conceived a most extraordinary liking to each other.

Though beauty in general doth not greatly recommend one woman to another, as it is too apt to create envy, yet, in cases where this passion doth not interfere, a fine woman is often a pleasing object even to some of her own sex, especially when her beauty is attended with a certain air of affability, as was that of Amelia in the highest degree. She was, indeed, a most charming woman ; and I know not whether the little scar on her nose did not rather add to than diminish her beauty.

Mrs. Ellison, therefore, was as much charmed with the loveliness of her fair lodger as with all her other engaging qualities.   She was, indeed, so taken with Amelia's beauty, that she could not refrain from crying out in a kind of transport of admiration, " Upon my word, Captain Booth, you are the happiest man in the world ! Your lady is so extremely handsome that one cannot look at her without pleasure."

This good woman had herself none of these attractive charms to the eye. Her person was short and immoderately fat ; her features were none of the most regular ; and her complexion (if indeed she ever had a good one) had considerably suffered by time.

Her good humor and complaisance, however, were highly pleasing to Amelia. Nay, why should we conceal the secret satisfaction which that lady felt from the compliments paid to her person ? since such of my readers as like her best will not be sorry to find that she was a woman.

CHAPTER VIII.

CONTAINING VARIOUS MATTERS.

A FORTNIGHT had now passed since Booth had seen or heard from the colonel, which did not a little surprise him, as they had parted so good friends, and as he had so cordially undertaken his cause concerning the memorial on which all his hopes depended.

The uneasiness which this gave him farther increased on finding that his friend refused to see him ; for he had paid the colonel a visit at nine in the morning, and was told he was not stirring ; and at his return back an hour afterward the servant said his master was gone out, of which Booth was certain of the falsehood ; for he had, during that whole hour, walked backward and forward within sight of the colonel's door, and must have seen him if he had gone out within that time.

The good colonel, however, did not long suffer his friend to continue in the deplorable state of anxiety ; for, the very next morning, Booth received his memorial enclosed in a letter, acquainting him that Mr. James had mentioned his affair to the person he proposed, but that the great man had so many engagements on his hands that is was impossible for him to make any further promises at this time.

The cold and distant style of this letter, and, indeed, the whole behavior of James, so different from what it had been formerly, had something so mysterious in it, that it greatly puzzled and perplexed poor Booth ; and it was so long before he was able to solve it, that the reader's curiosity will, perhaps, be obliged to us for not leaving him so long in the dark as to this matter. The true reason, then, of the colonel's conduct was this : his unbounded generosity, together with the unbounded extravagance and consequently the great necessity of Miss Matthews, had at length overcome the cruelty of that lady, with whom he likewise had luckily no rival. Above all, the desire of being revenged on Booth, with whom she was to the highest degree enraged, had, perhaps, contributed not a little to his success ; for she had no sooner condescended to a familiarity with her new lover, and discovered that Captain James, of whom she had heard so much from Booth, was no other than the identical colonel, than she employed every art of which she was mistress to make an utter breach of friendship between these two. For this purpose she did not scruple to insinuate that the colonel was not at all obliged to the character given of him by his friend, and to the account of this latter she placed most of the cruelty which she had shown to the former.

Had the colonel made a proper use of his reason, and fairly examined the probability of the fact, he could scarce have been imposed upon to believe a matter so inconsistent with all he knew of Booth, and in which that gentleman must have sinned against all the laws of honor without any visible temptation. But, in solemn fact, the colonel was so intoxicated with his love, that it was in the power of his mistress to have persuaded him of any thing ; besides, he had an interest in giving her credit, for he was not a little pleased with finding a reason for hating the man whom he could not help hating without any reason, at least without any which he durst fairly assign even to himself. Henceforth, therefore, he abandoned all friendship for Booth, and was more inclined to put him out of the world that to endeavor any longer at supporting him in it.

Booth communicated this letter to his wife, who endeavored, as usual, to the utmost of her power, to console him under one of the greatest afflictions which, I think, can befall a man, namely, the unkindness of a friend ; but he had luckily at the same time the greatest blessing in his possession, the kindness of a faithful and beloved wife. A blessing, however, which, though it compensates most of the evils of life, rather serves to aggravate the misfortune of distressed circumstances, from the consideration of the share which she is to bear in them.

This afternoon Amelia received a second visit from Mrs. Ellison, who acquainted her that she had a present of a ticket for the oratorio, which would carry two persons into the gallery ; and therefore begged the favor of her company thither.

Amelia, with many thanks, acknowledged the civility of Mrs. Ellison, but declined accepting her offer ; upon which Booth very strenuously insisted on her going, and said to her, " My dear, if you knew the satisfaction I have in any of your pleasures, I am convinced you would not refuse the favor Mrs. Ellison is so kind to offer you ; for, as you are a lover of music, you, who have never been at an oratorio, cannot conceive how you will be delighted." " I well know your goodness, my dear," answered Amelia, " but I cannot think of leaving my children without some person more proper to take care of them than this poor girl." Mrs. Ellison removed this objection by offering her own servant, a very discreet matron, to attend them ; but notwithstanding this, and all she could say, with the assistance of Booth, and of the children themselves, Amelia still persisted in her refusal ; and the mistress of the house, who knew how far good breeding allows persons to be pressing on these occasions, took her leave.

She was no sooner departed than Amelia, looking tenderly on her husband, said, " How can you, my dear creature, think that music hath any charms for me at this time ? or, indeed, do you believe that I am capable of any sensation worthy the name of pleasure when neither you nor my children are present or bear any part of it ?"

An officer of the regiment to which Booth had formerly belonged, hearing from Atkinson where he lodged, now

came to pay him a visit. He told him that several of their
old acquaintance were to meet the next Wednesday at a
tavern, and very strongly pressed him to be one of the
company. Booth was, in truth, what is called a hearty fellow, and loved now and then to take a cheerful glass with
his friends ; but he excused himself at this time. His
friend declared he would take no denial, and he growing
very importunate, Amelia at length seconded him. Upon
this Booth answered, " Well, my dear, since you desire
me, I will comply, but on one condition, that you go at the
same time to the oratorio." Amelia thought this request
reasonable enough, and gave her consent ; of which Mrs.
Ellison presently received the news, and with great satisfaction.

It may perhaps be asked why Booth could go to the tavern, and not to the oratorio with his wife ? In truth, then,
the tavern was within hallowed ground—that is to say, in
the verge of the court ; for, of five officers that were to
meet there, three, besides Booth, were confined to that air
which hath been always found extremely wholesome to a
broken military constitution. And here, if the good reader
will pardon the pun, he will scarce be offended at the observation ; since, how is it possible that, without running in
debt, any person should maintain the dress and appearance
of a gentleman whose income is not half so good as that of
a porter ? It is true that this allowance, small as it is, is a
great expense to the public ; but, if several more unnecessary charges were spared, the public might, perhaps, bear a
little increase of this without much feeling it. They would
not, I am sure, have equal reason to complain at contributing to the maintenance of a set of brave fellows who, at the
hazard of their health, their limbs, and their lives, have
maintained the safety and honor of their country, as when
they find themselves taxed to the support of a set of drones
who have not the least merit or claim to their favor, and

who, without contributing in any manner to the good of the hive, live luxuriously on the labors of the industrious bee.

CHAPTER IX.

IN WHICH AMELIA, WITH HER FRIEND, GOES TO THE ORA-
TORIO.

NOTHING happened between the Monday and the Wednesday worthy a place in this history. Upon the evening of the latter the two ladies went to the oratorio, and were there time enough to get a first row in the gallery. Indeed, there was only one person in the house when they came ; for Amelia's inclinations, when she gave a loose to them, were pretty eager for this diversion, she being a great lover of music, and particularly of Mr. Handel's compositions. Mrs. Ellison was, I suppose, a great lover likewise of music, for she was the more impatient of the two ; which was rather the more extraordinary, as these entertainments were not such novelties to her as they were to poor Amelia.

Though our ladies arrived full two hours before they saw the back of Mr. Handel, yet this time of expectation did not hang extremely heavy on their hands ; for, besides their own chat, they had the company of the gentleman whom they found at their first arrival in the gallery, and who, though plainly, or rather roughly dressed, very luckily for the women, happened to be not only well-bred, but a person of very lively conversation. The gentleman, on his part, seemed highly charmed with Amelia, and in fact was so, for, though he restrained himself entirely within the rules of good breeding, yet was he in the highest degree officious to catch at every opportunity of showing his respect, and doing her little services. He procured her a book and wax-candle, and held the candle for her himself during the whole entertainment.

At the end of the oratorio he declared he would not leave the ladies till he had seen them safe into their chairs or coach ; and at the same time very earnestly entreated that he might have the honor of waiting on them. Upon which Mrs. Ellison, who was a very good-humored woman, answered, " Ay, sure, sir, if you please ; you have been very obliging to us ; and a dish of tea shall be at your service at any time ;" and then told him where she lived.

The ladies were no sooner seated in their hackney coach than Mrs. Ellison burst into a loud laughter, and cried, " I'll be hanged, madam, if you have not made a conquest to-night ; and what is very pleasant, I believe the poor gentleman takes you for a single lady." " Nay," answered Amelia very gravely, " I protest I began to think at last he was rather too particular, though he did not venture at a word that I could be offended at ; but, if you fancy any such thing, I am sorry you invited him to drink tea." " Why so ?" replied Mrs. Ellison. " Are you angry with a man for liking you ? if you are, you will be angry with almost every man that sees you. If I was a man myself, I declare I should be in the number of your admirers. Poor gentleman ! I pity him heartily ; he little knows that you have not a heart to dispose of. For my own part, I should not be surprised at seeing a serious proposal of marriage : for I am convinced he is a man of fortune, not only by the politeness of his address, but by the fineness of his linen, and that valuable diamond ring on his finger. But you will see more of him when he comes to tea." " Indeed I shall not," answered Amelia, " though I believe you only rally me ; I hope you have a better opinion of me than to think I would go willingly into the company of a man who had an improper liking for me." Mrs. Ellison, who was one of the gayest women in the world, repeated the words, improper liking, with a laugh ; and cried, " My dear Mrs. Booth, believe me, you are too handsome and too good-

humored for a prude. How can you affect being offended
at what I am convinced is the greatest pleasure of womankind, and chiefly, I believe, of us virtuous women? for, I
assure you, notwithstanding my gayety, I am as virtuous as
any prude in Europe." "Far be it from me, madam,"
said Amelia, "to suspect the contrary of abundance of
women who indulge themselves in much greater freedoms
than I should take, or have any pleasure in taking; for I
solemnly protest, if I know my own heart, the liking of all
men, but of one, is a matter quite indifferent to me, or
rather would be highly disagreeable."

This discourse brought them home, where Amelia, finding her children asleep, and her husband not returned, invited her companion to partake of her homely fare, and
down they sat to supper together. The clock struck
twelve; and, no news being arrived of Booth, Mrs. Ellison
began to express some astonishment at his stay, whence she
launched into a general reflection on husbands, and soon
passed to some particular invectives on her own. "Ah,
my dear madam," says she, "I know the present state of
your mind, by what I have myself often felt formerly. I
am no stranger to the melancholy tone of a midnight
clock. It was my misfortune to drag on a heavy chain
above fifteen years with a sottish yoke-fellow. But how
can I wonder at my fate, since I see even your superior
charms cannot confine a husband from the bewitching
pleasures of a bottle?" "Indeed, madam," says Amelia,
"I have no reason to complain; Mr. Booth is one of the
soberest of men; but now and then to spend a late hour
with his friend, is, I think, highly excusable." "O, no
doubt!" cries Mrs. Ellison, "if he can excuse himself;
but if I was a man——" Here Booth came in and interrupted the discourse. Amelia's eyes flashed with joy the
moment he appeared; and he discovered no less pleasure
in seeing her. His spirits were indeed a little elevated

with wine, so as to heighten his good humor, without in the least disordering his understanding, and made him such delightful company, that, though it was past one in the morning, neither his wife nor Mrs. Ellison thought of their beds during a whole hour.

Early the next morning the sergeant came to Mr. Booth's lodgings, and with a melancholy countenance acquainted him that he had been the night before at an ale-house, where he heard one Mr. Murphy, an attorney, declare that he would get a warrant backed against one Captain Booth at the next board of green-cloth. "I hope, sir," said he, "your honor will pardon me, but, by what he said, I was afraid he meant your honor ; and therefore I thought it my duty to tell you ; for I knew the same thing happen to a gentleman here the other day."

Booth gave Mr. Atkinson many thanks for his information. "I doubt not," said he, "but I am the person meant ; for it would be foolish in me to deny that I am liable to apprehensions of that sort." "I hope, sir," said the sergeant, "your honor will soon have reason to fear no man living ; but in the meantime, if any accident should happen, my bail is at your service as far as it will go ; and I am a housekeeper, and can swear myself worth one hundred pounds." Which hearty and friendly declaration received all those acknowledgments from Booth which it really deserved.

The poor gentleman was greatly alarmed at this news ; but he was altogether as much surprised at Murphy's being the attorney employed against him, as all his debts, except only to Captain James, arose in the country, where he did not know that Mr. Murphy had any acquaintance. However, he made no doubt that he was the person intended, and resolved to remain a close prisoner in his own lodgings, till he saw the event of a proposal which had been made him the evening before at the tavern, where an honest gen-

tleman, who had a post under the government, and who was
one of the company, had promised to serve him with the
secretary at war, telling him that he made no doubt of procuring him whole pay in a regiment abroad, which in his
present circumstances was very highly worth his accept-
ance, when, indeed, that and a jail seemed to be the only
alternatives that offered themselves to his choice.

Mr. Booth and his lady spent that afternoon with Mrs.
Ellison—an incident which we should scarce have mentioned had it not been that Amelia gave, on this occasion,
an instance of that prudence which should never be off its
guard in married women of delicacy ; for before she would
consent to drink tea with Mrs. Ellison, she made conditions
that the gentleman who had met them at the oratorio
should not be let in. Indeed, this circumspection proved
unnecessary in the present instance, for no such visitor ever
came ; a circumstance which gave great content to Amelia ;
for that lady had been a little uneasy at the raillery of Mrs.
Ellison, and had upon reflection magnified every little compliment made her, and every little civility shown her by the
unknown gentleman, far beyond the truth. These imaginations now all subsided again ; and she imputed all that
Mrs. Ellison had said either to raillery or mistake.

A young lady made a fourth with them at whist, and
likewise stayed the whole evening. Her name was Bennet. She was about the age of five-and-twenty ; but sickness had given her an older look, and had a good deal
diminished her beauty ; of which, young as she was, she
plainly appeared to have only the remains in her present
possession. She was in one particular the very reverse of
Mrs. Ellison, being altogether as remarkably grave as the
other was gay. This gravity was not, however, attended
with any sourness of temper ; on the contrary, she had
much sweetness in her countenance, and was perfectly well
bred. In short, Amelia imputed her grave deportment to

her ill health, and began to entertain a compassion for her, which in good minds—that is to say, in minds capable of compassion—is certain to introduce some little degree of love or friendship.

Amelia was in short so pleased with the conversation of this lady, that, though a woman of no impertinent curiosity, she could not help taking the first opportunity of inquiring who she was. Mrs. Ellison said that she was an unhappy lady, who had married a young clergyman for love, who, dying of a consumption, had left her a widow in very indifferent circumstances. This account made Amelia still pity her more, and consequently added to the liking which she had already conceived for her. Amelia, therefore, desired Mrs. Ellison to bring her acquainted with Mrs. Bennet, and said she would go any day with her to make that lady a visit. " There need be no ceremony," cried Mrs. Ellison ; " she is a woman of no form ; and, as I saw plainly she was extremely pleased with Mrs. Booth, I am convinced I can bring her to drink tea with you any afternoon you please."

The two next days Booth continued at home, highly to the satisfaction of his Amelia, who really knew no happiness out of his company, nor scarce any misery in it. She had indeed, at all times, so much of his company, when in his power, that she had no occasion to assign any particular reason for his staying with her, and consequently it could give her no cause of suspicion. The Saturday, one of her children was a little disordered with a feverish complaint which confined her to her room, and prevented her drinking tea in the afternoon with her husband in Mrs. Ellison's apartment, where a noble lord, a cousin of Mrs. Ellison's, happened to be present ; for, though that lady was reduced in her circumstances and obliged to let out part of her house in lodgings, she was born of a good family and had some considerable relations.

His lordship was not himself in any office of state, but

his fortune gave him great authority with those who were. Mrs. Ellison, therefore, very bluntly took an opportunity of recommending Booth to his consideration. She took the first hint from my lord's calling the gentleman captain ; to which she answered, "Ay, I wish your lordship would make him so. It would be an act of justice, and I know it is in your power to do much greater things." She then mentioned Booth's services, and the wounds he had received at the siege, of which she had heard a faithful account from Amelia. Booth blushed, and was as silent as a young virgin at the hearing her own praises. His lordship answered, "Cousin Ellison, you know you may command my interest ; nay, I shall have a pleasure in serving one of Mr. Booth's character ; for my part, I think merit in all capacities ought to be encouraged, but I know the ministry are greatly pestered with solicitations at this time. However, Mr. Booth may be assured I will take the first opportunity ; and in the mean time, I shall be glad of seeing him any morning he pleases." For all these declarations Booth was not wanting in acknowledgments to the generous peer any more than he was in secret gratitude to the lady who had shown so friendly and uncommon a zeal in his favor.

The reader, when he knows the character of this nobleman, may, perhaps, conclude that his seeing Booth alone was a lucky circumstance, for he was so passionate an admirer of women, that he could scarce have escaped the attraction of Amelia's beauty. And few men, as I have observed, have such disinterested generosity as to serve a husband the better because they are in love with his wife, unless she will condescend to pay a price beyond the reach of a virtuous woman.

BOOK V.

CHAPTER I.

Booth's affairs were put on a better aspect than they
had ever worn before, and he was willing to make use of
the opportunity of one day in seven to taste the fresh air.

At nine in the morning he went to pay a visit to his old
friend Colonel James, resolving, if possible, to have a full
explanation of that behavior which appeared to him so mysterious ; but the colonel was as inaccessible as the best de-
fended fortress ; and it was as impossible for Booth to pass
beyond his entry as the Spaniards found it to take Gibraltar. He received the usual answers ; first, that the colonel
was not stirring, and an hour after that he was gone out.
All that he got by asking further questions was only to receive still ruder and ruder answers, by which, if he had
been very sagacious, he might have been satisfied how little
worth his while it was to desire to go in ; for the porter at
a great man's door is a kind of thermometer, by which you
may discover the warmth or coldness of his master's friendship. Nay, in the highest stations of all, as the great man
himself hath his different kinds of salutation, from an
hearty embrace with a kiss, and my dear lord or dear Sir
Charles, down to, well Mr ——, what would you have me
do ? so the porter to some bows with respect to others with
a smile, to some he bows more, to others less low, to others

not at all. Some he just lets in, and others he just shuts out. And in all this they so well correspond, that one would be inclined to think that the great man and his porter had compared their lists together, and, like two actors concerned to act different parts in the same scene, had rehearsed their parts privately together before they ventured to perform in public.

Though Booth did not, perhaps, see the whole matter in this just light, for that in reality it is, yet he was discerning enough to conclude, from the behavior of the servant, especially when he considered that of the master likewise, that he had entirely lost the friendship of James; and this conviction gave him a concern that not only the flattering prospect of his lordship's favor was not able to compensate, but which even obliterated, and made him for a while forget the situation in which he had left his Amelia; and he wandered about almost two hours, scarce knowing where he went, till at last he dropped into a coffee-house near St. James's, where he sat himself down.

He had scarce drank his dish of coffee before he heard a young officer of the guards cry to another, " Od, d—n me, Jack, here he comes—here's old honor and dignity, faith.'' Upon which he saw a chair open, and out issued a most erect and stately figure indeed, with a vast periwig on his head, and a vast hat under his arm. This august personage, having entered the room, walked directly up to the upper end, where having paid his respects to all present of any note, to each according to seniority, he at last cast his eyes on Booth, and very civilly, though somewhat coldly, asked him how he did.

Booth, who had long recognized the features of his old acquaintance Major Bath, returned the compliment with a very low bow; but did not venture to make the first advance to familiarity, as he was truly possessed of that quality which the Greeks considered in the highest light of honor, and which we term modesty; though indeed neither ours nor the Latin language hath any word adequate to the idea of the original.

The colonel, after having discharged himself of two or three articles of news, and made his comments upon them, when the next chair to him became vacant, called upon Booth to fill it. He then asked him several questions relating to his affairs; and, when he heard he was out of the army, advised him earnestly to use all means to get in again, saying that he was a pretty lad, and they must not lose him.

Booth told him in a whisper that he had a great deal to say to him on that subject if they were in a more private place; upon this the colonel proposed a walk in the Park, which the other readily accepted.

During their walk Booth opened his heart, and, among other matters, acquainted Colonel Bath that he feared he had lost the friendship of Colonel James; "though I am not," said he, "conscious of having done the least thing to deserve it."

Bath answered, "You are certainly mistaken, Mr. Booth. I have indeed scarce seen my brother since my coming to town; for I have been here but two days; however, I am convinced he is a man of too nice honor to do any thing inconsistent with the true dignity of a gentleman." Booth answered, "He was far from accusing him of any thing dishonorable." "D—m me," said Bath, "if there is a man alive can or dare accuse him: if you have the least reason to take any thing ill, why don't you go to him? you are a gentleman, and his rank doth not protect him from giving you satisfaction." "The affair is not of any such kind," says Booth; "I have great obligations to the colonel, and have more reason to lament than complain; and, if I could but see him, I am convinced I should have no cause for either; but I cannot get within his house; it was but an hour ago a servant of his turned me rudely from the door." "Did a servant of my brother use you rudely?" said the colonel, with the utmost gravity. "I do not know, sir, in what light you see such things; but, to me, the affront of a servant is the affront of the master; and if he doth not immediately punish it, by all the dignity of a man, I would see the master's nose between my fingers." Booth offered to explain, but to no purpose; the colonel was got into his stilts; and it was impossible to take him down, nay, it was as much as Booth could possibly do to part with him without an actual quarrel; nor would he, perhaps, have been able to have accomplished it, had not the colonel by accident turned at last to take Booth's side of the question; and before they separated he swore many oaths that James should give him proper satisfaction.

Such was the end of this present interview, so little to the content of Booth, that he was heartily concerned he had ever mentioned a syllable of the matter to his honorable friend.

[This chapter occurs in the original edition of Amelia, between the chapters numbered 1 and 2. It is omitted in Murphy's and all subsequent editions. Some slight alterations were made by the author on its omission in the text of the adjoining chapters to render the narrative consecutive. These have been retained here. See note in Biography prefixed to Joseph Andrews.

CONTAINING A BRACE OF DOCTORS AND MUCH PHYSICAL MATTER.

HE now returned with all his uneasiness to Amelia, whom he found in a condition very little adapted to relieve or comfort him. That poor woman was now indeed under very great apprehensions for her child, whose fever now began to rage very violently; and what was worse, an apothecary had been with her, and frightened her almost out of her wits. He had indeed represented the case of the child to be very desperate, and had prevailed on the mother to call in the assistance of a doctor.

Booth had been a very little time in the room before this doctor arrived, with the apothecary close at his heels, and both approached the bed, where the former felt the pulse of the sick, and performed several other physical ceremonies.

He then began to inquire of the apothecary what he had already done for the patient ; all which, as soon as informed, he greatly approved. The doctor then sat down, called for a pen and ink, filled a whole side of a sheet of paper with physic, then took a guinea, and took his leave ; the apothecary waiting upon him downstairs, as he had attended him up.

All that night both Amelia and Booth sat up with their child, who rather grew worse than better. In the morning Mrs. Ellison found the infant in a raging fever, burning hot, and very light-headed, and the mother under the highest dejection ; for the distemper had not given the least ground to all the efforts of the apothecary and doctor, but seemed to defy their utmost power, with all that tremendous apparatus of phials and gallypots, which were arranged in battle array all over the room.

Mrs. Ellison, seeing the distressed, and indeed distracted, condition of Amelia's mind, attempted to comfort her by giving her hopes of the child's recovery. "Upon my word, madam," says she, "I saw a child of much the same age with miss, who, in my opinion, was much worse, restored to health in a few days by a physician of my acquaintance. Nay, I have known him cure several others of very bad fevers ; and, if miss was under his care, I dare swear she would do very well." "Good heavens ! madam," answered Amelia, "why should you not mention him to me ? For my part I have no acquaintance with any London physicians, nor do I know whom the apothecary hath brought me." "Nay, madam," cries Mrs. Ellison, "it is a tender thing, you know, to recommend a physician; and as for my doctor, there are abundance of people who give him an ill name. Indeed, it is true, he hath cured me twice of fevers, and so he hath several others to my knowledge; nay, I never heard of any more than one of his patients that died; and yet, as the doctors and apothecaries all give him an ill character, one is fearful, you know, dear madam." Booth inquired the doctor's name, which he no sooner heard than he begged his wife to send for him immediately, declaring he had heard the highest character imaginable of him at the Tavern from an officer of very good understanding. Amelia presently complied, and a messenger was dispatched accordingly.

But before the second doctor could be brought, the first returned with the apothecary attending him as before. He again surveyed and handled the sick; and when Amelia begged him to tell her if there was any hopes, he shook his head, and said, "To be sure, madam, miss is in a very dangerous condition and there is no time to lose. If the blisters which I shall now order her should not relieve her, I fear we can do no more." "Would not you please, sir," says the apothecary, "to have the powders and the draught repeated?" "How often were they ordered?" cries the doctor. "Only *tertia* quaq. horâ," says the apothecary. "Let them be taken every hour by all means," cries the doctor; "and—let me see, pray get me a pen and ink." "If you think the child in such imminent danger," said Booth, "would you give us leave to call in another physician to your assistance—indeed my wife——" "Oh, by all means," said the doctor, "it is what I very much wish. Let me see, Mr. Arsenic, whom shall we call?" "What do you think of Dr. Dosewell?" said the apothecary. "Nobody better," cries the physician. "I should have no objection to the gentleman," answered

Booth, "but another hath been recommended to my wife."
He then mentioned the physician for whom they had just
before sent. "Who, sir?" cries the doctor, dropping his
pen; and when Booth repeated the name of Thompson,
"Excuse me, sir," cries the doctor, hastily, "I shall not
meet him." "Why so, sir?" answered Booth. "I will
not meet him," replied the doctor. "Shall I meet a man
who pretends to know more than the whole College, and
would overturn the whole method of practice, which is so
well established, and from which no one person hath pretended to deviate?" "Indeed, sir," cries the apothecary,
"you do not know what you are about, asking your pardon; why he kills everybody he comes near." "That is
not true," said Mrs. Ellison. "I have been his patient
twice, and I am alive yet." "You have had good luck,
then, madam," answered the apothecary, "for he kills
everybody he comes near." "Nay, I know above a dozen
others of my own acquaintance," replied Mrs. Ellison, "who
have all been cured by him." "That may be, madam,"
cries Arsenic; "but he kills everybody for all that—why,
madam, did you never hear of Mr. ——? I can't think
of the gentleman's name, though he was a man of great
fashion; but everybody knows whom I mean." "Everybody, indeed, must know whom you mean," answered Mrs.
Ellison; "for I never heard but of one, and that many
years ago."

Before the dispute was ended, the doctor himself entered
the room. As he was a very well-bred and very good-
natured man, he addressed himself with much civility to
his brother physician, who was not quite so courteous on
his side. However, he suffered the new-comer to be conducted to the sick-bed, and at Booth's earnest request to
deliver his opinion.

The dispute which ensued between the two physicians
would, perhaps, be unintelligible to any but those of the

faculty, and not very entertaining to them. The character which the officer and Mrs. Ellison had given of the second doctor had greatly prepossessed Booth in his favor, and indeed his reasoning seemed to be the juster. Booth therefore declared that he would abide by his advice, upon which the former operator, with his zany, the apothecary, quitted the field, and left the other in full possession of the sick.

The first thing the new doctor did was (to use his own phrase) to blow up the physical magazine. All the powders and potions instantly disappeared at his command ; for he said there was a much readier and nearer way to convey such stuff to the vault than by first sending it through the human body. He then ordered the child to be blooded, gave it a clyster and some cooling physic, and, in short (that I may not dwell too long on so unpleasing a part of history), within three days cured the little patient of her distemper, to the great satisfaction of Mrs. Ellison, and to the vast joy of Amelia.

Some readers will, perhaps, think this whole chapter might have been omitted ; but though it contains no great matter of amusement, it may at least serve to inform posterity concerning the present state of physic.]

CHAPTER II.

IN WHICH BOOTH PAYS A VISIT TO THE NOBLE LORD.

WHEN that day of the week returned in which Mr. Booth chose to walk abroad, he went to wait on the noble peer, according to his kind invitation.

Booth now found a very different reception with this great man's porter from what he had met with at his friend the colonel's. He no sooner told his name than the porter with a bow told him his lordship was at home : the door immediately flew wide open, and he was conducted to an antechamber, where a servant told him he would acquaint his lordship with his arrival. Nor did he wait many minutes before the same servant returned and ushered him to his lordship's apartment.

He found my lord alone, and was received by him in the most courteous manner imaginable. After the first ceremonials were over, his lordship began in the following words : " Mr. Booth, I do assure you, you are very much obliged to my cousin Ellison. She hath given you such a character, that I shall have a pleasure in doing any thing in my power to serve you. But it will be very difficult, I am afraid, to get you a rank at home. In the West Indies, perhaps, or in some regiment abroad, it may be more easy ; and, when I consider your reputation as a soldier, I make no doubt of your readiness to go to any place where the service of your country shall call you." Booth answered, " That he was highly obliged to his lordship, and assured him he would with great cheerfulness attend his duty in any part of the world. The only thing grievous in the exchange of countries," said he, " in my opinion, is to leave those I love behind me, and I am sure I shall never have a second trial equal to my first. It was very hard, my lord, to leave a young wife big with her first child, and so affected with my absence, that I had the utmost reason to despair of ever seeing her more. After such a demonstration of my resolution to sacrifice every other consideration to my duty, I hope your lordship will honor me with some confidence that I shall make no objection to serve in any country." " My dear Mr. Booth," answered the lord, " you speak like a soldier, and 1 greatly honor your sentiments. Indeed, I own the justice of your inference from the example you have given ; for to quit a wife, as you say, in the very infancy of marriage, is, I acknowledge, some trial of resolution." Booth answered with a low bow ; and then, after some immaterial conversation, his lordship promised to speak immediately to the minister, and appointed Mr.

Booth to come to him again on the Wednesday morning, that he might be acquainted with his patron's success. The poor man now blushed and looked silly, till, after some time, he summoned up all his courage to his assistance, and relying on the other's friendship, he opened the whole affair of his circumstances, and confessed that he did not dare stir from his lodgings above one day in seven. His lordship expressed great concern at this account, and very kindly promised to take some opportunity of calling on him at his cousin Ellison's, when he hoped, he said, to bring him comfortable tidings.

Booth soon afterward took his leave with the most profuse acknowledgments for so much goodness, and hastened home to acquaint his Amelia with what had so greatly overjoyed him. She highly congratulated him on his having found so generous and powerful a friend, toward whom both their bosoms burnt with the warmest sentiments of gratitude. She was not, however, contented till she had made Booth renew his promise, in the most solemn manner, of taking her with him. After which they sat down with their little children to a scrag of mutton and broth, with the highest satisfaction, and very heartily drank his lordship's health in a pot of porter.

In the afternoon this happy couple, if the reader will allow me to call poor people happy, drank tea with Mrs. Ellison, where his lordship's praises, being again repeated by both the husband and wife, were very loudly echoed by Mrs. Ellison. While they were here, the young lady whom we have mentioned at the end of the last book to have made a fourth at whist, and with whom Amelia seemed so much pleased, came in ; she was just returned to town from a short visit in the country, and her present visit was unexpected. It was, however, very agreeable to Amelia, who liked her still better upon a second interview, and was resolved to solicit her further acquaintance.

Mrs. Bennet still maintained some little reserve, but was much more familiar and communicative than before. She appeared, moreover, to be as little ceremonious as Mrs. Ellison had reported her, and very readily accepted Amelia's apology for not paying her the first visit, and agreed to drink tea with her the very next afternoon.

Whilst the above - mentioned company were sitting in Mrs. Ellison's parlor, Sergeant Atkinson passed by the window and knocked at the door. Mrs. Ellison no sooner saw him than she said, "Pray, Mr. Booth, who is that genteel young sergeant? he was here every day last week to inquire after you." This was indeed a fact; the sergeant was apprehensive of the design of Murphy; but, as the poor fellow had received all his answers from the maid of Mrs. Ellison, Booth had never heard a word of the matter. He was, however, greatly pleased with what he was now told, and burst forth into great praises of the sergeant, which were seconded by Amelia, who added that he was her foster-brother, and, she believed, one of the honestest fellows in the world.

"And I'll swear," cries Mrs. Ellison, "he is one of the prettiest. Do, Mr. Booth, desire him to walk in. A sergeant of the guards is a gentleman; and I had rather give such a man as you describe a dish of tea than any Beau Fribble of them all."

Booth wanted no great solicitation to show any kind of regard to Atkinson; and, accordingly, the sergeant was ushered in, though not without some reluctance on his side. There is, perhaps, nothing more uneasy than those sensations which the French call the *mauvaise honte*, nor any more difficult to conquer; and poor Atkinson would, I am persuaded, have mounted a breach with less concern than he showed in walking across a room before three ladies, two of whom were his avowed well-wishers.

Though I do not entirely agree with the late learned Mr.

Essex, the celebrated dancing-master's opinion, that dancing is the rudiment of polite education, as he would, I apprehend, exclude every other art and science, yet it is certain that persons whose feet have never been under the hands of the professors of that art are apt to discover this want in their education in every motion, nay, even when they stand or sit still. They seem, indeed, to be overburdened with limbs which they know not how to use, as if, when Nature hath finished her work, the dancing-master still is necessary to put it in motion.

Atkinson was, at present, an example of this observation which doth so much honor to a profession for which I have a very high regard. He was handsome, and exquisitely well made ; and yet, as he had never learned to dance, he made so awkward an appearance in Mrs. Ellison's parlor, that the good lady herself, who had invited him in, could at first scarce refrain from laughter at his behavior. He had not, however, been long in the room before admiration of his person got the better of such risible ideas. So great is the advantage of beauty in men as well as women, and so sure is this quality in either sex of procuring some regard from the beholder.

The exceeding courteous behavior of Mrs. Ellison, joined to that of Amelia and Booth, at length dissipated the uneasiness of Atkinson ; and he gained sufficient confidence to tell the company some entertaining stories of accidents that had happened in the army within his knowledge, which, though they greatly pleased all present, are not, however, of consequence enough to have a place in this history.

Mrs. Ellison was so very importunate with her company to stay supper that they all consented. As for the sergeant, he seemed to be none of the least welcome guests. She was, indeed, so pleased with what she had heard of him, and what she saw of him, that, when a little warmed with wine, for she was no flincher at the bottle, she began to indulge some freedoms in her discourse toward him that a little offended Amelia's delicacy—nay, they did not seem to be highly relished by the other lady ; though I am far from insinuating that these exceeded the bounds of decorum, or were, indeed, greater liberties than ladies of the middle age, and especially widows, do frequently allow to themselves.

CHAPTER III.

RELATING PRINCIPALLY TO THE AFFAIRS OF SERGEANT ATKINSON.

THE next day, when all the same company, Atkinson only excepted, assembled in Amelia's apartment, Mrs. Ellison presently began to discourse of him, and that in terms not only of approbation, but even of affection. She called him her clever sergeant, and her dear sergeant, repeated often that he was the prettiest fellow in the army, and said it was a thousand pities he had not a commission ; for that, if he had, she was sure he would become a general.

"I am of your opinion, madam," answered Booth ; " and he hath got one hundred pounds of his own already, if he could find a wife now to help him to two or three hundred more, I think he might easily get a commission in a marching regiment ; for I am convinced there is no colonel in the army would refuse him."

"Refuse him, indeed !" said Mrs. Ellison ; "no ; he would be a very pretty colonel that did. And, upon my honor, I believe there are very few ladies who would refuse him, if he had but a proper opportunity of soliciting them. The colonel and the lady both would be better off than with one of those pretty masters that I see walking about, and dragging their long swords after them, when they should rather drag their leading-strings."

"Well said," cries Booth, " and spoken like a woman

of spirit.   Indeed, I believe, they would be both better
served.

"True, captain," answered Mrs. Ellison ; "I would
rather leave the two first syllables out of the word gentleman than the last."

"Nay, I assure you," replied Booth, "there is not a
quieter creature in the world.   Though the fellow hath the
bravery of a lion, he hath the meekness of a lamb.   I can
tell you stories enow of that kind, and so can my dear
Amelia, when he was a boy."

"Oh ! if the match sticks there," cries Amelia, "I positively will not spoil his fortune by my silence.   I can answer for him from his infancy, that he was one of the best-
natured lads in the world.   I will tell you a story or two of
him, the truth of which I can testify from my own knowledge.   When he was but six years old he was at play with
me at my mother's house, and a great pointer-dog bit him
through the leg.   The poor lad, in the midst of the anguish
of his wound, declared he was overjoyed it had not happened to miss (for the same dog had just before snapped at
me, and my petticoats had been my defence).   Another instance of his goodness, which greatly recommended him to
my father, and which I have loved him for ever since, was
this : My father was a great lover of birds, and strictly
forbade the spoiling of their nests.   Poor Joe was one day
caught upon a tree, and, being concluded guilty, was
severely lashed for it ; but it was afterward discovered
that another boy, a friend of Joe's, had robbed the nest of
its young ones, and poor Joe had climbed the tree in order
to restore them, notwithstanding which, he submitted to the
punishment rather than he would impeach his companion.
But, if these stories appear childish and trifling, the duty
and kindness he hath shown to his mother must recommend
him to every one.   Ever since he hath been fifteen years
old he hath more than half supported her : and when my

brother died, I remember particularly, Joe, at his desire, for he was much his favorite, had one of his suits given him ; but, instead of his becoming finer on that occasion, another young fellow came to church in my brother's clothes, and my old nurse appeared the same Sunday in a new gown, which her son had purchased for her with the sale of his legacy."

" Well, I protest, he is a very worthy creature," said Mrs. Bennet.

" He is a charming fellow," cries Mrs. Ellison, " but then the name of sergeant, Captain Booth ; there, as the play says, my pride brings me off again."

> And whatsoever the sages charge on pride,
> The angels' fall, and twenty other good faults beside ;
> On earth I'm sure—I'm sure—something—calling
> Pride saves man, and our sex too, from falling.

Here a footman's rap at the door shook the room. Upon which Mrs. Ellison, running to the window, cried out, " Let me die if it is not my lord ! what shall I do ? I must be at home to him ; but suppose he should inquire for you, captain, what shall I say ? or will you go down with me ?"

The company were in some confusion at this instant, and before they had agreed on any thing, Booth's little girl came running into the room, and said, " There was a prodigious great gentleman coming upstairs." She was immediately followed by his lordship, who, as he knew Booth must be at home, made very little or no inquiry at the door.

Amelia was taken somewhat at a surprise, but she was too polite to show much confusion ; for, though she knew nothing of the town, she had had a genteel education, and kept the best company the country afforded. The ceremonies therefore passed as usual, and they all sat down.

His lordship soon addressed himself to Booth, saying, " As I have what I think good news for you, sir, I could not delay giving myself the pleasure of communicating it to you. I have mentioned your affair where I promised you, and I have no doubt of my success. One may easily perceive, you know, from the manner of people's behaving upon such occasions ; and, indeed, when I related your case, I found there was much inclination to serve you. Great men, Mr. Booth, must do things in their own time ; but I think you may depend on having something done very soon."

Booth made many acknowledgments for his lordship's goodness, and now a second time paid all the thanks which would have been due, even had the favor been obtained. This art of promising is the economy of a great man's pride, a sort of good husbandry in conferring favors, by which they receive tenfold in acknowledgments for every obligation, I mean among those who really intend the service ; for there are others who cheat poor men of their thanks, without ever designing to deserve them at all.

This matter being sufficiently discussed, the conversation took a gayer turn ; and my lord began to entertain the ladies with some of that elegant discourse which, though most delightful to hear, it is impossible should ever be read.

His lordship was so highly pleased with Amelia that he could not help being somewhat particular to her ; but this particularity distinguished itself only in a higher degree of respect, and was so very polite, and so very distant, that she herself was pleased, and at his departure, which was not till he had far exceeded the length of a common visit, declared he was the finest gentleman she had ever seen ; with which sentiment her husband and Mrs. Ellison both entirely concurred.

Mrs. Bennet, on the contrary, expressed some little dislike to my lord's complaisance, which she called excessive. " For my part," said she, " I have not the least relish for those very fine gentlemen ; what the world generally calls politeness, I term insincerity ; and I am more charmed

with the stories which Mrs. Booth told us of the honest
sergeant than with all that the finest gentlemen in the world
ever said in their lives !"

" O ! to be sure," cries Mrs. Ellison ; " ' *All for Love,
or the World well Lost,*' is a motto very proper for some
folks to wear in their coat of arms ; but the generality of
the world will, I believe, agree with that lady's opinion of
my cousin, rather than with Mrs. Bennet."

Mrs. Bennet, seeing Mrs. Ellison took offence at what she
said, thought proper to make some apology, which was very
readily accepted, and so ended the visit.

We cannot however put an end to the chapter without
observing that such is the ambitious temper of beauty, that
it may always apply to itself that celebrated passage in
Lucan,

> *Nec quenquam jam ferre potest Cæsarve priorem,*
> *Pompeiusve parem.*

Indeed, I believe, it may be laid down as a general rule,
that no woman who hath any great pretensions to admiration is every well pleased in a company where she perceives
herself to fill only the second place. This observation,
however, I humbly submit to the judgment of the ladies,
and hope it will be considered as retracted by me if they
shall dissent from my opinion.

CHAPTER IV.

CONTAINING MATTERS THAT REQUIRE NO PREFACE.

WHEN Booth and his wife were left alone together they
both extremely exulted in their good fortune in having
found so good a friend as his lordship ; nor were they wanting in very warm expressions of gratitude toward Mrs.
Ellison. After which they began to lay down schemes of
living when Booth should have his commission of captain ;
and, after the exactest computation, concluded that, with

economy, they should be able to save at least fifty pounds a year out of their income in order to pay their debts.

These matters being well settled, Amelia asked Booth what he thought of Mrs. Bennet? "I think, my dear," answered Booth, "that she hath been formerly a very pretty woman." "I am mistaken," replied she, "if she be not a very good creature. I don't know I ever took such a liking to any one on so short an acquaintance. I fancy she hath been a very sprightly woman; for, if you observe, she discovers by starts a great vivacity in her countenance." "I made the same observation," cries Booth: "sure some strange misfortune hath befallen her." "A misfortune, indeed!" answered Amelia; "sure, child, you forget what Mrs. Ellison told us, that she had lost a beloved husband. A misfortune which I have often wondered at any woman's surviving." At which words she cast a tender look at Booth, and presently afterward, throwing herself upon his neck, cried, "Oh, heavens! what a happy creature am I! when I consider the dangers you have gone through, how I exult in my bliss!" The good-natured reader will suppose that Booth was not deficient in returning such tenderness, after which the conversation became too fond to be here related.

The next morning Mrs. Ellison addressed herself to Booth as follows: "I shall make no apology, sir, for what I am going to say, as it proceeds from my friendship to yourself and your dear lady. I am convinced then, sir, there is something more than accident in your going abroad only one day in the week. Now, sir, if, as I am afraid, matters are not altogether as well as I wish them, I beg, since I do not believe you are provided with a lawyer, that you will suffer me to recommend one to you. The person I shall mention is, I assure you, of much ability in his profession, and I have known him do great services to gentlemen under a cloud. Do not be ashamed of your circumstances, my dear friend : they are a much greater scandal to those who have left so much merit unprovided for."

Booth gave Mrs. Ellison abundance of thanks for her kindness, and explicitly confessed to her that her conjectures were right, and, without hesitation, accepted the offer of her friend's assistance.

Mrs. Ellison then acquainted him with her apprehensions on his account. She said she had both yesterday and this morning seen two or three very ugly suspicious fellows pass several times by her window. " Upon all accounts," said she, " my dear sir, I advise you to keep yourself close confined till the lawyer hath been with you. I am sure he will get you your liberty, at least of walking about within the verge. There's something to be done with the board of green-cloth ; I don't know what ; but this I know, that several gentlemen have lived here a long time very comfortably, and have defied all the vengeance of their creditors. However, in the meantime, you must be a close prisoner with your lady ; and I believe there is no man in England but would exchange his liberty for the same jail."

She then departed in order to send for the attorney, and presently afterward the sergeant arrived with news of the like kind. He said he had scraped an acquaintance with Murphy. " I hope your honor will pardon me," cries Atkinson, " but I pretended to have a small demand upon your honor myself, and offered to employ him in the business. Upon which he told me that, if I would go with him to the Marshal's court, and make affidavit of my debt, he should be able very shortly to get it me ; ' for I shall have the captain in hold,' cries he, ' within a day or two.' I wish," said the sergeant, " I could do your honor any service. Shall I walk about all day before the door ? or shall I be porter, and watch it in the inside till your honor can find some means of securing yourself ? I hope you will not

be offended at me, but I beg you would take care of falling
into Murphy's hands; for he hath the character of the
greatest villain upon earth. I am afraid you will think me
too bold, sir; but I have a little money; if it can be of any
service, do, pray your honor, command it. It can never
do me so much good any other way. Consider, sir, I owe
all I have to yourself and my dear mistress.''

Booth stood a moment, as if he had been thunderstruck,
and then, the tears bursting from his eyes, he said, '' Upon
my soul, Atkinson, you overcome me. I scarce ever heard
of so much goodness, nor do I know how to express my
sentiments of it. But, be assured, as for your money, I
will not accept it; and let it satisfy you, that in my present
circumstances it would do me no essential service; but this
be assured of likewise, that whilst I live I shall never forget
the kindness of the offer. However, as I apprehend I may
be in some danger of fellows getting into the house, for a
day or two, as I have no guard but a poor little girl, I will
not refuse the goodness you offer to show in my protection.
And I make no doubt but Mrs. Ellison will let you sit in
her parlor for that purpose.''

Atkinson, with the utmost readiness, undertook the office
of porter; and Mrs. Ellison as readily allotted him a place
in her back-parlor, where he continued three days together,
from eight in the morning till twelve at night; during
which time, he had sometimes the company of Mrs. Ellison, and sometimes of Booth, Amelia, and Mrs. Bennet
too; for this last had taken as great a fancy to Amelia as
Amelia had to her, and, therefore, as Mr. Booth's affairs
were now no secret in the neighborhood, made her frequent
visits during the confinement of her husband, and consequently her own.

Nothing, as I remember, happened in this interval of
time more worthy of notice than the following card which
Amelia received from her old acquaintance Mrs. James:

"Mrs. James sends her compliments to Mrs. Booth, and desires to know how she does ; for, as she hath not had the favor of seeing her at her own house, or of meeting her in any public place, in so long time, fears it may be owing to ill health."

Amelia had long given over all thoughts of her friend, and doubted not but that she was as entirely given over by her ; she was very much surprised at this message, and under some doubt whether it was not meant as an insult, especially from the mention of public places, which she thought so inconsistent with her present circumstances, of which she supposed Mrs. James was well apprized. However, at the entreaty of her husband, who languished for nothing more than to be again reconciled to his friend James, Amelia undertook to pay the lady a visit, and to examine into the mystery of this conduct, which appeared to her so unaccountable.

Mrs. James received her with a degree of civility that amazed Amelia no less than her coldness had done before. She resolved to come to an eclaircissement, and, having sat out some company that came in, when they were alone together Amelia, after some silence and many offers to speak, at last said, "My dear Jenny (if you will now suffer me to call you by so familiar a name), have you entirely forgot a certain young lady who had the pleasure of being your intimate acquaintance at Montpelier?" "Whom do you mean, dear madam?" cries Mrs. James with great concern. "I mean myself," answered Amelia. "You surprise me, madam," replied Mrs. James : "How can you ask me that question?" "Nay, my dear, I do not intend to offend you," cries Amelia, "but I am really desirous to solve to myself the reason of that coldness which you showed me when you did me the favor of a visit. Can you think, my dear, I was not disappointed, when I expected to meet an intimate friend, to receive a cold formal visitant? I desire you to examine your own heart and answer me honestly if you do not think I had some little reason to be dissatisfied with your behavior?" "Indeed, Mrs. Booth," answered the other lady, "you surprise me very much; if there was any thing displeasing to you in my behavior I am extremely concerned at it. I did not know I had been defective in any of the rules of civility, but if I was, madam, I ask your pardon." "Is civility, then, my dear," replied Amelia, "a synonymous term with friendship? Could I have expected, when I parted the last time with Miss Jenny Bath, to have met her the next time in the shape of a fine lady, complaining of the hardship of climbing up two pair of stairs to visit me, and then approaching me with the distant air of a new or a slight acquaintance? Do you think, my dear Mrs. James, if the tables had been turned, if my fortune had been as high in the world as yours, and you in my distress and abject condition, that I would not have climbed as high as the monument to visit you?" "Sure, madam," cried Mrs. James, "I mistake you, or you have greatly mistaken me. Can you complain of my not visiting you, who have owed me a visit almost these three weeks? Nay, did I not even then send you a card, which sure was doing more than all the friendship and good breeding in the world required; but, indeed, as I had met you in no public place, I really thought you was ill."

"How can you mention public places to me," said Amelia, "when you can hardly be a stranger to my present situation? Did you not know, madam, that I was ruined?" "No, indeed, madam, did I not," replied Mrs. James; "I am sure I should have been highly concerned if I had." "Why, sure, my dear," cries Amelia, "you could not imagine that we were in affluent circumstances, when you found us in such a place, and in such a condition." "Nay, my dear," answered Mrs. James, "since you are pleased to mention it first yourself, I own I was a little surprised to see you in no better lodgings ; but I concluded you had your own reasons for liking them ; and, for my own part, I have laid it down as a positive rule never to inquire into the private affairs of any one, especially of my friends. I am not of the humor of some ladies, who confine the circle of their acquaintance to one part of the town, and would not be known to visit in the city for the world. For my part, I never dropped an acquaintance with any one while it was reputable to keep it up ; and I can solemnly declare I have not a friend in the world for whom I have a greater esteem than I have for Mrs. Booth.''

At this instant the arrival of a new visitant put an end to the discourse ; and Amelia soon after took her leave without the least anger, but with some little unavoidable contempt for a lady, in whose opinion, as we have hinted before, outward form and ceremony constituted the whole essence of friendship ; who valued all her acquaintance alike, as each individual served equally to fill up a place in her visiting roll ; and who, in reality, had not the least concern for the good qualities or well-being of any of them.

CHAPTER V.

CONTAINING MUCH HEROIC MATTER.

At the end of three days Mrs. Ellison's friend had so far purchased Mr. Booth's liberty that he could walk again abroad within the verge without any danger of having a warrant backed against him by the board before he had notice. As for the ill-looked persons that had given the alarm, it was now discovered that another unhappy gentleman, and not Booth, was the object of their pursuit.

Mr. Booth, now being delivered from his fears, went, as he had formerly done, to take his morning walk in the Park. Here he met Colonel Bath in company with some other officers, and very civilly paid his respects to him.

But, instead of returning the salute, the colonel looked him full in the face with a very stern countenance ; and, if he could be said to take any notice of him, it was in such a manner as to inform him he would take no notice of him.

Booth was not more hurt than surprised at this behavior, and resolved to know the reason of it. He therefore watched an opportunity till the colonel was alone, and then walked boldly up to him, and desired to know if he had given him any offence? The colonel answered hastily, " Sir, I am above being offended with you, nor do I think it consistent with my dignity to make you any answer." Booth replied, " I don't know, sir, that I have done any thing to deserve this treatment." " Look'ee, sir," cries the colonel, " if I had not formerly had some respect for you, I should not think you worth my resentment. However, as you are a gentleman born, and an officer, and as I have had an esteem for you, I will give you some marks of it by putting it in your power to do yourself justice. I will tell you therefore, sir, that you have acted like a scoundrel." " If we were not in the Park," answered Booth warmly, " I would thank you very properly for that compliment." " O sir," cries the colonel, " we can be soon in a convenient place." Upon which Booth answered, he would attend him wherever he pleased. The colonel then bid him come along, and strutted forward directly up Constitution Hill to Hyde Park, Booth following him at first, and afterward walking before him, till they came to that place which may be properly called the field of blood, being that part, a little to the left of the ring, which heroes have chosen for the scene of their exit out of this world.

Booth reached the ring some time before the colonel ; for he mended not his pace any more than a Spaniard. To say truth, I believe it was not in his power : for he had so long accustomed himself to one and the same strut, that as a horse, used always to trotting, can scarce be forced into a gallop, so could no passion force the colonel to alter his pace.

At length, however, both parties arrived at the lists, where the colonel very deliberately took off his wig and coat, and laid them on the grass, and then, drawing his sword, advanced to Booth, who had likewise his drawn weapon in his hand, but had made no other preparation for the combat.

The combatants now engaged with great fury, and, after two or three passes, Booth run the colonel through the body and threw him on the ground, at the same time possessing himself of the colonel's sword.

As soon as the colonel was become master of his speech, he called out to Booth in a very kind voice, and said, " You have done my business, and satisfied me that you are a man of honor, and that my brother James must have been mistaken ; for I am convinced that no man who will draw his sword in so gallant a manner is capable of being a rascal. D—n me, give me a buss, my dear boy ; I ask your pardon for that infamous appellation I dishonored your dignity with ; but d—n me if it was not purely out of love, and to give you an opportunity of doing yourself justice, which I own you have done like a man of honor. What may be the consequences I know not, but I hope, at least, I shall live to reconcile you with my brother."

Booth showed great concern, and even horror in his countenance. " Why, my dear colonel," said he, " would you force me to this ? for heaven's sake tell me what I have ever done to offend you."

" Me !" cried the colonel. " Indeed, my dear child, you never did any thing to offend me. Nay, I have acted the part of a friend to you in the whole affair. I maintained your cause with my brother as long as decency would permit ; I could not flatly contradict him, though, indeed, I scarce believed him. But what could I do ? If

I had not fought with you, I must have been obliged to have fought with him ; however, I hope what is done will be sufficient, and that matters may be discommodated without your being put to the necessity of fighting any more on this occasion."

"Never regard me," cried Booth eagerly ; " for heaven's sake, think of your own preservation. Let me put you into a chair, and get you a surgeon."

"Thou art a noble lad," cries the colonel, who was now got on his legs, " and I am glad the business is so well over ; for though your sword went quite through, it slanted so that I apprehend there is little danger of life : however, I think there is enough done to put an honorable end to the affair, especially as you was so hasty to disarm me. I bleed a little, but I can walk to the house by the water ; and, if you will send me a chair thither, I shall be obliged to you."

As the colonel refused any assistance (indeed he was very able to walk without it, though with somewhat less dignity than usual), Booth set forward to Grosvenor Gate in order to procure the chair, and soon after returned with one to his friend ; whom having conveyed into it, he attended himself on foot into Bond Street, where then lived a very eminent surgeon.

The surgeon having probed the wound, turned toward Booth, who was apparently the guilty person, and said, with a smile, "Upon my word, sir, you have performed the business with great dexterity."

"Sir," cries the colonel to the surgeon, "I would not have you imagine I am afraid to die. I think I know more what belongs to the dignity of a man ; and, I believe, I have shown it at the head of a line of battle. Do not impute my concern to that fear, when I ask you whether there is or is not any danger ?"

"Really, colonel," answered the surgeon, who well

knew the complexion of the gentleman then under his hands, "it would appear like presumption to say that a man who hath been just run through the body is in no manner of danger. But this I think I may assure you, that I yet perceive no very bad symptoms, and, unless something worse should appear, or a fever be the consequence, I hope you may live to be again, with all your dignity, at the head of a line of battle."

"I am glad to hear that is your opinion," quoth the colonel, "for I am not desirous of dying, though I am not afraid of it. But, if any thing worse than you apprehend should happen, I desire you will be a witness of my declaration that this young gentleman is entirely innocent. I forced him to do what he did. My dear Booth, I am pleased matters are as they are. You are the first man that ever gained an advantage over me ; but it was very lucky for you that you disarmed me, and I doubt not but you have the ' equanimity ' to think so. If the business, therefore, hath ended without doing any thing to the purpose, it was Fortune's pleasure, and neither of our faults."

Booth heartily embraced the colonel, and assured him of the great satisfaction he had received from the surgeon's opinion ; and soon after the two combatants took their leave of each other. The colonel, after he was dressed, went in a chair to his lodgings, and Booth walked on foot to his ; where he luckily arrived without meeting any of Mr. Murphy's gang ; a danger which never once occurred to his imagination till he was out of it.

The affair he had been about had indeed so entirely occupied his mind that it had obliterated every other idea ; among the rest, it caused him so absolutely to forget the time of the day, that, though he had exceeded the time of dining above two hours, he had not the least suspicion of being at home later than usual.

CHAPTER VI.

IN WHICH THE READER WILL FIND MATTER WORTHY HIS CONSIDERATION.

AMELIA, having waited above an hour for her husband, concluded, as he was the most punctual man alive, that he had met with some engagement abroad, and sat down to her meal with her children ; which, as it was always uncomfortable in the absence of her husband, was very short ; so that, before his return, all the apparatus of dining was entirely removed.

Booth sat some time with his wife, expecting every minute when the little maid would make her appearance ; at last, curiosity, I believe, rather than appetite, made him ask how long it was to dinner ? " To dinner, my dear !" answered Amelia ; " sure you have dined, I hope ?" Booth replied in the negative ; upon which his wife started from her chair, and bestirred herself as nimbly to provide him a repast as the most industrious hostess in the kingdom doth when some unexpected guest of extraordinary quality arrives at her house.

The reader hath not, I think, from any passages hitherto recorded in this history, had much reason to accuse Amelia of a blamable curiosity ; he will not, I hope, conclude that she gave an instance of any such fault when, upon Booth's having so long overstayed his time, and so greatly mistaken the hour of the day, and upon some other circumstances of his behavior (for he was too honest to be good at concealing any of his thoughts), she said to him after he had done eating, " My dear, I am sure something more than ordinary hath happened to-day, and I beg you will tell me what it is."

Booth answered that nothing of any consequence had happened ; that he had been detained by a friend, whom he met accidentally, longer than he expected. In short, he made many shuffling and evasive answers, not boldly lying out, which, perhaps, would have succeeded, but poorly and vainly endeavoring to reconcile falsehood with truth; an attempt which seldom fails to betray the most practised deceiver.

How impossible was it therefore for poor Booth to succeed in an art for which nature had so entirely disqualified him. His countenance, indeed, confessed faster than his tongue denied, and the whole of his behavior gave Amelia an alarm, and made her suspect something very bad had happened; and, as her thoughts turned presently on the badness of their circumstances, she feared some mischief from his creditors had befallen him; for she was too ignorant of such matters to know that, if he had fallen into the hands of the Philistines (which is the name given by the faithful to bailiffs), he would hardly have been able so soon to recover his liberty. Booth at last perceived her to be so uneasy, that, as he saw no hopes of contriving any fiction to satisfy her, he thought himself obliged to tell her the truth, or at least part of the truth, and confessed that he had had a little skirmish with Colonel Bath, in which, he said, the colonel had received a slight wound, not at all dangerous; "and this," says he, "is all the whole matter." "If it be so," cries Amelia, "I thank heaven no worse hath happened; but why, my dear, will you ever converse with that madman, who can embrace a friend one moment, and fight with him the next?" "Nay, my dear," answered Booth, "you yourself must confess, though he be a little too much on the *qui vive*, he is a man of great honor and good-nature." "Tell me not," replied she, "of such good-nature and honor as would sacrifice a friend and a whole family to a ridiculous whim. Oh, heavens!" cried she, falling upon her knees, "from what misery have I escaped, from what have these poor babes

escaped, through your gracious providence this day!''
Then turning to her husband, she cried, '' But are you sure
the monster's wound is no more dangerous than you say ? a
monster surely I may call him, who can quarrel with a man
that could not, that I am convinced would not, offend
him.''

Upon this question, Booth repeated the assurances which
the surgeon had given them, perhaps with a little enlarge-
ment, which pretty well satisfied Amelia ; and instead of
blaming her husband for what he had done, she tenderly
embraced him, and again returned thanks to heaven for his
safety.

In the evening Booth insisted on paying a short visit to
the colonel, highly against the inclination of Amelia, who,
by many arguments and entreaties, endeavored to dissuade
her husband from continuing an acquaintance in which, she
said, she should always foresee much danger for the future.
However, she was at last prevailed upon to acquiesce ; and
Booth went to the colonel, whose lodgings happened to be
in the verge as well as his own.

He found the colonel in his night-gown, and his great
chair, engaged with another officer at a game of chess. He
rose immediately, and, having heartily embraced Booth,
presented him to his friend, saying he had the honor to introduce to him as brave and as *fortitudinous* a man as any in
the king's dominions. He then took Booth with him into
the next room, and desired him not to mention a word of
what had happened in the morning, saying, '' I am very
well satisfied that no more hath happened ; however, as it
ended in nothing, I could wish it might remain a secret.''
Booth told him he was heartily glad to find him so well,
and promised never to mention it more to any one.

The game at chess being but just begun, and neither of
the parties having gained any considerable advantage, they
neither of them insisted on continuing it ; and now the colo-

AMELIA.

Drawn by R. Corbould & Engrav'd by W. Audinett for Cooke, Janu 1799.
Colonel Bath introducing Lieutenant Booth to
the acquaintance of his friend on recovering from
the wounds he had received from Booth in a duel.

Copyright 1902. Crowsup & Sterling Co.

He found the colonel in his night-gown and his great chair, engaged
with another officer at a game of chess.   He rose immediately,
and having heartily embraced Booth, presented
him to his friend.

Engraved by W. Audinett, from a drawing by R. Corbould (1799).

nel's antagonist took his leave, and left the colonel and Booth together.

As soon as they were alone the latter earnestly entreated the former to acquaint him with the real cause of his anger; "for may I perish," cries Booth, "if I can even guess what I have ever done to offend either you, or your brother, Colonel James."

"Look'ee, child!" cries the colonel; "I tell you I am for my own part satisfied; for I am convinced that a man who will fight can never be a rascal; and, therefore, why should you inquire any more of me at present? when I see my brother James, I hope to reconcile all matters, and perhaps no more swords need be drawn on this occasion." But Booth still persisting in his desire, the colonel, after some hesitation, with a tremendous oath, cried out, "I do not think myself at liberty to refuse you after the indignity I offered you; so, since you demand it of me, I will inform you. My brother told me you had used him dishonorably, and had divellicated his character behind his back. He gave me his word, too, that he was well assured of what he said. What could I have done? though I own to you I did not believe him, and your behavior since hath convinced me I was in the right; I must either have given him the lie, and fought with him, or else I was obliged to behave as I did, and fight with you. And now, my lad, I leave it to you to do as you please; but, if you are laid under any necessity to do yourself further justice, it is your own fault."

"Alas! colonel," answered Booth, "besides the obligations I have to the colonel, I have really so much love for him, that I think of nothing less than resentment. All I wish is to have this affair brought to an eclaircissement, and to satisfy him that he is in an error; for, though his assertions are cruelly injurious, and I have never deserved them, yet I am convinced he would not say what he did not him-

self think. Some rascal, envious of his friendship for me,
hath belied me to him; and the only resentment I desire
is, to convince him of his mistake."

At these words the colonel grinned horribly a ghastly
smile, or rather sneer, and answered, "Young gentleman, you may do as you please; but, by the eternal
dignity of man, if any man breathing had taken a liberty
with my character— Here, here—Mr. Booth (showing his
fingers), here, d—n me, should be his nostrils; he should
breathe through my hands, and breathe his last, d—n
me."

Booth answered, "I think, colonel, I may appeal to your
testimony that I dare do myself justice; since he who dare
draw his sword against you can hardly be supposed to fear
any other person; but I repeat to you again that I love
Colonel James so well, and am so greatly obliged to him,
that it would be almost indifferent to me whether I directed
my sword against his breast or my own."

The colonel's muscles were considerably softened by
Booth's last speech; but he again contracted them into a
vast degree of fierceness before he cried out, "Boy, thou
hast reason enough to be vain; for thou art the first person
that ever could proudly say he gained an advantage over
me in combat. I believe, indeed, thou art not afraid of
any man breathing, and, as I know thou hast some obligations to my brother, I do not discommend thee; for nothing more becomes the dignity of a man than gratitude.
Besides, as I am satisfied my brother can produce the
author of the slander, I say, I am satisfied of that, d—n
me, if any man alive dares assert the contrary; for that
would be to make my brother himself a liar. I will make
him produce his author; and then, my dear boy, your doing yourself proper justice there will bring you finely out
of the whole affair. As soon as my surgeon gives me leave
to go abroad, which, I hope, will be in a few days, I will

bring my brother James to a tavern where you shall meet us ; and I will engage my honor, my whole dignity to you, to make you friends."

The assurance of the colonel gave Booth great pleasure ; for few persons ever loved a friend better than he did James ; and as for doing military justice on the author of that scandalous report which had incensed his friend against him, not Bath himself was ever more ready, on such an occasion, than Booth to execute it. He soon after took his leave, and returned home in high spirits to his Amelia, whom he found in Mrs. Ellison's apartment, engaged in a party at ombre with that lady and her right honorable cousin.

His lordship had, it seems, had a second interview with the great man, and, having obtained further hopes (for I think there was not yet an absolute promise) of success in Mr. Booth's affairs, his usual good-nature brought him immediately to acquaint Mr. Booth with it. As he did not therefore find him at home, and as he met with the two ladies together, he resolved to stay till his friend's return, which he was assured would not be long, especially as he was so lucky, he said, to have no particular engagement that whole evening.

We remarked before that his lordship, at the first interview with Amelia, had distinguished her by a more particular address from the other ladies ; but that now appeared to be rather owing to his perfect good-breeding, as she was then to be considered as the mistress of the house, than from any other preference. His present behavior made this still more manifest ; for, as he was now in Mrs. Ellison's apartment, though she was his relation and an old acquaintance, he applied his conversation rather more to her than to Amelia. His eyes, indeed, were now and then guilty of the contrary distinction, but this was only by stealth ; for they constantly withdrew the moment they were discovered. In short, he treated Amelia with the greatest distance, and at the same time with the most profound and awful respect ; his conversation was so general, so lively, and so obliging, that Amelia, when she added to his agreeableness the obligations she had to him for his friendship to Booth, was certainly as much pleased with his lordship as any virtuous woman can possibly be with any man, besides her own husband.

CHAPTER VII.

CONTAINING VARIOUS MATTERS.

WE have already mentioned the good-humor in which Booth returned home ; and the reader will easily believe it was not a little increased by the good-humor in which he found his company. My lord received him with the utmost marks of friendship and affection, and told him that his affairs went on as well almost as he himself could desire, and that he doubted not very soon to wish him joy of a company.

When Booth had made a proper return to all his lordship's unparalleled goodness, he whispered Amelia that the colonel was entirely out of danger, and almost as well as himself. This made her satisfaction complete, threw her into such spirits, and gave such a lustre to her eyes, that her face, as Horace says, was too dazzling to be looked at ; it was certainly too handsome to be looked at without the highest admiration.

His lordship departed about ten o'clock, and left the company in raptures with him, especially the two ladies, of whom it is difficult to say which exceeded the other in his commendations. Mrs. Ellison swore she believed he was the best of all humankind ; and Amelia, without making any exception, declared he was the finest gentleman and most agreeable man she had ever seen in her life ; adding, it was great pity he should remain single. "That's true, indeed," cries Mrs. Ellison, "and I have often lamented it ; nay, I am astonished at it, considering the great liking he always shows for our sex, and he may certainly have the choice of all. The real reason, I believe, is, his fondness for his sister's children. I declare, madam, if you was to see his behavior to them, you would think they were his own. Indeed he is vastly fond of all manner of children." "Good creature!" cries Amelia ; "if ever he doth me the honor of another visit I am resolved I will show him my little things. I think, Mrs. Ellison, as you say my lord loves children, I may say, without vanity, he will not see many such." "No, indeed, will he not," answered Mrs. Ellison ; "and now I think on't, madam, I wonder at my own stupidity in never making the offer before ; but since you put it into my head, if you will give me leave, I'll take master and miss to wait on my lord's nephew and niece. They are very pretty behaved children ; and little master and miss will be, I dare swear, very happy in their acquaintance ; besides, if my lord himself should see them, I know what will happen ; for he is the most generous of all human beings."

Amelia very readily accepted the favor which Mrs. Ellison offered her ; but Booth expressed some reluctance. "Upon my word, my dear," said he, with a smile, "this behavior of ours puts me in mind of the common conduct of beggars ; who, whenever they receive a favor, are sure to send other objects to the same fountain of charity. Don't we, my dear, repay our obligations to my lord in the same manner, by sending our children a begging to him ?"

"O beastly !" cries Mrs. Ellison ; "how could such a thought enter your brains ? I protest, madam, I begin to grow ashamed of this husband of yours. How can you have so vulgar a way of thinking ? Begging, indeed ! the poor little dear things a begging ! If my lord was capable

of such a thought, though he was my own brother instead
of my cousin, I should scorn him too much ever to enter
his doors." " O dear, madam !" answered Amelia, " you
take Mr Booth too seriously, when he was only in jest ;
and the children shall wait upon you whenever you please."

Though Booth had been a little more in earnest than
Amelia had represented him, and was not, perhaps, quite
so much in the wrong as he was considered by Mrs. Ellison, yet, seeing there were two to one against him, he
wisely thought proper to recede, and let his smile go off
with that air of a jest which his wife had given it.

Mrs. Ellison, however, could not let it pass without paying some compliments to Amelia's understanding, nor
without some obscure reflections upon Booth, with whom
she was more offended than the matter required. She was
indeed a woman of most profuse generosity, and could not
bear a thought which she deemed vulgar or sneaking.
She afterward launched forth the most profuse encomiums
of his lordship's liberality, and concluded the evening with
some instances which he had given of that virtue which, if
not the noblest, is, perhaps, one of the most useful to society with which great and rich men can be endowed.

The next morning early, Sergeant Atkinson came to wait
on Lieutenant Booth, and desired to speak with his honor in
private. Upon which the lieutenant and sergeant took a
walk together in the Park. Booth expected every minute
when the sergeant would open his mouth ; under which expectation he continued till he came to the end of the mall,
and so he might have continued till he came to the end of
the world ; for, though several words stood at the end of
the sergeant's lips, there they were likely to remain forever. He was, indeed, in the condition of a miser, whom
a charitable impulse hath impelled to draw a few pence to
the edge of his pocket, where they were altogether as
secure as if they were in the bottom ; for, as the one hath

not the heart to part with a farthing, so neither had the other the heart to speak a word.

Booth at length, wondering that the sergeant did not speak, asked him what his business was ? when the latter with a stammering voice began the following apology : " I hope, sir, your honor will not be angry, nor take any thing amiss of me. I do assure you, it was not of my seeking, nay, I dare not proceed in the matter without first asking your leave. Indeed, if I had taken any liberties from the goodness you have been pleased to show me, I should look upon myself as one of the most worthless and despicable of wretches ; but nothing is farther from my thoughts. I know the distance which is between us ; and, because your honor hath been so kind and good as to treat me with more familiarity than any other officer ever did, if I had been base enough to take any freedoms, or to encroach upon your honor's goodness, I should deserve to be whipped through the regiment. I hope, therefore, sir, you will not suspect me of any such attempt."

" What can all this mean, Atkinson ?" cries Booth ; " what mighty matter would you introduce with all this previous apology ?"

" I am almost ashamed and afraid to mention it," answered the sergeant ; " and yet I am sure your honor will believe what I have said, and not think any thing owing to my own presumption ; and, at the same time, I have no reason to think you would do any thing to spoil my fortunt in an honest way, when it is dropped into my lap without my own seeking. For may I perish if it is not all the lady's own goodness, and I hope in heaven, with your honor's leave, I shall live to make her amends for it." In a word, that we may not detain the reader's curiosity quite so long as he did Booth's, he acquainted that gentleman that he had an offer of marriage from a lady of his acquaintance, to whose company he had introduced him, and desired his permission to accept of it.

Booth must have been very dull indeed if, after what the sergeant had said, and after what he had heard Mrs. Ellison say, he had wanted any information concerning the lady. He answered him briskly and cheerfully, that he had his free consent to marry any woman whatever ; " and the greater and richer she is," added he, " the more I shall be pleased with the match. I don't inquire who the lady is," said he, smiling, " but I hope she will make as good a wife as, I am convinced, her husband will deserve."

" Your honor hath been always too good to me," cries Atkinson ; " but this I promise you, I will do all in my power to merit the kindness she is pleased to show me. I will be bold to say she will marry an honest man, though he is but a poor one ; and she shall never want any thing which I can give her, or do for her, while my name is Joseph Atkinson."

" And so her name is a secret, Joe, is it ?" cries Booth.

" Why, sir," answered the sergeant, " I hope your honor will not insist upon knowing that, as I think it would be dishonorable in me to mention it."

" Not at all," replied Booth ; " I am the farthest in the world from any such desire. I know thee better than to imagine thou wouldst disclose the name of a fair lady." Booth then shook Atkinson heartily by the hand, and assured him earnestly of the joy he had in his good fortune ; for which the good sergeant failed not of making all proper acknowledgments. After which they parted, and Booth returned home.

As Mrs. Ellison opened the door, Booth hastily rushed by ; for he had the utmost difficulty to prevent laughing in her face. He ran directly upstairs, and, throwing himself into a chair, discharged such a fit of laughter as greatly surprised, and at first almost frightened, his wife.

Amelia, it will be supposed, presently inquired into the cause of this phenomenon, with which Booth, as soon as he was able (for that was not within a few minutes), acquainted her. The news did not affect her in the same manner as it had affected her husband. On the contrary, she cried, " I protest I cannot guess what makes you see it in so ridiculous a light. I really think Mrs. Ellison hath chosen very well. I am convinced Joe will make her one of the best of husbands ; and, in my opinion, that is the greatest blessing a woman can be possessed of."

However, when Mrs. Ellison came into her room a little while afterward to fetch the children, Amelia became of a more risible disposition, especially when the former, turning to Booth, who was then present, said, " So, captain, my jantee-sergeant was very early here this morning. I scolded my maid heartily for letting him wait so long in the entry like a lackey, when she might have shown him into my inner apartment." At which words Booth burst out into a very loud laugh ; and Amelia herself could no more prevent laughing than she could blushing.

" Heyday !" cries Mrs. Ellison ; " what have I said to cause all this mirth ?" and at the same time blushed, and looked very silly, as is always the case with persons who suspect themselves to be the objects of laughter, without absolutely taking what it is which makes them ridiculous.

Booth still continued laughing ; but Amelia, composing her muscles, said, " I ask your pardon, dear Mrs. Ellison ; but Mr. Booth hath been in a strange giggling humor all this morning ; and I really think it is infectious."

" I ask your pardon, too, madam," cries Booth, " but one is sometimes unaccountably foolish."

" Nay, but seriously," said she, " what is the matter ? something I said about the sergeant, I believe ; but you may laugh as much as you please ; I am not ashamed of owning I think him one of the prettiest fellows I ever saw in my life ; and, I own, I scolded my maid at suffering him to wait in my entry ; and where is the mighty ridiculous matter, pray ?"

" None at all," answered Booth ; " and I hope the next time he will be ushered into your inner apartment."

" Why should he not, sir ?" replied she ; " for, wherever he is ushered, I am convinced he will behave himself as a gentleman should."

Here Amelia put an end to the discourse, or it might have proceeded to very great lengths ; for Booth was of a waggish inclination, and Mrs. Ellison was not a lady of the nicest delicacy.

CHAPTER VIII.

THE HEROIC BEHAVIOR OF COLONEL BATH.

BOOTH went this morning to pay a second visit to the colonel, where he found Colonel James. Both the colonel and the lieutenant appeared a little shocked at their first meeting, but matters were soon cleared up ; for the former presently advanced to the latter, shook him heartily by the hand, and said, " Mr. Booth, I am ashamed to see you ; for I have injured you, and I heartily ask your pardon. I am now perfectly convinced that what I hinted to my brother, and which I find had like to have produced such fatal consequences, was entirely groundless. If you will be contented with my asking your pardon, and spare me the disagreeable remembrance of what led me into my error, I shall esteem it as the highest obligation."

Booth answered, " As to what regards yourself, my dear colonel, I am abundantly satisfied ; but, as I am convinced some rascal hath been my enemy with you in the cruellest manner, I hope you will not deny me the opportunity of kicking him through the world."

" By all the dignity of man," cries Colonel Bath, " the boy speaks with spirit, and his request is reasonable."

Colonel James hesitated a moment, and then whispered Booth that he would give him all the satisfaction imaginable concerning the whole affair when they were alone together ; upon which, Booth addressing himself to Colonel Bath, the discourse turned on other matters during the remainder of the visit, which was but short, and then both went away together, leaving Colonel Bath as well as it was possible to expect, more to the satisfaction of Booth than of Colonel James, who would not have been displeased if his wound had been more dangerous ; for he was grown somewhat weary of a disposition that he rather called captious than heroic, and which, as he every day more and more hated his wife, he apprehended might some time or other give him some trouble ; for Bath was the most affectionate of brothers, and had often swore, in the presence of James, that he would eat any man alive who should use his sister ill.

Colonel Bath was well satisfied that his brother and the lieutenant were gone out with a design of tilting, from which he offered not a syllable to dissaude them, as he was convinced it was right, and that Booth could not in honor take, nor the colonel give, any less satisfaction. When they had been gone therefore about half an hour, he rang his bell to inquire if there was any news of his brother, a question which he repeated every ten minutes for the space of two hours, when, having heard nothing of him, he began to conclude that both were killed on the spot.

While he was in this state of anxiety his sister came to see him ; for, notwithstanding his desire of keeping it a secret, the duel had blazed all over the town. After receiving some kind congratulations on his safety, and some unkind hints concerning the warmth of his temper, the colonel asked her when she had seen her husband ? she answered, not that morning. He then communicated to her his suspicion, told her he was convinced his brother had drawn his sword that day, and that, as neither of them had heard any thing from him, he began to apprehend the worst that could happen.

Neither Miss Bellamy nor Mrs. Cibber were ever in a greater consternation on the stage than now appeared in the countenance of Mrs. James. "Good heavens! brother," cried she, "what do you tell me? you have frightened me to death. Let your man get me a glass of water immediately, if you have not a mind to see me die before your face. When, where, how was this quarrel? why did not you prevent it if you knew of it? is it not enough to be every day tormenting me with hazarding your own life, but must you bring the life of one who you know must be, and ought to be, so much the dearest of all to me, into danger? take your sword, brother, take your sword, and plunge it into my bosom; it would be kinder of you than to fill it with such dreads and terrors." Here she swallowed the glass of water, and then threw herself back in her chair, as if she had intended to faint away.

Perhaps, if she had so, the colonel would have lent her no assistance, for she had hurt him more than by ten thousand stabs. He sat erect in his chair, with his eyebrows knit, his forehead wrinkled, his eyes flashing fire, his teeth grating against each other, and breathing horror all round him. In this posture he sat for some time silent, casting disdainful looks at his sister. At last his voice found its way through a passion which had almost choked him, and he cried out, "Sister, what have I done to deserve the opinion you express of me? which of my actions hath made you conclude that I am a rascal and a coward? look at that poor sword, which never woman yet saw but in its sheath; what hath that done to merit your desire that it should be contaminated with the blood of a woman?"

"Alas! brother," cried she, "I know not what you say; you are desirous, I believe, to terrify me out of the little senses I have left. What can I have said, in the agonies of grief into which you threw me, to deserve this passion ?"

"What have you said ?" answered the colonel : "you have said that which, if a man had spoken, nay, d—n me, if he had but hinted that he durst even think, I would have made him eat my sword ; by all the dignity of man, I would have crumbled his soul into powder. But I consider that the words were spoken by a woman, and I am calm again. Consider, my dear, that you are my sister, and behave yourself with more spirit. I have only mentioned to you my surmise. It may not have happened as I suspect ; but, let what will have happened, you will have the comfort that your husband hath behaved himself with becoming dignity, and lies in the bed of honor."

"Talk not to me of such comfort," replied the lady ; "it is a loss I cannot survive. But why do I sit here lamenting myself ? I will go this instant and know the worst of my fate, if my trembling limbs will carry me to my coach. Good-morrow, dear brother ; whatever becomes of me, I am glad to find you out of danger." The colonel paid her his proper compliments, and she then left the room, but returned instantly back, saying, "Brother, I must beg the favor of you to let your footman step to my mantua-maker ; I am sure it is a miracle, in my present distracted condition, how it came into my head." The footman was presently summoned, and Mrs. James delivered him his message, which was to countermand the orders which she had given that very morning to make her up a new suit of brocade. "Heaven knows," says she, "now, when I can wear brocade, or whether ever I shall wear it." And now, having repeated her message with great exactness, lest there should be any mistake, she again lamented her wretched situation, and then departed, leaving the colonel in full expectation of hearing speedy news of the fatal issue of the battle.

But, though the reader should entertain the same curiosity, we must be excused from satisfying it till we have first
accounted for an incident which we have related in this
very chapter, and which, we think, deserves some solution.
The critic, I am convinced, already is apprized that I mean
the friendly behavior of James to Booth, which, from what
we had before recorded, seemed so little to be expected.

It must be remembered that the anger which the former
of these gentlemen had conceived against the latter arose
entirely from the false account given by Miss Matthews of
Booth, whom that lady had accused to Colonel James of
having as basely as wickedly traduced his character.

Now, of all the ministers of vengeance, there are none
with whom the devil deals so treacherously as with those
whom he employs in executing the mischievous purposes of
an angry mistress ; for no sooner is revenge executed on an
offending lover than it is sure to be repented ; and all the
anger which before raged against the beloved object, returns
with double fury on the head of his assassin.

Miss Matthews, therefore, no sooner heard that Booth was
killed (for so was the report at first, and by a colonel of the
army) than she immediately concluded it to be James. She
was extremely shocked with the news, and her heart instantly began to relent. All the reasons on which she had
founded her love recurred, in the strongest and liveliest
colors, to her mind, and all the causes of her hatred sunk
down and disappeared ; or, if the least remembrance of any
thing which had disobliged her remained, her heart became
his zealous advocate, and soon satisfied her that her own
fates were more to be blamed than he, and that, without
being a villain, he could have acted no otherwise than he
had done.

In this temper of mind she looked on herself as the murderer of an innocent man, and, what to her was much
worse, of the man she had loved, and still did love, with

all the violence imaginable. She looked on James as the tool with which she had done this murder ; and, as it is usual for people who have rashly or inadvertently made any animate or inanimate thing the instrument of mischief to hate the innocent means by which the mischief was effected (for this is a subtle method which the mind invents to excuse ourselves, the last objects on whom we would willingly wreak our vengeance), so Miss Matthews now hated and cursed James as the efficient cause of that act which she herself had contrived and labored to carry into execution.

She sat down therefore in a furious agitation, little short of madness, and wrote the following letter :

" I hope this will find you in the hands of justice, for the murder of one of the best friends that ever man was blessed with. In one sense, indeed, he may seem to have deserved his fate, by choosing a fool for a friend ; for whom but a fool would have believed what the anger and rage of an injured woman suggested ; a story so improbable, that I could scarce be thought in earnest when I mentioned it ?

" Know, then, cruel wretch, that poor Booth loved you of all men breathing, and was, I believe, in your commendation guilty of as much falsehood as I was in what I told you concerning him.

" If this knowledge makes you miserable, it is no more than you have made the unhappy

" F. MATTHEWS."

CHAPTER IX.

BEING THE LAST CHAPTER OF THE FIFTH BOOK.

WE shall now return to Colonel James and Mr. Booth, who walked together from Colonel Bath's lodging with much more peaceable intention than that gentleman had.

conjectured, who dreamt of nothing but swords and guns and implements of wars.

The Birdcage-walk in the Park was the scene appointed by James for unburdening his mind. Thither they came, and there James acquainted Booth with all that which the reader knows already, and gave him the letter which we have inserted at the end of the last chapter.

Booth expressed great astonishment at this relation, not without venting some detestation of the wickedness of Miss Matthews ; upon which James took him up, saying, he ought not to speak with such abhorrence of faults which love for him had occasioned.

" Can you mention love, my dear colonel," cried Booth, " and such a woman in the same breath ?"

" Yes, faith ! can I," says James ; " for the devil take me if I know a more lovely woman in the world." Here he began to describe her whole person ; but, as we cannot insert all the description, so we shall omit it all ; and concluded with saying, " Curse me if I don't think her the finest creature in the universe. I would give half my estate, Booth, she loved me as well as she doth you. Though, on second consideration, I believe I should repent that bargain ; for then, very possibly, I should not care a farthing for her."

" You will pardon me, dear colonel," answered Booth : " but to me there appears somewhat very singular in your way of thinking. Beauty is, indeed, the object of liking, great qualities of admiration, good ones of esteem ; but the devil take me if I think any thing but love to be the object of love."

" Is there not something too selfish," replied James, " in that opinion ? but, without considering it in that light, is it not of all things the most insipid ? all oil ! all sugar ! zounds ! it is enough to cloy the sharp-set appetite of a parson. Acids surely are the most likely to quicken."

"I do not love reasoning in allegories," cries Booth; "but with regard to love, I declare I never found any thing cloying in it. I have lived almost alone with my wife near three years together, was never tired with her company, nor ever wished for any other; and I am sure I never tasted any of the acid you mention to quicken my appetite."

"This is all very extraordinary and romantic to me," answered the colonel. "If I was to be shut up three years with the same woman, which heaven forbid! nothing, I think, could keep me alive but a temper as violent as that of Miss Matthews. As to love, it would make me sick to death in the twentieth part of that time. If I was so condemned, let me see, what would I wish the woman to be? I think no one virtue would be sufficient. With the spirit of a tigress I would have her be a prude, a scold, a scholar, a critic, a wit, a politician, and a jacobite; and then, perhaps, eternal opposition would keep up our spirits; and, wishing one another daily at the devil, we should make a shift to drag on a damnable state of life, without much spleen or vapors."

"And so you do not intend," cries Booth, "to break with this woman?"

"Not more than I have already, if I can help it," answered the colonel.

"And you will be reconciled to her?" said Booth.

"Yes, faith! will I, if I can," answered the colonel. "I hope you have no objection."

"None, my dear friend," said Booth, "unless on your account."

"I do believe you," said the colonel; "and yet, let me tell you, you are a very extraordinary man not to desire me to quit her on your own account. Upon my soul, I begin to pity the woman, who hath placed her affection, perhaps, on the only man in England of your age who would not return

it. But for my part, I promise you, I like her beyond all
other women ; and, whilst that is the case, my boy, if her
mind was as full of iniquity as Pandora's box was of diseases, I'd hug her close in my arms, and only take as much
care as possible to keep the lid down for fear of mischief.
But come, dear Booth," said he, " let us consider your
affairs ; for I am ashamed of having neglected them so
long ; and the only anger I have against this wench is, that
she was the occasion of it."

Booth then acquainted the colonel with the promises he
had received from the noble lord, upon which James shook
him by the hand, and heartily wished him joy, crying, " I
do assure you, if you have his interest, you will need no
other ; I did not know you was acquainted with him."

To which Mr. Booth answered, " That he was but a new
acquaintance, and that he was recommended to him by a
lady."

" A lady !" cries the colonel ; " well, I don't ask her
name. You are a happy man, Booth, amongst the women ;
and, I assure you, you could have no stronger recommendation. The peer loves the ladies, I believe, as well as
ever Mark Antony did ; and it is not his fault if he hath
not spent as much upon them. If he once fixes his eye
upon a woman, he will stick at nothing to get her."

" Ay, indeed !" cries Booth. " Is that his character ?"

" Ay, faith," answered the colonel, " and the character
of most men besides him. Few of them, I mean, will
stick at any thing beside their money. Jusque à la Bourse
is sometimes the boundary of love as well as friendship.
And, indeed, I never knew any other man part with his
money so very freely on these occasions. You see, dear
Booth, the confidence I have in your honor."

" I hope, indeed, you have," cries Booth, " but I don't
see what instance you now give me of that confidence."

" Have not I shown you," answered James, " where you may carry your goods to market ? I can assure you, my friend, that is a secret I would not impart to every man in your situation, and all circumstances considered."

" I am very sorry, sir," cries Booth very gravely, and turning as pale as death, " you should entertain a thought of this kind ; a thought which hath almost frozen up my blood. I am unwilling to believe there are such villains in the world ; but there is none of them whom I should detest half so much as myself, if my own mind had ever suggested to me a hint of that kind. I have tasted of some distresses of life, and I know not to what greater I may be driven, but my honor, I thank heaven, is in my own power, and I can boldly say to Fortune she shall not rob me of it."

" Have I not expressed that confidence, my dear Booth ?" answered the colonel. " And what you say now well justifies my opinion ; for I do agree with you that, considering all things, it would be the highest instance of dishonor."

" Dishonor, indeed !" returned Booth. " What ! to prostitute my wife ! Can I think there is such a wretch breathing ?"

" I don't know that," said the colonel ; " but I am sure it was very far from my intention to insinuate the least hint of any such matter to you. Nor can I imagine how you yourself could conceive such a thought. The goods I meant were no other than the charming person of Miss Matthews, for whom I am convinced my lord would bid a swingeing price against me."

Booth's countenance greatly cleared up at this declaration, and he answered with a smile that he hoped he need not give the colonel any assurances on that head. However, though he was satisfied with regard to the colonel's suspicions, yet some chimeras now arose in his brain which gave him no very agreeable sensations. What these were, the sagacious reader may probably suspect; but, if he should not, we may perhaps have occasion to open them in the sequel. Here we will put an end to this dialogue, and to the fifth book of this history.

BOOK VI.

CHAPTER I.

PANEGYRICS ON BEAUTY, WITH OTHER GRAVE MATTERS.

THE colonel and Booth walked together to the latter's lodgings; for as it was not that day in the week in which all parts of the town are indifferent, Booth could not wait on the colonel.

When they arrived in Spring Garden, Booth, to his great surprise, found no one at home but the maid. In truth, Amelia had accompanied Mrs. Ellison and her children to his lordship's; for, as her little girl showed a great unwillingness to go without her, the fond mother was easily persuaded to make one of the company.

Booth had scarce ushered the colonel up to his apartment when a servant from Mrs. James knocked hastily at the door. The lady, not meeting with her husband at her return home, began to despair of him, and performed every thing which was decent on the occasion. An apothecary was presently called with hartshorn and sal volatile, a doctor was sent for, and messengers were dispatched every way; amongst the rest, one was sent to inquire at the lodgings of his supposed antagonist.

The servant hearing that his master was alive and well abovestairs, ran up eagerly to acquaint him with the dreadful situation in which he left his miserable lady at home, and likewise with the occasion of all her distress, saying that his lady had been at her brother's, and had there heard that his honor was killed in a duel by Captain Booth.

The colonel smiled at this account, and bid the servant make haste back to contradict it. And then turning to Booth, he said, "Was there evei such another fellow as this brother of mine ? I thought indeed his behavior was somewhat odd at the time. I suppose he overheard me whisper that I would give you satisfaction, and thence concluded we went together with a design of tilting. D—n the fellow, I begin to grow heartily sick of him, and wish I could get well rid of him without cutting his throat, which I sometimes apprehend he will insist on my doing, as a return for my getting him made a lieutenant-colonel."

Whilst the two gentlemen were commenting on the character of the third, Amelia and her company returned, and all presently came upstairs, not only the children, but the two ladies, laden with trinkets as if they had been come from a fair. Amelia, who had been highly delighted all the morning with the excessive pleasure which her children enjoyed, when she saw Colonel James with her husband, and perceived the most manifest marks of the reconciliation which she knew had been so long and so earnestly wished by Booth, became so transported with joy that her happiness was scarce capable of addition. Exercise had painted her face with vermilion ; and the highest good-humor had so sweetened every feature, and a vast flow of spirits had so lightened up her bright eyes, that she was all ablaze of beauty. She seemed, indeed, as Milton sublimely describes Eve,

> ——Adorn'd
> With what all Earth or Heaven could bestow
> To make her amiable.

Again :

> Grace was in all her steps, Heaven in her eye,
> In every gesture, dignity and love.

Or, as Waller sweetly, though less sublimely, sings :

> Sweetness, truth, and every grace
> Which time and use are wont to teach,
> The eye may in a moment reach,
> And read distinctly in her face.

Or, to mention one poet more, and him of all the sweetest, she seemed to be the very person of whom Suckling
wrote the following lines, where, speaking of Cupid, he
says,

> All his lovely looks, his pleasing fires,
>   All his sweet motions, all his taking smiles ;
> All that awakes, all that inflames desires,
>   All that sweetly commands, all that beguiles,
> He does into one pair of eyes convey,
> And there begs leave that he himself may stay.

Such was Amelia at this time when she entered the room ;
and, having paid her respects to the colonel, she went up to
her husband, and cried, " O, my dear ! never were any
creatures so happy as your little things have been this whole
morning ; and all owing to my lord's goodness ; sure never
was any thing so good-natured and so generous !" She then
made the children produce their presents, the value of
which amounted to a pretty large sum ; for there was a
gold watch amongst the trinkets that cost about twenty
guineas.

Instead of discovering so much satisfaction on this occasion as Amelia expected, Booth very gravely answered,
" And pray, my dear, how are we to repay all these obligations to his lordship ?" " How can you ask so strange a
question ?" cries Mrs. Ellison : " how little do you know
of the soul of generosity (for sure my cousin deserves that
name) when you call a few little trinkets given to children
an obligation !" " Indeed, my dear," cries Amelia, " I
would have stopped his hand if it had been possible ; nay, I
was forced at last absolutely to refuse, or I believe he

would have laid a hundred pound out on the children ; for I never saw any one so fond of children, which convinces me he is one of the best of men ; but I ask your pardon, colonel," said she, turning to him ; " I should not entertain you with these subjects ; yet I know you have goodness enough to excuse the folly of a mother."

The colonel made a very low, assenting bow, and soon after they all sat down to a small repast ; for the colonel had promised Booth to dine with him when they first came home together, and what he had since heard from his own house gave him still less inclination than ever to repair thither.

But, besides both these, there was a third and stronger inducement to him to pass the day with his friend, and this was the desire of passing it with his friend's wife. When the colonel had first seen Amelia in France, she was but just recovered from a consumptive habit, and looked pale and thin ; besides, his engagements with Miss Bath at that time took total possession of him, and guarded his heart from the impressions of another woman ; and, when he had dined with her in town, the vexations through which she had lately passed had somewhat deadened her beauty ; besides, he was then engaged, as we have seen, in a very warm pursuit of a new mistress, but now he had no such impediment ; for though the reader hath just before seen his warm declarations of a passion for Miss Matthews, yet it may be remembered that he had been in possession of her for above a fortnight ; and one of the happy properties of this kind of passion is, that it can with equal violence love half a dozen or half a score different objects at one and the same time.

But indeed such were the charms now displayed by Amelia, of which we endeavored above to draw some faint resemblance, that perhaps no other beauty could have secured him from their influence ; and here, to confess a

truth in his favor, however the grave or rather the hypo-
critical part of mankind may censure it, I am firmly persuaded that to withdraw admiration from exquisite beauty,
or to feel no delight in gazing at it, is as impossible as to
feel no warmth from the most scorching rays of the sun.
To run away is all that is in our power ; and in the former
case, if it must be allowed we have the power of running
away, it must be allowed also that it requires the strongest
resolution to execute it ; for when, as Dryden says,

All paradise is open'd in a face,

how natural is the desire of going thither ! and how difficult to quit the lovely prospect !

And yet, however difficult this may be, my young readers, it is absolutely necessary, and that immediately too :
flatter not yourselves that fire will not scorch as well as
warm, and the longer we stay within its reach the more we
shall burn.   The admiration of a beautiful woman, though
the wife of our dearest friend, may at first perhaps be innocent, but let us not flatter ourselves it will always remain
so ; desire is sure to succeed ; and wishes, hopes, designs,
with a long train of mischiefs, tread close at our heels.   In
affairs of this kind we may most properly apply the well-
known remark of *nemo repentè fuit turpissimus.*   It fares,
indeed, with us on this occasion as with the unwary travel-
ler in some parts of Arabia, the desert, whom the treacherous sands imperceptibly betray till he is overwhelmed and
lost.   In both cases the only safety is by withdrawing our
feet the very first moment we perceive them sliding.

This digression may appear impertinent to some readers ;
we could not, however, avoid the opportunity of offering
the above hints ; since of all passions there is none against
which we should so strongly fortify ourselves as this, which
is generally called love ; for no other lays before us, especially in the tumultuous days of youth, such sweet, such

strong and almost irresistible temptations ; none hath produced in private life such fatal and lamentable tragedies ;
and, what is worst of all, there is none to whose poison and
infatuation the best of minds are so liable. Ambition
scarce ever produces any evil but when it reigns in cruel
and savage bosoms ; an avarice seldom flourishes at all but
in the basest and poorest soil. Love, on the contrary,
sprouts usually up in the richest and noblest minds ; but
there, unless nicely watched, pruned, and cultivated, and
carefully kept clear of those vicious weeds which are too
apt to surround it, it branches forth into wildness and disorder, produces nothing desirable, but chokes up and kills
whatever is good and noble in the mind where it so
abounds. In short, to drop the allegory, not only tenderness and good nature, but bravery, generosity, and every
virtue are often made the instruments of effecting the most
atrocious purposes of this all-subduing tyrant.

CHAPTER II.

WHICH WILL NOT APPEAR, WE PRESUME, UNNATURAL TO ALL MARRIED READERS.

If the table of poor Booth afforded but an indifferent
repast to the colonel's hunger, here was most excellent entertainment of a much higher kind. The colonel began
now to wonder within himself at his not having before discovered such imcomparable beauty and excellence. This
wonder was indeed so natural that, lest it should arise likewise in the reader, we thought proper to give the solution
of it in the preceding chapter.

During the first two hours the colonel scarce ever had his
eyes off from Amelia ; for he was taken by surprise, and
his heart was gone before he [suspected himself to be in any
danger. His mind, however, no sooner suggested a certain
secret to him than it suggested some degree of prudence to

him at the same time ; and the knowledge that he had
thoughts to conceal, and the care of concealing them, had
birth at one and the same instant. During the residue of
the day, therefore, he grew more circumspect, and contented himself with now and then stealing a look by chance,'
especially as the more than ordinary gravity of Booth made
him fear that his former behavior had betrayed to Booth's
observation the great and sudden liking he had conceived
for his wife, even before he had observed it in himself.

Amelia continued the whole day in the highest spirits and
highest good humor imaginable, never once remarking that
appearance of discontent in her husband of which the
colonel had taken notice ; so much more quick-sighted, as
we have somewhere else hinted, is guilt than innocence.

Whether Booth had in reality made any such observations on the colonel's behavior as he had suspected, we will
not undertake to determine ; yet so far may be material to
say, as we can with sufficient certainty, that the change in
Booth's behavior that day, from what was usual with him,
was remarkable enough. None of his former vivacity appeared in his conversation ; and his countenance was altered
from being the picture of sweetness and good humor, not
indeed to sourness or moroseness, but to gravity and melancholy.

Though the colonel's suspicion had the effect which we
have mentioned on his behavior, yet it could not persuade
him to depart. In short, he sat in his chair as if confined
to it by enchantment, stealing looks now and then, and
humoring his growing passion, without having command
enough over his limbs to carry him out of the room, till decency at last forced him to put an end to his preposterous
visit. When the husband and wife were left alone together, the latter resumed the subject of her children, and
gave Booth a particular narrative of all that had passed at
his lordship's, which he, though something had certainly

disconcerted him, affected to receive with all the pleasure he could ; and this affectation, however awkwardly he acted his part, passed very well on Amelia ; for she could not well conceive a displeasure of which she had not the least hint of any cause, and indeed at a time when, from his reconciliation with James, she imagined her husband to be entirely and perfectly happy.

The greatest part of that night Booth passed awake ; and, if during the residue he might be said to sleep, he could scarce be said to enjoy repose ; his eyes were no sooner closed than he was pursued and haunted by the most frightful and terrifying dreams, which threw him into so restless a condition that he soon disturbed his Amelia, and greatly alarmed her with apprehensions that he had been seized by some dreadful disease, though he had not the least symptoms of a fever by any extraordinary heat, or any other indication, but was rather colder than usual.

As Booth assured his wife that he was very well, but found no inclination to sleep, she likewise bid adieu to her slumbers, and attempted to entertain him with her conversation. Upon which his lordship occurred as the first topic ; and she repeated to him all the stories which she had heard from Mrs. Ellison of the peer's goodness to his sister and his nephew and niece. "It is impossible, my dear," says she, "to describe their fondness for their uncle, which is to me an incontestable sign of a parent's goodness." In this manner she ran on for several minutes, concluding at last that it was pity so very few had such generous minds joined to immense fortunes.

Booth, instead of making a direct answer to what Amelia had said, cried coldly, "But do you think, my dear, it was right to accept all those expensive toys which the children brought home ? And I ask you again, what return we are to make for these obligations ?"

"Indeed, my dear," cries Amelia, "you see this matter

in too serious a light. Though I am the last person in the world who would lessen his lordship's goodness (indeed I shall always think we are both infinitely obliged to him), yet sure you must allow the expense to be a mere trifle to such a vast fortune. As for return, his own benevolence, in the satisfaction it receives, more than repays itself, and I am convinced he expects no other."

"Very well, my dear," cries Booth, "you shall have it your way; I must confess I never yet found any reason to blame your discernment; and perhaps I have been in the wrong to give myself so much uneasiness on this account."

"Uneasiness, child!" said Amelia eagerly. "Good heavens! hath this made you uneasy?"

"I do own it hath," answered Booth, "and it hath been the only cause of breaking my repose."

"Why then I wish," cries Amelia, "all the things had been at the devil before ever the children had seen them; and, whatever I may think myself, I promise you they shall never more accept the value of a farthing: if upon this occasion I have been the cause of your uneasiness, you will do me the justice to believe that I was totally innocent."

At those words Booth caught her in his arms, and with the tenderest embrace, emphatically repeating the word innocent, cried, "Heaven forbid I should think otherwise! Oh, thou art the best of creatures that ever blessed a man!"

"Well, but," said she, smiling, "do confess, my dear, the truth; I promise you I won't blame you nor disesteem you for it; but is not pride really at the bottom of this fear of an obligation?"

"Perhaps it may," answered he; "or, if you will, you may call it fear. I own I am afraid of obligations, as the worst kind of debts; for I have generally observed those who confer them expect to be repaid ten thousand-fold."

Here ended all that is material of their discourse; and a little time afterward they both fell fast asleep in one an-

other's arms, from which time Booth had no more restless-
ness, nor any further perturbation in his dreams.

Their repose, however, had been so much disturbed in
the former part of the night that, as it was very late before
they enjoyed that sweet sleep I have just mentioned, they
lay abed the next day till noon, when they both rose with
the utmost cheerfulness ; and, while Amelia bestirred herself in the affairs of her family, Booth went to visit the
wounded colonel.

He found that gentleman still proceeding very fast in his
recovery, with which he was more pleased than he had reason to be with his reception ; for the colonel received him
very coldly indeed, and, when Booth told him he had received perfect satisfaction from his brother, Bath erected
his head and answered with a sneer, " Very well, sir, if you
think these matters can be so made up, d—n me if it is any
business of mine. My dignity hath not been injured.

" No one, I believe," cries Booth, " dare injure it."

" You believe so !" said the colonel : " I think, sir, you
might be assured of it ; but this, at least, you may be assured of, that if any man did, I would tumble him down
the precipice of hell, d—n me, that you may be assured of."

As Booth found the colonel in this disposition, he had
no great inclination to lengthen out his visit, nor did the
colonel himself seem to desire it : so he soon returned back
to his Amelia, whom he found performing the office of a
cook, with as much pleasure as a fine lady generally enjoys
in dressing herself out for a ball.

CHAPTER III.

IN WHICH THE HISTORY LOOKS A LITTLE BACKWARDS.

BEFORE we proceed in our history we shall recount a
short scene to our reader which passed between Amelia and
Mrs. Ellison whilst Booth was on his visit to Colonel Bath.

We have already observed that Amelia had conceived an extraordinary affection for Mrs. Bennet, which had still increased every time she saw her ; she thought she discovered something wonderfully good and gentle in her countenance and disposition, and was very desirous of knowing her whole history.

She had a very short interview with that lady this morning in Mrs. Ellison's apartment. As soon, therefore, as Mrs. Bennet was gone, Amelia acquainted Mrs. Ellison with the good opinion she had conceived of her friend, and likewise with her curiosity to know her story : " For there must be something uncommonly good," said she, " in one who can so truly mourn for a husband above three years after his death."

" O !" cries Mrs. Ellison, " to be sure the world must allow her to have been one of the best of wives. And, indeed, upon the whole, she is a good sort of woman ; and what I like her the best for is a strong resemblance that she bears to yourself in the form of her person, and still more in her voice. But for my own part, I know nothing remarkable in her fortune, unless what I have told you, that she was the daughter of a clergyman, had little or no fortune, and married a poor parson for love, who left her in the utmost distress. If you please, I will show you a letter which she writ to me at that time, though I insist upon your promise never to mention it to her ; indeed, you will be the first person I ever showed it to." She then opened her scrutoire, and, taking out the letter, delivered it to Amelia, saying, " There, madam, is, I believe, as fine a picture of distress as can well be drawn."

" DEAR MADAM : As I have no other friend on earth but yourself, I hope you will pardon my writing to you at this season ; though I do not know that you can relieve my distresses, or, if you can, have I any pretence to expect that

you should.   My poor dear, O heavens—my——lies dead in
the house ; and, after I had procured sufficient to bury him,
a set of ruffians have entered my house, seized all I have,
have seized his dear, dear corpse, and threaten to deny it
burial.   For heaven's sake, send me, at least, some advice ;
little Tommy stands now by me crying for bread, which I
have not to give him.   I can say no more than that I am
          " Your most distressed humble servant,
                                        " M. BENNET."

Amelia read the letter over twice, and then returning it
with tears in her eyes, asked how the poor creature could
possibly get through such distress.

" You may depend upon it, madam," said Mrs. Ellison,
" the moment I read this account I posted away immediately to the lady.   As to the seizing the body, that I found
was a mere bugbear ; but all the rest was literally true.   I
sent immediately for the same gentleman that I recommended to Mr. Booth, left the care of burying the corpse
to him, and brought my friend and her little boy immediately away to my own house, where she remained some
months in the most miserable condition.   I then prevailed
with her to retire into the country, and procured her a
lodging with a friend at St. Edmundsbury, the air and
gayety of which place by degrees recovered her ; and she
returned in about a twelvemonth to town, as well, I think,
as she is at present."

" I am almost afraid to ask," cries Amelia, " and yet I
long methinks to know what is become of the poor little
boy."

" He hath been dead," said Mrs. Ellison, " a little more
than half a year ; and the mother lamented him at first
almost as much as she did her husband, but I found it indeed rather an easier matter to comfort her, though I sat
up with her near a fortnight upon the latter occasion."

" You are a good creature," said Amelia, " and I love you dearly."

" Alas ! madam," cries she, " what could I have done if it had not been for the goodness of that best of men, my noble cousin ! His lordship no sooner heard of the widow's distress from me than he immediately settled one hundred and fifty pounds a year upon her during her life."

" Well ! how noble, how generous was that !" said Amelia. " I declare I begin to love your cousin, Mrs. Ellison."

" And I declare if you do," answered she, " there is no love lost, I verily believe ; if you had heard what I heard him say yesterday behind your back——"

" Why, what did he say, Mrs. Ellison ?" cries Amelia.

" He said," answered the other, " that you was the finest woman his eyes ever beheld. Ah ! it is in vain to wish, and yet I cannot help wishing too. O Mrs. Booth ! if you had been a single woman, I firmly believe I could have made you the happiest in the world. And I sincerely think I never saw a woman who deserved it more."

" I am obliged to you, madam," cries Amelia, " for your good opinion ; but I really look on myself already as the happiest woman in the world. Our circumstances, it is true, might have been a little more fortunate ; but O, my dear Mrs. Ellison ! what a fortune can be put in the balance with such a husband as mine ?"

" I am afraid, dear madam," answered Mrs. Ellison, " you would not hold the scale fairly. I acknowledge, indeed, Mr. Booth is a very pretty gentleman ; heaven forbid I should endeavor to lessen him in your opinion ; yet, if I was to be brought to confession, I could not help saying I see where the superiority lies, and that the men have more reason to envy Mr. Booth than the women have to envy his lady."

" Nay, I will not bear this," replied Amelia. " You

will forfeit all my love if you have the least disrespectful opinion of my husband. You do not know him, Mrs. Ellison ; he is the best, the kindest, the worthiest of all his sex. I have observed, indeed, once or twice before, that you have taken some dislike to him. I cannot conceive for what reason. If he hath said or done any thing to disoblige you, I am sure I can justly acquit him of design. His extreme vivacity makes him sometimes a little too heedless ; but, I am convinced, a more innocent heart, or one more void of offence, was never in a human bosom."

" Nay, if you grow serious," cries Mrs. Ellison, " I have done. How is it possible you should suspect I had taken any dislike to a man to whom I have always shown so perfect a regard ? but to say I think him, or almost any other man in the world, worthy of yourself, is not within my power with truth. And since you force the confession from me, I declare, I think such beauty, such sense, and such goodness united, might aspire without vanity to the arms of any monarch in Europe."

" Alas ! my dear Mrs. Ellison," answered Amelia, " do you think happiness and a crown so closely united ? how many miserable women have lain in the arms of kings ? Indeed, Mrs. Ellison, if I had all the merit you compliment me with, I should think it all fully rewarded with such a man as, I thank heaven, hath fallen to my lot ; nor would I, upon my soul, exchange that lot with any queen in the universe."

" Well, there are enow of our sex," said Mrs. Ellison, " to keep you in countenance ; but I shall never forget the beginning of a song of Mr. Congreve's, that my husband was so fond of that he was always singing it :

> Love's but a frailty of the mind,
> When 'tis not with ambition join'd.

Love without interest makes but an unsavory dish, in my opinion."

"And pray how long hath this been your opinion?" said Amelia, smiling.

"Ever since I was born," answered Mrs. Ellison; "at least, ever since I can remember."

"And have you never," said Amelia, "deviated from this generous way of thinking?"

"Never once," answered the other, "in the whole course of my life."

"Oh, Mrs. Ellison! Mrs. Ellison!" cries Amelia; "why do we ever blame those who are disingenuous in confessing their faults, when we are so often ashamed to own ourselves in the right? Some women now, in my situation, would be angry that you had not made confidantes of them; but I never desire to know more of the secrets of others than they are pleased to intrust me with. You must believe, however, that I should not have given you these hints of my knowing all if I had disapproved your choice. On the contrary, I assure you I highly approve it. The gentility he wants, it will be easily in your power to procure for him; and as for his good qualities, I will myself be bound for them; and I make not the least doubt, as you have owned me yourself that you have placed your affections on him, you will be one of the happiest women in the world."

"Upon my honor," cries Mrs. Ellison, very gravely, "I do not understand one word of what you mean."

"Upon my honor, you astonish me," said Amelia; "but I have done."

"Nay then," said the other, "I insist upon knowing what you mean."

"Why, what can I mean," answered Amelia, "but your marriage with Sergeant Atkinson?"

"With Sergeant Atkinson!" cries Mrs. Ellison eagerly; "my marriage with a sergeant!"

"Well, with Mr. Atkinson, then, Captain Atkinson, if you please; for so I hope to see him."

" And have you really no better opinion of me," said Mrs. Ellison, "than to imagine me capable of such condescension? What have I done, dear Mrs. Booth, to deserve so low a place in your esteem? I find, indeed, as Solomon says, *Women ought to watch the door of their lips.* How little did I imagine that a little harmless freedom in discourse could persuade any one that I could entertain a serious intention of disgracing my family! for of a very good family am I come, I assure you, madam, though I now let lodgings. Few of my lodgers, I believe, ever came of a better."

" If I have offended you, madam," said Amelia, "I am very sorry, and ask your pardon ; but, besides what I heard from yourself, Mr. Booth told me——"

" O yes !" answered Mrs. Ellison, " Mr. Booth, I know, is a very good friend of mine. Indeed, I know you better than to think it could be your own suspicion. I am very much obliged to Mr. Booth truly."

" Nay," cries Amelia, " the sergeant himself is in fault ; for Mr. Booth, I am positive, only repeated what he had from him."

" Impudent coxcomb !" cries Mrs. Ellison. " I shall know how to keep such fellows at a proper distance for the future. I will tell you, dear madam, all that happened. When I rose in the morning I found the fellow waiting in the entry ; and as you had expressed some regard for him as your foster-brother—nay, he is a very genteel fellow, that I must own—I scolded my maid for not showing him into my little back room ; and I then asked him to walk into the parloi. Could I have imagined he would have construed such little civility into an encouragement ?"

" Nay, I will have justice done to my poor brother too," said Amelia. " I myself have seen you give him much greater encouragement than that."

" Well, perhaps I have," said Mrs. Ellison. " I have

been always too unguarded in my speech, and can't answer
for all I have said." She then began to change her note,
and, with an affected laugh, turned all into ridicule ; and
soon afterward the two ladies separated, both in apparent
good humor ; and Amelia went about those domestic offices
in which Mr. Booth found her engaged at the end of the
preceding chapter.

CHAPTER IV.

CONTAINING A VERY EXTRAORDINARY INCIDENT.

IN the afternoon Mr. Booth, with Amelia and her children, went to refresh themselves in the Park. The conversation now turned on what passed in the morning with
Mrs. Ellison, the latter part of the dialogue, I mean, recorded in the last chapter. Amelia told her husband that
Mrs. Ellison so strongly denied all intentions to marry the
sergeant, that she had convinced her the poor fellow was
under an error, and had mistaken a little too much levity
for serious encouragement ; and concluded by desiring
Booth not to jest with her any more on that subject.

Booth burst into a laugh at what his wife said. "My
dear creature," said he, "how easily is thy honesty and
simplicity to be imposed on ! how little dost thou guess at
the art and falsehood of women ! I knew a young lady
who, against her father's consent, was married to a brother
officer of mine ; and, as I often used to walk with her (for
I knew her father intimately well), she would of her own
accord take frequent occasions to ridicule and vilify her
husband (for so he was at the time), and expressed great
wonder and indignation at the report which she allowed to
prevail that she should condescend ever to look at such a fellow with any other design than of laughing at and despising
him. The marriage afterward became publicly owned,
and the lady was reputably brought to bed. Since which I

have often seen her; nor hath she ever appeared to be in
the least ashamed of what she had formerly said, though,
indeed, I believe she hates me heartily for having heard it.''

"But for what reason," cries Amelia, "should she deny
a fact, when she must be so certain of our discovering it,
and that immediately?"

"I can't answer what end she may propose," said Booth.
"Sometimes one would be almost persuaded that there was
a pleasure in lying itself. But this I am certain, that I
would believe the honest sergeant on his bare word sooner
than I would fifty Mrs. Ellisons on oath. I am convinced
he would not have said what he did to me without the
strongest encouragement; and, I think, after what we have
been both witnesses to, it requires no " great confidence in
his veracity to give him an unlimited credit with regard to
the lady's behavior.''

To this Amelia made no reply; and they discoursed of
other matters during the remainder of a very pleasant walk.

When they returned home Amelia was surprised to find
an appearance of disorder in her apartment. Several of the
trinkets which his lordship had given the children lay about
the room; and a suit of her own clothes, which she had
left in her drawers, was now displayed upon the bed.

She immediately summoned her little girl upstairs, who,
as she plainly perceived the moment she came up with a
candle, had half cried her eyes out; for, though the girl
had opened the door to them, as it was almost dark, she had
not taken any notice of this phenomenon in her countenance.

The girl now fell down upon her knees and cried, "For
Heaven's sake, madam, do not be angry with me. Indeed,
I was left alone in the house; and, hearing somebody
knock at the door, I opened it, I am sure thinking no
harm. I did not know but it might have been you, or my
master, or Madam Ellison; and immediately as I did, the

rogue burst in and ran directly upstairs, and what he hath robbed you of I cannot tell ; but I am sure I could not help it, for he was a great swingeing man with a pistol in each hand ; and if I had dared to call out, to be sure he would have killed me. I am sure I was never in such a fright in my born days, whereof I am hardly come to myself yet. I believe he is somewhere about the house yet, for I never saw him go out."

Amelia discovered some little alarm at this narrative, but much less than many other ladies would have shown, for a fright is, I believe, sometimes laid hold of as an opportunity of disclosing several charms peculiar to that occasion. And which, as Mr. Addison says of certain virtues,

> Shun the day, and lie conceal'd
> In the smooth seasons and the calms of life.

Booth, having opened the window, and summoned in two chairmen to his assistance, proceeded to search the house ; but all to no purpose ; the thief was flown, though the poor girl, in her state of terror, had not seen him escape.

But now a circumstance appeared which greatly surprised both Booth and Amelia ; indeed, I believe it will have the same effect on the reader ; and this was, that the thief had taken nothing with him. He had, indeed, tumbled over all Booth's and Amelia's clothes and the children's toys, but had left all behind him.

Amelia was scarce more pleased than astonished at this discovery, and re-examined the girl, assuring her of an absolute pardon if she confessed the truth, but grievously threatening her if she was found guilty of the least falsehood. "As for a thief, child," says she, "that is certainly not true ; you have had somebody with you to whom you have been showing the things ; therefore, tell me plainly who it was."

The girl protested in the solemnest manner that she

knew not the person ; but as to some circumstances she began to vary a little from her first account, particularly as to
the pistols, concerning which, being strictly examined by
Booth, she at last cried, " To be sure, sir, he must have
had pistols about him." And instead of persisting in his
having rushed in upon her, she now confessed that he had
asked at the door for her master and mistress ; and that at
his desire she had shown him upstairs, where he at first
said he would stay till their return home ; " but, indeed,"
cried she, " I thought no harm, for he looked like a gen-
tleman-like sort of man. And, indeed, so I thought he was
for a good while, whereof he sat down and behaved himself
very civilly, till he saw some of master's and miss's things
upon the chest of drawers ; whereof he cried, ' Hey-day !
what's here ?' and then he fell to tumbling about the
things like any mad. Then I thinks, thinks I to myself, to
be sure he is a highwayman, whereof I did not dare to speak
to him ; for I knew Madam Ellison and her maid was gone
out, and what could such a poor girl as I do against a great
strong man ? and besides, thinks I, to be sure he hath got
pistols about him, though I can't indeed (that I will not do
for the world) take my Bible-oath that I saw any ; yet to
be sure he would have soon pulled them out and shot me
dead if I had ventured to have said any thing to offend
him."

"I know not what to make of this," cries Booth.
" The poor girl, I verily believe, speaks to the best of her
knowledge. A thief it could not be, for he hath not taken
the least thing ; and it is plain he had the girl's watch in
his hand. If it had been a bailiff, surely he would have
stayed till our return. I can conceive no other from the
girl's account than that it must have been some madman."

" O good sir !" said the girl, " now you mention it, if
he was not a thief, to be sure he must have been a madman : for indeed he looked, and behaved himself too, very

much like a madman ; for, now I remember it, he talked to himself and said many strange kind of words, that I did not understand. Indeed, he looked altogether as I have seen people in Bedlam ; besides, if he was not a madman, what good could it do him to throw the things all about the room in such a manner ? and he said something too about my master just before he went downstairs. I was in such a fright I cannot remember particularly, but I am sure they were very ill words ; he said he would do for him—I am sure he said that, and other wicked bad words too, if I could but think of them.''

'' Upon my word,'' said Booth, '' this is the most probable conjecture ; but still I am puzzled to conceive who it should be, for I have no madman to my knowledge of my acquaintance, and it seems, as the girl says, he asked for me.'' He then turned to the child, and asked her if she was certain of that circumstance.

The poor maid, after a little hesitation, answered, '' Indeed, sir, I cannot be very positive ; for the fright he threw me into afterward drove every thing almost out of my mind.''

'' Well, whatever he was,'' cries Amelia, '' I am glad the consequence is no worse ; but let this be a warning to you, little Betty, and teach you to take more care for the future. If ever you should be left alone in the house again, be sure to let no person in without first looking out at the window and seeing who they are. I promised not to chide you any more on this occasion, and I will keep my word ; but it is very plain you desired this person to walk up into our apartment, which was very wrong in our absence.''

Betty was going to answer, but Amelia would not let her, saying, '' Don't attempt to excuse yourself ; for I mortally hate a liar, and can forgive any fault sooner than falsehood.''

The poor girl then submitted ; and now Amelia, with her

assistance, began to replace all things in their order ; and little Emily hugging her watch with great fondness, declared she would never part with it any more.

Thus ended this odd adventure, not entirely to the satisfaction of Booth ; for, besides his curiosity, which, when thoroughly roused, is a very troublesome passion, he had, as is, I believe, usual with all persons in his circumstances, several doubts and apprehensions of he knew not what. Indeed, fear is never more uneasy than when it doth not certainly know its object ; for on such occasions the mind is ever employed in raising a thousand bugbears and phantoms, much more dreadful than any realities, and, like children, when they tell tales of hobgoblins, seems industrious in terrifying itself.

CHAPTER V.

CONTAINING SOME MATTERS NOT VERY UNNATURAL.

MATTERS were scarce sooner reduced into order and decency than a violent knocking was heard at the door, such indeed as would have persuaded any one not accustomed to the sound that the madman was returned in the highest springtide of his fury.

Instead, however, of so disagreeable an appearance, a very fine lady presently came into the room, no other, indeed, than Mrs. James herself ; for she was resolved to show Amelia, by the speedy return of her visit, how unjust all her accusation had been of any failure in the duties of friendship ; she had, moreover, another reason to accelerate this visit, and that was, to congratulate her friend on the event of the duel between Colonel Bath and Mr. Booth.

The lady had so well profited by Mrs. Booth's remonstrance, that she had now no more of that stiffness and formality which she had worn on a former occasion. On the contrary, she now behaved with the utmost freedom and good-humor, and made herself so very agreeable that Amelia was highly pleased and delighted with her company.

An incident happened during this visit that may appear to some too inconsiderable in itself to be recorded ; and yet, as it certainly produced a very strong consequence in the mind of Mr. Booth, we cannot prevail on ourselves to pass it by.

Little Emily, who was present in the room while Mrs. James was there, as she stood near that lady, happened to be playing with her watch, which she was so greatly overjoyed had escaped safe from the madman. Mrs. James, who expressed great fondness for the child, desired to see the watch, which she commended as the prettiest of the kind she had ever seen.

Amelia caught eager hold of this opportunity to spread the praises of her benefactor. She presently acquainted Mrs. James with the donor's name, and ran on with great encomiums on his lordship's goodness, and particularly on his generosity. To which Mrs. James answered, " O ! certainly, madam, his lordship hath universally the character of being extremely generous—where he likes."

In uttering these words she laid a very strong emphasis on the three last monosyllables, accompanying them at the same time with a very sagacious look, a very significant leer, and a great flirt with her fan.

The greatest genius the world hath ever produced observes, in one of his most excellent plays, that

> Trifles, light as air,
> Are to the jealous confirmation strong
> As proofs of holy writ.

That Mr. Booth began to be possessed by this worst of fiends, admits, I think, no longer doubt ; for at this speech of Mrs. James he immediately turned pale, and, from a high degree of cheerfulness, was all on a sudden struck dumb, so that he spoke not another word till Mrs. James left the room.

The moment that lady drove from the door Mrs Ellison came upstairs. She entered the room with a laugh, and very plentifully rallied both Booth and Amelia concerning the madman, of which she had received a full account belowstairs ; and at last asked Amelia if she could not guess who it was ; but, without receiving an answer, went on, saying, " For my own part, I fancy it must be some lover of yours ! some person that hath seen you, and so is run mad with love. Indeed, I should not wonder if all mankind were to do the same. La ! Mr. Booth, what makes you grave ? why, you are as melancholy as if you had been robbed in earnest. Upon my word, though, to be serious, it is a strange story, and, as the girl tells it, I know not what to make of it. Perhaps it might be some rogue that intended to rob the house, and his heart failed him ; yet even that would be very extraordinary. What, did you lose nothing, madam ?"

" Nothing at all," answered Amelia. " He did not even take the child's watch."

" Well, captain," cries Mrs. Ellison, " I hope you will take more care of the house to-morrow ; for your lady and I shall leave you alone to the care of it. Here, madam," said she, " here is a present from my lord to us ; here are two tickets for the masquerade at Ranelagh. You will be so charmed with it ! It is the sweetest of all diversions."

" May I be damned, madam," cries Booth, " if my wife shall go thither.

Mrs. Ellison stared at these words, and, indeed, so did Amelia ; for they were spoke with great vehemence. At length the former cried out with an air of astonishment, " Not let your lady go to Ranelagh, sir ?"

" No, madam," cries Booth, " I will not let my wife go to Ranelagh."

"You surprise me!" cries Mrs. Ellison. "Sure, you are not in earnest?"

"Indeed, madam," returned he, "I am seriously in earnest. And, what is more, I am convinced she would of her own accord refuse to go."

"Now, madam," said Mrs. Ellison, "you are to answer for yourself; and I will for your husband, that, if you have a desire to go, he will not refuse you."

"I hope, madam," answered Amelia with great gravity, "I shall never desire to go to any place contrary to Mr. Booth's inclinations."

"Did ever mortal hear the like?" said Mrs. Ellison; "you are enough to spoil the best husband in the universe. Inclinations! what, is a woman to be governed then by her husband's inclinations, though they are never so unreasonable?"

"Pardon me, madam," said Amelia; "I will not suppose Mr. Booth's inclinations ever can be unreasonable. I am very much obliged to you for the offer you have made me; but I beg you will not mention it any more; for after what Mr. Booth hath declared, if Ranelagh was a heaven upon earth, I would refuse to go to it."

"I thank you, my dear," cries Booth; "I do assure you, you oblige me beyond my power of expression by what you say; but I will endeavor to show you, both my sensibility of such goodness, and my lasting gratitude to it."

"And pray, sir," cries Mrs. Ellison, "what can be your objection to your lady's going to a place which, I will venture to say, is as reputable as any about town, and which is frequented by the best company?"

"Pardon me, good Mrs. Ellison," said Booth: "as my wife is so good to acquiesce without knowing my reasons, I am not, I think, obliged to assign them to any other person."

"Well," cries Mrs. Ellison, "if I had been told this, I would not have believed it. What, refuse your lady an innocent diversion, and that too when you have not the pretence to say it would cost you a farthing ?"

"Why will you say any more on this subject, dear madam ?" cries Amelia. "All diversions are to me matters of such indifference that the bare inclinations of any one for whom I have the least value would at all times turn the balance of mine. I am sure, then, after what Mr. Booth hath said——"

"My dear," cries he, taking her up hastily, "I sincerely ask your pardon ; I spoke inadvertently, and in a passion. I never once thought of controlling you, nor ever would. Nay, I said in the same breath you would not go ; and, upon my honor, I meant nothing more."

"My dear," said she, "you have no need of making any apology. I am not in the least offended, and am convinced you will never deny me what I shall desire."

"Try him, try him, madam," cries Mrs. Ellison ; "I will be judged by all the women in town if it is possible for a wife to ask her husband any thing more reasonable. You can't conceive what a sweet, charming, elegant, delicious place it is. Paradise itself can hardly be equal to it."

"I beg you will excuse me, madam," said Amelia ; "nay, I entreat you will ask me no more ; for be assured I must and will refuse. Do let me desire you to give the ticket to poor Mrs. Bennet. I believe it would greatly oblige her."

"Pardon me, madam," said Mrs. Ellison ; "if you will not accept of it, I am not so distressed for want of company as to go to such a public place with all sort of people neither. I am always very glad to see Mrs. Bennet at my own house, because I look upon her as a very good sort of woman ; but I don't choose to be seen with such people in public places."

Amelia expressed some little indignation at this last speech, which she declared to be entirely beyond her comprehension ; and soon after, Mrs. Ellison, finding all her efforts to prevail on Amelia were ineffectual, took her leave, giving Mr. Booth two or three sarcastical words, and a much more sarcastical look at her departure.

CHAPTER VI.

A SCENE IN WHICH SOME LADIES WILL POSSIBLY THINK AMELIA'S CONDUCT EXCEPTIONABLE.

BOOTH and his wife being left alone, a solemn silence prevailed during a few minutes. At last Amelia, who, though a good, was yet a human creature, said to her hus-band, " Pray, my dear, do inform me what could put you into so great a passion when Mrs. Ellison first offered me the tickets for this masquerade ?"

" I had rather you would not ask me," said Booth. " You have obliged me greatly in your ready acquiescence with my desire, and you will add greatly to the obligation by not inquiring the reason of it. This you may depend upon, Amelia, that your good and happiness are the great objects of all my wishes, and the end I propose in all my actions. This view alone could tempt me to refuse you any thing, or to conceal any thing from you."

" I will appeal to yourself," answered she, " whether this be not using me too much like a child, and whether I can possibly help being a little offended at it ?"

" Not in the least," replied he ; " I use you only with the tenderness of a friend. I would only endeavor to conceal that from you which I think would give you uneasiness if you knew. These are called the pious frauds of friendship."

" I detest all fraud," says she ; " and pious is too good an epithet to be joined to so odious a word. You have

often, you know, tried these frauds with no better effect
than to tease and torment me. You cannot imagine, my
dear, but that I must have a violent desire to know the reason of words which I own I never expected to have heard.
And the more you have shown a reluctance to tell me, the
more eagerly I have longed to know. Nor can this be
called a vain curiosity, since I seem so much interested in
this affair. If, after all this, you still insist on keeping the
secret, I will convince you I am not ignorant of the duty of
a wife by my obedience ; but I cannot help telling you at
the same time you will make me one of the most miserable
of women.''

"That is," cries he, "in other words, my dear Emily,
to say I will be contented without the secret, but I am
resolved to know it nevertheless.''

"Nay, if you say so," cries she, "I am convinced you
will tell me. Positively, dear Billy, I must and will know.''

"Why, then, positively," says Booth, "I will tell you.
And I think I shall then show you that however well you
may know the duty of a wife, I am not always able to behave like a husband. In a word then, my dear, the secret
is no more than this : I am unwilling you should receive
any more presents from my lord.''

"Mercy upon me !" cries she, with all the marks of astonishment ; "what ! a masquerade ticket !''

"Yes, my dear," cries he, "that is perhaps the very
worst and most dangerous of all. Few men make presents
of those tickets to ladies without intending to meet them at
the place. And what do you know of your companion ?
To be sincere with you, I have not liked her behavior for
some time. What might be the consequence of going with
such a woman to such a place, to meet such a person, I
tremble to think. And now, my dear, I have told you my
reason of refusing her offer with some little vehemence,
and I think I need explain myself no farther.''

"You need not, indeed, sir," answered she. "Good heavens! did I ever expect to hear this? I can appeal to heaven—nay, I will appeal to yourself, Mr. Booth—if I have ever done any thing to deserve such a suspicion. If ever any action of mine, nay, if ever any thought, had stained the innocence of my soul, I could be contented."

"How cruelly do you mistake me!" said Booth. "What suspicion have I ever shown?"

"Can you ask it," answered she, "after what you have just now declared?"

"If I have declared any suspicion of you," replied he, "or if ever I entertained a thought leading that way, may the worst of evils that ever afflicted human nature attend me! I know the pure innocence of that tender bosom, I do know it, my lovely angel, and adore it. The snares which might be laid for that innocence were alone the cause of my apprehension. I feared what a wicked and voluptuous man, resolved to sacrifice every thing to the gratification of a sensual appetite with the most delicious repast, might attempt. If ever I injured the unspotted whiteness of thy virtue in my imagination, may hell——"

"Do not terrify me," cries she, interrupting him, "with such imprecations. O Mr. Booth! Mr. Booth! you must well know that a woman's virtue is always her sufficient guard. No husband, without suspecting that, can suspect any danger from those snares you mention; and why, if you are liable to take such things into your head, may not your suspicions fall on me as well as on any other? for sure nothing was ever more unjust, I will not say ungrateful, than the suspicions which you have bestowed on his lordship. I do solemnly declare, in all the times I have seen the poor man, he hath never once offered the least forwardness. His behavior hath been polite indeed, but rather remarkably distant than otherwise. Particularly when we played at cards together. I don't remember he spoke ten words to me all the evening ; and when I was at his house, though he showed the greatest fondness imaginable to the children, he took so little notice of me that a vain woman would have been very little pleased with him. And if he gave them many presents, he never offered me one. The first, indeed, which he ever offered me was that which you in that kind manner forced me to refuse."

"All this may be only the effect of art," said Booth. "I am convinced he doth, nay, I am convinced he must, like you ; and my good friend James, who perfectly well knows the world, told me that his lordship's character was that of the most profuse in his pleasures with women ; nay, what said Mrs. James this very evening ? 'His lordship is extremely generous—where he likes.' I shall never forget the sneer with which she spoke those last words."

"I am convinced they injure him," cries Amelia. " As for Mrs. James, she was always given to be censorious ; I remarked it in her long ago, as her greatest fault. And for the colonel, I believe he may find faults enow of this kind in his own bosom, without searching after them among his neighbors. I am sure he hath the most impudent look of all the men I know ; and I solemnly declare, the very last time he was here he put me out of countenance more than once."

"Colonel James," answered Booth, "may have his faults very probably. I do not look upon him as a saint, nor do I believe he desires I should ; but what interest could he have in abusing this lord's character to me ? or why should I question his truth, when he assured me that my lord had never done an act of beneficence in his life but for the sake of some women whom he lusted after ?"

"Then I myself can confute him," replied Amelia : "for besides his services to you, which, for the future, I shall wish to forget, and his kindness to my little babes, how inconsistent is the character which James gives of him with his lordship's behavior to his own nephew and niece, whose extreme fondness of their uncle sufficiently proclaims his goodness to them ? I need not mention all that I have heard from Mrs. Ellison, every word of which I believe ; for I have great reason to think, notwithstanding some little levity, which, to give her her due, she sees and condemns in herself, she is a very good sort of woman."

"Well, my dear," cries Booth, "I may have been deceived, and I heartily hope I am so ; but in cases of this nature it is always good to be on the surest side ; for, as Congreve says,

"' The wise too jealous are : fools too secure.' "

Here Amelia burst into tears, upon which Booth immediately caught her in his arms and endeavored to comfort her. Passion, however, for a while obstructed her speech, and at last she cried, " O Mr. Booth ! can I bear to hear the word jealousy from your mouth ?"

" Why, my love," said Booth, " will you so fatally misunderstand my meaning ? how often shall I protest that it is not of you, but of him, that I was jealous ? If you could look into my breast, and there read all the most secret thoughts of my heart, you would not see one faint idea to your dishonor."

" I don't misunderstand you, my dear," said she, " so much as I am afraid you misunderstand yourself. What is it you fear ? you mention not force, but snares. Is not this to confess, at least, that you have some doubt of my understanding ? do you then really imagine me so weak as to be cheated of my virtue ? am I to be deceived into an affection for a man before I perceive the least inward hint of my danger ? No, Mr. Booth, believe me, a woman must be a fool indeed who can have in earnest such an excuse for her actions. I have not, I think, any very high opinion of my judgment, but so far I shall rely upon it, that no man breathing could have any such designs as you have apprehended without my immediately seeing them ; and how I should then act I hope my whole conduct to you hath sufficiently declared."

"Well, my dear," cries Booth, "I beg you will mention it no more ; if possible, forget it. I hope, nay, I believe, I have been in the wrong ; pray forgive me."

"I will, I do forgive you, my dear," said she, "if forgiveness be a proper word for one whom you have rather made miserable than angry ; but let me entreat you to banish forever all such suspicions from your mind. I hope Mrs. Ellison hath not discovered the real cause of your passion ; but, poor woman, if she had, I am convinced it would go no farther. O heavens ! I would not for the world it should reach his lordship's ears. You would lose the best friend that ever man had. Nay, I would not for his own sake, poor man ; for I really believe it would affect him greatly, and I must, I cannot help having an esteem for so much goodness. An esteem which, by this dear hand," said she, taking Booth's hand and kissing it, "no man alive shall ever obtain by making love to me."

Booth caught her in his arms and tenderly embraced her. After which the reconciliation soon became complete ; and Booth, in the contemplation of his happiness, entirely buried all his jealous thoughts.

CHAPTER VII.

A CHAPTER IN WHICH THERE IS MUCH LEARNING.

THE next morning, whilst Booth was gone to take his morning walk, Amelia went down into Mrs. Ellison's apartment, where, though she was received with great civility, yet she found that lady was not at all pleased with Mr. Booth ; and by some hints which dropped from her in conversation, Amelia very greatly apprehended that Mrs.

Ellison had too much suspicion of her husband's real uneasiness ; for that lady declared very openly she could not help perceiving what sort of man Mr. Booth was : " And tnough I have the greatest regard for you, madam, in the world," said she, " yet I think myself in honor obliged not to impose on his lordship, who, I know very well, hath conceived his greatest liking to the captain on my telling him that he was the best husband in the world."

Amelia's fears gave her much disturbance, and when her husband returned she acquainted him with them ; upon which occasion, as it was natural, she resumed a little the topic of their former discourse, nor could she help casting, though in very gentle terms, some slight blame on Booth for having entertained a suspicion which, she said, might in its consequence very possibly prove their ruin, and occasion the loss of his lordship's friendship.

Booth became highly affected with what his wife said, and the more, as he had just received a note from Colonel James, informing him that the colonel had heard of a vacant company in the regiment which Booth had mentioned to him, and that he had been with his lordship about it, who had promised to use his utmost interest to obtain him the command.

The poor man now expressed the utmost concern for his yesterday's behavior, said " he believed the devil had taken possession of him," and concluded with crying out, " sure I was born, my dearest creature, to be your torment."

Amelia no sooner saw her husband's distress than she instantly forbore whatever might seem likely to aggravate it, and applied herself, with all her power, to comfort him. " If you will give me leave to offer my advice, my dearest soul," said she, " I think all might yet be remedied. I think you know me too well to suspect that the desire of diversion should induce me to mention what I am now going to propose ; and in that confidence I will ask you to let me accept my lord's and Mrs. Ellison's offer, and go to the masquerade. No matter how little while I stay there; if you desire it I will not be an hour from you. I can make an hundred excuses to come home, or tell a real truth, and say I am tired with the place. The bare going will cure every thing."

Amelia had no sooner done speaking than Booth immediately approved her advice, and readily gave his consent. He could not, however, help saying that the shorter her stay was there, the more agreeable it would be to him; for you know, my dear," said he, " I would never willingly be a moment out of your sight."

In the afternoon Amelia sent to invite Mrs. Ellison to a dish of tea; and Booth undertook to laugh off all that had passed yesterday, in which attempt the abundant good humor of that lady gave him great hopes of success.

Mrs. Bennet came that afternoon to make a visit, and was almost an hour with Booth and Amelia before the entry of Mrs. Ellison.

Mr. Booth had hitherto rather disliked this young lady, and had wondered at the pleasure which Amelia declared she took in her company. This afternoon, however, he changed his opinion, and liked her almost as much as his wife had done. She did indeed behave at this time with more than ordinary gayety; and good humor gave a glow to her countenance that set off her features, which were very pretty, to the best advantage, and lessened the deadness that had usually appeared in her complexion.

But if Booth was now pleased with Mrs. Bennet, Amelia was still more pleased with her than ever. For when their discourse turned on love, Amelia discovered that her new friend had all the same sentiments on that subject with herself. In the course of their conversation Booth gave Mrs. Bennet a hint of wishing her a good husband, upon which both the ladies declaimed against second marriages with equal vehemence.

Upon this occasion Booth and his wife discovered a talent in their visitant to which they had been before entirely strangers, and for which they both greatly admired her, and this was, that the lady was a good scholar, in which, indeed, she had the advantage of poor Amelia, whose reading was confined to English plays and poetry ; besides which, I think she had conversed only with the divinity of the great and learned Dr. Barrow, and with the histories of the excellent Bishop Burnet.

Amelia delivered herself on the subject of second marriages with much eloquence and great good sense ; but when Mrs. Bennet came to give her opinion she spoke in the following manner : " I shall not enter into the question concerning the legality of bigamy. Our laws certainly allow it, and so, I think, doth our religion. We are now debating only on the decency of it, and in this light I own myself as strenuous an advocate against it as any Roman matron would have been in those ages of the commonwealth when it was held to be infamous. For my own part, how great a paradox soever my opinion may seem, I solemnly declare I see but little difference between having two husbands at one time and at several times ; and of this I am very confident, that the same degree of love for a first husband which preserves a woman in the one case will preserve her in the other. There is one argument which I scarce know how to deliver before you, sir ; but—if a woman hath lived with her first husband without having children, I think it unpardonable in her to carry barrenness into a second family. On the contrary, if she hath children by her first husband, to give them a second father is still more unpardonable."

" But suppose, madam," cries Booth, interrupting her

with a smile, "she should have had children by her first husband, and have lost them ?"

"That is a case," answered she, with a sigh, "which I did not desire to think of, and I must own it the most favorable light in which a second marriage can be seen. But the Scriptures, as Petrarch observes, rather suffer them than commend them ; and St. Jerome speaks against them with the utmost bitterness." "I remember," cries Booth (who was willing either to show his learning, or to draw out the lady's), "a very wise law of Charondas, the famous lawgiver of Thurium, by which men who married a second time were removed from all public councils ; for it was scarce reasonable to suppose that he who was so great a fool in his own family should be wise in public affairs. And though second marriages were permitted among the Romans, yet they were at the same time discouraged, and those Roman widows who refused them were held in high esteem, and honored with what Valerius Maximus calls the Corona Pudicitiæ. In the noble family of Camilli there was not, in many ages, a single instance of this, which Martial calls adultery :

> *Quæ toties nubit, non nubit ; adultera lege est."*

"True, sir," says Mrs. Bennet, "and Virgil calls this a violation of chastity, and makes Dido speak of it with the utmost detestation :

> *Sed mihi vel Tellus optem prius ima dehiscat*
> *Vel Pater omnipotens adigat me fulmine ad umbras*
> *Pallentes umbras Erebi, noctemque profundam,*
> *Ante, pudor, quam te violo, aut tua jura resolvo.*
> *Ille meos, primum qui me sibi junxit, amores,*
> *Ille habeat semper secum, servetque Sepulchro."*

She repeated these lines with so strong an emphasis that she almost frightened Amelia out of her wits, and not a little staggered Booth, who was himself no contemptible scholar. He expressed great admiration of the lady's learning ; upon which she said it was all the fortune given her by her father, and all the dower left her by her husband ; " and sometimes," said she, " I am inclined to think I enjoy more pleasure from it than if they had bestowed on me what the world would in general call more valuable." She then took occasion, from the surprise which Booth had affected to conceive at her repeating Latin with so good a grace, to comment on that great absurdity (for so she termed it) of excluding women from learning ; for which they were equally qualified with the men, and in which so many had made so notable a proficiency ; for a proof of which she mentioned Madam Dacier and many others.

Though both Booth and Amelia outwardly concurred with her sentiments, it may be a question whether they did not assent rather out of complaisance than from their real judgment.

CHAPTER VIII.

CONTAINING SOME UNACCOUNTABLE BEHAVIOR IN MRS. ELLISON.

MRS. ELLISON made her entrance at the end of the preceding discourse. At her first appearance she put on an unusual degree of formality and reserve ; but when Amelia had acquainted her that she designed to accept the favor intended her, she soon began to alter the gravity of her muscles, and presently fell in with that ridicule which Booth thought proper to throw on his yesterday's behavior.

The conversation now became very lively and pleasant, in which Booth having mentioned the discourse that passed in the last chapter, and having greatly complimented Mrs. Bennet's speech on that occasion, Mrs. Ellison, who was as strenuous an advocate on the other side, began to rally that lady extremely, declaring it was a certain sign she intended to marry again soon. "Married ladies," cries she, "I believe, sometimes think themselves in earnest in such declarations, though they are oftener perhaps meant as compliments to their husbands ; but when widows exclaim loudly against second marriages, I would always lay a wager that the man, if not the wedding-day, is absolutely fixed on."

Mrs. Bennet made very little answer to this sarcasm. Indeed, she had scarce opened her lips from the time of Mrs. Ellison's coming into the room, and had grown particularly grave at the mention of the masquerade. Amelia imputed this to her being left out of the party, a matter which is often no small mortification to human pride, and in a whisper asked Mrs. Ellison if she could not procure a third ticket, to which she received an absolute negative.

During the whole time of Mrs. Bennet's stay, which was above an hour afterward, she remained perfectly silent and looked extremely melancholy. This made Amelia very uneasy, as she concluded she had guessed the cause of her vexation. In which opinion she was the more confirmed from certain looks of no very pleasant kind which Mrs. Bennet now and then cast on Mrs. Ellison, and the more than ordinary concern that appeared in the former lady's countenance whenever the masquerade was mentioned, and which, unfortunately, was the principal topic of their discourse ; for Mrs. Ellison gave a very elaborate description of the extreme beauty of the place and elegance of the diversion.

When Mrs. Bennet was departed, Amelia could not help again soliciting Mrs. Ellison for another ticket, declaring she was certain Mrs. Bennet had a great inclination to go with them ; but Mrs. Ellison again excused herself from asking it of his lordship. " Besides, madam," says she, " if I would go thither with Mrs. Bennet, which, I own to you, I don't choose, as she is a person whom *nobody knows*, I very much doubt whether she herself would like it ; for she is a woman of a very unaccountable turn. All her delight lies in books ; and as for public diversions, I have heard her often declare her abhorrence of them."

"What then," said Amelia, "could occasion all that gravity from the moment the masquerade was mentioned?"

"As to that," answered the other, "there is no guessing. You have seen her altogether as grave before now. She hath had these fits of gravity at times ever since the death of her husband."

"Poor creature!" cries Amelia ; "I heartily pity her, for she must certainly suffer a great deal on these occasions. I declare I have taken a strange fancy to her."

"Perhaps you would not like her so well if you knew her thoroughly," answered Mrs. Ellison. "She is, upon the whole, but of a whimsical temper ; and if you will take my opinion, you should not cultivate too much intimacy with her. I know you will never mention what I say ; but she is like some pictures which please best at a distance."

Amelia did not seem to agree with these sentiments, and she greatly importuned Mrs. Ellison to be more explicit, but to no purpose ; she continued to give only dark hints to Mrs. Bennet's disadvantage ; and if ever she let drop something a little too harsh, she failed not immediately to contradict herself by throwing some gentle commendations into the other scale ; so that her conduct appeared utterly unaccountable to Amelia, and, upon the whole, she knew not whether to conclude Mrs. Ellison to be a friend or enemy to Mrs. Bennet.

During this latter conversation Booth was not in the room, for he had been summoned downstairs by the sergeant, who came to him with news from Murphy, whom he had met that evening, and who assured the sergeant that if he was desirous of recovering the debt which he had before pretended to have on Booth, he might shortly have an opportunity, for that there was to be a very strong petition to the board the next time they sat. Murphy said further

that he need not fear having his money, for that, to his certain knowledge, the captain had several things of great
value, and even his children had gold watches.

This greatly alarmed Booth, and still more when the sergeant reported to him from Murphy that all these things
had been seen in his possession within a day last passed.
He now plainly perceived, as he thought, that Murphy
himself, or one of his emissaries, had been the supposed
madman ; and he now very well accounted to himself, in
his own mind, for all that had happened, conceiving that
the design was to examine into the state of his effects, and
to try whether it was worth his creditors' while to plunder
him by law.

At his return to his apartment he communicated what he
had heard to Amelia and Mrs. Ellison, not disguising his
apprehensions of the enemy's intentions ; but Mrs. Ellison
endeavored to laugh him out of his fears, calling him faint-
hearted, and assuring him he might depend on her lawyer.
" Till you hear from him," said she, " you may rest entirely
contented ; for, take my word for it, no danger can happen
to you of which you will not be timely apprized by him.
And as for the fellow that had the impudence to come into
your room, if he was sent on such an errand as you mention, I heartily wish I had been at home ; I would have
secured him safe with a constable, and have carried him
directly before Justice Thrasher. I know the justice is an
enemy to bailiffs on his own account."

This heartening speech a little roused the courage of
Booth, and somewhat comforted Amelia, though the spirits
of both had been too much hurried to suffer them either to
give or receive much entertainment that evening ; which
Mrs. Ellison perceiving soon took her leave, and left this
unhappy couple to seek relief from sleep, that powerful
friend to the distressed, though, like other powerful friends,
he is not always ready to give his assistance to those who
want it most.

CHAPTER IX.

CONTAINING A VERY STRANGE INCIDENT.

WHEN the husband and wife were alone they again talked over the news which the sergeant had brought; on which occasion Amelia did all she could to conceal her own fears, and to quiet those of her husband. At last she turned the conversation to another subject, and poor Mrs. Bennet was brought on the carpet. " I should be sorry," cries Amelia, "to find I had conceived an affection for a bad woman; and yet I begin to fear Mrs. Ellison knows something of her more than she cares to discover; why else should she be unwilling to be seen with her in public? Besides, I have observed that Mrs. Ellison hath been always backward to introduce her to me, nor would ever bring her to my apartment, though I have often desired her. Nay, she hath given me frequent hints not to cultivate the acquaintance. What do you think, my dear? I should be very sorry to contract an intimacy with a wicked person."

" Nay, my dear," cries Booth, " I know no more of her, nor indeed hardly so much as yourself. But this, I think, that if Mrs. Ellison knows any reason why she should not have introduced Mrs. Bennet into your company, she was very much in the wrong in introducing her into it."

In discourses of this kind they passed the remainder of the evening. In the morning Booth rose early, and, going downstairs, received from little Betty a sealed note, which contained the following words:

> Beware, beware, beware;
> For I apprehend a dreadful snare
> Is laid for virtuous innocence,
> Under a friend's false pretence.

Booth immediately inquired of the girl who brought this note? and was told it came by a chairman, who, having delivered it, departed without saying a word.

He was extremely staggered at what he read, and presently referred the advice to the same affair on which he had received those hints from Atkinson the preceding evening ; but when he came to consider the words more maturely he could not so well reconcile the two last lines of this poetical epistle, if it may be so called, with any danger which the law gave him reason to apprehend. Mr. Murphy and his gang could not well be said to attack either his innocence or virtue ; nor did they attack him under any color or pretence of friendship.

After much deliberation on this matter a very strange suspicion came into his head ; and this was, that he was betrayed by Mrs. Ellison. He had for some time conceived no very high opinion of that good gentlewoman, and he now began to suspect that she was bribed to betray him. By this means he thought he could best account for the strange appearance of the supposed madman. And when this conceit once had birth in his mind, several circumstances nourished and improved it. Among these were her jocose behavior and raillery on that occasion, and her attempt to ridicule his fears from the message which the sergeant had brought him.

This suspicion was indeed preposterous, and not at all warranted by, or even consistent with the character and whole behavior of Mrs. Ellison, but it was the only one which at that time suggested itself to his mind ; and however blamable it might be, it was certainly not unnatural in him to entertain it ; for so great a torment is anxiety to the human mind, that we always endeavor to relieve ourselves from it by guesses, however doubtful or uncertain ; on all which occasions dislike and hatred are the surest guides to lead our suspicion to its object.

When Amelia rose to breakfast, Booth produced the note which he had received, saying, " My dear, you have so often blamed me for keeping secrets from you, and I have so often, indeed, endeavored to conceal secrets of this kind from you with such ill success, that I think I shall never more attempt it." Amelia read the letter hastily, and seemed not a little discomposed ; then, turning to Booth with a very disconsolate countenance, she said, " Sure fortune takes a delight in terrifying us! what can be the meaning of this ?" Then, fixing her eyes attentively on the paper, she perused it for some time, till Booth cried, " How is it possible, my Emily, you can read such stuff patiently ? the verses are certainly as bad as ever were written." " I was trying, my dear," answered she, " to recollect the hand ; for I will take my oath I have seen it before, and that very lately ;" and suddenly she cried out, with great emotion, " I remember it perfectly now ; it is Mrs. Bennet's hand. Mrs. Ellison showed me a letter from her but a day or two ago. It is a very remarkable hand, and I am positive it is hers."

" If it be hers," cries Booth, " what can she possibly mean by the latter part of her caution ? sure Mrs. Ellison hath no intention to betray us."

" I know not what she means," answered Amelia, " but I am resolved to know immediately, for I am certain of the hand. By the greatest luck in the world she told me yesterday where her lodgings were, when she pressed me exceedingly to come and see her. She lives but a very few doors from us, and I will go to her this moment."

Booth made not the least objection to his wife's design. His curiosity was, indeed, as great as hers, and so was his impatience to satisfy it, though he mentioned not this his impatience to Amelia ; and perhaps it had been well for him if he had.

Amelia, therefore, presently equipped herself in her walking dress, and leaving her children to the care of her husband, made all possible haste to Mrs. Bennet's lodgings.

Amelia waited near five minutes at Mrs. Bennet's door

before any one came to open it ; at length a maid servant appeared, who, being asked if Mrs. Bennet was at home, answered, with some confusion in her countenance, that she did not know ; " but, madam," said she, " if you will send up your name I will go and see." Amelia then told her name, and the wench, after staying a considerable time, returned and acquainted her that Mrs. Bennet was at home. She was then ushered into a parlor and told that the lady would wait on her presently.

In this parlor Amelia cooled her heels, as the phrase is, near a quarter of an hour. She seemed, indeed, at this time, in the miserable situation of one of those poor wretches who make their morning visits to the great to solicit favors, or perhaps to solicit the payment of a debt, for both are alike treated as beggars, and the latter sometimes considered as the more troublesome beggars of the two.

During her stay here, Amelia observed the house to be in great confusion ; a great bustle was heard abovestairs, and the maid ran up and down several times in a great hurry.

At length Mrs. Bennet herself came in. She was greatly disordered in her looks, and had, as the women call it, huddled on her clothes in much haste ; for, in truth, she was in bed when Amelia first came. Of this fact she informed her, as the only apology she could make for having caused her to wait so long for her company.

Amelia very readily accepted her apology, but asked her, with a smile, if these early hours were usual with her ? Mrs. Bennet turned as red as scarlet at the question, and answered, " No, indeed, dear madam. I am for the most part a very early riser ; but I happened accidentally to sit up very late last night. I am sure I had little expectation of your intending me such a favor this morning."

Amelia, looking very steadfastly at her, said, " Is it possible, madam, you should think such a note as this would raise no curiosity in me?" She then gave her the note, asking her if she did know the hand.

Mrs. Bennet appeared in the utmost surprise and confusion at this instant. Indeed, if Amelia had conceived but the slightest suspicion before, the behavior of the lady would have been a sufficient confirmation to her of the truth. She waited not, therefore, for an answer, which, indeed, the other seemed in no haste to give, but conjured her in the most earnest manner to explain to her the meaning of so extraordinary an act of friendship; "for so," said she, "I esteem it, being convinced you must have sufficient reason for the warning you have given me."

Mrs. Bennet, after some hesitation, answered, "I need not, I believe, tell you how much I am surprised at what you have shown me; and the chief reason of my surprise is, how you came to discover my hand. Sure, madam, you have not shown it to Mrs. Ellison."

Amelia declared she had not, but desired she would question her no farther. "What signifies how I discovered it, since your hand it certainly is?"

"I own it is," cries Mrs. Bennet, recovering her spirits, "and since you have not shown it to that woman I am satisfied. I begin to guess now whence you might have your information; but no matter; I wish I had never done any thing of which I ought to be more ashamed. No one can, I think, justly accuse me of a crime on that account; and I thank heaven my shame will never be directed by the false opinion of the world. Perhaps it was wrong to show my letter, but when I consider all circumstances I can forgive it."

"Since you have guessed the truth," said Amelia, "I am not obliged to deny it. She, indeed, showed me your letter, but I am sure you have not the least reason to be ashamed of it. On the contrary, your behavior on so melancholy an occasion was highly praiseworthy; and your bearing up under such afflictions as the loss of a husband in so dreadful a situation was truly great and heroical."

"So Mrs. Ellison then hath shown you my letter ?" cries Mrs. Bennet eagerly.

"Why, did not you guess it yourself ?" answered Amelia ; "otherwise I am sure I have betrayed my honor in mentioning it. I hope you have not drawn me inadvertently into any breach of my promise. Did you not assert, and that with an absolute certainty, that you knew she had shown me your letter, and that you was not angry with her for so doing ?"

"I am so confused," replied Mrs. Bennet, " that I scarce know what I say ; yes, yes, I remember I did say so. I wish I had no greater reason to be angry with her than that."

"For heaven's sake," cries Amelia, " do not delay my request any longer ; what you say now greatly increases my curiosity, and my mind will be on the rack till you discover your whole meaning ; for I am more and more convinced that something of the utmost importance was the purport of your message."

"Of the utmost importance, indeed," cries Mrs. Bennet ; "at least you will own my apprehensions were sufficiently well founded. O gracious heaven ! how happy shall I think myself if I should have proved your preservation ! I will, indeed, explain my meaning ; but, in order to disclose all my fears in their just colors, I must unfold my whole history to you. Can you have patience, madam, to listen to the story of the most unfortunate of women ?"

Amelia assured her of the highest attention, and Mrs. Bennet soon after began to relate what is written in the seventh book of this history.

END VOL. I.